CALIFORNIA, HERE I AM

Also by Christopher Wood

A DOVE AGAINST DEATH

FIRE MOUNTAIN

TAIWAN

MAKE IT HAPPEN TO ME

KAGO

'TERRIBLE HARD', SAYS ALICE

JAMES BOND, THE SPY WHO LOVED ME

THE FURTHER ADVENTURES OF BARRY LYNDON

JAMES BOND AND MOONRAKER

DEAD CENTRE

JOHN ADAM, SAMURAI

SINCERE MALE SEEKS LOVE
AND SOMEONE TO WASH HIS UNDERPANTS

CALIFORNIA, HERE I AM

by

CHRISTOPHER WOOD

Published in Great Britain by Twenty First Century Publishers Ltd.

A catalogue record of this book is available from the British Library.

ISBN: 1-904433-21-9

To order further copies of this work or other books published by Twenty First Century Publishers visit our website:
www.twentyfirstcenturypublishers.com

To Adam and, of course, Caroline and Ben.

1.

"Crinkle winkle…Hut butt …Ninja nipples." My father reflects. "What do you think, a bit esoteric?"

"I don't really associate ninjas with nipples," I tell him. "Turtles, maybe."

"Hmn…. I suppose you're right. Pity, the phrase has a pleasing ring to it-" 'VRROOOOOM!!' My father's self-absorbed mumble is drowned in a staccato gunfire of revving engines. The lights change on Wilshire Boulevard and six lanes of neurotic metal narrowly fail to flatten a geriatric jogger in a fluffy pink track suit and matching knitted bonnet.

"Look at that woman," groans my father, the creative muse temporarily distracted. "Looks like a cashmere sea anemone. Must have needed a fork-lift truck to get that make-up onto her face. She starts to sweat and it'll slide off and break her foot." His gaze swivels to the line of flags outside the hotel. "Is that Union Jack upside down?"

I confess that I do not know.

"Well you should know, the fortune I've spent on your education." He sighs. "And that Canadian thing with the leaf. That's not a flag, that's a corn flakes packet. It's even worse than the yellow kangaroo."

I take a deep breath, which in the City of the Angels is probably highly injurious to my health. As in those time-exposed photographs of night time cityscapes with coloured worms of traffic, so one can visualise the heaving arteries of Los Angeles squirming with fuming entrails of mortal corruption like rusting wires crammed in a slimy flex. Sometimes I feel I can contain the rancid air within my hands, form it into balloon-like shapes, hear its plaintiff squeaks as it tries to wriggle from my fingers. I toss it aside and - plop! - it wrinkles out the crinkles and dives back into the murk.

"Buddha belly… Peanut pecker. Stoat parts…" My father reflects. "Do Americans have stoats? I don't mean in the biblical sense."

"I don't know," I say, and then add quickly before he can remind me that he has made a joke, "Racoons, maybe."

"'Racoon parts'." My father weighs the phrase and finds it wanting. "Hardly trips off the tongue, does it?"

I treat the question as rhetorical and search the lines of motorised effluent beating east and west for a sign of the car which is supposed to be picking us up. A lot of white teeth in Porsches out today. Money has been put where the mouth is.

"Hi, Mr Lock." Peter, the doorman, strokes each word towards us with equal stress and an ingratiating warmth dipped in pixie torpor. The Lotus-Eaters must have talked like this.

Peter is pulling a trolley full of matching luggage. Not the bloated reticules of the post bellum South but suitcases covered in a tufty fabric sprinkled with clusters of red roses. "Is this yours?"

"If it was, I'd travel separately."

"Suite four-o-five?"

"It's not ours," I say firmly.

My father never seems to get the message. This is Southern California. Simple answers to simple questions. Anything too complicated and life grinds to a halt. No substitutions.

I think Peter is waiting to be discovered. He has tight blond curls that shine with irrepressible lustre and his skin glows with vitality. I keep thinking of catfood commercials. His scarlet jacket is (on purpose?) slightly too small and his honed, toned frame seems about to explode from it at any moment. He smiles a lot and listens intently to everything that is said to him, sometimes leaning forward and nodding to emphasise his absorption in your words. This guy could take direction, or perhaps more importantly, give the impression that he could take direction. Sooner or later, the producer with the life-changing part will walk past the potted palms and - bingo! I keep meaning to ask him if Peter is his real name.

Now he is staring at my father. Perhaps he suspects that the luggage really does belong to us and that we are waiting to bundle it into a car and roar away without paying our bill. Perhaps he is merely puzzled. My father puzzles a lot of people.

"You guys going out to lunch?"

"That's the general idea," says my father watching the pink, fluffy one disappearing towards Beverly Glen. She is not jogging but walking robotistically and swinging her arms as it trying to shake them free from her shoulders.

"Nice day for it."

My father chews air. I can imagine the question that is forming itself in his mind: what would Peter consider a bad day to go out to lunch in the land of perpetual sunshine?

He says nothing so Peter looks at me. His face is not a catalogue of emotional responses but I think I recognise mild disgust tinged with sympathy. Doubtless, like the rest of the hotel staff, he suspects that I am my father's catamite and not his son. My father being English is bad enough. Californians consider themselves well-informed about the sexual proclivities of the male of the island race. That my father is a writer only tosses more fuel on the flames and if it is was generally known that he had a home in France - the country of Gide, Cocteau, Genet and umpteen other uncos sporting floppy berets and hooped matelot jumpers - then the evidence would be irrefutable. When not trawling the studios for writing assignments they have a pretty damn good idea what he gets up to.

Peter's thoughtful face suggests that he is wondering whether, if a future career depended on it, he would be prepared to submit himself to what I presumably undergo for a free lunch.

As if to resolve any lingering doubts about the nature of our relationship, my father extends his arm across my shoulders and draws me to him.

"Gnome nuts," he says cheerfully.

"Oh dear, I'm sorry I was so late." Constance spies a gap and her modest Japanese import bolts across Wilshire. There is a blare of horns and a screech of tyres. I glimpse braking drivers' mouths deformed into glistening gashes as they hurl obscenities.

"No worries," says my father, trying on an Australian accent for size.

"I had to drop someone off."

"Ermine," says my father. "I think they call them ermine. Or is it ermines? Remind to look it up when we get back."

Constance looks at me. I have a permanent role as interpreter to the outside world.

"We were talking about stoats," I say.

"Fart-breath?" says my father without conviction. "Americans are never very comfortable with farts, are they? I can never detect the fine line between what they consider gross and funny and what is merely gross and taboo."

"How's the script going?" asks Constance.

I like Constance. She is slender to the point of anorexia and wears a scent that reminds me of embalming fluid but most of the time she seems to divine the convoluted thought processes that gnaw at my father's utterances. It takes a weight off my shoulders.

"I'm trying to come up with an original but authentic-sounding teen-speak. You know, something that kids can relate to." Constance looks patient and interested, something she is very good at and an indispensable combination for anybody wishing to carve out a place in my father's life. "Sorry, Constance, I forgot you're a studio executive. You only go to screenings of Iranian movies without subtitles, don't you?" He sighs. "If you ever joined the great unwashed in an actual movie theatre you'd realise that these days people get bored before the end of a sentence. You have to hold their attention with little clusters of insults - usually connected with your sexual organs and their size - or lack of size and general repulsiveness. Chuck in a few permutations of the word 'fuck' and you've got a sporting chance of keeping the audience awake to the next car chase."

"That's so sad, isn't it?" says Constance dutifully as she narrowly fails to rear end a marauding jeep outside the Veterans Administration Cemetery.

"Yes, it is." My father thinks about it and laughs sadly, like a seal barking on a lonely rock.

I leave them to their middle-aged foreplay and prepare to enjoy myself. Handmaiden to my father's whims, Constance will shake off Wilshire and loop down to Santa Monica via San Vicente. This is about as good as Los Angeles gets for me. I love the poincianas along the grassy central divide with their bright red flowers like expensive Christmas tree decorations, the breaking waves of bougainvillea with the gables of distinguished houses glimpsed behind. There is a comforting hint of arboreal anarchy in this cheerful riot of colour that makes me think of homes rather than 'real estate'. Maybe it is because there are no manicured lawns with security patrol signs sprouting from the flowers. 'Armed response'. Step on the grass and someone will drive up and blow your head off. I don't want to think about that. Like I don't really want to be a member of the Brentwood Club. I just want to imagine how nice it must be in there behind the high fence.

I'm more at home out here with the ordinary folk. The joggers and the plodders. Thin men, fat men, very fat men, Greek gods sporting dumbbells. Beautiful girls prancing across the sward, more tick-tock, arm-pumping matrons in day-glo leotards, faces screwed up tighter than the spring in a toy locomotives. Glow, perspire, sweat, drip. No pain, no gain. Tinkle, tinkle, little cyclist. It makes me feel healthier to be in the presence of athletic endeavour.

Tenth Street. Now begins the countdown to the sea. Ninth, seventh, fourth. Ahead are the palm tree on Ocean Avenue with the palisades and the Pacific beyond. It gets me every time, that first glimpse of the ocean. Just as it did when I was a child. I could be living here. If - as they say in the movies - things had turned out differently.

Constance eases out onto Ocean - only mild hooting - and the traffic closes in around us. More joggers flit through the palms and the glorious bright Californian light crashes off the facades of the buildings along the seafront. The ocean is probably full of coughing fish but today it looks magical, dressed with silver sails and distant haze - haze, please God, not smog. Now the pier comes into view, already mentally booked for the obligatory post-prandial stroll. Beside me, people are selling junk art, gazing out to sea or stretched out on the grass behind the beach. A lot of them look lonely. This is a good place to come when you don't want to be lonely by yourself.

"I can never remember-" begins Constance.

"Over there. Where is says Valet Parking."

The restaurant we are going to has an awning that projects over the sidewalk and a wall with plants along the top of it so that you are protected from the hoi-polloi as you fork your Louisiana crab cakes.

Constance pulls across the traffic and a stream of curses and parks more or less in the middle of the road. More screeching brakes and a faint whiff of burnt rubber. The Hispanic car jock at the entrance to the underground garage gesticulates frantically.

"If you can't get any closer, maybe we can find a cab." My father is nervously patting the bonnet of the car that has stopped two inches from Constance's wing mirror in a 'nice doggy, please don't bite' manner.

"Oh dear." Constance does something with her foot and the car leaps forward onto the sidewalk like an electrocuted frog.

The car jock rips open my door. "Enjoy y'meal." Difficult to avoid the feeling that the words could have been uttered with more sincerity.

"I'll do my best." My father graciously accepts the parking ticket and gallantly extends an arm to Constance. They precede me towards the restaurant. Behind us, I hear the screech of tortured rubber as our car meets the first bend of the ramp.

We walk through an archway of shrubbery and meet two sets of perfect white teeth detonated by our arrival into welcoming smiles.

Behind them, and of only marginally lesser impact, are sparkling eyes, cute button noses, lightly tanned skin and ultra-healthy blond hair, the standard facial accoutrements of the Southern Californian greeting girl.

"Hi! And how are you guys today?" exults the taller of the duo. She manages to make it sound like she twisted and turned all night wondering what the next twenty-four hours held in store for us.

"I'm expiring from terminal ennui," says my father.

"Great!" The fair one drops her head preparatory to studying a list of names. "Have you guys made a reservation?"

"Lock. Twelve-thirty. On the terrace."

"Gotcha!" She strikes out the name with satisfaction. "Your table's not quite ready yet. Would you care for a drink at the bar while you wait?"

My father sighs, and for a moment I fear that he is going to read her a lecture about the whole point of booking being that the table is ready when you get there. Luckily he looks from Constance to me and reads the silent pleading in our eyes. Satisfied that at least he has someone in his power he grudgingly agrees to go to the bar. The greeters look after him without warmth. My father has not responded with the obligatory spontaneous enthusiasm that would have made them feel appreciated and at ease.

"What do you want?"

"Oh dear," says Constance. "What are *you* going to have?"

She turns to me as I try to mount a bar stool gracefully. I shunt it two feet backwards and have to snatch behind me to stop it from falling. In the background I hear a tiny tinkle of suntanned laughter.

"I'll have a margarita, up, with salt." My father, impatient, is explaining his needs to the barman. "Shaken not blended. Spare me the explosion in the detergent factory."

The barman stares at my father coldly, digesting his words, breaking them down into sections that impart relevant information. He reaches for a glass.

"In a tumbler."

The barman slowly inclines his head and reaches for another glass. This guy is what Peter at the hotel could aspire to on his ruthless slog to the summit. He is groomed to the max. Every pore open to sunshine down to the corium, no gleaming lash out of place. He wears the restaurant tie and a spotless white shirt and a dazzling white starched apron and he looks so - so white. He does not so much mix my father's drink as beatify the ingredients that go into it.

"Your table is ready now. You requested the patio?"

Greeter Two is looming with three menus on boards. I know that my father would rather suffer a vasectomy with a rusty tuning fork than allow the word 'patio' to pass his lips but he merely grunts and tosses a bill onto the counter.

"That's eight dollars, sir."

Constance finds another five dollar bill immediately and we are led out to the patio, or the terrace, or the bit under the awning. Diners glance up immediately to see if we are famous. Their faces give us the answer.

"Enjoy."

"Thank you."

"You're welcome." Greeter Two willows away towards the desk.

I have noticed that 'Thank you' is a flummox phrase in Southern California. The locals reveal themselves uneasy in its presence, uncertain how to deal with it. It has no established role in the rituals of everyday life. Its appearance is almost a source of embarrassment. 'Uh huh', is a fairly common response. 'Urhh' is more frequent.

"You didn't order any drinks." My father's tone is accusing. He looks more relaxed now. Ensconced. The right table in the right place. Child opposite. Drink and mistress to hand.

"A glass of wine would be lovely," says Constance. I agree with enthusiasm.

"Why not?" My father's eye is already roaming over the wine list like a shepherd checking a well-loved flock. "What do you think? The Edna Valley or shall we try something else. I had a Grgich-"

"Hi! I'm Michael. I'd like to tell you about today's specials."

Michael is presumably addressing someone swimming towards Santa Catalina Island. As he reels off a list of dishes that sound like colour schemes dreamed up by a lunatic interior decorator on acid, his gaze is fixed on a point somewhere far beyond the end of the pier. I don't have to look at my father to know that a small, black cloud is forming over his head.

"...with a blueberry and béchamel sauce. That's a special favourite of mine." Michael lights upon us beneath him and salutes the discovery with a benign smile. "Do you folks have any questions?"

"No," I say hurriedly.

"Great. I'll give you a few moments to think about it." He disappears in a crackle of starch.

"Impertinence! Fellow should be dragged to the oubliettes and thrashed with oak staves." My father grinds his teeth. "Why should I give a tinker's toss what his name is? And why do they always have to interrupt you just when you're saying something really important?" He racks his brains before staring at me accusingly. "You've probably forgotten what I was talking about."

"You were going to order some wine."

"Oh yes." He drains his margarita. Salt from its rim has rhinestoned his beard. Mildly repulsive but there will be worse to come. "And why should I give a damn if he likes that filthy pudding? If he told me he liked sodomising frogs, would I start sprinting for the nearest swamp?"

The turbaned woman at the next table turns her head.

"It's no big deal," I grunt.

"'No big deal'," he mimics. "You sound just like your mother.

"That figures, doesn't it?" I say. "Given the choice, I don't have to sound like you all the time."

"It's tomorrow you're seeing Jim, isn't it?" Kind Constance gallops to the rescue.

"Yes. Ten thirty." Jim Zaiferts is a Senior Vice President at the studio she works for. Or is he just a Vice President? Or an Executive President? It probably doesn't matter very much when you are applying for a job as a reader or - come on, let's glamorise it a little - Script Analyst.

"I think you're going to like Jim. He's..." Constane hesitates and her long bony figures enclose air and start to sculpt a crude human form imbued with qualities both manifold and manifest.

"Yeah," I say. Of course, it doesn't really matter a hill of beans what I think about Jim Zaiferts. The important thing is that he should feel orgasmically good about me.

I wonder how old he is. The way the movie business is going I am probably a bit long in the tooth for this job. I haven't liked to ask but I'd wager that Zaiferts is under thirty. In his mid-twenties maybe. Separated from me by three years, a desk and one hundred thousand dollars. Youth is king and queen in Hollywood, and being over forty a disease worse than the Big C. My father is now what they call 'a veteran' - if they bother to call at all. Ho ho. I ponder. How old is he? Fifty-two? Fifty-three? When you get to that age the odd year or two can't make much difference.

Now he is looking chastened. Maybe it is because of our little brush. Maybe he is thinking about my mother.

"Toad-tool." He looks at us for a reaction. "Toadstool?? Get it?" Constance's smile is that of a freshly qualified psychiatric nurse struggling to survive her first week on the ward. My father sighs and shakes his head. "What do you want to eat?"

Around an hour and a half later things have deteriorated predictably. The chardonnay is nose down in the ice bucket and my father and Constance are on their second Cointreau and double espresso. 'Decaffeinated' is an anagram of 'snivelling wimp' as far as my father is concerned. Constance's hands pump up and down, occasionally thumping the table and her jaws bounce open like a gin trap as she mouths utterances like "No!!" and "Out-rage-ous!!" in response to my father's increasingly crazed ramblings. She looks like a happy seal. My father's face glistens with sweat and food that has got displaced in his beard. His napkin is a gouache, his glass like a vessel used to test a sample of the Ganges at Benares. No need to perform an autopsy; the ingredients of his meal jostle in its depths: a plankton of Caesar salad and soft-shell crab. Not eye candy, but it pales beside the oil slick of black leaking down his coffee cup. In contrast, Constance has flecked her china with nimbus smudges of puce lipstick. There is no justice. They are committing gastronomic murder and I am the one who is suffering.

Constance reaches across the table and playfully pushes my father in the chest. Oh dear. I can read the signs. Desperate for something else to look at, I gaze out onto the street. I am worried about tomorrow. Not just about the interview with Zaiferts but about the whole direction I am taking. Do I really want to work in the movie industry? Am I doing it because of my father or because I don't want to not do it because of my father?

Maybe my mother has something to do with it. It is difficult to separate yourself from your parents, even when they separate themselves from each other. If I don't do this what am I going to do? The people I was at university with are already standing in line to be cabinet ministers. Funny that: how I automatically think 'standing in line' rather than 'queuing up'. I guess I'm becoming a kind of chameleon, changing my colour/colour according to which of my parents I am feeling closer to. My mother is one of the few people you will ever meet who came from Nebraska.

A chair scrapes back and I turn hopefully. The woman with the turban is standing up. She takes a long, severe look at my father which I field before he can ask her where she parked her elephant. Her disgusted eyes sift through the detritus of our meal and she shakes her head. A disapproving 'tch' and she swings her Versace bag over her skinny shoulder and marches out ahead of her husband whilst he directs jerky papal benediction gestures at the staff as he struggles to keep up with her. He has to be her husband. I didn't hear them exchange a word throughout their meal. It's funny the couples that stay together.

"How are you guys doing here?" Michael's affable inquiry reeks of sincerity. In fact, it means 'fuck off, I want to go home'. To my relief, my father asks for the check. It comes fast and whilst my father empties a McDonald's carton of food from his dangling specs I check out the scene on Ocean. Quite a crowd out there now. Kids with skateboards. An old man on roller blades. Some blacks with a throbbing ghetto-blaster the size of a coffin. Two Lance Armstrong look-alikes with razor thin racing bikes, lurex tights, bulbous space-baddie helmets and skin-tight advertising board tunics - the Tour de France seen as a life-style. A bush-bearded mutterer fossicking in the trash bins. All human life is here. Enriched by the bonus of a very beautiful girl. She appears suddenly as her bicycle squeaks to a halt outside the restaurant. What eyes. Like a startled falcon's - or something redolent of strength tinged with vulnerability. She starts to get off and her long skirt snags on the saddle. I glimpse exquisite white thigh as our gaze meets through the wisteria. She blushes and thrusts her skirt down before wheeling her bike briskly out of sight. I feel strange. Turned over like a spadeful of earth. 'Laura, on the train that is passing through'. The girl makes me think of Lucy. Makes me think that I have not thought of Lucy for a couple of days. Something else to ponder.

Constance is huddled over a small card that tells her what fifteen percent of the bill is. My father groans, writes in the sum she tells him, achieves a laborious addition, signs the top slip and starts to extract carbons and tear them up. He deposits the tiny pieces in a coffee cup and stares at his smudged fingers for several seconds.

"A man comes home and finds traces of carbon on his wife's nipples. He knows that she's had lunch with a lover."

"Doesn't sound like a mainstream Hollywood movie to me," says Constance.

"The French would appreciate it," says my father. "I can see Emmanuelle Béart in the bath, screaming. Except they don't tear up their carbons. Shit! People always have to make things difficult, don't they?"

I nod and stand up. He is absolutely right.

I am glad to be outside but sad that there is no sign of the beautiful girl and her bike. I had constructed a modest fantasy in which her supple body would be bent over a punctured tyre. I would arrive to detect the tiny fizz of escaping bubbles, apply a patch like a soothing Band-aid, reveal controlled brute strength as I levered the taut rubber over the rim. It's strange. I can't even remember what she looked like. Lightish hair. Tawny,

I think. But it's no big deal. I'm always suspicious of writers who can reel off every detail of the beloved two seconds after she is encountered. If the first impression is overwhelming that should be enough for the moment. The nuances can be assimilated later.

Constance is now clinging to my father's arm. Unfettered child of nature, free spirit, drunk, he wishes to plunge across the street against the 'Don't Walk' sign. They look like a couple of middle-aged juvenile delinquents ready to tip over a trash can at the drop of a tab.

Constance must be getting on for fifty. She was a famous English actress who came to Hollywood and stopped being famous. She married an actor and became an American citizen before discovering that her husband was gay. This might have daunted some people but Constance was a game kid and, fortunately perhaps, bisexual. She tried to fight fire with Fire Island and my father hints at scenes of unbridled lust and titillating debauchery. Drugs, orgies, a gallant Constance gamely sharing the nuptial couch with her husband and a series of other men, none of whom, apparently, particularly interested in her. The marriage collapsed with her acting career and she became an agent and then a studio executive. She has the power to say 'no' to projects but not 'yes' and is valued because having been born a foreigner she is judged to have particular insights into overseas material which are useful but which can always be overruled because, having been born a foreigner, she can never really understand what Americans like.

I join the jostling throng heading down the causeway towards the pier. The sidewalk is a narrow ledge against the wall, as if someone remembered that people might want to walk rather than drive onto the pier only as an afterthought. Taking precedence beside me is a long line of slowly moving automobiles. Some of them I haven't see since I was a kid. Huge, semi-inflated balloons of dented metal with bits missing and rust at the corners. These families have come to the seaside from Downtown, Boyle Heights and East L.A. Places where dollar bills are counted in singles.

My father and Constance are skirting the milling crowd in front of the sideshows. There is a ritual to the after lunch Sunday walk. A brisk stroll to the end of the pier where the crusty fishermen are observed and the sea inspected. Then a slow return that takes in the break dancers, the escapologists, the half-naked man who dives onto a bed of broken glass, a couple of sideshows, the big wheel and the carousel.

The Santa Monica State Beach is peppered with a dust of families stretching away towards the Babylonian haze of Malibu. Kids dash in and out of the water like it might bite them. People loll and luxuriate in the sunshine. Smooch, schmooze, snooze.

How easy it is when all the clouds live over England. I remember the day trips to the seaside resort of Cromer. Looking out of the window all the time to see if it had stopped raining. Digging in against a damp breakwater to seek protection from the wind. Christ, that wind. All the way from Scandinavia. Swifter than the Norsemen but no less cruel. And the obligatory dip. If the undertow didn't get you then pneumonia would. Once my father had to save me from drowning. The day the rubber ring blew half way to Sheringham. Was there ever a sea more grey and cold? I can still run my fingers down my arm and feel the goose pimples. You had to build sand castles to keep the blood pumping through your body. And the sandwiches - 'because of the sand which is in them', the beach cricket with my mother faking a pitcher's wind-up, the tiny scuttling crabs, the starfish you weren't allowed to take home, popping seaweed, rock pools, saucy postcards, the final plod up the cobbled slipway with the sand itching between your toes. Happy days.

Now I am tailing my father past the Buccaneer's Inn - 'Cocktails - No Thongs'. As a child I used to think that Thongs were Chinese gangsters probably forbidden to mix with pink ladies. Here, where the steps go down to the beach, you can have your photo taken next to the cut-out of a famous person. Clint Eastwood, Marilyn Monroe, Antonio Banderas - probably here for the Hispanic contingent from East L.A. There is also President Bush as 'Top Gun'. Do I crave a permanent memorial of myself pressing the flesh with Dubya? Hmn. Let me think about it.

Leaning against a shed are two battered cut-outs of Laurel and Hardy, presumably en route to the scrap heap. This saddens me. One of my most enduring childhood memories is watching television with my father. Or rather, watching my father shaking with body-threatening laughter as Oliver Hardy sprawled in a fireplace and bricks released by Stan on the roof fell noisily on his head. I had never heard my father make noises like that before. Was he all right? Was something terrible happening? There seemed to be no relation between my father's reaction and what I saw happening on the screen. It was pretty scary.

I catch up with my father at the end of the pier. He is staring into infinity and gripping the rail in his 'Capten, art tha sleepin' there below?' pose. Constance is peering into the fishermen's bait buckets and making tiny 'ugh' noises. Two pipes on the bosun's whistle and they could be setting sail for China.

"Funny to think that the Don got here before us," says my father to no one in particular.

I make a non-committal noise that I have perfected over the years and become absorbed in a circling seagull. The pier used to be longer but a storm carried a large piece of it away. Now it is being 'redeveloped'. This will probably mean one hundred and fifty identical boutiques selling plastic mugs with your name on them whilst Micky Mouse drifts about in the background with a pooper-scooper. Sad. Come back squalor, all is forgiven. Nostalgia has no future in California.

"Right," says my father briskly. It is the voice of Scott having reached the South Pole. 'We've done our best, chaps. Pity about Amundsen. Now its time to go back and die heroically'. His paternalistic eye sweeps over the natives, no doubt pitying them - poor devils - for no longer having a queen to worship, and he takes a last deep breath, probably inspired by my grandmother: "ozone, dear," she would hiss whenever we got without sniffing distance of the sea.

Constance takes my arm but, sensing an involuntary tension, immediately releases it. My father is already striding down the pier and we follow him in single file.

A large crowd is watching a fire eater. At least, I think he is a fire eater. It seems increasingly possible that he might be an unhinged vagrant. He staggers, swigs from a bottle, splutters through a flame. Nothing. Either this is a very clever routine or the man is in imminent danger of grisly self-immolation. The crowd seems to be waiting patiently for the latter. Constance, sensitive soul, draws us away.

We move on to the rubber frogs. The idea is to hit a crude metal catapult with a wooden mallet so that your frog soars clumsily into the air and thwacks down on a rubber lily in a little pond. It becomes obvious immediately that the game would make a very effective sobriety test. My father's first carefully-rehearsed tap barely lifts the frog off its platform. His second lands it on the roof of a booth thirty yards away.

"Let me have a go," I say hurriedly. I manage to land one frog almost on a lily leaf and Constance thinks I'm wonderful.

My father is sulking, looking around for the rifle range and revenge but it seems to have disappeared. Perhaps the city fathers have taken advantage of the redevelopment to sweep it aside. Possibly a prudent measure. Things can get out of hand at the seaside. Near Venice Beach, my father saw a man drive a car backwards and forwards over another man until you could hear and see the bones breaking through his flesh.

There being nothing more virile for my father and I to compete at than hurling fluffy balls at empty matchboxes, we trudge on towards the carousel.

I am sad to notice that the pottery has closed. Sad but not surprised. The average meringue case bore more resemblance to a work of art than their Madonna heads, doves and puppy dogs, but therein lay their charm. They were so downright, outrageously awful that they shone out like beacons of originality amidst the rest of the tacky, derivative rubbish. I press my nose to the grubby window. Nothing. Empty shelves and a few sheets of dust-covered wrapping paper. Now I will never own a clay bulldog with a seam running down its nose.

The line for the wheel is daunting and Constance and my father are already waiting by the entrance to the merry-go-round. It is kind of them but there is no danger of me getting lost. At the end of the pier walk there is only one place to go. I can hear the hurdy-gurdy already, glimpse the rhythmic up-and-down of the painted horses, see the good little children clinging on through the glass. You only see good little children on a carousel.

My father has bought the tickets and we join the expectant line behind the barrier. Slowly, slowly, so very slowly, the merry-go-round glides to a halt. The horse you want is always on the other side. But no matter. You are a big boy now and you can walk with unforced dignity and accept a mount on the outside. One of the ones that does not go up and down. Your little friends and their assertive parents have pushed ahead to grab the best stuff. My father turns in the saddle and levels two fingers at me. His thumb cocks an imaginary hammer. Bang! Bang! Billy the Kidalong's mouth jumps open and his hands clutch at his heart. You got me, pop! The music cranks into laboured sound and we are under way. Constance rides side-saddle. She looks attractive, and happy. Everybody looks happy. This is such good therapy. Something about the honky-tonk music, the cosy shared experience, the expressions on the kids' faces, the expressions on the parents' faces as they watch the expressions on the kids' faces. Everybody thinking - like in a good dream - 'I am having the best time. This is so great'.

And, of course, this is the carousel in 'The Sting'. The movie with Paul Newman and Robert Redford and the catchy piano music by Scott Joplin. I could be sitting on Paul Newman's horse - only he would have had one that went up and down. 'I-want-to-be-happy-but-I-can't-be-happy' the honky-tonk music still crashes out but it's beginning to ring a little hollow and the good feelings are ebbing away, not too fast but just around the edges.

It must be because I'm thinking about tomorrow. Once the meeting with Zaiferts is over I'll feel better.

But then, I always feel sad on Sunday afternoons.

2.

I went to Nebraska once. With my mother to visit her family. Her 'folks'. I can't remember much about it because I was too small. The age when grown-ups' faces swoop down at you like frightening birds, always a little out of focus. It was cold, I remember that. Cold and flat. The house was a big bungalow with lawns front and back. I couldn't figure why they bothered to have them because they were always covered in snow and nobody ever walked on them except to put scraps on the bird table held by a carved wooden Indian propped up with a rock.

It was dark in the house and the furniture was big and scary. It loomed at you. My grandfather's breath smelt and they had an Airedale that bit me. I can still hear the creak of its wicker basket as it stirred in its sleep. Its breath smelt too.

The bite was the high point of our visit. My mother shouted at my grandmother and the dog was driven out of the house and ran round and round the wooden Indian making patterns in the snow. I think my mother went back for the funerals.

Now, the only time I think of Nebraska is when I see the college football results. I can imagine all those folks huddled together in some huge bowl under the freezing grey sky, getting off on the Cornhuskers beating the shit out of Kansas State. Driving their pick-ups home afterwards along those straight, straight roads, back to Wahoo or Weeping Water or where my grandparents lived. Everything is so far away in America.

I am lying in bed at the hotel. My father has gone to the movies with Constance. It is now three o'clock in the morning so let us treat that as a euphemism. I cannot sleep because I am worrying about tomorrow and my meeting with Zaiferts at the studio. Recently I have not been sleeping well because I have been worrying about what every tomorrow holds. They roll in, one after the other, like sullen black waves. This is bad. I should be sleeping like a log at my age. I am scarcely more than a growing boy.

Sleeping in the bed next to my father does not help. I wonder sometimes if, because there isn't enough room in his brain for all the demons, they hop over into mine. Normally he is so drunk when he retires that he is out like a light the moment his head touches the pillow. The sound of a saw mill cranking into log-splintering action starts immediately and gains in intensity. Then, just when I have drifted into sleep I am inevitably awoken by the sound of him creeping towards the bathroom. Out of consideration for me, he does not turn the light on so I wait in tortured anticipation until he stubs his toe on the door jamb or blunders into the television. 'Click'. Light floods the room and the bathroom door closes hurriedly and, usually, noisily. Then, a lusty thunder of Niagra in spate - quickly truncated - indicates that he has thoughtfully directed the relieving stream against the porcelain. Gratefully, I begin to close my eyes - 'BANG!' - he has dropped the lavatory seat. By now I have become a jangling bundle of nerves. But father is not insensitive. Tutting his clumsiness, he will retire to the icebox and slurp orange juice for ten minutes until satisfied that I have drifted off again. Then he will tiptoe back to bed and knock over a reading lamp.

I turn over for the umpteenth time and push my head into the pillow. No problems with space. This single bed could scoff most English double beds for breakfast and still feel hungry. And it is firm. Not like a sagging, elastic hammock. And the air conditioning purrs, keeping you at a perfect temperature. Like a tomato ripening in the darkness. 'Crump!' Another night owl motorist thumps past over the storm drain and, down towards the Santa Monica Freeway, there is the dismal wail of a police car siren. This is when all the things you read about in the L.A. Times are happening. Rapists shinning up and down drainpipes in Sherman Oaks. Drug-crazed deadbeats desperate for a fix prizing open Westchester windowsills with their switchblades. Hear that creak? You could be next, buddy.

Why can't images of good cheer and optimism fill my brain at this hour? Why does it always have to be gloom and uncertainty, a familiar parade of scythe-bearing skeletons pouring out of the closet and jostling to be the first to spark off a nightmare?

I remember once - it was when we were renting the house in Westwood - waking up in the middle of the night and finding the curtains radiant with brilliant light. A voice from above was telling me to come out with my hands up or they were going to send in the dogs. I had started off thinking 'E.T'. but this was rather blacker. This was it. What my English grandmother had told me was going to happen if I went on biting my fingernails. God can get very nasty with people who bite their fingernails. But it was not God come to drag me away to purgatory. It was an LAPD chopper with a searchlight. They had cornered a burglar in the garden of the house next door. Lucy wanted to know if the dogs would have been dropped out of the helicopter; and if they would have been issued with parachutes? She hoped so. Otherwise it would have been cruel.

Lucy. Uhm. Yes. I will ring her tomorrow - or rather, later today. Around twelve if I get back from the meeting in time. That will be eight o'clock in the evening in merrie olde England. It never seems right that England is ahead of the States. It should be dragging its heels in some temporal backwater, Roman numerals of leafy hours behind. Or maybe I will send a postcard. Except that all the postcards are out of focus or make L.A. look like downtown Detroit after a nuclear strike. Of course, I could send the hotel letter card with its photo of Peter in his scarlet uniform beside a white Rolls Royce against a background of exotic tropical foliage with the swimming pool glimpsed in the background, but this seems a trifle ostentatious. The English side of my nature craves something more low key - but in focus.

Good. Lucy has been dealt with in depth. Now what shall I think about? That nagging pain in my chest that I suspect is cancer, especially when it leaps to my left testicle? Having to cut off my penis because I have pissed in the Amazon and a minute candiru has swum up the stream of uric acid and activated its retrorse spines in the mouth of my urethra so that my bladder will explode? Alas, poor uric. My English grandmother would have understood. God has no time for people who piss in the Amazon.

When I was a child I spent the whole of one afternoon sobbing my heart out because I realised I was going to die. Not immediately. Just sometime. Grandma had told me about heaven but I couldn't handle the concept of living for ever and ever and ever with lots of people, many of whom I didn't want to see any more. I thought I would prefer it down here with mummy and daddy and more holidays. But you don't get a choice.

Should I look at my father's Penthouse again? The one he thought he'd hidden on top of the closet? Would this help me to sleep? Probably not. There is something very unpleasant about staring at the same beaver as your father, reading the same invented letters about guys with humungous dicks that cream off like fire hoses every two seconds. And then - NO! - it is too disgusting. Night, bring on new tortures.

I throw my thoughts up for grabs and, for a few seconds, glimpse the girl outside the restaurant; her irresistible look of peeved hauteur, that delicious white thigh, soft but with a sunlight ripple of muscle. I wish she could stay longer but she quickly decides that she does not belong in a mind like mine and disappears. Probably just as well. I should not be seeing her whilst I am still technically involved with Lucy. Lucy. Who I am going to talk to later today. Or whenever.

I twist my neck painfully to gaze at the clock with the luminous red digits. It is screwed to the bedside fixture, presumably so that you cannot hurl it into the middle of the pool when, for no particular reason, it starts playing 'I just called to say I love you' at five o'clock in the morning.

Now it is four o'clock. That means that it is midday in London. Maybe my mother will be reading at home. My mother is a literary agent. 'Twas not always so. When she married my father she was a potential housewife - or homemaker if you prefer it. She didn't. She and my father split up.

Now, most days, she goes into the office. But sometimes she stays at home with a pile of manuscripts and an apple. She saves the apple to the last manuscript. She is very conscientious.

I get out of bed and go into the spacious sitting room. Just a few words to tell her that I am all right. I can remember when you had to call the operator and give them the number: 'Thank you for calling AT&T'. I never knew what to do when they said that.

Should I have said something? : 'No. Thank you'. Or, 'It's a pleasure'. It seemed so off hand just to leave it there until the dialling tone. I have woken up this man in the middle of the night and he is thanking me and I am saying nothing. Maybe he was being ironic but this is America and that would have seemed very unlikely. I guess my concern was just the British half of my character showing through. Like those English tennis matches when you knock the word 'sorry' into the net for three sets.

The number rings and I have the momentary sensation of something tightening in my chest. Then 'click'. Disappointment. The answering machine. "Hi, I'm sorry you've got a recorded message but don't hang up. Leave a message after the bleep and I'll get back to you as soon as I can." I could hang up immediately but I continue to listen until the message is over. My mother has a beautiful voice. Very modulated. She cossets each word so that you believe that she really is sorry, that she really does want to talk to you.

I blurt a few words and put the phone down. It's funny but it's almost better like this. If we had talked there would have been a risk of some glitchy grains of sand getting into the words. A misunderstood remark, a shading of the voice. This way my mother has been just how I wanted her. Beautiful, warm, serene. More there than there. I am almost tempted to call her back. Just to hear her voice again.

She met Philippe at Club Med. So did we, I suppose. He was, and still is, fifteen years younger than her, and her friends were shocked. It was not abnormal to have an affair with a handsome young Frenchman - on the contrary, it was probably enviable - but to fall in love with him. To leave your husband and live with him. Well.

I subsequently discovered that most of the tutting ladies had been tupped by my father, but that did not seem to change anything. They were still disapproving and he was bitterly upset. "I'm a one woman man," I once heard him say plaintively to a male friend, "except for sex, of course." I think this is true. He does still love my mother and he will remain a 'one woman man'. Except for sex, of course.

Footsteps are approaching the apartment. Slap, slap, slap. I recognise the weary tread. Like a lame walrus with a hangover. My father must have had a row with Constance. Or maybe he couldn't face the thought of breakfast conversation. I have seen his features contort in pain at the first whirr of a juicer. The reason doesn't matter. He is coming through the door in a few seconds and I do not want to see him. I turn off the light and run into the bedroom. I am just pulling up the sheet when I hear the apartment door opening. Shit. I should have left the light on. He probably saw it being turned off. I feel guilty and annoyed that I feel guilty. I wait but he does not come to bed before I have fallen asleep.

"Do you want to dance like the monkeys do in France?" I awake to the muffled sound of my father singing in the bathroom. 'Singing' is another euphemism. I always imagine that other people's fathers sing well-known ballads like 'Old Man River' or 'Oh what a beautiful morning' but my father composes his own tuneless dirges that always include references to monkeys and something called Nosgra Trees. No, I have no idea what they are either. While he is splashing water or misdirecting piss everywhere, he attacks the morning with these one-line ditties usually bawled aggressively in the manner of a football chant. There is never a hint of melodic inspiration, nothing to suggest that he could compose a hummable nursery rhyme if he lived another thousand years.

"Why do nosgra trees dance every day…?" In nearly every case, the lay contains a question that is never answered. This clearly infuriates the singer so that he repeats the words with mounting intensity until they eventually force their way through his tightly-clenched teeth as unintelligible mumbles spattering the bathroom mirror in toothpaste.

I could do without that this morning. As is always the case when it is time to get up I have just purged the demons of the night and entered the magic kingdom of dawn doze. Like a drowsy drone on a honeycomb, I am steeped in delicious half-sleep, pampering myself with languid feline stretches, able at will to drift into deep slumber should I weary of the warm shafts of sunlight gently patting my cheek. At least, that is the general idea. The idyll is shattered when my father marches into the room behind his bulging stomach and tosses discarded clothes on my bed. "Don't forget you've got a meeting," he says.

When I go into the living room he is sitting by the window reading the Los Angeles Times. Or rather, he is staring at one section of it. The other three hundred and sixty-odd pages stick out of the wastebasket. My father goes through the L.A. Times like a customs official with Tourette syndrome on piecework. He calls it 'The Tree-Murderer', curses it for making his fingers filthy, accuses the editors of intentionally hiding the sports section so that he can never find it, says that you could learn more about world affairs by reading the graffiti on a shithouse wall in Pensacola. He even boos the paper's commercials when he goes to the movies.

"Listen to this," he says. "'The first person to jump 210 feet to his death from the Japanese-built bridge over the Bosphorus was a Japanese tourist, Mr Hiroshi Eguchi'. That's very sad, isn't it? So why do I laugh?"

"Because you're a very sick human being," I tell him.

"That's not the only reason. It's something to do with the fact that he's a Japanese tourist and that it's in Turkey. It has to do with nationalities. I don't think it would work with an Englishman or an English bridge."

"That's because you're English," I say. "The Japanese would probably find it hysterically amusing."

"Possibly." My father ponders. "I wonder if he knew."

"That he was jumping off a Japanese bridge?"

"Exactly."

"Maybe his wife had ditched him for the man who built it."

"Too obvious."

In this life there are earthquakes, typhoons, mudslides and tidal waves. Air crashes, train derailments, explosions in ammunition factories, leaks from chemical plants, burnouts in nuclear reactors, space rockets and senior executives. People caught up in these catastrophes think of themselves as being victims of a human tragedy. They are wrong. In reality they are auditioning for a part in one of my father's movies.

"You think there's a movie in it?"

My father - he can direct, just ask him - frames a screen with his thumbs and forefingers. "We start with these Japanese eyes, very clear, very intense. Sort of young Tishiro Mifune. Then-"

"You're going to stick with a Japanese hero?"

"He's in love with Nicole Kidman. She comes in later. This is a flash forward."

"Obviously."

"We see the eyes and then there's an almost imperceptible blink and - they've gone. Hold on the empty sky. Now we pull back, back, back. We start to see the bridge, and the mosques, and the minarets, start hearing the mysterious watery sounds of Istanbul. Maybe some of that music... you know..."

"'Midnight Express?'"

"Something like that. Back into the Golden Horn and the souks and whatever. And then-"

"Wait a minute," I say. "If it's Nicole Kidman, she's going to want to be on the bridge."

My father looks at me. He knows I am right. "Are you going like that?" he says.

The path that guided my father towards the movies was long and arduous - and probably not a path at all, just stepping stones of happenstance...screen ripples and dissolves, dates flutter down from a calendar....a locomotive chugs towards us....

On the train pulled by that locomotive my father, then a struggling advertising executive commuting from our humble dwelling in the poverty belt, wrote unsuccessful adventure novels. Once a year he was invited to lunch by his publisher in a second rank (as befitted his status) Soho restaurant. Emboldened by adequate wines, to which at that time he was not so accustomed, he dared to suggest that perhaps there was a way to make money from books that, so far, few publishers had deigned to try: give the reader what he wanted. Sucking the nectar from his second Cointreau he postulated that a book entitled 'The Sexy Diary of a Window Cleaner' would sell a million copies. His publisher, then desperately trying to catch the eye of a waiter for the bill, froze like the key of a cash register nipped by a Pleistocene frost. "Write it," he breathed

My father was wrong about a million copies. It sold nearer three million. And 'The Dirty Diary of a Driving Instructor' did even better. ('Sexy Diary' was changed to 'Dirty Diary' because the title promised more of the kind of sex that people were beginning to admit that they really enjoyed and because the alliteration stopped it sounding too dirty dirty as opposed to cheerful rugger club smutty.)

Andy Groper was the eponymous hero of the books and they delivered what they promised. When Andy's potent pussy-pounder was not penetrating the promised gland, his throbbing amber mamba would be spearing the hairy clam. Or his pocket-rocket exploding in the - I think the flavour has been conveyed. It was not that Andy was promiscuous. He was a victim. First of his penis, which seemed to have a life completely independent of the rest of his body, and secondly, of all womankind who, typical of their predatory nature, had only to clap eyes on our hero before ripping off their clothes and attempting to impale their quivering dilly pots, love grottos and furry dells on his rampant giggle stick, love truncheon, loin leopard, throbbin' robin etc., etc.

In each book, Andy pursued a different profession chosen because of its association in the public mind with opportunities for sexual shenanigans. 'Hotel Porter', Travelling Salesman'; 'Taxi Driver' tumbled after each other and he had written about ten before sales began to drop off, at which point the movies arrived to relaunch interest. At the beginning, the 'Dirty Diaries' were like a blight on the bookshop shelves, a swarm of colourful midges. You could watch them winging towards the cash desks as the sales staff struggled to restock the fast-emptying shelves.

In the wake of this success, my father, already disenchanted with advertising - a reciprocal feeling, I understand - gave up his job to write full time. The money from the 'Dirty Diaries' was going to buy him the time to produce something more serious, something worthwhile. In fact he produced even more 'Dirty Diaries'. It seemed insane not to when the market was there and everybody told you how fickle public taste could be. The good stuff could come later. We moved house and my mother was presented with a scarlet convertible about which she had mixed feelings.

A 'film producer' - more specifically a second hand car salesman and dealer in 'exotic' films - emerged as if from under a golden stone and my father started writing film scripts. Or rather, the same script over and over again. My father did not know it then but Bernie Bowman could not afford a real writer and nobody saw any future for the films. This is how my father ended up with points instead of money. A wonderful deal as it turned out.

After a million tribulations, the movie of 'The Dirty Diaries of a Window Cleaner' was made and released. This was a terrible time. The paperback books had never been released. The film was. The critics universally announced that it made the cheapest, most offensive smut hitherto palmed off on the British public seem like 'Sense and Sensibility'.

It made no difference to the public. Outside treacherous London they formed queues around the block, and for the sequels, to the farthest corners of the English-speaking world, apart from America where they could not understand what anybody was saying - not that this was very relevant. My mother was relieved that at least nobody in Nebraska was likely to see the film and by this time had locked her fur coat in the cupboard and given up using the convertible to go shopping. When the accountants announced that we had a choice between giving most of the money to the government or going abroad she was almost happy to start packing.

My father had no qualms. He did the work. He drove to the studio gates to a reserved parking spot and watched the sets being built. He had lunch with his publisher - much more frequently these days. He was intimately and profitably involved in something that had been his idea and that was a huge success. He hardly had time to mix with people outside the circle he was working with and that happy band had nothing but positive things to say about what he was doing. My mother could spend the money, and sip coffee with her comparatively indigent friends. Also, she had already left home once. I was uneasy and sorry to leave my prep school, but life abroad was going to be an adventure and I would have my parents with me.

"Did you hear what I said?" My father is still smarting about Nicole Kidman. "Are you going to go like that?"

My world-weary sigh strives to forgive him for being so bourgeois. "This is the only clean shirt I've got."

"I was talking about the shoes."

"They're my Reeboks."

"They look as if you found them on a rubbish dump."

"Everybody wears them."

"Not when they're falling apart."

"Do you want me to wear a suit?"

"No! Nobody wears a suit in California, unless they're going to their agent's funeral. Anyway, you'd probably sweat and that would be fatal. You should wear something just like everybody, else only slightly different. Something you feel good in."

"I was feeling pretty good like this," I tell him.

Now it is my father's turn to sigh. "Okay. Go like that. Go in pair of velvet bloomers with a feather up your bum if you want to."

"Fine."

A long pause. "Just change the shoes."

An hour and a half later I am screaming (literally) east along Wilshire. the stretch past the L.A. Country Club where you can slam your foot down for all of three hundred yards before meeting another light. My father had put the car keys somewhere safe. Somewhere where it would be impossible to miss them: an ash tray on top of the icebox as it turned out after we had been looking for half and hour and he had accused me of losing them. The result of this typical paternal cock-up is that I am now seriously L-A-A-A-T-E!! for my date with cinematographic destiny in the Valley. Every light will be against me. Shit! There goes the first one. Hundreds of hard-faced women in convertibles are pouring across the road from Beverly Hills like flying foxes en route to the fruit groves. It is strange. The older they are, the bigger the car. Some of these babes are so small and wizened that the only evidence of their presence in the car is a pair of bejewelled hands thrust up to grasp the steering wheel. They must need mirrors in the roof to bird dog each other into Robinsons. Good hunting, ladies. May there be enough diamante clothes pegs for all of you.

I burn the lights at Santa Monica - AND YOU, ASSHOLE! - and burrow into the phalanx of superior motor vehicles that congests the bosky purlieus of Beverly Hills. Fortunately, reading the local road signs has a calming influence - like watching fifty dollar bills drift down before your eyes in a dream: Roxbury, Bedford, Camden, Rodeo - yes, the Rodeo Drive where you have to make an appointment to get into a shop and buy twelve of everything if you want to get your parking validated. Beverly, Canon, Crescent. The traffic will thin out a bit when I get to West Hollywood. I turn on the radio: '-and as Nasrula, the great Persian poet tells it to us, we are the knowledge, we are the truth, we are the-' Boy, I wonder who rented this car before my father. No doubt about it, L.A. does provide listening for ever taste. Stations that only play The Grateful Dead's greatest hits to those that survive on selected readings from the Book of Deuteronomy: '-so remember, friends. The reward is in the giving, not the gift. Let me give you that number one more time-'. I flick on hurriedly. A D.J. is bemoaning that there are four whole days 'count 'em' to the next weekend and that he cannot wait that long. Suicide seems a serious option. Go ahead, friend, make my day. One more try: 'Barbie, I know this is difficult but I want to ask you a serious question. Do you think it would be a good thing for society in general if serial sex offenders were castrated?' 'Gee, well. I don't know. I mean, I guess, if you could do it without hurting them too much' - I turn off. Better to hum along with the air conditioning. All these stations, all these people playing music you never liked and telling you things you don't want to know in order to sell you things you don't need. All that choice. Still, that guy by himself in the car beside yours at the lights is laughing his head off. What is he listening to? Why not lower the window and ask him? ARE YOU CRAZY!!! He might think it was a stick-up and whip out his magnum. BOOM! BOOM! Lots of facial rearrangement before the loved ones filed past the open coffin.

Commander Chuck is the one I like. He is up there in his little plane, looking down at us - and after us. A Sig Alert on the Pomona Freeway, a ten mile tailback on the Harbor Freeway south of Slauson, an abandoned bedstead on the north lane of the Long Beach Freeway just south of Firestone - what is it with these bedsteads? Why is it never an icebox or a washing machine? Why are they always dumped on the freeway? Who does it? When? Are they a religious cult? Anyway, Commander Chuck is up there peering down at all this confusion and frustration and people picking themselves out of mangled bed springs and he stays so twinkly and chirpy and folksy and calm. Just like God on a really great ecumenical Sunday. I try and take a lesson from Commander Chuck. Try and stay above it all.

I am now in West Hollywood. A part of L.A. that has a large gay population. My father would be swift to point this out to you, though perhaps not in quite those terms. He normally checks the fuel gauge when approaching the city limits and drives past the outdoor cafés and colourful clothes shops looking neither right nor left. Only when reaching the unashamedly feminine contours of the Beverly Hills Post Office does he begin to loosen up a little. Perhaps the local lights perceive the presence of my father's car. They turn red every time it comes within fifty yards of them.

Stay calm. There is nothing you can do about it. Just take a few deep breaths, turn up the air conditioning and hate your father. My eyes wander over to the sidewalk. How sad. The pasty-faced youth standing by the doughnut stand: 'Some say' - crossed out - 'the best donuts in the world'. You usually see these kids further along Santa Monica, emerging around dusk. This guy must be desperate. His jeans are too small, not promiscuously tight, small. The grubby white T-shirt has the sleeves rolled up almost to the armpits. He looks Swedish with all that blond hair. Probably comes from Minnesota. They have a lot of Swedes up there, don't they? Or is it Michigan? No, that's where Michael Moore comes from. I wonder what brought this sad kid to L.A. And to this. Maybe somebody told him he looked like a movie star. He does remind me of someone. Maybe his father split and his mother married again - or got involved. Time to move on. He hitched towards the sun but nothing worked out. Lousy, dirty, go-nowhere jobs - when he was lucky enough to find one. So he started doing drugs because they gave dead time a little edge and because everybody did them. Then he had a habit. Then a more expensive one. No problemo. Just do a trick occasionally. It's real easy. After a while, you don't think about it. So he did. And he didn't. And now he's standing there with the white skin of Death in an Ingmar Bergman movie and that moist, staring look as if his eyes have been removed and replaced with shiny stones; scratching himself, carrying his hands over the lumps on his arms, waiting for the car to slow down and the 'over here, baby' look from the trick.

Our eyes meet and-shit! He's coming over. Surely he can't - not me - the lights change and I nearly strip the gearbox in my panic to get away. The fucking car stalls. Now he is bending down towards me. Oh, God. I can feel the hot flush igniting my cheeks.

"How amazing, I dreamt about you last night." Original approach although I'm not flattered and-wait a minute. There is something familiar about that face. "Hadiscomb. We were at Rockingham together." Christ. The old school. Small world. "Small world."

"Yes," I say. "What-what are you doing here?"

"Holiday. Well, sort of. I'm with my parents." He has a flat English Midlands accent, poshed up a bit like Margaret Thatcher's. I vaguely remember him fainting when he went up to collect the divinity prize. Or maybe it was somebody else. I can be a bit hazy about the past. Especially when it concerns Rockingham.

"You're just the guy I need. Somebody who knows the lie of the land. I'm looking for a shop called Esprit."

I am wrestling with conflicting emotions. This is becoming my main source of exercise. Relief gets the decision by a grudging submission from irritation and anxiety.

"Get in," I hear myself saying. "I'm going past the door."

Encouraged by angry hooting from redneck Angelinos who resent being held up by the trade of perverts, he scrambles into the car. He wears the kind of cologne that a maiden aunt might give you for Christmas and rubs his hands nervously. "Thanks a lot. I always get confused by the street numbers. They don't seem to follow sequentially - if that's the right word."

"You should ask for a cross street," I tell him. "Sorry if I seem a little preoccupied. I'm late for an appointment."

"Gosh, I'm sorry." His hand leaps to the door handle. "Let me off here."

"Stay put, it's okay."

"No, seriously. Drop me off. I'll find my way."

He is almost scrambling out of the car and I can imagine the guys in the truck behind thinking that there has been a disagreement about the price of his services.

"Sit tight!" I am surprised how psychotic my voice sounds. "It's all right."

I wish I could find it in myself to be more friendly but I have things on my mind and you don't expect phantoms from the satanic mists of your English public - equals private - school to swirl towards you on Santa Monica Boulevard. Now I come to think about it I'm pretty certain that he broke an ankle in a house match.

"Where are you staying?"

"The Beverly Hilton. It's pretty nice. Got a swimming pool." A strange piece of information to impart. In Beverly Hills where the average gardener's mutt has its own swimming pool. Still, I suppose when you come from England. "How long are you going to be here? We could-er-you know-um…"

Luckily, being half-British, I know what he is trying to say. "Yes, we could."

I give him the name of my hotel and we pull up outside the concrete bunker that Esprit might have bought from Hitler. There is a high-pitched, mocking wolf whistle from the truck as it overtakes us. "Give me a ring."

"I will." He says it very firmly and holds onto the hand he has insisted on shaking. "I'm glad I've caught up with you."

"Sure." I pull out onto La Cienega - GO PISS IN THE AMAZON, BUDDY!! - feeling a new phase of unease. 'I'm glad I've caught up with you'. Strange choice of words. And why did I say the British 'give me a ring' instead of 'call me'.? The chameleon in me, I suppose.

I scoot along Fountain for a few blocks and turn up towards Franklin. Sunset and Hollywood are hurdled and hillside homes pepper the skyline ahead as if they have been dumped by a tidal wave. You have to have nerves of steel to live in the canyons. Flash floods, bush fires, coyotes that can eat your dog, maniacs - molto maniacs. A lot of the houses are poised on stilts like they have limped away from a painting by Dali. At last, Highland and the Hollywood Bowl. I must go to a concert. Just once so I can get it out of my system. I have the choice of the Hollywood Freeway but I chicken onto Cahuenga Boulevard. I have to be in the right mood for the freeway. Very up. Very brave. Sometimes it can seem that you are in a birch bark canoe approaching a huge, fast-flowing river. You tremble on the slip road and - slomp! You're in it. Sucked into a moving log jam of thunder. Pick-ups, trucks, articulated trucks, juggernauts. Threadbare tires, shot brakes, fifty mph-? - you must be kidding. Barham Boulevard. Already!? That's where you want to get off but you're in the wrong lane. Try and get over. Come on! I'm signalling, aren't I? Please let me in. Please! BLARE!! All right, all right! This time. Scr-e-e-e-ch! Squeal! BLARE!! FLASH!! What's that guy screaming? He looks crazy. Has he got a gun? Fuck it. It's too late. You've missed it. Now the next turn-off is Lankershim. LOOK OUT!!! There's one of those fucking bedsteads. A-A-A-A-A-RGH!!! SKID! CRUNCH! SMASH! Tinkle, tinkle, tink...

The studio is near Forest Lawn Memorial Park. The cemetery. Though, of course, nobody ever uses that word. It has unpleasant connotations. It suggests death. Death is a taboo word in Hollywood. It suggests that you're not going to live forever. And not living forever is hostile to the whole concept of being Californian. It is another nasty word like 'age' which has difficulty shaking off its grisly doppelganger 'old'. Old age has the unenviable reputation here of being the harbinger of the aforementioned unmentionable.

I pass over - or perhaps pass away is more appropriate - from the Hollywood Freeway and weave down Barham. Soon, I can see the sound stages like aircraft hangars and the hand-painted billboards that proudly announce the studio's recent releases. Three no-nos and a so-so. The colours on the posters are still lustrous but the dreams must be beginning to fade. What effect will these turkeys have on my chances of being hired? Will they be combing the Filofax for new blood to redress the balance, or retrenching whilst they lick their wounds? Probably neither. The movie industry keeps going on a kind of dogged, cock-eyed optimism; the belief that somewhere in that labyrinth of greed and paranoia there must be a couple of guys whipping up a script that is going to be the next E.T.

I get to the appropriate gate five minutes late. Not bad. I can schmooze with Zaiferts about how bad the traffic was. Maybe even embellish the Hadiscomb incident into an amusing little vignette. Maybe not.

The security guy lolls out of his little hut. "Yessir?"

"William Lock. I have a meeting with Jim Zaiferts." Not 'Mr Zaiferts'. This is America. By the same token I should probably have called myself 'Bill'. With a name like William you have choices. Very handy for us chameleons. 'William' is stern and dignified. A little austere and unapproachable. He conquers things. It is what my mother calls me when she is angry with me. 'Will' is more sensitive and artistic. It is what girls who like me call me. Before they call me William. Will turns his profile to the evening light and scribbles poetry. 'Bill' is a pretty average sort of chap. Solid, Reliable. Plays games. Somebody to share a beer or go into the jungle with. 'Billy' is a 'good ol boy', always itching to rip open a six-pack in front of the Monday night football game. He shouts 'Y-e-e-e-e-a-a-a-hhh!!' and 'A-L-L-L-R-R-R-I-I-I-I-GHT!!!' and loves to do high fives. Don't introduce him to your sister. Don't lend him your car.

Yes, I should have been friendly, clean cut Bill not stand-offish William. Still, it's not too late to change. The security man doesn't give a shit what I call myself. He stops thumbing through a sheaf of passes. "Haven't got anything for Lock. You'll have to pull over there and call the office."

Great! Some moronic underling has goofed off. I consign them to a date with Vlad the Impaler and nearly knock an elderly messenger off his bike as I dump the car and pelt to the phone - occupied by a man who seems to be translating the Bible into Serbo-Croatian from memory and who occasionally flicks his wrist at me to go away like I am some annoying insect. By the time I get to the phone, find Zaifert's number and get an authorisation to see him I am running twenty-five minutes late. Not running, driving rather faster than the 5m.p.h. speed limit along a winding blue line towards Executive Plaza West. It is not glamorous around here; a hinterland of prefabricated buildings that give the impression they have arrived in the night; a trailer park without the mud and the barking dogs.

The blue line ends and I have to find somewhere to park. Not easy. All the parking places have stencilled names attached to them - few of them are fading which suggests something slightly alarming - and I reason that it would not be a smart career move to leave my modest Japanese import in the Studio Head's slot. At last. 'Visitors Parking'. Yes, Lynn Truss, I know it sounds like a statement but I don't have the time. 'Taken'. 'Taken'. 'Taken'. Fuck! What are all these sodding people doing here!?

I dump the car at the end of the line and stride towards the block of concrete with the blue windows. It is important that I stay calm. I take a few remedial deep breaths. Sweat is dribbling down from my armpits but hopefully nobody will notice unless I leap into the air and try and leave my hand prints on the ceiling. Past the dusty shrubbery and through the swing doors. Push not pull, Will. Interesting character revelation there, but the guy behind the desk in the middle of the atrium does not look like a psychiatrist. More like a retired (corruption? brutality?) police captain which he probably is. He must have seen it all. The great, the not so great, me. People leaving in exaltation, despair, floods of tears, handcuffs. People like my father chanting incredulously: 'They bought it! They bought it!'

I blurt out Zaifert's name and he jerks his thumb over his shoulder towards the stairs and goes back to reading The National Inquirer: 'Two-headed Martian was my dream lover!' I was expecting more security but I am not going to argue. I mean, when was the last time you read the headline 'Famous movie producer slaughtered at desk!'? Strange when you think of the nature of the business.

Up the stairs, two at a time, and down the long, long corridor hung with framed stills from the Oscar-winning roles of the immortals. I recognise her. And him. And he's in that TV series playing the grandfather. Can't remember what his name is. And that movie's on every Christmas. 321, 322, - I want to go to the bathroom but there isn't time and it's probably only nerves - 323. The name tag catches my eye. Constance Powell. That's our Constance, my father's Constance. But the office is empty and there is only a sagging patchwork cat burying its face in the sofa as certain proof of her studio existence. 325. Here we are. I take a couple of deep breaths and try and empty my mind of negativity. I walk into the outer office.

My father who visits these places all the time says that there are two kinds of secretary, although they are always called 'assistants'. One of them is the surrogate mother. She is round and cuddly. She feeds you candy and gossip, describes what happened on her last date, her trip to Europe, provides details of her sister-in-law's hysterectomy, plies you with drinks and magazines. After five minutes you can feel that you have known each other all your life, that you ought to swap addresses so that you can exchange birthday cards.

Then there is Jim Zaifert's secretary, the Pope's mitre. The spiritual guardian of the great one's entity. The almost him. She is so integrated into the persona of her boss that symbiosis has taken place. She is that person purged of weakness. Cross this woman at your peril.

"Bill Lock," I say. "I may be a bit late."

Zaifert's secretary winces as if this information is redundant, and finishes what she is typing before replying. "He's in a meeting," she says coldly. "Take a seat."

I am heading for the comfortable sofa glimpsed through the open door to the large inner office when she jabs a finger towards the chair in front of her desk. I sink into it obediently like she has said 'basket'.

"Can I get you something?"

The words are spoken without eye contact, and with such lack of enthusiasm that I feel it would be presumptuous to ask for a Coke.

"No thanks."

She nods briskly and goes back to her typing. She is attractive in a haughty sort of way and wears a simple, high-necked, grey dress, trimmed with blue ribbon around the vertical slit that plunges towards her breasts. I have plenty of time to check this out in the half hour that elapses whilst she fields non-stop phone calls and scribbles messages. I am impressed. Zaiferts must be at the hub of the Hollywood universe.

Just as I am wondering whether to go to the men's room for a little light relief, a tall, shirt-sleeved guy in his late twenties, with a jacket slung over his shoulder, breezes into the office and sticks out his hand. A sheaf of messages is thrust into it by the amanuensis who speaks without looking up. "The screening's at six. Ray's going to call you at home. I've booked Le Dome for lunch tomorrow." This must be the great man. I wonder whether to spring to my feet or at least rise, but he is already heading into his office swinging his arm forward from the shoulder in a gesture reminiscent of John Wayne scrambling out of a foxhole: 'Let's go get those little slit-eyed bastards!' Is this directed at me? I look to the assistance for guidance but she has eyes only for her computer. I hurry after Zaiferts and wonder whether to close the door behind us. Better not. It might suggest that I was anal-retentive or bent on assassinating him.

Zaiferts hurls his jacket across the room and collapses into a black leather and chrome Eames chair, throwing his head back and gripping the arms with both hands. His knees are wide apart with his raised heels under his thighs. He is wearing cowboy boots with scrolly bits around their scalloped tops. He lets out a rebel yell and jerks forward so that for a moment I think he is going to spring at me. "Ellie!" He swivels in my direction. "Siddown." Tough call. Should I go for the sofa or the armchair? The armchair might be his. On the other hand, am I being unassertive, wimpish even, by failing to occupy the throne of power and authority? The most important thing is to make a decision. I sit on the sofa.

She who must be Ellie has appeared in the doorway, her face devoid of emotion. One feels that human beings are merely blank screens on which she projects her thoughts.

"Book my table at Mortons. Nine-no-nine-thirty-no-nine. Three people. You want something?" His words slam into each other like wagons in a train crash and it takes Ellie's bored stare to make me realise that the last three were directed at me.

"Er..." This time I had better have something. It would be friendly. The fist step towards our bonding. But what? Juice? Juvenile. Perrier? Flakey. Club Soda? Dull. Say something, dummy! "A coffee would be great."

"Cream? Sugar?" The words are snapped out like the last two tickets for a ride on her patience.

"Black, please."

Genies have disappeared slower.

Behind his desk, Zaiferts is leafing through his messages, body thrust forward, elbows resting lightly, a jungle cat poker player examining his hand. Occasionally he tosses his head back and his long hair - it could be described as a tawny mane - taps the nape of his neck. Bounce.

I steal a glance around the room. The desk is across one corner and rises in tiers giving the impression of an organ in an old-fashioned movie theatre. I can imagine Zaiferts rising from the depths pumping out 'The Stars and Stripes for ever', up, up until he floats above everybody else in the room. Beside the desk is a state of the art V.C.R. and music system plus a ton of DVDs. Nice. A low table supports a small robot, a never-ending spring that walks down stairs, a diabolo, several separate-the-bits-of-metal conundrums and a jar of pistachio nuts. A miniature basket ball net is attached to one wall with a small sponge basketball waiting nearby. The executive den par excellence. Zaiferts does not need a home. He could rent his apartment and stay here and play with his toys and scoff pistachios. And that freezer in the outer office must be groaning with supplementary nutriment. Ellie would make sure you never starved.

She walks in and hands me a small mug of coffee as if she wished it was the contents of a pooper-scooper. "Thanks."

"Hmhuh." She goes out.

As if her departure was a signal, Zaiferts tosses his messages aside and springs to his feet. He flails his arms for several seconds and charges to the centre of the room. A big stretch and he flops into the armchair with his legs dangling over one of its arms. His hand thrusts out for the nuts. "Okay. Procrastination is the - who gives a shit? Let's cut to the chase. I am Tootorey."

Several seconds pass. Who the hell is Tootorey? Have I come to the wrong office? Maybe he is inviting me to call him by some arcane nickname: 'Tootorey' Zaiferts. It seems a bit of a mouthful.

He sees that I am confused. "As the French would say."

Further thought is necessary. Then I get it! What he said was 'I am *toutes oreilles*': 'I am all ears' in French. I am glad we have got this little mystery cleared up but it hardly constitutes a giant stride forward in our relationship. "Er-yes," I say. "Aaaargh!"

I say "Aaaargh!" because I have just taken a sip of the coffee and it is scalding hot.

"Hot, huh?" Zaiferts' tone is not unsympathetic but he glances at his Patek Philippe watch and gobbles a pill that has materialised from nowhere. Vitamins, no doubt. I sense that I am in danger of losing him before I have even started.

I put my coffee down quickly, spilling it. "It's about that job as a reader, or a script analyst. You see-" I break off because Zaiferts is staring at me strangely. The pistachio shells drop from his fingers before he can continue hurling them in the general direction of the wastebasket. His eyes widen. "Are you British?" There is a kind of building incredulity in his voice. As if, the more he thinks about it, the more it seems incredible that such a human condition could exist.

"My father's English. My mother's American."

"Really?" He is still staring at me. "Go ahead."

I try to talk persuasively about my all-consuming passion for the movies but I read the perplexed wonder in his eyes and am conscious of only one thing: how English I sound. How effete. How totally lacking in verbal vigour - I mean, vigor - how affected, how supercilious, how fumbling, how utterly devoid of even one jot, tad or iota of the raw, untamed dynamism that spouts from every pore of Jim 'Mr Motion' Zaiferts as he lopes puma-perfect across his den and glances at a desk diary the size of the Doomsday Book. It is as if Hadiscomb had been some ghastly succubus, lurking en route to slink into my body, neutralise my mother's red-blooded Yankee genes and substitute them with a metastasis of banal, insipid, empire-losing bromides.

"You're not Larry Bannof - 'Forbidden Dreams'? Shit!" Zaiferts shouts towards the outer office like a spoilt child pissed with his mother. "This isn't Larry Bannof!"

"Do you wanna speak to Jeff?" Ellie's voice comes right back at him.

"Yes, no, yes." He snatches up a phone, swears at it, grabs another one. "Howyadoin, asshole?" He throws himself back in his swivel chair and the tawny mane spanks the back of his neck. Bounce. "Fuck you too." He listens cheerfully. "Did she? Well, fuck her!" He sucks his teeth and juggles a remote control. "The fuck I did! The guy's out of his fuckin' mind!" I listen, fascinated. I have never heard the word 'fuck' used with such good humour before. It sounds as if it is being belted around a squash court by gleaming jocks. "You know what you can do? You can fuck yourself!!" He slams down the phone positively rejuvenated. "What a guy!" He is bounding towards me again.

"Constance-" I begin.

He stops dead and snaps his fingers at me. "La Belle Mère Constance." His arms spread wide and he raises his knees daintily like a ballet dancer tiptoeing over eggs. "Gotcha! She told me all about you. Your old man used to be a writer, right? Excellent. Ellie!" He is steering me towards the outer office. "You shoulda said something. I thought you were going to pitch me a fuckin' movie. Jesus." Ellie is standing beside her desk patiently. "Give," - he wiggles a finger in my direction - "give him…." he indicates a shelf bulging with scripts. "Whatever." Ellie selects a script and hands it to me. "And he'll need one of those...those..."

"I'll get one from Constance."

"Yeah." He turns back to me. "We'll see how you make out. Nice talking to ya."

By the time I can tell him that it was nice talking to him too, his back is disappearing into his office. I hesitate and all I hear is the soft scuff of a sponge basketball dropping through an undersized hoop. Bounce.

3.

We are dining at The Ivy and my father has just offered to feel Sharon Stone's breasts for irregularities. No, he can't have done. He must have made it up. Though the two sleek men in Thiery Mugler suits at the table with her are glaring our way. He must have said something on the way back from the men's room. I fear he may be in one of his moods. I began to sense it when I got back from Zaiferts.

He had been sitting in the living room with a towel around his waist, staring at the remains of a bar of soap. Like Hamlet with Yorick's skull. No sooner had I guessed what was in his mind than he was off. "Just think of it," he breathed. "You are this bar of soap and you have just burst refulgent from your double-bonded, glistening wrapping paper – the world is your oyster. Imagine the glow of pride as you glimpse your noble, embossed crest reflected in the bathroom mirror. How every milligram of your saponified triglycerides must exalt at that moment. Surely, no tiny cloud of doubt could cast the most minute shadow over your bevelled roseate flanks? Not for you a furtive glance to where your gilded paper lies discarded amongst a detritus of wasted bathroom products. Poor soap, visions of immortality. How can you begin to guess what the future holds in store? The shock of suddenly finding yourself thrust into armpits and crotches, of languishing in half-full bidets and abandoned basins; of turning to furry pap or being left to crack and wither on a sun-scorched hardwood shelf, your embossment no more than a memory like the faded escutcheon of some once-noble family fallen on hard times. Alas, that is just the beginning. As the days pass, so you will find yourself increasingly dropped, slipping through fingers that once held you proud and firm, darting like a panicked fish as fumbling fingers pursue you through dark, subaqueous labyrinths too horrible to mention. Now, your balmy scent will have fled and will barely discern hot from cold, scarcely exude a lather. The end will be in sight. One more tumble to the harsh white tiles; one more impatient grunt and your wasted cadaver will be consigned to the depths of a bin in a sordid tangle of discarded dental floss A shiny new wrapper will flutter down to cover you like a shroud. The ruthless cycle of ablution will grind on."

"That's sad," I say.

"I've tried to mould the old scraps into the new soap - a kind of life graft-" he gazes at the pink sliver between his fingers "-but the new soap always rejects it." He sighs. "It's probably something that the manufacturers put in it. How low can human beings sink?"

My father harbours strange affinities. No creature or object is so blighted as to forfeit his indulgence. Ordinary children are weaned on 'Cinderella' and 'Jack and the Beanstalk'. My father eschewed such hackneyed fare and nourished me with his own more arcane creations. 'Bertie the Benevolent Bedbug' and 'Rudolph the Faithful Mosquito' were two I remember. I forget what happened to poor Bertie, except that he got squashed, but Rudolph left a permanent impression. He was a gentle fellow, typical of his vegetarian kind, never happier than when sinking his proboscis into a soothing draft of flower or fruit juice. It was his wife, Florence, who was the problem. She had the unquenchable craving for blood of her sex. Many a time when they went down to the swamp to breed, Rudolph would try and persuade Florence to take a refreshing sip of Marsh Marigold or Mimulus but his wife could think only of Farmer Honker, his chimney stacks poking up but a few fields away, and refuse all his blandishments. There was a lot of Madame Bovary in Florence.

One night, when Rudolph was looking after the children as usual, Florence buzzed off to Farmer Honker's farm - there was a subplot about three little pigs called Basher, Bosher and Abstinence but I never felt it integral to the main thrust of the narrative - and hours passed. Florence did not come back. Rudolph suddenly remembered something and alarm bells began to ring. A friendly daddy longlegs who lived under the next door dock leaf (and had no blood worth speaking of) had heard that Farmer Honker had received planning permission to build bungalows on one of his fields. Supposing he had sold the land to a rich property developer and used the cash to replace his old plastic fly swatter with a giant can of new-improved-formula-twenty-five-percent-extra-special-trial-purchase-offer insecticide? Rudolph's blood turned cold and, finding a neighbourly earwig to look after the children, he sped towards Farmer Honker's bedroom. A faint, staccato buzzing confirmed his worst fears even before he saw the outline of the huge aerosol spray in the moonlight. The air was still heavy with nauseous fumes but brave Rudolph closed his eyes and flew towards the sound of his wife's feeble susurration. He found Florence crumpled in a heap by the bed. She was in a pitiful condition, and for a moment he thought that he had arrived too late, but his miraculous appearance seemed to cheer her. "My darling Rudolph," she breathed. "If we can escape from this nightmare I swear that I will never suck blood again." That was all Rudolph needed to hear, and gritting his probiscis, he slung Florence's inert body across his shoulders. Summoning up all his remaining strength, he started to fly to safety. Alas! In her semi-conscious state, Florence could not help but revert to her old ways. She started to buzz. Farmer Honker woke up. His head turned. At any second he would grab the aerosol spray and they would be finished. Benefiting from Florence's extra weight Rufus forgot his male scruples and plunged down on Farmer Honker emitting a chilling buzz. Thinking that he was being attacked, the old man jerked away and in his confusion knocked the aerosol to the floor. By the time he could retrieve it, Rudolph and Florence were out of the window and skimming back to their little (in fact quite large) family. The cool night air quickly brought Florence back to her senses and she hugged her brave, loyal husband to her bosom in gratitude. From that day onwards she was as good as her word and nothing but plant juice passed her pretty proboscis and she and Rudolph lived happily ever after. The end.

"I wish they'd cart some of this bloody debris away."

Tonight, there is also the booze to worry about. If my father has yet to discover the really great Californian Cabernet Sauvignon, it is not through want of trying. Have we really drunk two bottles of the stuff? And that after two rounds of margaritas and before we started on the Cointreau.

"Another sticky?"

I should say no, but what the hell? I am pleasantly drunk, the lights are low, the muted buzz of conversation is like muzac, people's faces are soft and hazy, much, much more beautiful than they were three hours ago. Three hours? Have we really been here three hours?

"I asked you if you wanted another drink. How can a sprig of my loins be deaf to such a question?"

"Sure. Why not?"

"Waiter!"

I wonder if he gets deafer as he gets drunker - or should it be 'more drunk'? Probably yes in both cases.

"Two more large Cointreaus and a couple of double espressos, please. And if you could inject a teeny hint of warmth into the espressos? Grazie." He watches our waitress disappear. "Sour-faced little trollop. I expect she's got the curse."

"She didn't have a clue what you were talking about," I tell him. "All you needed to say was 'hot'."

My father sighs. "God, it's frustrating being in a town that has a vocabulary of twelve words and a few shrill shrieks." He looks around. "Do you think these people are having a good time?"

"They're having a great time," I say firmly. What this evening does not need is my father trying to lead everyone in community singing.

"They don't look as if they're having a good time. They look like accountants with piles, dining with their mothers in law. And look what they're drinking, that ghastly Lambrusco stuff. The poor man's Mateus Rose." He feeds his snobbery a dismissive snigger.

Normally this sort of stuff would get on my nerves but alcohol renders me relaxed and tolerant. I am squatting at the mouth of my insulated cave watching the fuzzy people go by, my mind in limbo, feeling good. Beside me is grouchy old father bear munching into a honeycomb and grumbling about the bees.

"Two large Cointreaus, two double espressos. Enjoy." The waitress finds some room on the table and disappears.

"Cheers." My father separates his sticky fingers from one glass and attaches them to another. "Here's to the enterprise." He is not referring to me but to the fact that he has almost finished the re-write of the teen movie he is penning for his agent, Larry Sabel, operating in the illegal (a word open to interpretation in Hollywood) guise of producer. I can't remember the title but it has 'High School' in it.

"Cheers," I say dutifully. After all, he is paying for all this. I don't like it. But I don't not like it.

"And here's to your meeting with what's-his-name. I hope it all works out."

"Zaiferts," I say. "Thanks."

"Nice of old Constance to have set that up. She's a good egg, isn't she? I should have invited her along."

What seems like hours later, I am beginning to think that this would not have been such a good idea: after my father has discovered that his credit card has not been stolen, worked out the tip three different ways and left too little, kept the wrong credit card slip and then risen unsteadily to his feet. At first I imagine, with acute embarrassment, that he is performing some kind of obscure ceremonial dance for the amusement of the other customers. Two small steps to the left, two to the right, hands extended away from the body, knees flexing to the point of collapse. Perhaps he is trying to evoke the spirit of some ancient Native American potlatch. It is only when he plucks the flowers out of a vase and tries to support himself with them that I realise that he is hopelessly drunk.

"Are you all right?" I hiss. People are looking, waiters are closing in.

"Fine." He draws himself up to his full height and walks through the dessert trolley.

The terrible thing is that he does not stop. Like Captain Oates walking into the blizzard or Virginia Woolf filling her lungs with Ouse he just keeps going. An Old Testament rain of gateaux, meringues and berries plunges towards the floor and his progress is only impeded when he blunders into another table and plants his hand in somebody's gazpacho.

"They've changed the layout," he says, as if suspecting a carefully laid trap. "That's the problem with these places when they get too popular. They try and fit in too many tables."

I grab his arm and support him out onto the terrace with only the loss of a tray of drinks. I can sense that he is trying to appear normal but this is not easy when you are wearing most of The Ivy's dessert trolley down the front of your Giorgio Armani. The al fresco diners have only heard my father coming; now they get to meet him for the first time. "This way!" I bleat as he tries to enter the kitchens.

"Very nice." My father is addressing the greeter who gapes at him from behind his lectern like a pixilated rabbit discovering a starving polecat on the doorstep. Our erratic progress through the flambeaux is a Calvary. I have never felt more mortified in my life. *Le tout Hollywood* observing this scene of flesh-creeping humiliation. Thank God that Zaiferts is breaking bread sticks at Mortons this evening.

"Sorry." My father has lurched from my grasp and stumbled onto a woman's lap.

"These bloody torches suck the oxygen out of the air."

The woman is making spluttering noises redolent of imminent apoplexy and her escort is on his feet; a bottle shatters as a wine bucket crashes to the ground.

"Why are these people staring? Haven't they ever seen a genius before"

"Not this close, perhaps," I tell him. I drag him upright as the woman gasps and clutches at her throat. "I'm sorry. My father isn't feeling very well."

"Premenstrual tension," he explains to her. "It's transmissible. You should talk to your doctor."

More waiters than we have seen during the whole of our meal close in like the jaws of a gin trap and we are hustled towards the low white, paling fence, feet barely touching the ground. I think they would kill us if there were not so many witnesses.

"All right, all right. So I'm not a big tipper. You should work in Europe!" We are thrust out onto the sidewalk and the waiters retire, rubbing dessert off their hands. "And your Gumbo Ya-Ya sucks!!"

Deciding to show a bit of class, the diners return to their mesquite-grilled Louisiana redfish and whipped summer squash and we are left alone on the sidewalk. All I want to do is put two or three hundred miles between myself and the place, then have therapy.

"We need to take a little walk," I say through teeth clenched so tight that they seem to be fitting into each other like Russian dolls. My father seems amenable to this suggestion but before he has completed one step, a car jock materialises out of the darkness and sticks out a hand. Instinctively, my father delves in a swage of meringue around his breast pocket and hands over a cream-covered parking ticket. Barely fazed, the car jock glances at it for a second and lopes away.

"Hey!" I shout. But he has gone. Open-mouthed, my father has his head tilted back as if studying the stars. He is taking deep breaths. Very deep breaths. "You can't drive," I tell him.

"I'll be fine once I sit down." He takes some more breaths and starts coughing. "You know something? That lesbian bitch must have spiked my drink."

I hardly have time to start disabusing him of this notion when there is a screech of brakes and our car appears like the wicked witch in a pantomime.

I glance towards The Ivy. Diners are still looking at us and there is a small staff conference around the nearest telephone. Definitely time to move on.

"Money." In the manner of royalty my father never seems to travel with any loose cash and is extending a hand in my direction. He steps off the sidewalk and nearly collapses in the gutter. Dutifully, I fumble for some dollars and get them into his hand at the third attempt.

Most people would just hand the cash to the car jock and drive off but my father, though prepared to lay out fortunes on meals, always considers that the price for parking his car is iniquitously high and is loath to add any additional sum that might be construed as a tip He argues that valet parkers get away with millions because people are too embarrassed to ask for their change in case they appear as a cheapskate in front of their date. My father, a stickler for principle, is not afraid to appear as a cheapskate in front of anybody if it establishes a moral principle and saves himself fifty cents.

Normally this kind of performance makes me feel distinctly uncomfortable, but on the scale of tonight's embarrassment it pales into insignificance. I also calculate that the longer the period of time before we get into the car the better. I am not feeling so chipper myself. It is therefore with relative equanimity that I observe the scene in which the car jock mutters darkly and gestures from the clearly inadequate sum nestling in his palm to the filth spattering my father's person. My Spanish is not good but I think he is saying that, in his country, a man who wears his food as clothing and clings to his last centavo as a starving flea cleaves to the genitals of a diseased rat is not held in great respect.

None of this has any effect on my father, who, before I can stop him, has slumped behind the wheel and managed to turn the windshield wipers on. The telephone activity around the greeter's lectern shows no signs of abating and there are gestures being made in our direction. I get into the car hurriedly. Now my father seems to have taken a violent dislike to the safety belt which he is attacking with a ferocity worthy of Laocoon in his problems with the sea monsters. A vicious grunt and he forces the clip into my socket.

Still grumbling, the car jock stumps off behind the car. I have considerable sympathy for the man, the more so when my father accidentally finds reverse and nearly turns him into two people.

"Fucking automatics!" Now we are rocketing forward at sixty miles an hour. "Why can't they give you a proper car? I hate this bastard! Good lock though."

He proves this with an illegal U-turn that turns my stomach into a double helix and nearly grafts us to the line of cars parked along Robertson.

"Stop!" I scream. "Stop!!" I glimpse a blur of gaping faces as we hurtle past The Ivy.

"Bloody brake doesn't work!"

"Your foot's on the accelerator!!"

A red light looms and we hurtle through it across Beverly. My heart stops and I contract my body preparing for the impact. There is a terrifying screech of brakes and a blast on the horn like a shell exploding beside my head. A wraith of swaying metal whistles past within a paint lick of us. Crack! I am hurled forward and my head hits the windshield so hard I can feel the glass flex. My father has found the brake.

"Sodding automatics!!" He sees me checking my forehead for blood and genuine concern enters his voice. "Are you all right? You ought to put your safety belt on."

Before I have time to curse him and tell him why I cannot put my safety belt on, a black and white shape whips past us and stops as if dropped from a crane. Two doors fly open and two figures explode onto the street. One drops to the ground with arms outstretched and the other covers the ground between us like igniting gasoline. He too has his arms thrust out and what seems like the largest handgun I have seen outside a 'Dirty Harry' movie hovers before my father's nose. "Good evening, officer," he says.

"Whadafuckyassholesthinyadoin!!?" I can smell the cop. It is a mixture of adrenalin, fear and bad contract laundering. The huge badge on his chest dazzles. It is practically a breastplate. His face looks as if it was hewn from weathered anthracite and reveals less propensity for tenderness than Clint Eastwood's left buttock. I think of some of the episodes of 'The Shield' I have seen and wish that I hadn't. "Yujusrunafuckinredlite!!"

"'Gatsby believed in the green light'" says my father for no particular reason.

"Wadafuckutalkinbout!!?" The cop pushes the gun a little closer to my father's temple. I don't think my father's accent helps. Could we sound Muslim? That would not be good. "ID!!"

My father looks blank and then realises this is neither an arcane local greeting nor an expression of abuse but a request. He reaches towards the glove compartment.

The cop's finger tightens on the trigger. "No!" I scream at my father. "He thinks you're going for a gun!"

"A gun? Don't be ridiculous."

I am about to explain that if my father seems a little strange it is because he is hopelessly drunk when I realise that, in our present situation, this would probably be counter-productive.

"It's at the hotel," I say, accentuating the husky reassuring timbre of a one hundred percent - yes sirree! - home-grown All-American boy. The other cop has approached us warily and I notice how crisp and new everything he wears looks. Even the creases have creases in them. The white T-shirt, the chevrons, the gleaming belt with its tool for getting boy scouts out of horses' hooves. Everything except his holster. That looks scuffed and I know why. Because it gets a lot of use. And it gets a lot of use because a gun keeps being whipped out of it. And that's not just to nail Halle Berry pin-ups to the precinct wall. It's to blow huge, living lumps of flesh out of low-life scumbags like my father and me. I wish daddy could realise this.

"Getout!!"

At the back of my mind I had always known that, one fatal day, something like this was going to happen. Totally innocent but implicated in a serious crime thanks to the malice or stupidity of some feckless imbecile, probably my father. Now the two of us are going to be handcuffed and taken down to the police station; locked up with violent criminals and obliged to take showers with depraved AIDS-ridden drug addicts. If there is any justice they will ask my father to pick up the soap first.

"MOVEIT!!!"

"Really," says my father.

I am starting to open the door - slowly, very slowly - when there is a crackle from the police car radio and a voice gabbles urgency. One cop runs back and I hear him acknowledging something. He shouts to his partner and dives into the car. The engine roars into life. I cannot believe this. Perhaps there is a God. Perhaps Grandma was right. The first cop stares at us and hesitates. I can read his mind: 'What kind of sick society is it that prohibits me wasting these two snivelling punks and leaving them for the garbage collector?'

"Fuckenshit!!"

There is another shout and he takes off running, diving into the police car as it starts to accelerate. The red light throbs and the siren starts to wail. In three seconds it has disappeared.

My father sighs. I imagine that it must be relief, but I am wrong. "Did you hear the way that fellow talked to us? Absolutely appalling. Can you imagine an English policeman speaking to you like that?"

"Get out!" I shout at him. "Get out! I'm going to drive."

"Are you sure you feel up to it? You seem a little tense."

"Get out!!" I resist punching him and after a clumsy game of blind man's musical chairs I am behind the wheel. "We'll park the first place we can and get a taxi."

My father, sulking, says nothing but stares out the window. There is a parking space a hundred yards down the road. That is where we are going.

We nearly make it.

My foot welded to the brake pedal, I am slowing down when there is a banshee wail and an ancient sedan swings round the corner, leaning away from its suspension like it has bad breath. One headlight has been reduced to a gaping black socket and the mangled fender is buried in the radiator grill. The shuddering wreck is so close to the ground that it seems to have no wheels and is striking sparks from the road surface. It is also on our side of the street. CRUNCH! I glimpse a goldfish bowl of crazed faces and the sedan carries away one of our headlights and rips along the body work like a drunk trying to open a tin of sardines with an axe. The impact bunts us sideways and the sedan roars away into the night.

"Shit!" exclaims my father. "Now see what you've done."

"What do you fucking mean!?" I scream at him. "They were on the wrong side of the road! They were probably the reason the cops took off!"

"All right, all right. No need to get your knickers in a twist." He tries to open his door but it is jammed by the force of the impact. "Oh, my God."

"What is it?"

"I think I'm paralysed. I can't move."

"Try releasing your safety belt!"

Eventually, he does so and slides across the seats huffing and puffing and nearly sodomising himself on the gear shift. "Jesus." He hauls himself up and stands beside me surveying the damage. "It looks like a write-off."

"Did you take out the extra insurance cover?"

"No."

"Christ!"

"Stop being such a bloody tragedy queen. You have to stay calm and collected in a situation like this." He lashes out at the car with his foot. "Fucking bastard!"

Our feet crunching on rust and broken glass, we wrench the fender away from the offside tyre. The parking space nearby has now been taken. A police car screams past at the end of the street.

"Do you want me to drive?" asks my father.

"Are you crazy?"

The car starts at the third attempt and we ease forward. Something bad has happened to the suspension but it is capable of being driven. Rows of cars line both sides of the street. Opportunities for parking equal nil.

"Where shall we go, back to the hotel?"

"No. You know how people talk."

"So where?"

"Beverly Hills?"

"No. They phone the cops if they see a dog approaching a fire hydrant."

"So where then?"

"I don't know! Just keep going. We need to go somewhere where I can think."

He takes a deep breath through his mouth and closes his eyes. "This area is teeming with criminals."

Another police car flashes by at the end of the street and he may be right. I am not in the mood to argue I am exhausted, I am scared; the world is too much with me. It would be nice to drive beyond civilisation and emerge somewhere else.

That is how we arrive at the top of a canyon in the Santa Monica Mountains. I have no idea how we got there. Some hitherto unencountered manifestation of myself must have been driving.

When we pull off the road, there is a drop into darkness before us and Los Angeles spread out as if the Milky Way has just dropped out of the sky. We seem to be alone. The silence is unsettling. 'Crack!' My father throws his weight against the door and it springs open with a satisfying noise like the seal on a giant tin of instant coffee being ruptured. He struggles out and swings his arms vigorously three or four times before spreading them wide and adapting the pose of the giant statue of Christ that looks down on Rio de Janeiro from the Corcovado.

"Look at that," he says. "Beyond beautiful, isn't it? All those lights, so pure and innocent." He pulls open his fly and releases a noisy torrent of urine. "That's what it should be like all the time. Bugger!" He has just splashed himself via a treacherous plant with large leaves. "'Or like stout Cortez, when with eagle eyes he stared at the Pacific - and all his men looked at each other with a wild surmise - Silent upon a peak in Darien'." He shakes his penis dry enthusiastically. "I wonder where Darien is. I bet Keats had to look it up. Poor sod never got out of Europe, did he? He should never have got on that boat."

"That was Shelley," I tell him.

"Was it? Oh well, it was Italy anyway. I've never felt completely safe there myself. The important thing is that they were both too young to die." He rounds on our car. "Not like you, you bastard! It's tragic, isn't it? This huge, wondrous, ethereal landscape blighted by the motor car; God knows how many people are doomed to cough out their lives with an exhaust pipe stuffed up their nostrils. It's disgusting. The motor car should be abolished. We should all have bicycles. Can you imagine the freeways humming to the cheerful buzz of millions of derailleurs? A fitter, happier Los Angeles. People would burst through their office doors slavering to do a good day's work.

All it needs is someone with the guts to take the first step." He pokes the unfortunate car with his toe. "We don't need you, you polluter, you septic haze-maker, you environmental mugger, you-you murderer!" He reaches inside the car and releases the hand brake. "Come on, we'll push it over the cliff."

"What!? You're crazy."

"We're crazy if we don't. Don't you see!? That's what this evening was all about, only we didn't recognise it. 'There is a tide in the affairs of men, which taken at the-'" he waves his arms - "something, you know. We need to do this for humanity." He strains against the trunk and the car squeaks pitifully and moves forward a couple of inches. "Do you like this car after what it's tried to do to us tonight?"

"No." I have to confess to myself that I do not like this car.

"Then let's get it before it gets us."

"How are we going to get home?"

"'How are we going to get home?'" My father simulates a mincing pipe. "Did Alexander the Great say that when he set sail from - from wherever? No he just went right on and conquered-" I wait "-everything."

"This is crazy." I am saying that, but with the tone of a man happily embracing insanity. I have never pushed a car into a canyon before and right now it seems the kind of thing that everybody ought to do at least once in their lifetime. Also, I have drunk a lot and I am a sucker for lousy rhetoric. I have a nasty suspicion that I might have been a natural for the Nazi Youth Party. Just for the uniform and the chance to bonk beautiful blonde maidens in a chalet in the Bavarian Alps, of course. Nothing ideological.

"I see this great scene in a movie." My father explodes into a self-congratulatory laugh. "Arnold Schwarzenegger pushes this car over a cliff. He waits a couple of seconds and says 'Valley Parking'. You get it? Valley parking. Valet parking? I can just hear him saying it, can't you? That voice? I think I'll get Larry to call his agent and set up a meeting."

"Arnold Schwarzenegger is Governor of California," I explain carefully.

"It's just a phase he's going through," says my father confidently. "He'll be back. Okay, you swine!" He is addressing the car again. "Now!"

What the hell? We thrust together and the car suddenly bucks like an escaping animal and surges forward into darkness. There is the crunch of undergrowth being flattened and a second's silence before a violent 'THUMP!' segues into the staggered rumble of an avalanche. More seconds pass and the noise eventually dies away in a skitter of tiny stones. There is no dramatic fireball or final explosion.

All I hear is a sound like a human voice crying out.

4.

Please God. Tell me I dreamt it.

That is the life-line I toss myself when I wake up with a cack-handed plasterer's mate chipping neurones off the inside of my brain with a sledge-hammer. The pain is second only to the dull ache in the pit of my stomach. The ache of guilt. Why? Why? Why did I do it?

"'Your placent-a will present-a view of meadows green'," my father is crooning away to the tune of 'The Folks who live on the Hill'. They don't write songs like that any more he is always telling me. His cheery warble induces a glimmer of hope. Maybe I did dream it.

"I've sorted out the car situation." His voice booms from the doorway.

"Brilliant." My heart soars. A miracle. "How?"

"I've rented another one."

"Western have rented you another one?"

"Not Western. Last Hope."

"They didn't ask any questions?"

"Why should they? Anyway, Last Hope don't ask questions. That's how they stay in business. Have you ever driven past their lot? The first time I thought it was a junkyard."

"But what are we going to do about the other car?"

"Nothing."

"Nothing!? We pushed it into a canyon."

My father shakes his head slowly, as if explaining something to a child, which of course he is. "Do you know how many cars are stolen in Los Angeles every day?"

"No."

"Neither do I. But it must be in the hundreds."

"But if it was stolen we'd report it, wouldn't we? How did we get home? I mean, I know in reality we got a lift with those two guys you said were male prostitutes but-"

"You didn't know it was stolen." I stare at him. "Listen to me, William, and I'll tell you what really happened. The truth as you're going to tell it to the rental people."

"Me!?"

"Last night you went to a party where there was valet parking."

"But-"

"Hear me out, Will. You had a little too much to drink so, like a solid citizen, you took a taxi home. This morning you had to leave town on urgent business. You with me so far?"

"Yes, but why is it 'me'? Why can't it be 'us'?

"Because it works better that way, you'll see. Besides, it's a young man's story. I visualise you being played by Leonardo DiCaprio."

"Thanks, but-"

"When you got back to town you called your host and he put you on to the valet parking people and you asked them where they'd parked your car and they said they'd call you back which, of course, they didn't, so you rang again - you're a conscientious guy, it's one of the things I've always liked about you - and this time they say that they can't trace the guy who parked your car - he's probably on his way back to Guatemala - so the car's mislaid somewhere. You comb the local streets - that admirable conscientious streak again - but there's no sign of it. It must have been stolen."

"Why did you rent another car?"

"Because I need one for business. I thought you had the other one."

"But they're going to want to talk to the valet parking people."

"Fine. Give them anyone in the Yellow Pages."

"But they won't know anything about it."

"Exactly. They wouldn't anyway. Valet parkers don't remember anything on principle - or rather, lack of it. This is Indian country, Will. Not the John Birch Society. Have you ever been so racked by tedium that you've started to read the conditions on that receipt they give you? You have no rights. They could drive your Chevvy straight round to the local car press and have it cast as an altarpiece in the chapel of Our Lady of Santa Cruz and you couldn't do a thing about it. Most car jocks are failed Mexican stock car racers. The turnover is terrific. Like I said, the guy who parked your car has probably been deported or opened a taco stand in Pico Rivera. We're not talking pension schemes here."

"I don't know." But I sense myself weakening. When he goes on like this it seems more like reckless high spirits than anything criminal. But still. "Okay, just suppose they buy all this and I don't actually go to prison. They're going to find the car and charge it to your credit card."

"That particular card was stolen ten minutes ago, when I went down for a swim. Naturally, I cancelled it immediately. All Western can get is the month I've already paid for." My father smiles his smug smile and pats me on the shoulder. "Don't worry. These people insure their budgies against the clap. Millions of dollars are written off every day. They're not going to blink an eye."

The phone rings and my father answers it. Immediately I feel uneasy. "Yes?" He listens and his voice becomes mannered and waffly. Almost a caricature of a British accent. He seems to think that this impresses the locals. I am not so sure. People often ask me if I am Australian. "I'll have to talk to my son. He's off gallivanting somewhere. You know what the young are like….About another couple of weeks with any luck. I'll give you a buzz when I have a better idea….Splendid. Cheerio." He puts the phone down with a flourish. "Talk of the devil. That was Western. They wanted to know how much longer you wanted the car."

"I thought I heard a scream."

My father looks puzzled and gazes out of the window towards the pool. "I didn't-"

"After we pushed the car."

"Come on! Don't start imagining things. I didn't hear anything." His voice becomes more soothing. "Look, with a bit of luck they might never find the car. Or by the time they do - we'll be out of the country."

"You'll be out of the country. I'm trying to get a job here, remember?"

"All right, all right. No point in getting yourself in a state. You should have thought of all this before you put your shoulder to the wheel, so to speak The best thing you can do is channel your imagination into that script analysis." He glances at his watch. "I've got to go and pick up the new car." He calls reception for a cab and squeezes my shoulder.

"You must show me the script they've given you. I'll probably be able to come up with some sage observations. "Buckle down to it, Will. I know you've got it in you."

When he has gone I have some breakfast and continue to feel physically and mentally awful. The future, never short of a few clouds, has now darkened perceptibly. Where can I turn? Suddenly, the thought of calling Lucy seems like a balm rather than a penance. I know that she would be wonderfully sympathetic. But do I want to plough through all the details? Maybe I'll try ma again. But that, too, seems pretty defeatist.

Come on, Will. You are a big boy now. Best to follow father's advice: tackle the script.

I stare at the buff envelope. How am I going to handle this? I want to come over as bright and perceptive but not - heaven forbid - as an intellectual; someone who lacks the common touch; that vital ability to make the great American public purr with delight and roll over waggling their paws in the air. I must not use words like 'mymidon'. I must keep things terse, punchy. At Disney they hold seminars on whether '- -' whips the eye towards the punch line faster than ':'. Of course, all this depends on whether I can get a handle on the script in the first place. If it is 'Finnegan's Wake' this could be a problem. But it will not be 'Finnegan's Wake'. It will be something aimed at Mr and Mrs America, or rather Master and Miss America, or rather anyone still left with enough pocket money to buy their way into the multiplex after they've trawled the mall. I must also be careful not to give offence. I have presumably been given something that the studio has - or had - in development. They might even be making it. If I say that it is a piece of drek I am insulting their taste. However, it may be a piece of drek that George Clooney has brought to the studio and they may be crazy to forge a relationship with him. I must cover that contingency too.

But first, the report form I have been given to fill in. I withdraw it from the buff envelope and peruse. The first page has official stuff at the top and than a heading 'PREMISE'. There is space for a response and then a grid in which you have to rate 'PREMISE', 'STRUCTURE', CHARACTERISATION' and 'DIALOGUE' with a choice of 'EXCELLENT', 'GOOD', 'FAIR' or 'POOR'. I can do that. I turn over. A page headed 'SYNOPSIS'. Okay. I turn over again to find 'COMMENT' and at the bottom: 'WRITER RECOMMENDATION': YES—NO—OTHER. Wait a minute. 'OTHER'? What other could there be? Surely you recommend that they either make the movie or they don't. Perhaps you can suggest that the writer, though not belting the ball out of the park this time, shows promise; or that a particular aspect of his talent is worth noting; or that the theme might be worthy of development in other hands.

Hmn. If I make a positive suggestion that they either do or do not make the movie then I avoid this dilemma. Probably do not make it. I don't want to sound too easily impressed. Someone prepared to fritter away scores of millions of the studio's dollars on every script that comes through the door. On the other hand, if I say that they should make it then I am revealing myself as a man of courage and integrity prepared to back his own creative judgement. Difficult.

Maybe it would be better if I read the script first. And slowly. Taking in the descriptions as well as the dialogue. My father is always complaining that studio executives, or 'stupid illiterate cretins' as my father calls them, do not do this. 'You didn't make that clear' is what they say reproachfully because the hero did not express in words his intention to blow the safe, steal the jewels, shoot the villain in the nuts, and slide down a telegraph wire to safety with the heroine across his shoulders.

A shape appears against the window. Maria, the Mexican room maid, is shading her eyes and trying to peer through the reflected sunlight and into the suite. Maria has high cheekbones, slightly protruding lips and piercing brown eyes. So do all the women in the first drafts of my father's screenplays. I wonder if there is any connection. If Maria thought that the suite was empty she would immediately enter and cover every available surface with book matches, shower caps and sewing kits furnished with a thread so fine that only fairies bent on weaving bodices for kindly elves would think of using it.

Maria is in love with my father. She is unaware of this but, according to my father, the woman is often the last to know. He has spotted the tell-tale signs: our lavatory is 'hygienized' every morning with a cheerleader's sash and the space beside the basin littered with small plastic phials of something that the flaking gold lettering suggests is shampoo. By such unguarded gestures do women apparently reveal the depths of their infatuation. The French baker's wife at Pulignac gave herself away by always - sensitive readers may wish to skip a couple of lines - sliding my father's baguette into a thin plastic snood rather than wrapping it in a fold of tissue paper as she did with all the other customers. He used to find it difficult to meet the husband's eyes when the poor cuckold, floury arms laden with warm *couronnes*, slammed through the doors from the bakery to catch his wife *in flagrante delicto*.

It is fortunate perhaps that the language barrier prevents Maria from giving full vent to her feelings. Her only word of English seems to be 'v-a-a-c-u-u-m'? delivered molto fortissimo. I say 'no' automatically; a habit probably picked up from my mother. When we lived in France as a family, she always cleaned the house from top to bottom before the maid arrived.

It is now nine-thirty. Five-thirty in the evening in London. Mother will be reading her umpteenth manuscript or, at lightening speed, assembling the ingredients for the dinner party she will be hosting for a gaggle of embryonic writing talents and rising young publishers - the spoken and bespoken word. An occasion for Philippe to fill glasses and raise his eyes to hers with melting adoration as he swoops to substitute a plate. A shame I can't drop in for an after dinner mint and a stab at a *bon mot.* Or at least approach the glowing bay window at the corner of the square; enjoy the comforting sense of warmth and home behind the drawn curtains. But in dreary reality I know that, if beyond them, I would soon be nudged to the edge of the hip-lit conversation, an observer rather than a participant; a family pet that has been let in from the cold to assume its familiar position by the fireside. I would start to wish I was back here. Doing something.

The phone rings. They have found the car. Panic. What was I supposed to say? I can't remember. Stay put. The phone will go away. But it might be something important. Something positive. I don't have to speak until I know. I pick up the phone and prepare a 'wrong number' voice, disturbed, irritated, peremptory.

"Hello…?" Tentative. Female. I know who it is but I wait, giving them the chance to become someone else. They do not avail themselves of the opportunity. "Hello? Hello?"

"Hi, Lucy. I wasn't expecting you." Not strictly true. After Western rental and anyone with news of a family bereavement, Lucy was always high on the list of potential callers.

"Mr Lock? I'm sorry to disturb you. I was trying to get hold of Will."

"This is he. Me. It. Son of Adrian Lock. In the flesh." Despite the fact that it happens all the time I am still annoyed. How can people be so, so unobservant? I have heard my voice recorded and listened to my father on the phone interminably and our voices have nothing in common.

"Will? Really? You sound so like your father."

"What time is it with you? It must be late."

"Not really. I've just come off the ward. I felt like talking to you." And reproachfully. "I haven't heard a word since you left."

"Didn't you get my postcard?" I wish I could make my lies sound more convincing. Or perhaps I don't. Because I lie badly I don't feel so guilty about doing it. There is a kind of underpinning honesty in me that cannot be subverted.

"No. When did you send it?"

"I can't remember. Not so long ago. Maybe it hasn't got there yet."

"You could have rung."

"I was waiting to have something positive to tell you." There is an element of truth in this.

"Just to tell me you were all right. I was quite worried. You read such awful things in the papers."

I know what she means. The British press makes everyday life in the States seem like the last twenty minutes of 'Alien'. "Don't believe all that stuff. I haven't been mugged for days. How are things with you? How's Mr Thomas?"

"Thompson. He died."

"Oh dear. I am sorry. Still, it can't have been a total surprise."

"It was really. We thought he'd turned the corner. Then he walked to the television room and haemorrhaged."

"How awful." I had been hoping to avoid the details but no chance. Now I can see a river of blood rushing down the twenty-two inch screen like something from a Kurosawa movie

"Yes, it was. It was his birthday too. "Do you know when you're coming back?"

"No. I went for an interview yesterday." Her inquiring voice comes in but I ride over it. "Not bad. I've got to analyse a script. Basically, tell the studio whether they should make this film or not." I wait for her to sound impressed.

"When will you know?"

"About the job?"

"When you're coming back."

"It'll depend on how they react to my script analysis - and what else turns up."

"When's your father coming back?"

This is a slightly more sophisticated version of her original question. She is aware that I am living on my father's largesse and that he will not be subsidising my stay after his departure. He has finished the meetings associated with his current project and is only hanging on to taste the waters and in the hope that his agent will be able to dredge up a few more meetings that might net further assignments. These to be dragged back to Pulignac and ingested at leisure until the next bout of starvation sends him jetting over to the New World. Father is now picking up his own tab which is a repellent, almost unthinkable, thing for a writer to do. He will not be gracing these portals for much longer.

"Difficult to say. He seems to have a lot on his plate at the moment."

Silence. Her voice wavers between concern and doubt. "Are you all right?"

"I'm fine."

Pause. "Oh dear. You don't sound like my Will."

This would be a good moment to take the bull firmly by the testicles and tell her that I am no longer 'her Will' and that our relationship has entered a new phase - one of final and irreconcilable rupture. But I am a coward and I do not want to feel any guiltier or sorrier for myself than I do at the moment. Also, at the back of my disgusting mind is the feeling that I might need her again. Like some garment tucked away in the back of a closet that might just come back into fashion.

"It's not easy on the phone."

"Have you met someone else?"

The more Lucy behaves like this, the easier it is to be hard. It is not an endearing trait but I seem to lose respect and affection in inverse proportion to the need I evoke in others. At the same time, I sense that if Lucy was here and if she started to cry then I would want her sexually. Her vulnerability would be a turn on. I can see her smudged cheeks, the matted lashes. Smell the warm, earthy, dewy smell. I feel a twinge of lust and start to get an erection.

"Don't be ridiculous, Lucy. Apart from anything else I've only just got here."

"What do you mean? It seems like weeks. Did you get my letters?"

"Yes, thanks." Say something, Will. "Listen, Lucy. This call must be costing you a fortune. I'll write, I promise. If I sound a bit odd it's because I'm so wrapped up in this job thing."

"You do miss me a bit?"

"Of course I do."

She begins to sound a mite happier. "Because I miss you awfully, Will."

"So do I. Look, I'll write. I promise." I inject urgency into my voice. "My father's coming. Look after yourself. I'm sorry about Mr Thomas."

I put the phone down, realising that it should have been 'Thompson'. Oh well, it doesn't really change anything. Especially for the unfortunate Mr Thompson. And Lucy and myself are exactly where we were before her call except that I now have half an erection which, of course, is twice as useless as nothing at all.

Poor Lucy. Her big problem is an over abundance of tender feeling. When she starts to care about a patient, he inevitably sickens and dies. It has got so that she has to steel herself not to get involved. And, perhaps, that wariness is spreading over into our relationship. She cares therefore she senses that it must be doomed. 'It', I hope, not me, though there was an echo of personal concern in her words. Oh dear, as she would say; it would probably be better for us both if she found another vocation.

Maria is still hovering with her trolley so I take the script down to the pool via the new wing. This has a tasteful waterfall-cascade running down its middle that descends to a small pond full of goldfish and cigarette butts. There is also a Jacuzzi much frequented by British pop groups. The staff always peer into its depths as they go past so I suspect that there was once a tragedy. It is a *sine qua non* of any successful Beverly Hills hotel that someone famous should have taken an overdose there.

Peter is manoeuvring a trolley load of luggage and his face slowly ignites into a smile as he sees me.

"Hi, Mr Lock. Have a good one." His words move so slowly that if you didn't like them you would have time to duck.

I raise a cheerful thumb in acknowledgement and glance into the pond. These goldfish are survivors. The last time I looked they had been joined by a giant human stool adorned with a small Union Jack; probably the gift of one of those British pop groups. Worse, the goldfish were nibbling at it. I found this pretty gross but my father thought the scene highly symbolic and drags it into any conversation concerning the Royal Family.

Usually the pool is surrounded by bored women ploughing through Sidney Sheldon novels, and tense men reading scripts while they wait for the phone to ring and someone to give them more money. Today there is no one about except for a tiny, elf-like man unloading trays of pansies from a trolley. This is José, the happiest employee in the hotel - if not the world. "Hi, meesta!" His head starts at a point and its widest part is his smile. He seems to have more teeth than other people and looks as if he tried to swallow a sweet corn sideways. He performs many tasks but seems to have a special affinity with flowers. Since you never see any butterflies or moths in Los Angeles, I sometimes wonder if he pollinates them himself. It is not difficult to imagine him flitting from plant to plant with a pair of gossamer wings attached to his narrow shoulders. And his nose would be useful too. I had always thought of it as a beak, but it could easily double as a proboscis.

"You wanna tow-wells?" He is speeding towards the pile before I can say no, so I give my British genes their head and accept a couple with too many words of thanks, before draping them over the uncomfortable plastic thongs of a lounger. Even happier perhaps, José returns to his pansies humming what I choose to interpret as an old Mexican lay. Above, Maria slowly pushes her trolley along the balcony that skirts the first floor apartments and he calls to her but there is no response. Perhaps she didn't hear him.

The sun has nearly disappeared behind the palms but it is still warm. The calm surface of the pool trembles with enough refractions to give David Hockney the other half of my wasted erection. I sit in shadow, my destiny between my hands. The script has no title page, so I do not know who wrote it or what it was called. No problem, this will give me the chance to come up with a snappy title, hopefully better than the one that exists at the moment. Good thinking, Lock. I start to read.

Twenty minutes later I am called to the phone. After dawdling round the conversational block three times Hadiscomb wonders whether I would care to accompany him to a concert given by Mahlathini and the Mahotella Queens.

Actually, it is Mahlathini and the Mahotella Queens backed by the Makgona Tsohle Band, 'The Band That Knows Everything' and, much to my surprise, they are terrific. The best Mbaganga-Township Jive group to come out of South Africa and that is not just Hadiscomb's opinion. It says so on the cover of the DVD I have just bought.

'King Groaner' Mahlathini, naked except for a few beads and meerkat tails over the frolicsome parts, attacks with a low-pitched, rasping roar that sounds like a blocked smokestack gargling with paint stripper. Whilst he growls up a storm the Queens are belting out layers of close harmony that must buckle the aerials on cars parked several blocks away. They are big girls and wear nylon brassieres like hammocks beneath skimpy leopard skin tops. Mosaics of brightly-coloured beads dazzle on their micro-mini skirts, belts, mop caps, necklaces and anklets that shake, shudder and bounce as they dance, sway and stamp. In the background the band bellows like cows in labour and blazes away with guitars, sax, pennywhistle and drums. Squalls of sweat break over the crazed audience who are hurling themselves around like Indian clubs. The atmosphere is charged with sweat and pot. The bouncers look worried but they have their hands full holding back the crowd still trying to fight its way in off Sunset. Even the barmen are dancing. My estimation of Hadiscomb rises. He has even offered me grass. I look around but I cannot see him. He must be one of the people doing the splits and banging their heads on the ground. What a scene. Today Zululand, tomorrow the world.

To my surprise, I recognise someone. A small, bug-like man in a baggy Italian suit who is ignoring the performers and staring intently at the audience as if eager to assess every nuance of their reaction. This is Larry Sabel, my father's agent. I met him once - beside a swimming pool inevitably. 'Agent' is now the wrong word because Larry has become a producer and they are not allowed to be agents. Presumably there is a limit to how much money you are allowed to make even in Hollywood. Larry is now my father's manager. I think my father rather likes this. It makes him feel that he has a literary Don King on his side as opposed to those poor scribblers who only have agents, the butt of almost as many industry jokes as writers.

I do not know if Sabel has a slice of M.M.Q.M.T.B., but I sense that he would like to. His highly sensitive nostrils scent potential. He is not listening to the music but establishing a demographic of the market responding to it. He will surely be bearing a firm handshake backstage, placing a few strategic calls in the morning.

Our eyes meet and, for a second, I think he has recognised me. This would be unusual because I am not important. My DNA is not in the shape of a dollar sign. Even infrequent visits to Tinseltown have revealed to me that the natives possess a built-in screening device that renders lesser (e.g. poorer) beings invisible, even if they have once been introduced as equals. Sabel's eyes flash intensity and his stare deepens. I turn away hurriedly. I think he fancies me.

"Had enough!?" Hadiscomb has to shout as he burrows out of the mêlée, dripping with sweat. He has been investing quality time with the true aficionados, those who cluster round the stage, dancing to shed a limb as they bond with the artists, siphoning off a little of their glory.

I nod. It is always a good idea to quit while you are ahead at this kind of event. Before the encores and the fights, and the guy who ODs, and the paramedics. We nearly pick up two girls outside the 'Señoritas'. The stoned one thinks that Hadiscomb's accent is 'utterly cute' but her friend wants to stay so we leave them arguing and thrust out onto Sunset. It greets us with a halitosis of exhaust fumes but at least it is reminiscent of air. My clothes are clinging to me like Scotch tape.

Hadiscomb is still regretting the girls but I persuade him to settle for a hamburger and we find a Mr Fat Boy that is still open. We order and Hadiscomb, John Travolta for the new millennium, scans my DVD and croons about something called 'mggashiyo'.

"Where did you hear about these guys?" I humour him.

"When I was at Rockingham."

That figures. At the dear old school it was vital to be into some fringe group that nobody had ever heard of to stand any chance of achieving musical street cred. Anyone saying the words 'George Michael' risked being lapidated with field hockey balls and it was rumoured that the body of a naïve fourth former suspected of once owning a 'Wham' cassette had been found in the local canal.

"Really?" I say.

"Yes. I trudged round Leicester and found this back street record shop - probably a front for something. You know, selling drugs, that kind of thing. Anyway, it was exceedingly ethnic so in I plunged. Hadn't the first clue about what I was buying except that it was African and different. Then I got to like it. Now it looks as if it's going to take off." He smiles. "If they really happen I'm going to be able to tell people I discovered them ten years ago."

"Was it ten years ago?"

"Yes." He bites into his hamburger and a big blob of mustard drops onto his plate. He nods towards it. "It's a shame about American food, isn't it? The advertisements taste much better."

Funny about Hadiscomb. I can't really get a fix on him. "Your father made supermarket trolleys, didn't he?"

"He's a brain surgeon." Hadiscomb munches doggedly. "Chambers was the supermarket trolleys. You know, Voyce's friend."

He stage delivers the additional information - pause, stress - like it means something. Like I am supposed to respond.

"I don't remember," I say. This is becoming irritating. "I'm not a genius when it comes to names and places. And Rockingham wasn't a particularly good time for me."

"Me neither. You might recall that?" He dabs at the mustard with a piece of bread from his discarded hamburger. "Does your father still write those books?"

A well-plied rod, but none the less still painful - even in the unexpected hands of Hadiscomb.

"No. He hasn't written one for years. He writes scripts for movies that never get made." I feel a surge of anger. Sending me to fucking Rockingham against my mother's wishes and turning out hack screenplays whilst Hadiscomb's father is a brain surgeon. Just think what I could have achieved if my father had been a brain surgeon. "What are you doing these days?"

"I haven't made up my mind. I tried banking but it didn't work. Medicine, maybe. Though I'm aware what everybody is going to say." He flicks the spent mustard sachet across the table. "Voyce had a terrapin."

An hour later I am stretched out on my bed and listening to the traffic sounds. I usually slip into sleep pretty quickly but not tonight.

The car, Lucy, my future. These things are clear in my mind but without resolution. Only Santa Monica girl survives as a vestige of hope nourished by positive imagination. Perhaps an all-pervading sense of melancholy is the permanent travelling companion of the young. If nobody said that then they should have done. And if the future is not enough to worry about, then there is always the past sneaking up behind you. My father stirs in his sleep and emits a tiny squeak. Like a noose tightening. Voyce. I close my eyes in search of darkness but something moves across its liquid surface in a V of approaching motion; the head of a small monster with something lodged in the corner of its ugly, lipless mouth.

Damn you, Hadiscomb. I don't want to go back there. I have enough problems where I am.

5.

I awake to my father singing one of his favourite compositions. 'I like Big Ones'. The lyrics could be memorised in the womb. "I like big ones, you like big ones, she likes big ones, he likes big ones-" and so on until the thundering - and perhaps inevitable - climax: "We like big ones -YES!!!" I think he will probably be chanting that when I beat him to death with a copy of 'The Rogers & Hart Songbook'. Certainly, if my mother ever had any qualms as she was packing her suitcase for the last time under the family roof then the thought that she would never have to listen to that dirge again must have bought the lid snapping down with the force of a bear trap. The only positive thing is that it suggests that he has entered a manic phase with hope in the ascendant.

For me, hope is the jangling Californian sunlight behind the curtains and being able to stand upright. Rising to the vertical tips all the festering poisons of the night down my body to tumble out of my toes and wriggle on the carpet. I stamp them to death and fling back the drapes to be bathed in golden warmth. Grrrh! Today I will fall on the script like a famished wolf, excoriate its very essence, subject it to such intense, coruscating analysis that Zaiferts' hands will tremble as he reads.

But it is not to be. My father informs me that we are toddling up the coast to Santa Barbara - should I wish to accompany him. A house party at this salubrious watering place could apparently launch his career in a spectacular new direction. "'There is a tide in the affairs of men'," he begins, before drying up. 'Good old Constance' has come into contact with a Russian film producer who has access to unlimited wealth and a notion he wishes to turn into a movie. All he needs is a writer. Said producer, his Russian director, the obliging Constance and the mercurial Larry Sabel will all come together like favourable constellations under the roofs of an art-loving multi-millionaire at the aforesaid Santa Barbara and money will shower down in torrents. He will explain more in the car.

I am only half-listening as I grapple with the pros and cons. A little quiet time with the script in congenial surroundings will more than compensate for that lost on the journey; and this is a good moment to get out of L.A. Sooner or later - probably sooner - somebody is going to find the car and I'd rather be somewhere else when the phone rings.

Peter, in earnest conversation with Maria, is summoned to store luggage that we do not need and my father profits from the occasion to explain that the bath plug does not achieve a snug closure unless you wrap a wash cloth round it. He points out sternly that in Europe a family of five could live for a year on the electricity wasted in producing the water that leaks away. Peter listens patiently but without giving any sign that he understands my father's convoluted argument. I think he is left with the impression that Europeans drink their bath water, something he probably suspected already.

Driving Highway 101 to Santa Barbara is hardly hitching up a couple of mules and pointing them west but it is travel and I still respond to the magic of the American road. You can always get in a car and go somewhere better. From empty spaces to teeming cities. From plains to snow-capped mountains. From burning deserts to freezing forests. Nowhere will you be too far from the fundamental values that underpin America and if you come back there will be no reproaches. It didn't work out. The timing wasn't right. You will try again. The road will still be there. It is your birthright. Your escape. It is freedom. You start the engine and you hit the road, and have the feeling of America in your bones; of something that is going on for ever and has already come a long, long way in a very short time.

We run out of gas eight hundred yards from the hotel, near Wilshire and Westwood, which is reputed to be the busiest intersection in the States. I now believe this. I am deputed to find the nearest gas station because my father believes that his English accent and amiable manner will fend off problems with the police and other road users. I leave him smiling vacuously whilst Angelinos slow down to see if they can spot any mangled bodies and bat obscenities at each other. When I eventually trudge back with a can of gas that has cost an arm and a leg, three other drivers are filling in insurance forms beside their dented vehicles and a woman is having hysterics because a truck has backended her brand new Toyota MR2 Roadster which carries a licence plate reading 'MOMSTOY'. We pull away in a vengeful cloud of blue language just as the police are arriving.

"Fucking people!" says my father.

Thus, in two words, does he succinctly encapsulate his attitude to his fellow human beings; an attitude which achieves its sharpest definition when he is driving. My father has a theory that most of the anger in the world is generated by people trying to be nice to each other. He believes that this is unnatural and can only lead to an escalation of tension that will inevitably explode into violence. This accumulation of stress, he argues, is at its most dangerous when one is at the wheel of a car in a major industrial city. Luckily, my father has come up with a solution. It consists of him heaping unstinted abuse on every other road user in which no physical characteristic, nuance of skin tincture or perceived creed or religious persuasion escapes denigration.

Fortunately for the preservation of his theory and himself, the recipients rarely hear his words as the expletives are spluttered through clenched teeth as his overtaking foot savages the accelerator pedal.

One advantage of our personal energy crisis is that a strained silence prevails until we are past Ventura and the rolling green countryside undulates towards the Santa Ynez mountains. By then the traffic has fallen away behind like a pack of dogs that chased us out of town and my father's abhorrence of vacuums has led him into a more detailed description of the putative new project. He is enthusiastic about the idea of a European producer: "Imagine," he says, "the joy of working with someone who doesn't think that Wittgenstein is a tax haven." He is also optimistic about the source of the money: the Russian Mafia. This is a wonderful new font of production money that Hollywood has barely tapped. And the Russian authorities, apparently a branch of the aforesaid R.M., are prepared to be co-operative should a subject be found that reflects well on their country and provides the means to recoup their as yet unspecified administrative expenses. And yes! Let joy be unconfined. A subject has been found: a remake of 'War and Peace' - in space. The heroes will be pioneer soviet astronauts battling against an invading galaxy which will represent Napoleon's army. It will cost millions and millions of roubles, deutschmarks and dollars and possibly break down into several films. My father will become colossally rich from the Chinese television rights alone.

Perhaps I am still smarting at being despatched for the gas but I ask why they do not get a Russian writer who knows something about space. My father considers this question redundant - "Fucking stupid" is how he actually puts it. Apparently, everybody except me knows that the Russians only make art films directed by tortured (often literally) long-haired, dissident intellectuals with unpronounceable names you can never remember. They have no real knowledge of commercial cinema, something they had the grace to admit when they came, cap in hand, to the Mecca of commercial film-making. And they do not have Larry Sabel as manager. Wonderful, prescient Larry who can walk on water and turn bread into much more bread minus ten percent.I think of mentioning Larry's presence at the concert but decide against it. Any comment is likely to be interpreted as an attack and with father in mellow mood it is best to leave him to his fantasies.

"Constance has turned up trumps again," is all I content myself with saying.

"Yes," he says shortly. "She's a brick."

Yes. Useful for building one's career if available in sufficient quantity, I muse. He could be a little more effusive. Especially since she helped him land his last big writing assignment. Perhaps he feels guilty. Sometimes I wonder if he still entertains the notion that he will get back together with my mother.

I am still mulling over this when, to my surprise, we pull off 101 just before Santa Barbara and enter the slightly peeling, sun-bleached gates of the Magnolia Hotel. It transpires that though we have visiting rights to the house party we are not actually part of it. We are going to stay here. This is a slight letdown socially but no real hardship because I have good memories of the Magnolia from way back when my mother was on the team. It is really a motel and straggles down to the sea in a series of chalets and lanai rooms with names like 'Oceanview' and 'Sea Foam'. There is a private beach, a boardwalk, a couple of pools, and ping-pong and shuffleboards and paddle tennis and everything needed to make you feel slightly exercised before heading for the Eucalyptus Cocktail Lounge and Dining Room. The clientele is family, taking a breather from the L.A. hinterland, and veering towards middle-aged and beyond. The kind of richly coiffured matrons with dangling rhinestone spectacles who snatch up hideous garments in the gift shop and hold them against each other crooning, "Isn't this just to die for?" There is a cheerful patina of all-prevailing shabbiness that the European side of my nature finds reassuring and can equate with tradition.

I wait in the car while my father sorts out the reservation. This is an unspoken convention that shields us, temporarily, from the consequences of people misconstruing the true nature of our relationship. A misconception fuelled by my father's habit of frequently addressing me as 'darling' in crowded places. Something he has done since childhood.

I am relieved to see him emerge without a porter and we drive through swaying palm and nodding hibiscus to 'Bamboo Song' where a large suite with bedroom, verandah, bathroom and kitchenette awaits us - 'Beach umbrellas, back rests, mats, bicycle rental and massage appointments -

Dial operator and ask for the lifeguard'. The guy must have his hands full. You would need to pick the right moment to start drowning. My father says he has some calls to make and seems happy when I tell him I am going for a walk.

Like a lemming, I head for the sea; past 'Arroyo' and 'Las Flores' as the geriatric, nut brown tennis pro creaks by on his ancient bike. I think I remember him from last time. His whites stand out like the peak of Kilimanjaro. 'Plink-plonk' from the tennis courts and beside them the Railroad Diner/Coffee Shop is doing good business with paper napkins blowing away in the breeze. Just beyond is a real railroad track which you have to cross to get to the beach and the more sought after ocean front rooms along the boardwalk. Sometimes a train comes through. A real old-fashioned one with flatcars and lots of rattling. It moves just about faster than a man can run and you can imagine cowboys slugging it out on the roofs of the boxcars; a tribe of whooping indians galloping in pursuit.

The munchers stare at me aggressively as they wrap their mouths round satchels of beef. They have already staked their claim while I am recognised as a newcomer who has barely set foot in the place. I pass over the track, hearing again that imagined hum of the great American distance, and stare at the Pacific with my own personal wild surmise. Like a boil on the face of a beautiful woman, an offshore drilling rig disfigures what was once an uncluttered path to the horizon. Others are scattered along the coast with the air of sinister extra-terrestrials awaiting the signal to wade ashore and exterminate all human life. My heart sinks. Do we really need oil that badly? Wouldn't it be easier to simply annex another middle eastern country? Nothing personal, of course. It's just that oil rigs look better sticking out of deserts.

At least there is the boardwalk beneath my feet. The wood bleached so white that it has become like weathered pumice stone. The rail is warm and slightly rough to the touch with the reassuring feel of a familiar human body.

I walk to the end where there is a small patch of lawn and take the steps down to the beach. Stretches of sand and shingle with outcrops of rock. The tide is on the ebb, small waves plopping down to send tongue-licks of clear water chasing each other across hissing shingle. Sandpipers skip in and out of the waves, the delicate tracery of their footprints melting into the washed sand. I take off my shoes and socks and head up towards the town, struggling through the deep sand. There are a few interesting houses beyond the motel. Some sleek and modern with balconies and white wooden shutters. Others like untidy piles of squat lanterns or weathered packing cases with windows let into them. I remember my parents talking about buying one. It would have been a good idea. New playmates arriving every day at the Magnolia, and all its amenities to fall back on. My parents were great at dreaming up schemes like that. Too bad they never came to anything. Perhaps because there was a nagging fear in both their hearts. They lived from day to day keeping their options open. Perhaps that is why there is only me.

I pick up a piece of driftwood that looks a little like a duck's head. That was another of my mother's games. Comb the beach and produce five objects that resemble something. Anything. Anything that will win you words of praise and make you feel a little bit clever and loved. I miss my mother. I miss the three of us.

The beach comes to an end in a cliff and a tumble of sea-splashed rocks and I descend to the water's edge and then turn back. The water is freezing cold when it snaps at my toes and a million motes of sunshine tingle above the wavelets. Facing south, the sand stretches away without interruption and in the distance a couple with a dog are walking arm in arm. Occasionally, the man breaks away to hurl a ball and the dog soars skywards to catch it on the bounce, throwing up flurries of sand as it skitters and slides. I envy that couple. I would be that man with someone to love on his arm. With the right girl I would walk on and on, never leaving the beach, through the Americas until we reached Tierra Del Fuego where we would be married in Ushuaiai because it sounded like the west wind in rut, and then walk up the east coast to Rio for our honeymoon. 'Great Beach Walks of the World'. It would not be easy because the coastline of Chile is crumbling cheese. But it would be the project that forged our union. There would be frontiers to cross, and military installations, and no-go zones and nuclear reactors and vast private domains but we would pass beyond them as if invisible and carry on quietly to the unspoilt places where we would lie in each other's arms beneath full moons and cloudless skies. Perhaps it would take all our lives. Never having lost sight of the sea, our ageing limbs would march doggedly into a wall of cold around the Hudson Strait and we would expire together, spying mortality through the transparent flesh of our tightly clasped hands and gazing into each other's eyes and out towards Greenland and the northern lights.

Ahead of me, the couple go up the beach and disappear into one of the private houses. I am glad I have not got close to them because now they can remain perfect in my imagination. I walk on and on and the houses become less imposing until they cease to exist. The last is an unfinished bungalow poking out from a jumble of orange and violet convolvulus that trails out onto the beach tracking the merest vestige of a stream. The water dies away in the sand like a tear drying on a cheek.

When I get back to 'Bamboo Song' my father is pacing up and down impatiently. He is a hymn to Georgio Armani in faded creams and yellows. The look of weathered Eurotrash that he clearly hopes is going to tap the mother lode. He utters the inevitable groans at my choice of clothing and we take the car and burrow into the bosky purlieus of the Santa Barbara fringe. Houses are invisible, shielded by winding driveways of tall pines, oaks and shaggy eucalypts. Nice neighborhood. I could be happy here. The right wrought iron sign eventually looms up and we turn through griffin-topped stone pillars into a wide drive that rises in gentle curves for about half a mile.

A final bend and we are in a square, gravelled courtyard dotted with statues and fragments of doric pillars that enclose an ornate pool and its fountain in the shape of a glaucous Poseidon stabbing a sea monster with his gushing trident. The Italian villa beyond must have left a gaping hole in the hills above Florence. Eleven shuttered windows stretch across its broad facade beneath a gently sloping red-tiled roof surmounted by helmeted statues who stare down warily from ornate plinths. From the courtyard, two curving stone staircases rise to converge before a recessed central doorway lost in shadow and, on either side, the lower windows sprout lintels like bushy eyebrows and are protected by iron grills. The walls are decorated with patterns of pastel stucco-work that includes friezes of snarling lions, classical heads and cheerful suns with myriad serpentine rays, and at their foot nestle vases and urns and large earthenware pots containing small orange and lemon trees.

The villa is the colour of tired sunshine. Staring at it in its setting of ilex, dogwood and cypress, I feel as if we have driven through a time warp. The fountain tinkles reassuringly and grouped around it is a cluster of exotic automobiles that might have been created as prototypes for an exclusive European motor show.

My father sighs and drinks in the scene. "But are they really happy?" he ponders.

I am surprised by the lack of security. And where is everybody? There is music wafting from somewhere but it is not coming from the terrace at the side of the house, where a major domo figure stares down at us impassively. The man withdraws and my father gets out of the car and moves his balls to a more comfortable position. "I'm not saying this again," he warns. "So don't forget it. This could be the most important social event of your life."

"Uuuhuh," I say.

He sighs in a different register and leads the way up the weathered sandstone steps towards the side terrace. The view of the ocean beyond the primary horizon of pines, oaks and cypresses is marred only by the marauding oil derricks. Comfortable, cushioned wicker chairs are arranged in groups and fans turn slowly in the high-vaulted dark interior. Two cute Filipino maids are tidying up piles of glossy magazines and my father's eyes kerb-crawl their slender bodies before alighting on a well-stocked bar. The major domo figure is behind it, now beaming like a man who lives to give satisfaction.

"Why not?" says my father.

I leave him debating whether to go with the Absolut or the Stolychniya and head down another flight of step and into the descending gardens. The music intrigues me. It sounds like a sitar or some other kind of esoteric Indian instrument probably already featuring large in Hadiscomb's CD collection. The high box hedge gives the impression of entering a maze. Marble statues of warriors and goddesses lurk in alcoves and at the bottom of a flight of steps a semi-circular pool is sprinkled with fans of water lilies amongst which drift fat, mottled goldfish with ragged tails. Along the edge of the pool, a line of stone naiads gesticulate wildly like competitors in a swimming race complaining about a false start.

The sitar has now been joined by a humming sound which comes from from the far side of an archway cut in a Maginot line of ilex. A continuous "m-m-m-m-m-m-" from human voices, rising and falling. "Mar-mar-mar-mar-". A man's voice is overlayed. Soft. Strained. Urgent. I edge forward and peer through the gap in a pleached section of the hedge behind a statue of Alexander the Great - all right, so it could be Hector. I am looking down into a sunken lawn surrounded by rose-sprinkled screens of dogwood and pomegranate and divided by waist-high box hedges like the family pews in the kind of church my English grandmother likes to visit. About thirty men and women are enclosed in the box pens and I cannot help thinking of sheep dog trials. Despite their situation they have the hue of lightly tanned well-being, the healthy sheen of newly-printed bank notes. Crisp white cotton sits well on their glowing skins. Most are squatting with their eyes closed and their hands extended with the palms upwards. They could be anticipating a communion wafer. Their lips tremble as they hum and they face the mouth of a dark grotto where a man commands a large stone seat and tilts his head back towards the heavens. It is he who is chanting the "mar-mar-mar-" refrain.

I recognise Constance in a pink that matches her state of faint embarrassment and, beside her, Larry Sabel wearing the expression of a man suffering withdrawal symptoms because he has not taken a telephone call in more than ten minutes. There are also two other men who I assume must be Constance's Russian proteges - though this seems too epicene a word for fellows with the rough-hewn features of hurriedly peeled potatoes and ill-fitting suits worn the way sofas wear dust sheets. One is fat and hirsute, the other thin and bald with the air of someone who once moonlighted for the Borgias. Neither of them is humming.

"-MAH!" The chant is bitten off in a shriek and the man before the grotto snaps his head upright and rises slowly to his feet. The hummers stop as one - except Larry who is a little late. "Let us look inside ourselves...deeper...deeper....Growth is our personal agenda . We are growing, growing....As one....As many...."

The man is about thirty and looks and dresses Indian. But an Indian designed by the team that gave you Michael Jackson. He is incredibly good looking - beautiful might be a more appropriate word - and emphatically androgynous so that he represents no direct challenge to your sexuality but could be everything that you ever wanted in a lover, counsellor or tax consultant. Even as I look at him I begin to wonder if he is Italian rather than Indian. He has an international face, a universal face. He would make a great God.

"We need to undertake a physical commitment to this growth. Open our arms to it, embrace it, feel it happening inside us. Feel it... Feel it!.....FEEL IT!!!"

Oh dear, something tells me that father does not know what he has let himself in for. This is not his cup of tea - not that any cup of tea is his cup of tea when I come to think about it. The speaker rambles on about 'inner voices' and 'higher minds' in his strange, indefinable accent and then, suddenly, as if scenting an alien presence, his gaze swivels and sweeps the surrounding foliage. I step back hurriedly and collide with the haft of he who might be Alexander the Great's sword. The statue wobbles and starts to topple.

Shit! I grab it round the bust and try to wrestle it back onto its plinth. It weighs a ton. Behind me, I hear a light tread descending the ilex alley.

"You should have taken one from nearer the gate," says a female voice. "The bronzes have more class and you wouldn't have had so far to carry it."

I dump Alex more or less back in position and turn to face the newcomer. My heart jumps. This is the girl Santa Monica girl was auditioning for. She is not blonde but dark-haired with a wide, slightly-pouting mouth, delicate nose and huge violet eyes. She makes me feel strange. Like I know her already from a photograph. Like she was always going to turn up one day and it was just a question of time. She is wearing tennis kit of impeccable whiteness that sets off perfectly her trim, honey-coloured limbs. I don't think I have ever seen a girl more beautiful. She looks at me suspiciously.

"You're not the guy who's been breaking in to fondle the caryatides? I mean, poor women, as if they didn't have enough problems supporting a roof."

"Of course not." I realise that my hand is resting on Alexander's fig leaf and remove it hurriedly. "I just bumped into it, that's all."

"Easily done. It's real difficult to squeeze past them."

"Uhm," I say. I extend a hand. "Look, my name's Will."

The vision eyes my hand for a second like there might be something unpleasant concealed in it and then extends her own with less than total enthusiasm. "Rashmi," is what I think she says.

Further strain on my conversational powers is avoided by the arrival of a huge, glistening jock also in tennis kit. He bounds down the steps carrying a sheaf of rackets and ignoring me, slaps Rashmi playfully on the butt with several hundred dollars worth of fibre glass before leaping on his way. Rashmi falls in behind him. "See you later," I say.

She responds with a little over the shoulder wave that could mean anything and skips nimbly on her way. I would like to watch her play tennis, hell, I would pay to watch her skin a three month old German shepherd - and it wouldn't have to be a dog - but maybe I can do that later. Right now it might be more sensible and career enhancing to check that father is behaving himself.

When I get back to the terrace, he is clutching the inevitable goldfish bowl of vodka and staring sternly at a glossy brochure. "Look at this," he says, "'Cymirid'. Sounds like a pesticide or a Welsh Nationalist party, doesn't it? 'Discovering you. The most important person you'll ever meet'. Four thousand dollars for the weekend. Mind you, that does include accommodation and meals. You can probably count on a glass of hot water bulked up by the essence of a dunked prune."

I am still tingling with thoughts of Rashmi. Not emotions that I feel like sharing with my father. Who was that jock she was with? Could he be important in her life?

There is a babble of voices from the gardens and Larry Sabel appears pouring untapped minutes of frustration into his cell phone. Raised consciousnesses are returning to lower a few drinks. Constance drifts to my father's side and kisses him on the cheek. With her is a slim beauty in a turquoise turban who I remember being in the first rank of the acolytes. My father perks up and beckons to me.

"Esme. This is my son, William. Esme is our hostess."

"How wonderful." Esme positively glows, her enthusiasm seemingly transcending the trivial detail of my arrival on earth and transforming it into a universal metaphor for the miracle of birth and consanguinity. She lays slender hands on my shoulders for an instant and then joins them together and squeezes; as if cracking an invisible walnut.

"Welcome to peace, William."

The English side of my nature is about say something nice about the house but she has already moved on to accept a glass of iced tea from the shaman, healer, spiritual guide or whatever he is. I note that he is looking at me unlovingly. This is puzzling. People usually have to know me for at least five minutes before they start to take a dislike to me.

"Adrianski!" The larger of the two men in tent-struck suits has brushed away the ministrations of a waiter and is more than half-filling a cut glass tumbler with brandy. This he slops towards my father in a messy toast. I am introduced and explained and learn that the speaker is Bronski and his thin, bald friend with the demeanour of a mediaeval court poisoner, Igor. I think that Igor is the director though I am never sure

The two Russians and my father are the only people availing themselves of the bar. The seekers and purveyors of inner wisdom cluster round a table in the tesselated interior sipping iced tea or designer bottled waters. I note that they clutch each others arms every time they say something.

"I believe you're over here to make a movie," I say dutifully to Bronski.

"I am over here to fuck some thin women." He casts an eye over the Filipino maids like a farmer preparing to bid at a livestock auction. "The potato in its liquid form is no friend to the woman's hips."

"Vodka is the central heating of the Russian woman," opines Igor, lugubriously. "Poor, fat, ugly britches."

"Bitches," corrects Bronski. He nods towards my father. "Why we need fuckin' writer." He smacks down his glass and half-swallows a belch. "The little boys' room is my next heaven-haven-fuck it!!" He lurches towards the interior and Igor follows.

"What a couple of mensches," exults my father as soon as they are out of earshot. "I'd follow them into the jungle any day." Yes, just to get my wallet back, I think; but he is still beaming in their direction. "And did you see those teeth?" - Igor must have the worst teeth I have ever flinched from. A neglected graveyard of lopsided yellow tombstones peppered with shotgun bursts of lead. At least, I suppose, they are - "Real teeth! That's the mouth of a human being. Not some synthetic Henry Ford orifice - 'Any colour you like as long as it's white'. What's wrong with Americans? What are they scared of? What statement are they trying to make? Who'd inflict the tortures they do on their children unless they were fundamentally sick? Those cow-catcher braces must be a last resort against an impulse to commit incest. What's wrong with a little crookedness here and there? It lends character and charm. Why this desperate yearning for conformity? Can't they see that a hint of yellow suggests that you have real teeth that have lived a little rather than a set of plastic majong tiles screwed into your gums?" He leans forward as if I am directly responsible for all this. "Perhaps we're dealing with some real psychosis here. Some morbid association with other parts of the body and their functions. Or is it just the mad march to perfection spurred by money-grabbing quacks prepared to fan any insecurity so that they can recycle your features and scare you into buying anything from a nostril douche to a tequila-flavoured vaginal spray?"

I wipe the spittle from my face and make a mental note to put off introducing him to Rashmi for as long as possible. "I'm going to explore a little," I tell him.

I do not get very far. Barely am I approaching the nearest staircase that might lead towards the tennis courts than a hand drops on my sleeve.

"Hi." Larry Sabel is smiling at me. Not a pretty sight. At first I think that he recognises me, then I reject the notion. I remember how he stared at me at the concert and feel uneasy. "Some place, huh?"

"Impressive," I say, stiffly.

"Mind you, I've been to better,"

"Really?" There is not a lot of emphasis on the question mark.

"Yeah. And the home help. Not bad, huh?" He gestures towards one of the tiny Filipinos who is emptying the only ashtray of its single butt. "Couldn't you fuck the ass off that?"

"Eruum.." I falter.

"If that's your kind of thing." He is giving me that stare again.

"I saw you at that concert. You know, 'Maha-Ma-Ma-'" I wrestle with the name and give up. "The group from Soweto."

"You were there? Well, well. Small world. What a way to go, huh? All that black pussy whipping you to death. And that lead guy. Must be hung like a horse." Again, his eyes are burning into me. I look across the terrace for a means of escape. Esme smiles at me sweetly.

"They were good," I say weakly.

"Great body." Sabel has run his fingers across my stomach. Who is he talking about? "Have you taken a stroll round this place? You could lose yourself. Do you want to see my room? I found this weird book. Photos of statues. Greek, I guess. Guys doing some strange stuff. You wouldn't believe it."

"No, thanks." I try to draw away but he is clinging to my arm and I am reminded of those dogs that take a fancy to your knee.

"You want to loosen up, you know that? Do you smoke? Come on, I've got some good stuff. The best. Or would you like something else? Name it, sweetheart." He follows my eyes as they search for help. "Don't tell me you're hanging out with that old jerk."

"You mean, my father?"

"Your father?" I can almost feel the little whirring cogs in Sabel's brain turning white hot. "Hey, come on! I was talking about the bald guy. No, hey, Adrian Lock. Listen, I represent him. I'm his ag-manager. Very talented guy. We go back-boy, it must be-"

"Excuse me." I retrieve my arm and flee down the steps. My armpits are damp. I feel like I've put a wet finger up a light socket. What a shame that had to happen just when I've meet the girl of my dreams - or rather, the kind of girl who has up until now never deigned to set toe in my dreams.

The tennis court is at the edge of the formal gardens and surrounded on all sides by walls of green canvass. There are portholes and I peer through one to see the jock yelping with frustration as he lashes a ball into the bottom of the net. He looks hot and harassed. Rashmi has yet to break glow and appears totally relaxed as she hunches and sways from side to side, awaiting the next serve. Her profusion of dark hair is now swept back in a bandeau and cute little pompoms dangle from the back of her cashmere socks. Her legs are lightly muscled so that they gleam appealingly in the dying sun and each time she belts the ball she purses her lips and emits a delicate little 'ouf' noise that makes my toes tingle. The jock is good but she gets everything back and works him round the court until he becomes exasperated and loses the point trying to hit a risky winner.

It makes me think of the games between my mother and father at Pulignac. On the municipal court between the swimming pool and the camping site. He always used to hit the ball doggedly to her backhand, something she had difficulty dealing with. After five minutes of this my mother was prone to lash the ball viciously into the bleachers and demand whether my father was more interested in a game of tennis or in initiating a protracted exercise in sadism. My father would apologise profusely, suggesting that perhaps there was a basic difference in their interpretation of the rules. He had always imagined, obviously erroneously, that the idea was to deliver the ball into the opposing court in such a manner that the opponent could not return it. Perhaps he had misunderstood something. He would then apologise again and hit every ball softly to her forehand until she screamed and lifted one over the communal showers shouting that she was not so feeble that she needed to be patronised and made the butt of his infantile sarcasm. All she wanted was a game in which there was some variety and not a pathological desire to win at all costs. My father would then try and spread the ball around the court with the result that his game went completely to pieces and my mother beat him and told him that he had a faulty service action and should take lessons.

The jock serves a perfect ace to the back hand corner. "Long," says Rashmi without flickering an eye lash.

The jock double faults and hurls his racket at the canvass a few feet from my head. Perhaps he is trying to blame me. I take the hint and withdraw, pausing only to lavish on Rashmi a look of uncomplicated adoration. She waves her racket at me cheerfully. God, I hope she is part of the house party and not just passing through.

When I return to the terrace, my father appears preoccupied. Separating from Constance, he steers me and another pail of vodka with a twist away from the throng. "I've been talking to Larry," he says in a schoolmasterly voice. "He asked me if you were gay."

I snort. "That doesn't surprise me."

"What's that supposed to mean?"

"It means he's trying to get it in first." My father looks alarmed. "He's the one's who's gay. He just made a pass at me."

"Larry is my agent."

"That has nothing to do with his sexual orientation." I wait. "Surely you don't think I've been hiding something all these years?"

My father's silence is not encouraging. He sighs. "How does one ever know? Your mother never wanted you to go to boarding school. Maybe she was right."

"I can't believe this. You think I'm gay?"

"Nobody's blaming you, Will. I mean, I'm not blaming you. Maybe it's my fault. Not that it is a fault, of course." He gazes towards the Pacific Ocean. "It's just a pity that you couldn't talk to your mother."

"Ask Larry yourself. He was offering me drugs as well."

"Perhaps my own attraction to the fair sex is some kind of sublimation." My father has stopped listening to me. "I remember the school play when I was about seventeen. Richard II. I was Bushy, or was it Green? 'Expedient manage must be made, my liege, e'er further leisure yield them further-' I'll look it up. Anyway, there was this fourth former playing the queen's attendant. Blandford, I can still remember his name. He's borrowed his sister's brassiere and stuffed it with the Daily Express. I remember him sitting on my knee in the wings and me fondling his breasts underneath his dress. But, of course, it wasn't 'him', it was 'her'. You know what I mean? It wasn't homosexual. I was imagining that Blandford was a woman. So…I can…I have...you know…I do see…."

It may sound as if my father is extending the hand of shared experience and paternal solidarity but I know that in reality he is merely exploring the dramatic possibilities of the situation. That and ensuring I do not stake a claim to supremacy in some new field of experience. If I killed someone he would immediately confess to several unsolved murders committed for reasons that would qualify for the Nobel Peace Prize.

"Then there's the whole American thing."

"What do you mean?"

"Well, part of you belonging to an alien culture. The shock of adjustment could have triggered off the very reaction your mother was worried about. I don't know. I'm a hundred percent British. I don't know how it would have affected me."

That is another problem with being the child of a mixed marriage. You are two people. Each parent automatically attributes any positive trait to their own nationality, heritage and upbringing. Anything vaguely nebulous, questionable or incomprehensible is the province of the other party. When you are good you are them. When you are bad you are the other one.

"Dad," I say patiently. "Hold the psychobabble. This is blatant bullshit. I'm no more gay than you are."

"It doesn't matter if you are," says my father nobly. "I've never had a homophobic bone in my body. And you'll always be my son. Maybe it's just a phase you're going through. I told you about Blandford. Mind you, he was wearing make-up-"

"I don't give a shit about Blandford!"

My father looks hurt. "No need to adopt that tone. Especially after I've just wangled you an invite to the vegan barbecue."

I am about to tell him what he can do with it when I see Rashmi coming up the steps.

6.

"Who won?

"Who won what?"

"The tennis."

"Oh, that." She stares at me like it would have been nice if I had been talking about something more interesting. "I did. I always win against Parrish. It's the main reason I play him.

"And do you always cheat?"

"Only when the other guy does - or when I need to to win. Gee, this food is really foul."

We are on the terrace. Rashmi. Moi. A cast of thousands all playing extras. It is evening. Chinese lanterns stir in a gentle breeze. Cicadas warble. The air is heavy with the scent of an unseen shrub, or maybe a visible woman. I am in love.

Rashmi was talking about the buffet. Not a repast I will forget in a hurry. It looked like the bits you throw away when you make a salad and tasted like the bits you throw away when you make a salad curdled in stale yak's milk.

"Not good," I agree. "Are you staying at the house?" What I really mean is: 'I have adored you from the first moment I set eyes on you. I look upon you as Turner gazes upon a sunset. Only a pucker of your lips and my heart is torn apart as if by wild beasts. Each breath you take-'

"Are you all right?"

"I'm great."

"You just looked kinda - I thought it might have been food poisoning. No, I'm not staying. Parrish brought me over. He lives up the road." She looks around. Maybe for Parrish. Maybe for anyone.

I gaze at her, critically aware that I need to say something. It is not just that she is beautiful. Lots of girls are beautiful. It is the feeling that I get when I look at her beauty. As if each separate feature forms part of a combination that unlocks my heart. Yes, it's as serious as that.

"Do you live in Santa Barbara?"

Squint-eyed, lock-jawed John Wilkes said that it took him but five minutes conversation with a pretty woman to put himself on terms with the handsomest man in Europe. Two minutes with Rashmi and I feel I am talking like John Wilkes looks.

"No, I'm up from L.A."

My heart gives a little jump. A positive jump. At the same instant, I see the tennis jock approaching. He who must be Parrish. He carries a lemon jacket which is several sizes too small for him and the ideal accompanying garment to the flesh-revealing, halter necked, primrose number that Rashmi is wearing. He is going to take her away from me.

"Doyouhaveatelephonenumber?" The words sodomise each other.

"I have several."

Luckily, Parrish has been waylaid by Esme and the beautiful androgynous one who I now know is called Ganna.

"If you could spare one, I'd like to see you again in L.A."

"I was beginning to wonder if you worked for a communications company." She knocks back her drink. "Okay. You can try me under J.P.Rand. It's been known to work. Tell me, are you Australian?"

Before I can reply, Parrish is upon us and she is backing into the jacket he holds out like a matador extending a cape.

"Seeya." He nods and takes her firmly by the upper arm. Within two seconds they have disappeared into the crowd. I stare at the space where she stood and conquer a desire to run after her; just so I could watch her get into a car and off the premises. 'J.R.Rand'. I start patting my pockets for a pen.

"I sometimes think I'm descended from a French woman who was raped by an English soldier in the Hundred Years War," says a loud, familiar voice. "Or maybe it was an English woman raped by a French soldier." A world-weary sigh that invites complicity. "It was that kind of war"

My father is holding court, fortified by the excellent claret that Esme produced to wash down the buffet. Drink is a great leveller and he is now prepared to swap psychological insights with those whose comments he would normally ridicule. Or, more realistically, he is ready to pounce upon any subject that arises so that he can relate it to his own experience and talk about himself interminably.

I am relieved that Rashmi left before she could perceive that there was some kind of bond between us. Constance has gone too. She left before dinner. She may have known something about the food but I suspect it was because my father had barely exchanged a word with her since we arrived. This is not good news career-wise.

"I feel it every time the train approaches Limoges," continues father.

"The rape?" asks a dark, intense woman of the type that frequently seems to appear in my father's life at this time of the evening.

"No, a feeling of belonging. I feel *bien dans la peau* - 'good inside my skin' - as the French say."

"That's beautiful," says a pale woman who is sitting hand in hand with a thin, balding man attached to a goatee beard. "Don't you think so, Keaton? It makes me want to go to France."

Keaton is more circumspect. "I'd have thought that the residual legacy of the rape experience would have had a counter-productive influence on your environmental polarity," he observes.

"Rape was much more common in those days," says my father cheerfully. "People took it in their stride. And it was a long time ago. The fourteenth century? The fifteenth century?" He muses. "Funny, when a war lasted for a hundred years you'd think you'd remember when it was."

"I doubt if women ever took rape in their stride," says the dark woman sternly. "You seem to have a rather dated perception of life. Has it ever occurred to you that you might harbour a fund of unfocussed aggression?"

"I always thought it was pretty focused most of the time," says my father. "Anyway, it probably comes from working in Hollywood."

"What to you do?" says Keaton suspiciously. "Are you a director?"

"I haven't the patience," says my father dismissively. "I write."

"You're a screenwriter?" The pale woman releases Keaton's hand. "That's fascinating. What have you written that we might have seen?"

"Nothing, probably," says my father. "I mainly write for people who think 9/11 is a cut-price convenience store."

"We all have violence in us." Keaton has spotted danger. "It's a question of how we handle it, that's all. I have to control my own feelings sometimes."

"That's right, dear," says the pale woman.

"The motion picture industry is blatantly failing in its responsibilities," says the dark woman sternly. "Young people are being raised on an endless diet of gratuitous sex and violence."

"You don't have to worry about me, "says my father. "My moral standards are beyond reproach. I've never advocated sex on a first date - not unless you're really in love."

I gaze out beyond the terrace into the soft Pacific night. The ugly oil rigs have disappeared to be replaced by clusters of fairy lights. They look like candelabra ranged along the dark banqueting table of the horizon or Spanish galleons standing off to load fresh treasures from the new world. Around one hundred and fifty years ago this was part of Mexico, all the way up to San Francisco. Just down the road, Spanish heels clattered up the steps of El Presidio Real and the great, great grandparents of the people around me, if they were not heaving in a boat labouring round the Horn or wondering whether to eat each other in a snow-bound pass east of the Sierra Nevadas, could have been trading with fur trappers in the San Joaquin valley. Less than two hundred years. A temporal hiccup. A flicker of coonskin caps, Stetsons, stove pipe pants, billycock hats, Eton collars, elastic-sided boots, flared jeans and Levi 501s and we are there to here, screaming down the tunnel towards the brilliant light and suddenly discovering we're in a gun barrel. Shot into the future before we've had time to digest the past.

Once upon a time, the settlers in their covered wagons gazed in awe and trepidation at the endless, rolling prairies and distant snow-capped mountain ranges because there was no alternative. Now we swallow our surroundings with a cup of coffee and the newsflash on 'Good morning, America'. Now, even buildings emigrate. One morning you are stones and mortar embedded in the Tuscan hills, the next - or nearly - you are outside Santa Barbara. I am sitting in an immigrant. An immigrant staring at strange creatures who arrived after it did, sucking sustenance from a colder, alien sea. No wonder people get confused.

What made my mother's folks, the Chabbicks, choose that patch of what is now Nebraska as their stopping place? Did they just pull up the wagon and say: "This seems like a nice spot, dear. Let's kill a few Indians and start planting corn." Did they even come by wagon? Maybe they got a train from New York via Chicago. Or sailed through the Great Lakes. Perhaps they came up the Mississippi-Missouri on a riverboat. Oh, America. You are so vast and rich and wonderfully exciting. What a shame you are happening so fast. Sometimes I feel that the best parts disappeared before anybody noticed. That they live only as memories diluted into images on the walls of dusty art galleries.

I must ask my mother about the Chabbicks when I next talk to her. It is too late to call now. She and Philippe will be in bed.

I move along the terrace to the group that includes Esme, Ganna, Bronski, Igor and the largest number of acolytes. Larry sees me coming and whispers in Esme's ear. She studies me and gives a little wave. Boy, despite the fact that I am in love with Rashmi, I have to concede that she is very beautiful. Ganna leans forward to hear what Larry is saying and his face hardens. Sensing bad vibes, I check out the blush-pink damask in the nearest lavatory before limping back to the terrace. I wonder what Rashmi is doing now?

"-deformed midget!" My father could be inveighing against anyone but I quickly detect that he has lit upon one of his favourite bugbears: philosophers. As a breed he hates them even more than producers, critics, taxmen, bank managers, stock brokers, Lloyds underwriters, accordionists and Morris dancers. To him, they are posturing, arty-farty pedants answering questions that only a psychiatrist would be interested in asking. My father is suspicious of ideas that have to be thought about. He prefers them to arrive pre-packaged, preferably with the minimum amount of wrapping.

"-tortured, miserable git." Having dispensed with Kant he moves on to Kierkegaard who quickly gives way to Jung: "Spent all his life moping in a mental home"; Schopenhauer: "Makes Kierkegaard seem like a children's party entertainer. What can you say about a man who founded 'Systematic Modern Pessimism'?; Nietzsche: "Difficult to spell, syphilitic Nazi nutter who died hopelessly insane," and ending triumphantly with Rousseau: "Spawns the Romantic Movement but dumps each of the five babies he has with a serving wench he refuses to marry on the doorstep of a foundlings' hospital! The man is a complete monster!"

"Have you read any of these people?" asks the dark woman accusingly.

"Of course I have," lies my father. "As far as it's possible for any more or less sane person to wade through their wafflings without reaching for a shotgun." He fixes her with a stern eye. "You know what Nietzsche said?: 'When a woman becomes a scholar there is usually something wrong with her sex organs'. Mind you, I doubt that the diseased little rat ever got close enough to form an opinion."

"That's awful," says the pale woman, referring I imagine to Nietzsche's statement rather than his postulated lack of success with the opposite sex.

What puzzles me most is the source of my father's information. To the best of my knowledge, most of his education took place long after school and university in my bedroom, where as a small boy I would frequently find him sitting on my bed wrapped up in one of the Ladybird series of educational books for small children purchased for me by my mother. I remember 'Kings and Queens of England (Book 1)' and 'Alexander the

Great' in the 'Adventures from History' series, but not a slim volume dedicated to the great philosophers. The sparse, economical style favoured by L. du Garde Peach, M.A., Ph.D., D.Litt. would also have militated against the kind of detail furnished by my father.

"W-e-ell," says Keaton. "It's been real interesting talking to you, but I think-"

"And it's been really interesting talking to you." My father stands up. "And now I'm going to the lavatory."

He stumps off and Keaton hurriedly takes his wife by the arm and starts saying good byes like he is worried he may not have finished before my father gets back. Only the dark woman from our little group is not seizing the chance to escape. She twitches like an angry cat searching for something to vent its wrath on and then goes into the house. Perhaps she is staying the night. We are not, I know, but I sense that it will not be easy to prise father away from surroundings that he clearly finds congenial. I move to the balustrade and gaze down at Poseidon, now discretely floodlit. A line of cars is beginning to glide away down the drive. A hand plucks at my sleeve and I instinctively prepare my face for Larry Sabel.

"Are you okay?" Esme looks at me, concerned.

I switch off the expression of someone about to heave his vegan barbecue over an unwanted admirer.

"You look-"

"I'm fine. Really."

"You sure? Some people had problems with the tofu scramble."

"Not me," I insist. "It was delicious."

"Let's go for a walk." She glances over her shoulder and steers me down some steps that lead to the gardens. "You can never say goodbye to everyone. They'll call if they had a good time."

"I've had a great time."

"I'm so glad." She squeezes my arm and her shoulder rubs against mine. Maybe she stumbled. She is wearing a long white robe, bunched on one side at hip level and held by a clasp at the shoulder and I realise that she is dressed exactly like some of the statues we are passing. As if she had stepped down off a pedestal. The walls of box close in and the sky is a narrow pathway of stars above our heads. Behind us, the buzz of the house fades as we descend deeper into the gardens.

"Ganna was very receptive to you."

"Good." I immediately feel stirrings of unease.

"He's such a sensitive person and he knows so much."

"Yes." Is she about to try and sign me up for a course of 'Cymirid'?

"He thinks you may be living in the wrong body experience."

"That's interesting," I lie.

"What happened with Larry Sabel-"

"I'm not gay." It comes out as one word.

"Whatever. You can be exactly what you want to be. It's a time-space thing."

"I don't think it's as complicated as that." Maybe I should come right out with it and tell her that I do not have four thousand dollars.

"It's not complicated at all." She is touching me again.

"Yes, but-"

"I believe your karma could relate to a different period in your sun-dance. When you were living in ancient Greece, maybe."

"Esme, can we get this straight?" Freud might have been intrigued by my choice of word. "I'm not-"

"How can I explain it? It's like a giant wheel of fortune. Everybody needs to try real hard to jog their balls into a different prize slot." She takes my hand in hers. "You see what I'm getting at? It doesn't sound so crazy, does it?"

It does but - "No, of course not." How beautiful she looks in the moonlight. Not like Rashmi, of course. Still…

"Ganna would explain it so much better than I do. He has this great instinct. Whatever happened, you must never feel guilty about it. It wasn't wrong. It was just out of synch with your restructured temporal unity." She draws me after her. "C'mon, I want to show you something."

I feel her soft fingers against mine and begin to surrender to the mood. On and on we go, through gardens within gardens where there are fountains like wedding cakes and ghostly white statues peering from sculpted bushes: Venus wringing her hair, Hercules strangling somebody he doesn't like.

A petrified Neptune, covered in icicles, crouches in a pool beneath an overhanging glacier of stones, and cypresses soar like artists' brushes touching in stars against a blue-black sky. When I used to lie on my rackety, iron cot at Rockingham, listening to the assorted coughers, snorers, farters and masturbators polluting the night, it was this kind of fantasy that kept me going: myself and a beautiful woman, hand in hand, gliding through a landscape of legend. I have had to wait a few years. But still.

A lancet arch leads to a circular pool surrounded by tall yew hedges with trees jostling behind as if trying to peer in. The pool is full of huge stone frogs and they gaze open-mouthed and ready to spout water at a row of atlantes supporting the entrance to a stone recess. Each telamon is a malevolent head of Bacchus garlanded with grapes and grimacing in drunken agony under the weight he has to carry. Tongues protrude, eyeballs roll. There is wildness, pain and rage in the faces. They are like mad, chained beasts desperate for one last bite.

Esme leads me towards the dark opening and I am her shadow. Beyond the pillars are more carved figures, and as she fiddles in an alcove for what I discover are matches, I begin to make out a huge marble bath from which sprout stone and bronze animals: a unicorn, a wild boar, an antlered stag, a monkey squatting on a camel's back. She lights two candles and I see that we are in a vaulted grotto with walls sculpted in pumice and travertine to give the appearance of lichen. The bath has gaping, sharp-toothed fishes mouths for feet and rampant lobsters support its rim flanked by bulging embellishments of shells. The ceiling joins the walls in an arabesque of masks and painted flowers.

"This is Jim's place," says Esme.

For a moment I assume that she is referring to a member of the staff. It seems a little over the top for a gardener's hut.

"Real horn." She is indicating the tusks of a wild boar. I nod, feeling that any statement is superfluous.

Esme sighs and moves into the shadows. The bust of a man is revealed, posed on a remnant of Doric pillar. It could be Julius Caesar except that he is wearing bifocals. Esme sniffs. I sense that I am in the presence of Jim.

"Your husband?" Esme nods. I peer closer. "Is that a wig?"

"No. It's his real hair. He was losing it so he had it all shaved off when he went on his journey."

"To the next world," I say sadly, trying to get into the spirit of things.

"No, to China. Selling combine harvesters. He thought it would make it grow again, you know, and China isn't a very hair place so it wouldn't matter as much as if he was going to, say, for instance..." She tries to think of a hair place.

"Fiji?" I suggest.

"Yeah, somewhere like that. But it never grew again. Not an itsy-witsy bit. But, luckily, I'd kept his old hair in a casket for sentimental reasons so we were able to use that."

"That was lucky," I say, and then, feeling that this statement requires embellishment: "I mean, if his hair had gone on falling out bit by bit you probably wouldn't have kept any."

Esme does not appear to have heard me. She continues to gaze at the bust and then turns towards me very slowly. Her eyes capture mine without resistance. "You know something incredible? Your mind gives off measurable radiations that escape through the follicles and become impregnated in your hair. And it doesn't matter about washing it or what shampoo you use. They stay there. They're a blueprint of your ongoing development. One hair provides enough information for a personalized mind radiation report. Isn't that incredible? You can find out exactly where you are in the overall spiritual evolutionary process."

"It must be very expensive." Why did I have to say that?

"One hair. One tiny hair. And the amazing thing is that its power survives virtually undiminished, even after you've terminated a particular life experience." She smiles and a tiny tear glistens at the corner of one eye. "That's what's so wonderful. I never thought that Jim's trip to China would be his most precious gift to me - apart from the financial benefits, of course. It was if he knew he was moving on and wanted to leave me a map."

"You had one of his hairs analysed?"

"Of course. Ganna organised it. They placed it in this conductor that bombarded it with re-energised neutrons - though I guess you're not interested in the details?" I make noises that suggest I would be more than interested in the details but that if she wants to skip to the doubtless fascinating conclusion, that is fine by me too. "It was even better than I could possibly have hoped for. You see, William, some people are polymorphs. That means they have many different layers of being that become separated when they move on. 'Like particles dropping from a butterfly's wing' is how Ganna describes it. These particles catch the light and they're the same particles but you're experiencing them in a different way - like you're looking through a kaleidoscope or something. They can alight anywhere, any time. But when they do, something happens inside you. You feel it." A touch of the Jims, I think. "It happens in the form of very intense bondings and I can totally identify with that in relation to Jim because I often used to feel closest to him when I was furthest away physically - or should that be farthest? - anyway, it doesn't matter. You see what I mean?" I have no idea what she is talking about but she sounds convinced and, in my present state, that's good enough for me. "Up close there was almost too much of him to handle and I was getting confused. But now that I know that I haven't really lost him and that he's just spread himself around and I'm going to meet bits of him again and again and again so that I can ingest them into my own spiritual evolution, well, that's a really joyous feeling."

"Yes," I say.

"To find part of someone you love in a stranger who ceases to be a stranger and becomes that person, that's truly wonderful." She rests her head against my shoulder and squeezes my arm. I can feel her body from knee to breast. "Welcome home."

My heart is beating so strongly that I feel I ought to apologise for the noise. I want to say something but I am afraid of breaking the spell. I turn my head and my lips are brushing her forehead. Her hand drops to my thigh. She draws a little closer. "I'm not wrong, am I?"

This is an easy question to answer. There are others more complex hovering in the vicinity - like haven't I just fallen in love with Rashmi? for instance - but they can be dealt with later. If I have been designated protean Jim, so be it. It is a just recompense for all the rotten things that have happened to me in my life. "No, of course not."

"Do you want to stay here or shall we go outside?"

Another easy question. Jim the First is not projecting a truck load of empathy through his bifocals and if he and I are to be truly one I would prefer that whatever happened between Esme and me took place behind our back.

"Come on then." Esme interprets my silence correctly and draws me after her, pausing to blow out the candles with two delicate puffs. Farewell original Jim. Past the hunchbacked Bacchi and we are skirting the mass of rock that encloses the grotto. A fountain in the shape of a satyr's head lunges from the wall. The eyes are Mongol slits, the nose beaked, the whiskers curly and the forked goatee beard black and stained where water dribbling from the pendulous lower lip has corroded the bronze. I stare at it and realise where I am. It is the huge ears protruding from the cluster of sculpted locks that are the giveaway. I am starring in my own personal production of 'A Midsummer Night's Dream'. I am some happy sprite who lurked in the corridors of Shakespeare's imagination and is now thrust from the wings to make love to Titania, Queen of the Fairies. The Athenian glades have become Florentine going on Californian but that only compounds the magic.

"I know a secret place," breathes Esme.

"'A bank where the wild thyme blows…'" I murmur, following her through a gap in the cypresses. How incredible all this is. Now, all we need is a Bottom.

In fact there are two bottoms. The largest and wobbliest, shuddering like a vat of jelly being emptied into a funnel belongs to Bronski who is energetically servicing one of the maids glimpsed on the terrace. Beside him is Igor, similarly engaged with another female member of the domestic staff. As I look on, bemused, Bronski stretches out an arm and, in a bizarre conjunction, meets Igor's hand which is reaching towards his. They clasp hands and continue to thrust away in unison. Nothing in the tableau deserves high marks for artistic merit but my reaction to the hand-clasping puzzles me. I find it distasteful.

What Esme thinks I never find out as she is already striding briskly towards the house.

I feel sad and let down, but in a funny way relieved. I have not been unfaithful to Rashmi and, miraculously, my father is not involved in what I see before me.

Life teaches one to be thankful for small mercies.

7.

"I thought it went pretty well on the whole," says my father, cheerfully. "Mind you, I don't know why I'm a writer when I could be a Hawaiian Shaman specialising in colonic horoscopes with free disposable speculums." He sniggers. "'You pass your future'. Which reminds me, I've had a great idea for a gay organisation to stand up to The National Front. It's going to be called The National Behind."

'Sensitivity' has never been a candidate for my father's middle name. I can still see the expression on the Swedish paediatrician's face when he told her that the best way to test if the bath water is too hot for your elbow is to dip a baby in it.

We are back at the hotel and Santa Barbara is already sinking into the quicksands of my memory. It might have been a dream. Esme. The Gardens. Rashmi. No, Rashmi was real. She has to be real.

"Of course, Constance is playing up. I never understand what gets into women. Time of life, I suppose."

"Being treated like shit doesn't help," I moralise.

"But now that I'm close to Bronski it doesn't matter so much."

As usual, he has ignored my words. "You hardly spoke to Bronski."

"That was intentional, *mon petit brave*. You never want to look as if you're grovelling for work in this town. It diminishes your market value. Play hard to get and they beat a path to your door." He rubs his hands and shows his teeth. "I've never known Larry so bullish about anything. We're probably going to Sun Valley to get the feeling of the snow. I see white as the leitmotif of the piece. It's so Russian, isn't it? The link between the book as it lives in our imaginations and its new incarnation. Snowy spheres in some distant galaxy." He starts to flick through the sections of the L.A. Times. "What did you think of Karen?"

I am still thinking of Rashmi. I could call her immediately but, as daddy would doubtless suggest, that could be a bad idea. Too eager. And, if she passed, it would cast a blight on my other designs: all the things I need to do to get my life in gear: write the script analysis, sort out my mid-Atlantic crisis, face up to the Lucy situation, find a job and get away from my father. No, I will make a start on the script analysis, then call her. "Karen?"

"The dark-haired one at the party." His voice softens. "Interesting woman. Confrontational, but she sort of grows on you. I mean, you have to concede that you can't be right all the time, don't you? She's a journalist. Writes for one of those free papers they dump in the lobby. Rather attractive, don't you think?"

"I didn't really notice."

He's in the mood to talk; but when was the last time you hunkered down and had a good old chinwag with your father? About anything. And especially anything connected with sex. I find the thought that he ever did it pretty repugnant, let alone the thought that he still does it, let alone the thought that he is prepared to talk about it. If he wants to chat about things like this he should lean on a male friend, though there aren't lots of those about, especially out here. Larry Sabel, maybe though it's difficult to associate him with the word 'friend'. Maybe I'm the only candidate. 'The only friend a father truly makes' - if I allow myself to think like the editorial board of The Readers' Digest. As you get older, parents are like signposts. Not to be talked to but to be read for distances and destinations. Usually of places you do not want to go to.

"Oh, no!" My father lets the paper drop from his hands.

"What is it!?" But I know. They have found the car. Lying on top of a nun.

"The Lakers lost again. Golden State Warriors! How can you lose to a team with a name like that?" He kicks the paper across the room. The Lakers play basketball. Like fish swim. My father supports them which means that he is never able to watch them. Not a whole game; just little bits on television. If he watches them for too long they become lacklustre, turn over the ball and start missing free throws, and he feels responsible. He has led them to back-to-back-to-back world titles by swimming up and down the pool while the finals were being played, generating energy that Shaq O'Neal and Kobe Bryant turned into baskets. It was tough going, but somebody had to do it.

He also supports the Oakland Raiders, though bemoaning the fact that they no longer seem to recruit players exclusively from the ranks of schizophrenic psychopaths, demonic circus strongmen, recidivist drug addicts and men who rip the heads off live pigs not just to prove that they are unpleasant but because it is the quickest way to the chitlings. 'Commitment to excellence' is the Raiders' motto. 'Excellent to be committed' is what my father says it ought to be.

The phone rings and my heart jumps. I must stop reacting like this. "Hello?" My father has answered it and his face becomes serious. "Yes. Yes, he is." He looks towards me and draws a finger across his throat. Tired of jumping, my heart starts pounding. "You want to talk to him? Very well." He beckons to me and thrusts out the phone. Oh, God. Why did I have to do it? If only I could live five minutes of my life again - as an orphan. He thrusts the phone into my hand. "Don't forget what I told you."

"Hello?"

It is Hadiscomb calling for news of the weekend and wondering if I would like to go to 'the flicks' later. My father chortles in the background and I wonder what you get for patricide in California these days. Probably a citation from 'The Friends of Euthanasia'.

I had been contemplating giving Hadiscomb the brush off but now I am not so sure. After a weekend with my father he seems like a cylinder of oxygen. We agree to meet later and I take the script down to the pool. Maria is there, flicking her feather duster outside the sought-after poolside suites and apparently deep in conversation with José. I am surprised when she suddenly swings her trolley through a hundred and eighty degrees and stalks off, obviously pissed about something. I wonder if they are related in some way. Maybe he is her father.

"Hi, meesta!" The volume is there, but today I don't feel like I am the sole focus of José's attention. He sinks his trowel into the earth and grabs a pansy from his tray like he is going to bury it rather than plant it. Our eyes meet and he awards me the obligatory teeth feast before getting on with his work. This must be the most thickly planted poolside on earth. José has to push flowers aside to get new ones in. No wonder they die in droves and keep having to be replaced.

I open the script feeling a tinge of righteousness laced with excitement. I always savour the roll-up-your-sleeves moment, the artist face to face with the naked canvas, the round the world navigator staring across empty ocean. Challenge. I have read the script once so I have a good fix on what happens. It is not a bad piece of work and I can see why they gave it to me. A comedy adventure about two young guys who come together and steal a car which turns out to belong to a Mafia capo and contains the clues to a fortune so that they have both the cops and the Mafia after them, plus the involvement of a sultry, sexy, spunky girl who you know immediately must work for the Mafia, though they never suspect this and both fall in love with her which helps because she changes sides at the last minute when a lot of bad guys get blown away and the heroes killed, except that they have not really been killed but faked their deaths so that they can ride off into the sunshine with the money and bonk the heroine to death for the rest of their lives. The end. Everything is okay, including the bit where you think that the heroine has double-crossed them and gone off with the money, but it is not vastly different from scores of other movies one has seen. Maybe this is a good thing. The script is not going to lead the audience into Ingmar Bergman territory where they might become confused, succumb to terminal angst and stage a collective suicide. On the other hand, it is a tad 'ho hum'. If not exactly screaming out to be raped by an idea it could at least be goosed by a notion. Everything is predictable within its genre: wise-cracking buddies, car chases, lots of damage to public property. Little sign of Harold Pinter having been flown in to oversee the re-writes. However, people obviously go for this stuff and there are some good things. The chase in the condom factory, for instance. Or the scene where the three heroes are forced to enter a drag queen contest and the girl doesn't win. Hmn.

I plough on, my eyelids becoming heavy. It is amazing how taxing it is to maintain concentration on the written word. Like going round an art gallery. After half a dozen paintings I am asphyxiated by total torpor, barely capable of dragging one foot in front of the other. At the Tate gallery I have a clearer recollection of the leather banquettes (yum) than of the paintings. And if I get the job I will have to read hundreds of these things each week. Oh well, I suppose that with practice my faculties will sharpen up. And some of the scripts will be better than this. On the other hand, I fell asleep reading 'Hamlet'. Mind you, that is a bit heavy despite all the quotable bits. Maybe I am not cut out for this. Oh God, why do I have to depress myself? I have only read twenty-two pages this time round. I must think of it as an apprenticeship. With any luck, after a couple of months I will be promoted and scrambling onto the executive ladder, within a few rungs of touching Zaiferts' turn-ups. I will be covering other people's coverage and attending script conferences, nodding thoughtfully and occasionally tossing out an observation that reveals trenchant insight. Of course, right now, the sun is not helping. It is creeping under the parasol and embalming me in delicious, soporific warmth. With the second reading under my belt I had intended to call Rashmi, but, but…I close my eyes. This is so nice. Flop. I feel the script dropping from my fingers that have already gone bye-byes. A split second later, the rest of me follows.

The movie I see with Hadiscomb is not unlike the script I am reading and we both agree that we should have seen the Hungarian film at the Nuart. That is the trouble with art films. They are like the leftovers you keep in the back of the icebox until they turn bluey-green and you can throw them away with a clear conscience. You keep intending to see Ladislas Szlabov's epic right up to the moment that you discover with relief that it isn't on any more.

After the movie we wander through throbbing young Westwood and eat at the Hamburger Hamlet which we share with U.C.L.A. cheerleaders and their huge, glowing escorts.

L.A. is a very departmentalised town. If we had been eating at Santa Monica and Fairfax, everybody would have been Jewish and a hundred and ten. Maybe it is a reaction against all the testosterone in the air but I find myself lurching towards the morbidly metaphysical. "Have you ever thought about killing your parents?"

Hadiscomb brushes some of the salt from his margarita off his lips and reflects. "When I was younger, I thought about killing my father - well, not exactly killing him. I just thought it would be nice if he wasn't there any more. You know, nothing painful or lingering. A car accident maybe. Then I could be alone with my mother. I suppose I was in love with her. That's quite normal, isn't it?"

"The best," I tell him. It is weird but most Europeans automatically assume that every American is an expert on anything associated with psychiatry or drugs.

"I didn't think about what we'd do for money with him gone. Pretty stupid really."

"Love is blind," I comfort him.

"That lasted about ten years I suppose. Now we get on pretty well. Without having anything to do with each other, of course." I nod sympathetically. "Now I have more problems with my mother. She's getting very vocal. You know, all the sacrifices she made for the family, and what's she got to show for it? She never had a career, et cetera, et cetera. It's tough but there's nothing I can do about it. If you suggest she takes up painting she thinks you're being patronising. She ought to be talking to my father. It's not my responsibility. I wasn't in a position to do anything when I was a child."

Even though you were your mother's lover? How does she feel about that now? Betrayed, perhaps. Yes, I think I could begin to enjoy this. "Perhaps she can't talk to him," I say, sounding very serious, even to me.

"Probably not. He's lucky of course having his career. He'd wade through brains for nothing. I don't think he's really happy unless he's got a scalpel in his hand. That's why we're over here at the moment. Lectures, visits to hospitals. My mother's not happy. She doesn't like the heat and she feels she's just along for the ride; that people are only being nice to her because she's his wife and chattel. A car was supposed to take her somewhere yesterday but it never turned up."

"Tough." All this sounds vaguely familiar and depressing and I begin to have second thoughts about a career as a counsellor. As far as one can ever be completely certain why one says anything I had intended the subject of patricide to segue into to the revelation that my foolish father stupidly pushed our car into a canyon. Now I am not so sure. Hadiscomb is more self-confident and assertive than when I first bumped into him. He is looking better too. Time has obviously been spent beside that pool at the Hilton. I notice one of the cheerleaders checking him out and whispering to her equally cute friend who looks our way. This is not what I am searching for. I want the certainty of unquestioning sympathy not the possibility of probing analysis.

"What about you? says Hadiscomb politely.

"I had a dream when I kept hitting my father and he wouldn't die. No matter what I did he kept bouncing up again like a ninepin. And he never stopped smiling."

"That's horrible."

"It cuts to the chase, doesn't it? It's not heavy with abstruse symbolism."

"Best to get it out of your system in dreams, I suppose. I used to dream I was making love to my mother."

"That's more normal - common, I guess I should say - or maybe normal's okay."

"But I always woke up before I came."

"I used to masturbate over my mother-you know-"

"Yes, of course." A faint blush colours Hadiscomb's cheeks. "So did I - I mean, I masturbated over my mother, not-"

"Sure."

A Pause. The blush deepens. "I don't think I ever saw your mother."

We digest the implications of all this and the impassive Mexican commis finishes replenishing the iced water and withdraws. Hadiscomb looks after him. "Do you think he understood what we were talking about?"

"He probably masturbates over his mother too."

"In Catholic cultures it must be like a religious experience." He taps a knife on the table. "I suppose the nearest I ever came to wanting to kill him was when he wouldn't take me away from Rockingham. That fucking place!" He speaks with a venom that startles me and people at surrounding tables turn and stare at us. I have never heard him use the word 'fucking' before and he makes it sound strange, as if it has been lodged at the back of his throat for a long time and he has just hawked it up. "When all he would do was arrange for me to change houses." He stares at me challengingly. "You remember that? You must remember that."

And suddenly I do remember. Some of it. More than I want to. Hadiscomb was in my house. With Voyce.

When I was a child, the local vicar came to my grandmother's house with a weighted sack and I followed him down to the river bank where he threw it in under the leaning chestnut trees. And as the sack sank it shook and shuddered and bucked and I realised that he was drowning something. It was a cat. And the awful struggling and the streams of bubbles went on and on and on. And I did nothing but watch in fascinated horror until the bubbles stopped and the Reverend Webdale patted me on the shoulder and went back over the dyke and across the meadow to take tea with my grandmother.

"Voyce had a terrapin," I hear myself say. "He used to feed it baby mice."

Hadiscomb continues to look through me. What more does he expect me to say? It was a terrible time for both of us. No arguments. My parents' marriage was breaking up and I was trying to come to terms with an English public school after the comparative freedom of having lived in France. It was probably the worst time of my life. Why dwell on it?

"You're right," I say. "It was a fucking place." I try to make 'fucking' sound the way Hadiscomb makes it sound but it doesn't have the same intensity. Hadiscomb doesn't say anything. He just continues to stare at me. Then, eventually, he nods.

One positive result of the evening is that I write to Lucy. Well, I send her a long postcard referring to a letter which, in fact, I have not written. In this way she will feel, in a sense, that she has received two communications and part of my conscience - the part that doesn't go to church on Sundays - will be eased a little. I also send a postcard to my mother and read the script again, this time to the finish.

Despite all this I feel on the defensive. No sign of the actual Indians but I can see smoke signals all along the ridge. Maybe if I keep my head down and keep going they will attack somebody else's wagon train.

Hadiscomb accompanies his parents to a medical conference at San Diego and the next few days pass without incident. Beverly Hills is not designated as a dumping ground for toxic waste and any bits that fall off passing aeroplanes miss me as I bear the script down to the pool. I even call Rashmi at 'J.P.Kahn' which turns out to be some kind of fancy answering service, but she is out of town. I am almost relieved. I can continue to hope that she hasn't fed me a crock of numbers that add up to 'get lost'.

She cannot call me because - perturbed by the lack of news about the car - my father has deemed it best that we no longer receive calls. He has told the switchboard that we are experimenting with a course of intensive internalisation and that the unexpected sound of a telephone ringing could destroy the balance of our psychic crystals with the result that we might be unable to order room service for at least twenty-four hours. If they will take messages, we will return all calls when the *nada* permits it.

Anywhere else in the world they would think he was joking or search for the number of the nearest funny farm but this is California. My father's request borders on the mundane. We are staying in a hotel where a man wearing a suit made out of hair nets checked in with a pile of 'Spiderman' comics and asked that a hammock be slung in his room; where a woman demanded birdseed for breakfast because she was eating for the stuffed canary that sat in a cage on her TV set. My daddy eccentric? Puh-leease!

Whilst I tweak my analysis, my father hands in his re-write, the 'Crinkle winkle' piece, and takes meetings with 'studio children' as he calls them. 'War and Peace' in space is threatening to become a definite contender and his mood mellows accordingly.

It is therefore no surprise when, one fine morning (one that wasn't fine would be a surprise) I find him bristling before me, rubbing his hands together to start a fire and demanding to see the script. "I've nothing to do until my power lunch," he chortles. "Larry and Bronski at Le Dome - you should try the '99 Montagny if they ever let you though the door. Let me cast an eye over this piece of crap. I might be able to bestow a few wrinkles."

"Thanks," I say, handing over the script.

He tosses it on top of a copy of 'Variety' - no mention of him again - and pats me proprietarily on the shoulder. "The way this Russian thing is going, who knows what might happen. I'm going to get a producer credit, did I tell you?" Three times, actually. "With you sitting pretty in a studio and my name in lights from Newark to Nishnynovgorod, this could mean hot and cold running gold mines for both of us, you know what I mean?"

"Did Larry bite you?"

"What are you talking about?" He picks up my script and weighs it in his hand. "Last time we ate in the back part of the room on the left. That's where you want to be. And Mike Medavoy said hello to me. I don't think he knew who I was but he knew I was somebody - he's never been great for names anyway. It was strangely pleasing. God forbid that I should ever become sentimental about this town but it is nice, just sometimes, when you can entertain the tiniest feeling that you're part of it all. Not a large part, not a particularly important part, just a part. Now, where are my specs?"

He pats his chest but he hasn't hung them round his neck so we spend five minutes searching before they are discovered in the bathroom where he was headed anyway.

I must say, I had never realised what a fast reader my father was. It only seems like a little longer than the time normally reserved for 'choking a darky' as he still unfortunately insists in calling the function, before he has returned, brusquely slapping the script against his thigh. "Right," he says. "Shoot."

"Well," I say, eager to show my paces. "First of all I've dreamed up a title. I thought it might be a good idea to show a little initiative."

He nods. "Why not?"

"'One Hot Sunday'," I wait, but his face tells me nothing. "You get it? It's a double meaning. Like, it happened on a Sunday and more colloquially - WOW! 'One Hot Sunday'!" I snap my fingers.

"Interesting. What did you actually think of it?"

I hesitate. "It's difficult to know where to start."

"Just plunge in."

"Well, the big problem for me is the girl. Apart from the fact that you know immediately she must have been planted by the bad guys, she has no character. She just makes squeaking noises and loses her clothes. We never learn anything about her…her-"

"Concerns?"

"Yes, her concerns. And what her background is - I suppose that's part of the same thing. And it's never clear what she sees in the heroes. A few wisecracks and she's in the sack with each of them, one after the other.

She ought to feel differently about them as individuals. And I didn't like her swearing all the time. And-"

"What about the relationship between the guys?"

"That was better but it was still pretty unoriginal. I mean, the rich kid from the broken home, the poor kid who had nothing but the love of his family. I knew they were going to turn up at that Thanksgiving dinner. And the crippled sister. At least Dickens-"

"What about the plot?" It is strange but he is twisting the script tighter and tighter, like he is yearning to thrust it into a very small opening.

"It's a variation on a theme we've seen a thousand times before. A buddy movie in which the heroes don't know why they're being chased and nobody believes them and everybody's against them."

"Like 'North by Northwest'."

"But 'North by Northwest' had Hitchcock and Cary Grant - and James Mason - and Eva Marie Saint."

"This could have Spielberg and Toby Maguire, fuck it!"

"Yes, but the script of 'North by Northwest' was so much better. It was touching as well as clever and exciting and funny."

My father sniffs. "What a shame they didn't give you something by Jean-Luc Godard. Something that might play to three Trotskyite art students in a condemned fleapit off the Boulevard St Germain."

"Of course, I haven't written all this down. I've tried to find some positive things-"

"I wonder if it ever occurs to you that the cinema is a mass market medium. If we all nourished our own little private art house fantasies, the industry would grind to a halt."

"Do you want to see what I've written? I did say that if they found a decent-"

"Apart from the fact that this...this intellectual dross that you so patently despise appeals to millions of poor devils around the world who lack your expensively honed critical factors, there is the trifling detail that its creation pays for the fucking food you stuff down your throat!" He stands by the window with his fists clenched and a red glow suffusing the area around his beard. What has got into him? Has the possibility of working on something that might actually get made encouraged him to see himself as the new guardian of 'The Seventh Art'? Or has he merely started on the booze a little earlier than usual?

He throws himself into an armchair. "It's not easy, you know. Nobody ever asks you to write a bio of Mother Theresa." He shakes his head and a horrible suspicion begins to sneak into my mind. "I sometimes wonder how Dostoyevsky would have made out in this town. The man couldn't even hit on the best way to spell his own name."

"Let me tell you about all the things I liked," I say hurriedly.

"If you want to educate people you have to engage their attention first."

"I thought the chase in the condom factory was great."

"You need to sugar the pill a - what are you talking about!?" He stares at me as if I am mad.

"When the testing machine goes bananas and they all start inflating and exploding, and the gunge spurts-"

"'Gunge'? Where!?" He starts rifling through the script.

"Towards the end. Just after the drag queen contest."

"'Drag queen contest'?" He stares up from the pages.

"Which, incidentally, I thought was another great scene. It's a very subtle way of suggesting the sexual imbalance between-"

"The bastards!!" He hurls the script across the room. "They've had a fucking rewrite done behind my back! And Jeff Lieberstein swore to me that Jim Carrey wanted this for his next picture - LOVED IT! Jesus Christ! Is there no decency? No integrity?" He sinks lower into the armchair. "And handing out the script like an I.Q. test for retarded teenagers. They can't do that. What are the Writers' Guild there for?" He is not a member of the Writers' Guild but this hardly seems the moment to point that out. However, I need to say something. Some remedial balm is clearly called for.

"What I said about 'North by Northwest'-"

"Will you shut up about fucking 'North by Northwest'!?" He surges to his feet.

"I just wanted to say that I don't think it's perfect either. I have problems-"

"*Tu me fais chier avec tes problèmes*!!" In moments of stress it is not unusual for my father to lapse into a flow of French invective. I think it makes him feel that his rage is not merely personal but an expression of cosmic concern that speaks in many tongues on behalf of the whole sensate universe. It also sounds better. "They're going to love you at the studio. They'll never make another film and you'll be a bloody genius!"

"I'm sorry," I say.

"I'm going to ring Larry." He stumps towards the bedroom and kicks the cover off the script as he passes. "And you didn't like Ditsie. What did you want her to do, translate 'Paradise Lost' into Yiddish?"

I don't have the chance to reply because he has slammed the bedroom door. Oh dear, this is all so unfortunate. My father can be very sensitive about his female characters. I remember, a long time ago, watching him read a review in which a critic had accused him of being incapable of getting inside the mind of a woman. At first he had looked annoyed, then a thin Will-o'-the-wisp smile had appeared on his lips - I guess it was a smirk really - as he acknowledged that this was possibly the only part of a woman he had never tried to get into.

Five minutes later he returns via the bathroom. "What did he say?" I ask.

"He was outraged, naturally - swore he knew nothing about it. He's going to call the studio and get back to me." He sighs as reality kicks in. "I know what he's going to say anyway. They can print my script on a roll of used bog paper if they want to. They can get a brain dead chimpanzee to do a rewrite. They can turn it into an underwater musical. Forget the small print - read the big print. I get paid. That's the bottom line. If you want to make art go and live in Provence. If you want to make money, stay here. And if that means swimming up a sewer full of human botulins - so be it." He fixes me with a bloodshot eye and I suddenly think how old he looks - just like after he has done his push-ups. "You do understand that, don't you? You are Gulliver and they do things differently here. They don't speak English, they speak money. And money has a limited vocabulary. It doesn't include words like 'candour' and 'taste' and 'integrity' - probably because nobody's ever made a large enough profit out of them. And if you stay here you've got to get used to different temporal unities. 'Never' seldom lasts longer than three weeks and 'always' can be much shorter. And the mental process is different too. You don't hire a seal. You fly in a pregnant duck-billed platypus from a zoo in Yokohama and teach it to balance a ball on its bill. Make-up will fit it with flippers and take care of the details. And never complain that you've been ripped off or betrayed. People will have no respect for you. Enter into the spirit of things. It's not 'Don't get mad, get even', it's 'Don't get mad, get even more'. If you're in the movie business, whingeing about moral issues is like an embalmer complaining that he's found an eyelash on his elbow." He pats me on the shoulder. Remember some of this and you'll have a nice time here. The unhappy people in Hollywood are those who can't come to terms with their misconceptions." He heads for the door. "And now I'm going to get very drunk."

Listen," I say. "I really am very sorry."

But he has gone.

8.

"Who?"

"Bill - Will Lock."

"'Billwill'?"

"We met at Santa Barbara a couple of weeks ago. Esme's place. I've been tied up."

"So have I. It's kinda fun for a change, isn't it?"

"I thought we might go out to dinner, see a movie or something."

"I'm sorry, Billwill. I don't remember you."

"You were on the way to the tennis court. I was fondling a statue."

"Oh, yeah. You're the Australian guy."

"Not really. I'm actually half American, half English."

"'Actually'." She mimes an outrageous British accent. "Okay, what have I got to lose that I haven't lost already? There's a new place on Melrose that's supposed to be good. We could meet there. Thursday? It's the only free night I've got."

I pretend to be consulting a diary jam-packed with engagements. "Yeah, I can do that."

We confirm the time and place and I put the phone down before she can change her mind. Ye-es! I had felt it would be a positive moment to call, just after messengering my script analysis to Zaifert's at my father's expense. A date with Rashmi must be a good omen, the warrant of divine approval. Of course, I can always refuse the job if they offer me one but I don't think I will do that. The time has come for me to settle down in one place. I can't keep flitting to and fro between continents. Not flitting, fleeing. If I stay in one spot long enough I will adapt to it, put down roots, stabilize. In America you can do that. People are used to you not being exactly the same as they are.

That was the hell of arriving at Rockingham. Two years behind everybody else, half-American and having lived in 'Frogland'. Every nuance of speech or term of reference was mercilessly picked on, ridiculed or sneered at. To have non-British blood in your veins automatically made you a 'wog'. To have lived abroad was like pissing in the latest coronation mug. Anything you said was either 'showing off' or revealing your lack of affinity with the innate rules of conduct that are the birthright of all natural born Englishmen. This prickly paranoia, this relentless raking over of the ashes of the past reduced me to tears and to days and nights of misery.

And that was before the discovery of the connection between my father and Andy Groper.

France had previously promised less and yielded much more. Approached from the road, Rockingham seemed an impressive, cheerful place with its mellowed, warm stone buildings and ivy-girt walls. Not, as it subsequently turned out to be, a leper colony with fives courts.

By contrast, the village school at Pulignac had seemed like a crumbling chapel set in a misty graveyard the first day I found myself deposited before it. Small French boys and girls peered out from behind trees like hobgoblins. I heard a breathless whisper pass the rounds: "*L'Anglais arrive!*" There was one young master, Monsieur Buge, one classroom, four classes. On the first day, whilst Monsieur Buge was engaged in one corner, a tiny girl left her seat, squatted on the floor, pulled down her pants and started to piddle. Without breaking off his discourse, Buge picked her up by the collar, still in motion, and deposited her outside like a puppy. I could not believe what I was witnessing. This was about the earthiest event involving a member of the opposite sex that I had ever participated in.

To my astonishment, my classmates were kind and welcoming. They actually seemed proud to have '*un Americain*' - once my mother's country of birth had been ascertained I was promoted to what, in French eyes, was the most prestigious nationality - in their school. And Monsieur Buge was indulgent of the fact that I barely spoke a word of French and did not automatically start my '*dissertations*' exactly two centimetres from the left hand ruled margin - at least, at first.

In two months I was speaking with sufficient fluency to hold my own in local café society and I had seen all the girls in the school '*faire pipi*' whilst they had been afforded the chance to feast their eyes on my '*zizi*'. I was eleven years old and a man of the world.

Maybe France is the place. But as somebody observed, she is like a woman. You can adore her but you can never be her. She is not of my blood like England and America and I do not have my father's facility for transmogrification through the ages. She is also dangerously perfect. To stay in Pulignac all the time would be like living on a diet of candy. I would become bilious. That is what happened to my mother. She used to complain that Pulignac was not 'the real world' and this made my father mad because he visited the real world a lot and he knew that Pulignac was much better. It was beautiful and calm and you ate well and did not get mugged. My mother said nothing and went on painting and reading and writing letters and helping me with my homework.

Mr Buge was making progress with both of us. My mother had started off tentatively, but now the essays and criticisms that she presented in my name - with a little input from me - were increasingly well received and her confidence was growing. I felt slightly guilty about the way that she involved herself in my work; and when Monsieur Buge sometimes called in the evenings I was always scared that it was to complain of her obvious assistance. I remember the twinge of apprehension when I answered the telephone and heard the familiar voice - and my relief that my father never seemed to be there when he called.

It is two days after the delivery of the script that I bump into Constance at Gelson's in Century City. This is an up-market supermarket where you might catch rising young executives in carefully co-ordinated casuals doing their weekend shopping. 'Flush yuppies in Hush Puppies' my father calls them. It caters for the kind of person who knows that origami is not a type of pasta and is clean to the point of making a European feel that he might have wandered into an embalming parlour. It is also slightly precious, the sort of gastronomic Bloomingdales where Basil might go to buy Tarragon.

I am staring intently at the freshly squeezed orange juice. All orange juices in Los Angeles are freshly squeezed but some are more freshly squeezed than others. Unless you actually see the juice being squeezed - which seems to be a secret ritual like elephants dying, or doing virtually anything else apart from standing around looking big - it is difficult to know whether the containers nearest the front are the freshest or whether the old ones have been moved forward so that you think they are the freshest whereas, in fact, the fresh ones have been placed at the back where they sit on a sludge of melting ice. Sometimes there is a demarcation line where the mashed peel has separated from the juice and sunk to the bottom of the container and this is a clear indication that the stuff has been around for a while. However, it is not in the laid-back spirit of Gelson's to be spotted holding up a carton to the light as if proposing a vegetarian toast and I am about to make a random choice when I spy Constance pushing her almost empty trolley along one of the brimming aisles.

My first reaction is one of surprise. I know that senior movie executives have to eat but I had always imagined that this ritual took place in expensive restaurants or roped-off sections of the commissary. To discover one in the comparatively humble purlieus of a supermarket - even one as salubrious as Gelson's - is slightly disconcerting. Like bumping into the Virgin Mary at the dry cleaners. Constance is now peering at the cookie section, twisting her head to read the small print. She looks confused. Perhaps she is short-sighted and on a diet.

"Hi, Constance."

My voice makes her jump and she stares at me. For a few seconds I think she must have problems realising who I am. It is not often that she sees me without my father lurking a few feet away. She looks tired and preoccupied. "Hi," she says without the enthusiasm normally packaging the word in California.

"These are good."

"What?"

"These cookies." I point to some next to the ones she was looking at. "I've tried them."

"Really?" She puts the first ones into her basket. She seems tense.

"I've submitted the script analysis."

I am hoping that she will express interest, even say that, yes, she knows, because she's read it and it's brilliant, but she merely nods. "Good. Jim's in New York at the moment."

"I'll just have to be patient."

"Like the rest of us." She weighs a packet of herbal tea bags in her hand and then replaces it on the shelf. "And how is your dear father?" A little catch in the voice.

"He's fine. I guess Jim Zaiferts has a lot of scripts to read."

"As do we all."

She is pushing her trolley away from me. I have to lengthen my stride to keep up. "It's funny, I don't know if you're aware of this but they gave me one of my father's scripts to analyse. I guess it must have been an accident."

"It must have been." She stops sharply so that I blunder into her trolley. "Nobody could have had that much of a sense of irony."

"I suppose not."

"We were going to make that script at one stage."

"But you're not any more?"

"Oh no." The lines around her mouth purse into what might be a smile.

"That's a pity. It had some good things in it - I mean, lots of good things - you know-"

"Yes, I know." She is gripping the handle of her trolley very tightly. "Your father's new best friend came in the other day."

"Really." I wonder what she is talking about

"Yes, Bronski. He wanted to talk about a distribution deal."

"Great." I hope I emphasise the word in a way that conveys genuine interest but there are other careers at stake here. Mine, for instance. I need to keep the pressure on, show Constance what a bright spark I am. "What was it called originally?"

"What?"

"My father's script. The one I was given to-"

"'Running Wild'."

"Not bad. I called it 'One Hot Sunday'. I probable don't need to-"

I break off because there are tears running down her cheeks. She stares into my eyes and starts trembling. "Are you a chip off the old block, William?" She shakes her head.

"I don't really know" One of the shelf loaders in a long white starched coat is staring our way. "It's...look, it was just a thought. 'Running Wild' is a good title. Very good. I was only trying-"

"Don't!" She has closed her eyes and clenched her fists tightly. Her sparse make-up is running. A woman in a cloche hat bangs carts in her eagerness to get past. I feel awful.

"I'm sorry. Is there anything I can-"

"No! Just leave me alone."

Poor Constance. Studio life is never less than a ball-breaker, and it is even worse for women. My father has pointed this out to me many times. Things are clearly not going well for Constance at the moment and it is getting to her. From all points of view it behoves me to show understanding and compassion. Words have not done the trick so...I cast about and light upon a stack of Kleenex. Plucking a pack from the shelf, I tear it open and hand her one - Sir Walter Raleigh for our times. She hesitates, accepts it, blows her nose and peers at me through red, glistening eyes. Then she starts laughing, or crying, or both.

I begin to back away. "We're out of juice. I mean, my father and-" She starts to sob. "It was...I'll see you."

I am turning away when I realise that I still have the pack of Kleenex in my hand. Should I put them in her trolley because she needs them? Or does this saddle her with the financial burden of paying for them? Difficult. It would probably be more gentlemanly and make a better impression if I paid for them. "I'll tell dad I bumped into you," I say, trying to exit on an upbeat but she only starts crying even louder, so I wedge a clump of tissues between the bars of her trolley and head for the nearest check-out. At a pinch, we can make do with the juice that is left in the icebox.

When I get back to the hotel, my father is on the floor doing the aforementioned push-ups. Sort of push-ups in which the stomach rarely risks vertigo by straying too far from the carpet. Even in trying times, my father is a stern guardian of his physical condition.

He actually ran the inaugural Los Angeles Marathon. 1986. Well, it's a young country. If you have a couple of hours to spare he will tell you about it. It is one of my first childhood memories. The bleeding nipples (ninja nipples?), the raw inside thighs, the blisters the size of lamp bulbs. The pain barrier, the wall, the dehydration, the cramps, the long periods of doubt, the brief moment of euphoria when he hobbled across the finishing line. Your average early Christian martyr enjoyed a day at the races compared to what my father went through to get a small bronze medal and a scroll that never arrived.

"Am I prone or supine?" he gasps.

"Supine sounds more appropriate," I tell him. He grunts and grinds out ten more jerky, flopping movements before collapsing in a pool of sweat. The veins on his temples stand out like a relief map of the Himalyas. Eventually, he forces himself onto one knee.

"What are fibre optics?"

"I don't know." This eternal general knowledge quiz drives me mad. "I bumped into Constance at the supermarket."

"Really. How was she?"

"A bit strange. Sort of distant. Then she suddenly started crying. Overwrought, I guess you could say."

He makes 'tch, tch' noises. "She's a studio executive. When was the last time you saw one who was underwrought? The trouble with Constance is that she's too tender for this town. She should go back to England and open a dolls' hospital in Littlehampton." He scrambles to his feet and catches a glimpse of himself in the mirror as he reaches for a comb. "Look at that. A Greek god trapped in the body of a fifty-five year old man. What do you think? A movie?"

"I didn't know you did horror."

"Very funny, Will. But don't give up the day job, if you ever get one."

"Constance said Bronski had been to the studio to talk about a distribution deal."

"Did she now?" Father runs a comb through his hair and it comes away looking like a starved Yorkshire terrier. "Well, I suppose it would be civil to give her a buzz. See how she is. Why don't you pop down and check if we've had any calls?"

I have already checked on my way up but I am only too happy to accommodate his desire for privacy when talking to Constance. Anything he does to cheer her up can only improve my job prospects.

There is a new girl on the switchboard in reception. English, pretty, eager to please. We have made discreet eye contact and she associates my face with my name. This is my undoing. Hardly have I checked that our pigeonhole is empty save for a message informing me that Hadiscomb is back in town than she is speaking into the phone and holding up a restraining hand. "Yes, hold on a minute." She turns to me and indicates the house phone. "It's for you." I feel a pang of fear like a rabbit picked out in a car's headlights. I can only think of bad news: Zaifert's assistant telling me I am unemployable, Rashmi cancelling our date - and of course- I pick up the phone.

"Hello?"

"This is Western Rentals." A-a-argh! The damp finger probes the light socket. "Your lease on Honda-" blah, blah, blah "-expires tomorrow. Dyawanna renew?" He has the bank teller's deadpan I-do-this-a-thousand-times-a-day-and-boy-will-I-be-glad-when-it's-Saturday-and-if-you're-having-a-heart-attack-would-you-mind-not-leaning-against-the-grill-thank-you voice.

"Er-um, well, sure. Fine. Yes."

"Okay. Bring it in tomorrow before midday."

"BRING IT IN!?" I moderate my voice. "I have to bring it in? Can't we just do this over the phone?"

"No. We need to check the car over and draw up a new agreement." His voice tightens a notch. "You got a problem?"

"No." Such insouciance. "It's just that - no, it doesn't matter. Midday, you said?"

"I did." He rings off.

"Shit!" says my father when I tell him. "Why did you have to answer the sodding phone?"

"How could I refuse?"

"Easily! For hygienic reasons. Think of the number of people who use those desk phones. Bacteria breed like flies - much, much faster. You need to have a death wish to touch one." He takes a couple of deep breaths. "Still, we mustn't panic. It's too late to worry now. We'll just have to stall them for a bit. Typical shitty luck, just when everything is coming together."

"Everything? You mean 'One Hot' - I mean 'Running Wild'."

"I mean 'War and Peace in Space'. You can't live in the past. Pragmatism is the name of the game even if nobody here knows what it means. Tomorrow is another day, if you can live that long. Incidentally, there was no answer from Constance. Bloody woman doesn't even have an answering machine. Can you imagine that? No answering machine, no television, no PC, and she never goes to the cinema. How pretentious can you get? It's ridiculous. You can't carve out a permanent career in this town by being the only person who's actually read Gabriel Garcia Márques."

"Talking of careers. I'm becoming terminally worried about the effect on mine of having shoved a rental car over a cliff."

My father sniffs. "Hardly a cliff. And do we have to wade through all that again? We didn't push it over anything. Whoever stole it did that. All you did was mislay a car. Start getting that into your head and believing it. And if you did push a car over a cliff it was just an explosion of boyish high spirits. You'll find people around here remarkably forgiving when it comes to excusing human frailty. Of course, it helps if you're head of a studio but the sentiment permeates down. It's part of a collective symbiosis of not feeling negative about yourself. You're already suffering guilt about what you did. God knows, isn't that suffering enough!?" He cups his chin in his hand. "And when I think about it, I'm not sure that pushing a car over a cliff ought to be an obligatory life experience for a young exec. It demonstrates a feral, streetwise 'up yours!' contempt for establishment values which is pulse beat perfect for the contemporary teenage Zeitgeist. By the way, I think Anthony DiCaprio's getting a bit long in the tooth for you. We should go with Gael Garcia Bernal - or one of those kids who fucked the apple pie."

Sometimes my father scares me. As he gets older, his imagination is beginning to atrophy and he actually has to live the experience before he can write about it with conviction. And once the idea begins to take shape it becomes the property of the page and says goodbye to reality so there is no moral stigma attached. I just hope he never contemplates a project about infanticide.

"I don't think you realise quite how serious this is. It isn't an exercise in style. Both our careers could be ruined. We could go to prison."

"Good," says my father with relish." Then I could get down to my novel. The trouble is that you can't get into a prison any more. They're too crowded. Throw a hand grenade into a McDonalds and you'd get thirty days visiting old ladies, with time off if you brought cookies. It's a problem. I've often thought that if I had an incurable disease and twelve months to live I'd go and kill someone really evil so that I'd have the backbone of the *roman à clef* that I'd write as a gesture to posterity after they put me away. Mind you, it would probably take more than twelve months to sort through the contenders - I mean, you'd need a year just for the politicians, wouldn't you? - and I doubt if they'd lock me up even if the prisons weren't full. Two weeks parole and I'd be out, a national hero - on the cover of People, chatting to Jay Leno and David Letterman and all the other talk show hosts. I'd never be able to get around to the novel. What a tragedy after all that great publicity. I'd be dead before the ink was dry on the contracts. But maybe - listen to this - during the twelve months, they might have come up with a cure for my incurable disease!-"

"I think we should change hotels."

"-or maybe they made the wrong diagnosis. That's better. It would take less time to spell out-"

"And return your car immediately so that it looks as if we've left town."

"-and yes, yes! Here's the twist. I find out that I'm perfectly healthy, but just as I'm walking out of the hospital towards the girl of my dreams - I gave her the hope to live when we both thought we were dying - I get run over by a car."

"I like that bit," I tell him. "Have you been listening to a word I said?"

"Of course. What did you say?"

"That we should get out of here immediately."

"Are you crazy? That's the action of someone who's guilty. Do you want the rental company to think you're a criminal? You haven't done anything wrong. You've got to get that into your head. It's the curse of valet parking. It's ghettoised teenage delinquents from broken homes who never had a chance, it's the society we live in, it's someone else. And, if it's any consolation, we're leaving here anyway in a couple of days." He lets the news sink it. "How would you like to step into a pair of skis?"

"Sounds better than leg irons." I watch the placatory smile flit across his lips. "You mean we're actually going to Sun Valley?"

"I'm going to Sun Valley. And because I'm a wonderful father and a great human being I'm going to take you with me. Larry, Bronski, Igor and me: Team Tolstoy. We're going up there to schmooze with the mooze and tickle the story line into shape."

"Why Sun Valley?"

"Because it has class and that's what this project is all about. And, of course, the snow. I told you how I saw snow as being the leitmotif-"

"Yes, yes," I say hurriedly.

"-drawing us back remorselessly to the gilded bedrock of the book. Also-" he lowers his voice "-I think the Godoroski have a stake in a hotel there."

"The who?"

"The Godoroski. The *ne plus ultra* of the Russian Mafia."

My mind permits itself a boggle. "I've never heard of them."

My father taps his nose sagely. "It just shows how discreet they've been, doesn't it?"

"In Sun Valley?" I grapple with the concept. "Sun Valley doesn't have gambling and prostitution, does it?"

"Not yet."

"Why would they want to go there?"

"I'm only guessing, but I suspect they're looking for new image, something more youthful. I mean, snow is very teen, isn't it? Clean, fun but dangerous, and it's the colour of cocaine. What could be more appropriate? And, these days, if I say Mafia, what do you think of? Brando mumbling, right?"

I allow this to percolate. "It's scary."

"Look at the way art thrived under the Borgias."

I wonder what 'Ladybird' book he got that from. "But taking money from murderers and pimps and drug peddlers."

"Don't you ever watch 'The Sopranos'? These people can be very human. And don't start getting political, for God's sake. Politics and art don't mix."

"Who said that?"

"I did."

"Great. I thought it sounded like you."

"Just concentrate on the skiing. Apparently, the hotel's just opposite the lifts. And they have a French chef."

"Not Italian?"

"Fine. Have it your way." He withdraws his hand from my shoulder. "Stay here if you like. Check into the local church hall. I don't want you to corrupt your principles."

I know I should tell him to get stuffed, but once you've taken Andy Groper's dollar, how far behind are the Russian Mafia? It's the complacency that I can't stand.

"I still think I heard someone cry out." I watch him digesting this. The eyes close, the jaws chew imaginary bile. "When we pushed the car over-"

"Oh, for Christ's sake!" I savour the reaction. Predictable, but a child still likes to enjoy the odd moment of power. "I really can't go on with this." He is heading for the door. "You need to get a grip on yourself!" Slam!!

I wait for him to realise that he has forgotten something but minutes pass and he does not come back. A sense of triumph is short-lived. I am uneasy and unhappy, and probably several other 'un' words. I would like to talk to somebody sympathetic who might help me feel better. Candidates, in order of seniority include:

1.) My grandmother. "Hello, Gran. Will, here. No, Will. Your grandson. Yes, that's right. Listen, I just pushed a car over a cliff." "Did you, dear? That's nice. It's been lovely weather here."

2.) My mother. She would listen intently occasionally muttering 'the bastard!' When I was finished she would ring my father and they would have a terrible row. My father would feed me withering looks and shake his head for two days.

3.)Lucy. She would be incredibly understanding and make me feel a shit for fancying Rashmi - and for still contemplating the thought of sex with her whilst fancying Rashmi.

4.) Peter, Maria and José. Sympathy guaranteed but comprehension of situation probably akin to my grandmother's. Long term repercussions of revelation a problem.

5.) Hadiscomb. Hardly a possibility. Already he stares at me as if I am the static on the screen of a TV set and he is waiting for a picture to appear.

6.) Rashmi. Are you kidding?

"Maybe she got the date wrong."

Hadiscomb and I are in a Thai restaurant on Melrose. The restaurant where I was supposed to meet Rashmi. She has not shown up. I am feeling pissed off. Hadiscomb was not part of the dating arrangement but had been informed that if he wanted to see the most beautiful girl in the world he need only walk past the aforementioned restaurant at nine o'clock to see her dining with me. Inquisitive and in the area, Hadiscomb had peered through the dwarf palms to see a solitary Lock shovelling bean shoots round his plate. It is all his fault. The man is a Jonah. I should have waited fifteen minutes and hit the streets.

"Maybe she confused the restaurant."

"She chose it."

"She could still have made a mistake."

"Maybe she's stood me up." I can only stand so much of Hadiscomb being nice to me.

"Ye-es." He makes it sound like a very distant possibility.

I should have seen this coming. I did see it coming. Rashmi was hardly crawling all over me. I was making all the running. Stupid me. She can get stuffed. Who needs her?

I do.

I stare at the flock wallpaper, trying to turn the evening into supper with Hadiscomb.

When I came in, it was a Thai restaurant. By the time we leave it could be a stir-fry wok takeout or a singles bar for gay seniors. Premises go up and down on Melrose like the hammers on a steam organ. Setting up in business here is like being a tomato plant in the Florida Everglades. You can grow to twelve feet overnight and the next day be a puddle of putrefaction. It's the street that never changes because it's always different. You can buy anything here, from a third-rate rip-off of a haut couturier dress, to a fourth rate rip-off of a haut couturier dress, to a rip-off that is so grotesque and poorly made that even the boutique owner's mother-in-law who put up half the collateral and stole the design from an old Vogue she found at her tantric yoga class was amazed when somebody bought it.

But Melrose is not just fashion. A lot of eating takes place here in establishments catering for every taste in restaurant name. The food itself is less distinctive. Although Californian cuisine reputedly borrows from many international sources - as opposed to sauces which are less popular - it is mainly in the realm of description that it makes its most flamboyant statement. The shock of the new is not what tempts the dollar out of the customer's pocket, unless it relates to decor, and in the *Gesamtkunstwerk* of local gastronomy it has never been deemed the place of the food to thrust itself ostentatiously before its fellow muses of presentation, service and ambience. A restaurant is a place where you go to be seen and meet people. If the food has a nice colour, that's a bonus.

I glance around. Rashmi is not the only one conspicuous by her absence. So are a lot of other customers. The Thai family, huddled in layers along the back wall, look worried rather than inscrutable. Maybe they can read the writing on the wall. The writing that says 'Remove wall and install pasta machine for the opening party on Saturday night'.

"We were talking about the car."

"I know we were." There is a flurry of movement outside the door and, for an instant, I think that I see Rashmi. But it is only Santa Monica girl and a bunch of jocks deciding that the place doesn't have enough bezazz. They stumble away down the street and the sad waiters shrink back against the walls.

"I thought you were worried."

"I am worried, that's why I mentioned it," I say, wishing that I hadn't. Hadiscomb seems obsessed. I can see his father in him as he stares at me; mental scalpel in hand, eager to make an incision.

"We could go and have a look." He waits. "It would set your mind at rest."

"I'm not certain I could find my way back there."

"We could try. Look, if you'd killed somebody, they'd have discovered the body by now." He waits some more. "Wouldn't they?"

"I suppose so."

"So let's go. We can take my car. I've got a torch." He can see that I'm still hesitating. "Once you know that you haven't killed anyone, the big worry will be out of the way. Everything else will seem less dramatic. Your father's probably right about the car hire company." He smiles to himself. "Does he still have those boots?"

"Boots?"

"The blue Wellingtons."

I have to think for a moment and I remember. Those terrible, shame-conferring, Iranian rubber boots bought at once mega-fashionable Biba. Peacock blue, of course, with a little shimmering star effect. "Where did you see those?"

"When he came up for the house matches. You know, when you broke your ankle."

Ten minutes later, I am sitting beside Hadiscomb in his car. It is a strange sensation. Like he is the sheriff and I am going to show him where I committed the murder and buried the body. I don't remember him like this at Rockingham. Assertive. There he was withdrawn, intense, picked upon. Voyce used to make his life hell.

"Can you remember any landmarks?"

"There was a long white house with a lot of dogs barking behind the wall. But that was at the top. When we'd started walking. Walking back."

Now I am not certain whether I want to find the place or make a noble effort and then get dropped at the hotel but some interior compass steers me remorselessly into a familiar landscape. I recognise the house like a white homage-to-Taos brick kiln, the foundations of a new mansion thrusting up like a copse of jackstraws. They seem like fragments of a dream. The one where you return to a familiar place with a sense of dread, knowing what is going to happen.

"Are you all right?"

"Yeah. I was just trying to get my bearings."

"You'd have gone up, wouldn't you?"

He is right. Any road that went up, we took it. It was like the instructions for finding your way to the centre of a maze.

Hadiscomb has barely pulled forward when a security patrol car comes towards us down the hill. There is one guy inside and I feel his eyes giving us the once over as he slows down. Hadiscomb's car doesn't have the neighbourhood profile, especially after dark when the maid has gone home and only your friends would be calling. Maybe the guard is already calling the cops, asking them to check us out. Maybe I am paranoid. The tail lights are wiped away by the next bend and a long, white wall comes into view.

"I think we're getting close."

"Fantastic views."

"Yup."

"Tell me-"

"Pull off the road here-careful!" My nerves laugh. What a joke if we drove over the edge and ended up on top of car number one.

"Okay!" Hadiscomb noses into the foliage and switches off the engine and lights. I sniff the acrid, baked-sweat smell that comes as a free gift with every rented car. There is a chirr of insects and somewhere, not so far away, a dog is barking. Probably behind the long, white wall. The darkness closes in and I jump when a moth suddenly flutters against the windshield.

"This is where you did it?" It does sound like a murder.

"I think so. You've got your flashlight?"

We get out and I walk back to check how easy it is to see the car from the road. Not very, unless you were looking very hard. I hope the security guard is curled up in a lay-by somewhere with a burrito and his favourite smoky-voiced lady DJ on the radio. There is the sound of a car approaching and I run back and duck down in the bushes beside the drop. The headlights bathe the grass a few feet away and the engine note purrs away into the night.

"Give me the flashlight." He hands it over and I lead the way down the slope. Bushes sprout out at right angles and, further down, the beam picks out the silvery silhouettes of small, stunted trees. I swing the flashlight, looking for signs of crushed undergrowth.

"Are you sure this is the place?"

I ignore him and continue down the incline. It is steeper than it looks and the grass is dry and slippery. I nearly lose me footing and set off a small avalanche of stones that skitter away into the darkness. Maybe what didn't seem like a very good idea is a very bad idea. We could be approaching a precipice. Behind me, Hadiscomb moves easily. I never remember him being this fit at Rockingham. I stop to get my breath and swing the flashlight about. February rains have gullied parts of the hillside so that in the strange, white light it looks like worm-eaten timber.

"Over there."

Hadiscomb is indicating a flattened bush. He could be right. The shadowy mass of trees further down the slope is punctured by a jagged crenellation. I look back up the hillside but all I can see is an uneven line of black topped by stars. I start to edge along the fall line.

"Careful! It's getting steep."

We talk in whispers like we suspect someone might be listening. It does not require great imaginative powers to see crouching figures in the clumps of bushes and sprouting grasses. Hadiscomb stumbles and another Paul Revere of stones gallops away into the darkness. The last pebble comes to rest and I start forward. Then stop. Did I hear something? I turn off the flashlight and we listen. I can hear Hadiscomb's breathing. Nothing else. For a second I can see myself in the garden at Rockingham with the black mass of the sleeping house looming above me. It must be Hadiscomb who makes me think of that.

"Behind!"

I swing the flashlight towards the rustling sound up the slope. A dark shape melts into the grass at ground level. A snake? A rat? Something more exotic? I wait and then move on carefully, following the contour of the slope until we reach a narrow gully, scored knee-deep in the crumbling earth. It makes a natural path with irregular, descending steps like the bed of a dried-up waterfall. I start to edge down towards the gap in the tree line.

"Watch out for poison ivy." I don't think there is any and we would never see it, but something makes me want to assert myself at Hadiscomb's expense. The flashlight picks out a white shape where a sapling has been snapped in two and the splintered wood is showing through the bark. No doubt about it. This must be where the car came down. A sharp jab of fear. It's true. It wasn't a dream. We did do it.

Beyond the trees, the flashlight kliegs into darkness. The ground must fall away sharply. I crane forward warily and make out a sagging wire fence interlaced with dead creepers. A section of it has been carried away and ruptured wires point down the hill. Fear chooses each foothold carefully as I edge forward and direct the beam into the void. A line of concrete posts drops down a precipitous slope. We are at the edge of somebody's property. Despite the weeds it is obvious that the ground has been tended in the not too distant past. Shit. What are we going to find down there? Do I really want to know? Bugger Hadiscomb. I listen hard. There is no sound. No chink of light to suggest a dwelling with people in it.

"Sorry."

Hadiscomb has farted. This at least relieves tension and provides an incentive to move forward. A single wire joins the concrete posts and we cling to it awkwardly, our backs to the void, our hands burning as we try to stop ourselves sliding. We are lowering ourselves into space with the earth carved into steep steps like the tiers of a mountain vineyard. As my back scrapes against each post, I turn and look down. At last I see something. A silvery rectangle smudged by patches of black. The roof of a house set amongst trees. I freeze and listen to my heavy breathing.

"What's the matter?"

"Wait."

If there is anybody in the house, they would have to be deaf not to have heard us. Deaf or dead.

"God!"

I do not want to go any further but Hadiscomb scrambles past me and lowers himself to the next post. I make myself follow.

"Jesus!!" Hadiscomb continues to run through the Holy Trinity.

I crane to see what he is looking at. Another grey rectangle set against the foot of the bluff. A swimming pool. A black shape rears from it. We have found the car. I let out a cry. There are dark shapes floating in the water. Dark, bloated shapes. Bodies. Putrefying corpses swollen with the gasses from their rotting tripes. A sweet, sickly smell wafts towards. I want to be sick.

Hadiscomb presses forward and I am alone. "Had-" But he has already reached the spot where the slope levels out. He brushes through the foliage and I wait for something to happen. Poor devils, they must have been enjoying a midnight dip when the car struck. The lucky ones probably died instantly; the others must have dragged their mangled bodies clear only to drown in agony. I will never, ever, be able to forgive myself. I can hear my heart beating faster. I want to get away, but at the same time, something is drawing me towards the pool.

When I get there, Hadiscomb is staring at the car that shares the pool with four inflatable rubber mattresses. It is standing on its nose in the shallow end and there is a shuttered bungalow in the background. The water is brown, and creatures that I do not want to think about scuttles to and fro as I probe the depths with a flashlight. There is the musty, rotting vegetable smell of stagnant water. A million moats of matter; but mattresses not bodies.

Hadiscomb watches me expectantly as I sink to my knees. "You do some weird things, don't you?" he says.

"It runs in the family," I tell him.

9.

When I get back to the hotel, my father is in the bar. This is a clear sign that something is wrong. He does not normally waste his sweetness on the common herd. It takes an event of dramatic proportions to make him seek the solace of human company. After an air crash he would have scruples to overcome before he allowed himself to join the circle of survivors warming their hands around the smouldering wreckage.

"There you are." He knocks back his drink, ignores the bartender who is desperately signalling to him to sign for it - and God knows how many others - and wobbles unsteadily across the foyer. "Nice of you to come back from whatever manner of debauchery you've been engaged in. No!-" he can see I am about to say something important "-it doesn't matter. I just want you to know that we're in the most terrible shit."

"That's amazing," I tell him. "I've discovered a new form of ventriloquism. I just have to think something long enough and you say it. Now, I've-"

"This is serious." My father seldom finds other people's attempts at humour amusing. "No sooner had you disappeared this afternoon than they were waiting in the foyer."

Mounting stress, plus sudden shock, equals cardiac arrest. "Western Rentals?"

"Not Pol Pot and Nancy Sinatra!" He takes me by the elbow and marches me towards the pool area. The foyer is filling as a convention of Cyndie Lauper look-alikes pours out of the elevator. "What a bunch of psychotics. And racists to boot. I got the impression that they hated the English. Apparently, one of them had a great uncle who was tortured by the British in Palestine. I asked him if he'd ever heard of a place called Iraq. That went down like a lead balloon. But anyway, if we did torture the fellow, there must have been a reason, mustn't there? He must have done something. And we didn't want to be there in the first place, did we? It was a United Nations mandate - or was it the League of Nations?

Remind me to look it up. Anyway, we were there in a strictly peacekeeping capacity. But did they want to know about that?-"

"Probably not," I interrupt. "What did they want?"

His voice becomes steeped in noble sacrifice. "You don't have to worry. Thanks to you swanning off to amuse yourself, I was obliged to take everything on my own shoulders." I begin to feel a little better. "I told them your story, just as you told it to me when you broke down and confessed this morning."

"What!?"

"So don't forget the details. We'll go over it again in a minute. God, and I'm so exhausted."

"So I'm implicated?"

"If you choose to use the word. Yes, you always were. It's what we agreed."

I turn away and find myself looking through the window of one of the poolside apartments. A middle-aged man and what I assume is his wife are sitting side by side on a sofa and watching television. How snug and peaceful and happy they look in the sombre half-light, like Mr and Mrs Norman Rockwell painted by Millet. Budge up, folks; I want to be your son.

"It's the xenophobia that gets me." My father witters on. "Sometimes I wonder why we bothered to have an empire. All you get is resentment. And when you think what we've done for these people. For heaven's sake. What was America before we got here? Just a few red Indians jumping up and down around a bonfire. Now look at it: motorways, skyscrapers, soft ice-cream. And have we ever had a word of thanks? Never. And dressing up as Red Indians to throw that tea in Boston harbour. I mean, what a ridiculous thing to do. Utterly childish and a complete waste of-"

"Shut up!!" My voice reverberates off the four enclosing walls of apartments and Peter and Maria who are gliding past as one in the shadows, separate like balls of mercury. "Just tell me what the fuck is happening!"

"There's no need for that kind of language. Losing your head isn't going to help us."

I look in the pool and think of what Hadiscomb said about his own father. Nothing painful but - Ophelia, Gatsby, William Holden in 'Sunset Boulevard'. Floaters. But all d-e-a-d.

"It's funny - well, not funny, bizarre. The thing that really seems to piss them off is that the bloody car hasn't been found. Maybe it's something to do with their insurance cover. They seem to be suggesting that we stole the car - or rather, you did. Strange, huh?"

"Very."

"Because we'd always thought that it would be better if they didn't find the car, hadn't we?"

"I've never encouraged myself to have much of an opinion either way."

"No. Well, having Mr Gallow and his chum standing on your nuts would concentrate your mind wonderfully. Shouting and screaming and making threats. And the other one's got B.O. Bloody wonderful white teeth, of course."

"I rang Larry and he suggested that we got a lawyer. Going to cost an arm and a leg, obviously."

"You told Larry what happened?"

"I told him the truth. Our truth. The one we made up."

"You made up."

"Don't start that. It's so immature. I have enough problems as it is. I'm going to talk to the lawyer before we leave tomorrow."

"We can leave?"

"I gave them our passports."

"What!?"

"I had to. That and a call from the lawyer are the only things stopping them from pressing charges.

"Oh my God. We're never going to get out of the country."

"Don't be melodramatic. All is not lost. I've been thinking-"

The middle-aged man is drawing the curtains of his apartment. Another day of blameless human existence is coming to a fruitful close. He and his wife will probably not make love but lie side-by-side, holding hands and watching the moonlight reflected on the ceiling before they peck each others lips, draw apart a little, and drift into decent, honest sleep. Happy dreams, folks.

"-if they find the car, they're going to be more sympathetic - well, not exactly sympathetic. Their idea of a humane gesture is probably to beat your face into a *shaped* pulp. No, let's just say they'll be more inclined towards reason."

"Talking of which-"

"Please, Will. I'm trying to think. We don't know how far the car went down the slope. It could be wedged in some brushwood."

"Or in a-"

"Will! This is important. What I'm trying to say is that we might be able to recover it and leave it somewhere where it has to be discovered. You see what I mean; we can't very well say that we've had a flash from outer space that suggests it might be in a fold of the Santa Monica Hills."

"No, that would be pretty dumb." I wait a few seconds. "Actually, it's in a swimming pool in a fold of the Santa Monica Hills."

His face jumps a couple of frames. "What?"

"I just got back from there. The good news is that we didn't kill anybody."

"Why didn't you say something before?" He holds up a long-suffering hand. "It doesn't matter. Is it driveable?"

"Not unless you've got scuba gear. It's a giant paperweight. The engines probably in the trunk. It's going to need a crane to get it out."

"Well if there's a pool, there must be a house."

"There is. A bungalow. But it's all shut up and overgrown. We had a look round."

"We?"

"Hadiscomb and I."

"Hadiscomb?"

"The Brit who was at Rockingham with me. He's over here with his parents. I told you, the famous brain surgeon. If you ever wanted-"

"Yes, yes, I remember. Why the hell has he got involved in this?"

"I wasn't going there by myself. And you didn't seem very interested."

"Jesus Christ! Why didn't you put an ad in the L.A. Times? I hope he can keep his mouth shut, this…this-"

"Hadiscomb."

"Right. So tell me more about the bungalow. Why's it empty? Did you check the outside?"

"Yes. There're no 'To Let' or 'For Sale' signs. Looks like a private road leading to it. There's creepers growing over the front fence. It could be on an estate. Doesn't look as if anyone's been there for a while."

"Which is why no one's reported the car. Shit! Typical Lock luck. Dump a car in a pool and you'd expect it to be on the six o'clock news nationwide. Somebody up there must hate us. Now, let's think. How can we tip off Western without them suspecting it's us?"

"It's got to be found sooner or later. Maybe the people who own the bungalow are on vacation."

"More likely it's been sold for redevelopment. We could have to wait months." He snaps his fingers. "Can you see the pool from outside the property?"

"Yes, from the hillside above."

"Great, here's what we do. You ring up the police and tell them you were hunting possums or coons or whatever it is, and that they should haul thar weary asses down thar ri-ight pronto 'cos thar's this hah itsy-bitys aut-o-mo-bile stickin' out of this hah pool, yes sirreee!." I listen to this in full wince. I suspect that the Queen Mother would have done a better American accent than my father. "Then put the phone down before they can ask any questions."

"Why don't you do it?"

"Because you're better qualified by birth. Come on, there's no risk attached. You can use a pay phone. Do it tomorrow if you like. It could make all the difference to when we see Europe again."

"When you see Europe again. I'm trying to get a job here, remember?

"Of course." He smiles, confident that I am going to do what he wants. I wish he wasn't right. The middle-aged couple's suite is now in darkness. The surface of the pool calm as a guiltless dream. "Are you sure you can rely on this Hadiscomb fellow?"

"An Old Rockinghamian? What a question. Funny, he remembered your god-awful rubber boots. By the way, do you remember me breaking an ankle?"

"Yes, in a house match, wasn't it? One of your own side. Clumsy great lout stood on your foot coming into a loose scrum. You don't remember?" He pats me on the shoulder. "Just shows you how easy it is to put the bad stuff behind you."

"I hope so." How wrong can he be?

"I know so." He steers me back towards the bar. "Now, it's slipped my memory. Would you like to come to Sun Valley or not?"

Airports take up so much space. When I have walked across the huge hall and checked in and taken the escalator to the long tunnel that leads to the satellite where you get on the moving walkway that connects with the corridor that leads to the galleries, I am almost surprised to find people waiting for an airplane. I have the feeling that I ought to be there already. That I should be coming through the doors into the welcoming arms of my loved ones at Houston, Denver or wherever. All those pale blue walls with white doves frozen in flight are probably placed there to take your mind off the possibility of having to pluck white hot pieces of metal out of your body, but they lull me to sleep. I expect to open my eyes and be at my destination. But it is really like a visit to Father Christmas's grotto. When you sit in the little train and suddenly realise that it is the scenery winding past while you stay put.

And the airport at Salt Lake City, where we change on the way to Hailey on the way to Sun Valley, seems even bigger because there are no people there. And not many planes, either. Just my father and I and a few rubbernecks who I suspect are not going anywhere but have just turned up on the off chance that something interesting might happen. Like a hijack or an armed raid on the cuddly toy concession. In the old days they would have turned up to see the stage pull out of town.

I am intrigued to be in Salt Lake City because this, of course, is where the Mormons come from, or rather, came to. My eyes are peeled for obedient groups of bovine women in the company of powerful, bearded men with bags under their eyes but the few people I see look disappointingly normal. Mormons clearly go to more pains to melt into the background than, say, Hassidic Jews.

"I love the Mormons," says my father, looming up beside me with a rime of ice-cream on his beard. "What a bunch of wacky, wonderful guys."

For once I have to agree with him. All religions demand faith but to hook up with The Church of Jesus Christ of Latter-Day Saints, you need the kind of unquestioning commitment that makes your average Jehovah's Witness seem like Brer Rabbit on laudanum. Take, for instance, young Joseph Smith of Fayette, New York who started it all. It is 1827 and you're sitting there waiting for someone to draw up the rules of baseball when an angel called Moroni arrives - I always have problems with that name - bearing tidings of golden plates inscribed with his father's work: 'The Book of Mormon' apparently concealed for some reason around 400 A.D. So far, so unbelievable, but does Joseph hesitate? Not for one second. He merely borrows some special spectacles the angel has thoughtfully brought along and sets to translating the plates which turn out to be written in something called 'Reformed Egyptian' - a language hitherto unknown to Egyptologists and containing quotations from Shakespeare and the Authorised Version - or maybe it should be the other way around.

The job done, Joe hands back the specs and the plates to the angel and promptly sallies forth to spread the good news. Not so easy. Converts are hard to find and people are sceptical - not to say hostile - and after considerable controversy - including the failure of a bank he starts - Joe and his brother Hyrum are tossed into jail in Carthage, Illinois. The next day it gets worse. A mob breaks in and lynches them. (Ironic perhaps that fifty miles down the Mississippi, in Hannibal, Missouri, the nine year old Mark Twain was growing up as Samuel Langhorne Clemens. Hannibal, Carthage. Strange coincidence. Strange names for that America, though Memphis, Alexandria and Cairo were not far away along the Mississippi. Maybe young Twain read about the lynching in the Missouri Courier on which he subsequently worked, the word 'lynch' being courtesy of Justice of the Peace, Charles Lynch, who had departed this life rather more peacefully less than fifty years before five hundred miles east in Virginia).

With the death of Joe and Hyrum, the Mormons were booted out of Illinois and the hour brought forth the man. Brigham Young became president of the church and led his flock from Nauvoo on the banks of the Mississippi to the new Jerusalem, Deseret, the Great Salt Lake valley where, having wandered half way across America for three years, they started work on their settlement the day they arrived.

Seventeen years before the Civil War, thirty-two before Custer was wiped out at the Little Bighorn. Through what is now Missouri, Nebraska - did my mother's folks stop off here, or were they on the Overland Stage Trail to the south? - Wyoming and into Utah, over the Rockies and through the Devil's Gate. Frontier settlements, six shooters, injuns. Mountains, plains. Freezing cold, burning heat. You can't beat a good trek for forging team spirit and belief into conviction. The suffering becomes part of the dogma. When you have been through that amount of suffering it must have been for a good reason, otherwise what was the point? Ask the Israelites, or the Boers - or anyone who attended an English public school.

What a shame that Hollywood's eventual homage to the ultimate 'Trekkie' was called 'Brigham Young - Frontiersman' and not 'Brigham Young - Megabonker'. In the movie, the number of wives was reduced to four - which presumably reduced production costs as well as conveying a more wholesome image - and Jagger - Dean, unfortunately, not the more plausible Mick - spent more time fighting off Indians and plagues of locusts than doing what Brig was best at. In reality, at his death, Brigham Young left seventeen grieving widows, fifty-six children and, for 1877, the huge sum of two and half million dollars.

Those were the days. Why couldn't I have been out there with just a few hundred thousand Sioux and Comanche to worry about rather than in L.A. meeting with Western Rentals?

The lawyer provided by my father has the sleek, healthy sheen of a thrusting young rat - I don't get the chance to see if his eyes are pink because he never removes his shades. One look at me and I can tell what is passing through his mind: plea bargaining. It's a problem I have. I look guilty even when I'm innocent and when I'm guilty it's a miracle that arrow stigmata don't start erupting all over my flesh.

Pitching for Western Rentals are small, plump Mr Shankel and his relief, Mr Gallow, equipped with a face that only a smotherer could love. They have the air of men who have seen plenty of suffering over the years and have long ago mastered the art of coming to terms with it. Their lawyer was scheduled to attend but made only an intermittent contribution, being stuck in a traffic jam on the Pomona Freeway where his car phone - supplied by Western - broke down.

'Don't say any more than you have to' is my lawyer's advice and I take it gladly spending most of the meeting staring at the carpet. Whenever I do bump into the eyes of Shankel or Gallow it is to be faced with the irrefutable certainty that they regard me as a liar and a cheat. The fact that they are absolutely right does not build confidence, any more than the growing suspicion that when telephoning the police I had failed to specify the whereabouts of the pool. I had been so busy trying to disguise my voice, and so worried that the call might be traced, and so unconvinced by my invented reason for being in the area, that I had barely mumbled a few clumsy sentences containing the word 'pool' and 'car' before jamming down the phone.

Out of consideration for my father's feelings, I do not share the news of my possible dereliction. His mood has darkened with the information that our flight, once delayed, is now cancelled. He postulates that the local airline is approaching bankruptcy and that the plane will only take off when enough passengers have bought tickets to pay for the fuel. This could take days. I leave him explaining to a totally disinterested official that never, not once, not a single time in a lifetime of travelling first class from Transylvania to Timbuktu has he ever, ever been subjected to such abysmal, mind-boggling, incompetence and flagrantly iniquitous corporate dishonesty. Not to mention...

His voice dies away and I find a door in the glass and go outside. The cold air slaps me across the face and I can see my breath dancing on a spider's web of crystals. On all sides, obvious Mormons are still in short supply. Maybe they have gone skiing. The town is surrounded by snow-capped mountains and instead of struggling up to Sun Valley we could rent a car and be in Park City within an hour; or weaving down the slopes with Robert Redford at Sundance. I take a few deep breaths and begin to feel better. My knees flex, I start to adjust my weight downhill.

What a country. Two hours ago I could have been dangling my sun-warmed toes in a palm-fringed pool. Now I am in a different world. Yet it is still America. One continent. One self-contained empire that rolled west like a series of overlapping maps unfurling across a vast table. In 1783, barely more than three million people with half the land mass in the hands of foreign powers. A hundred years later, a population larger than any European nation and the most productive economy in the world. So fast. Maybe I was wrong about the past dying. Perhaps in that momentum the frontier spirit never had the chance to die. It is still being borne forward, symbol and reality, an especially American feeling that change and movement are inevitable, that hope allied to perseverance and invention will always prevail and lead to happiness.

As a child, I was taken to the Air Space Museum in Washington D.C. where I saw the battered canister that had deposited Armstrong and Aldrin on the moon. I was impressed, but my most enduring memory remains the jukebox in one of the adjacent corridors. It was playing Frank Sinatra singing 'Come fly with me'. All the songs related to flight or to the sky. In Europe, this would have been considered frivolous, demeaning to the spirit of a great achievement, but to me it was comforting and illuminating. It showed how eclectic man could be. How very simple things could exist beside scientific marvels, perhaps even provide stepping stones towards them. How minds that could expand wide enough to consider any possibility could solve any problem. It made me very warm towards America. Very glad that I was half-American.

I go inside to learn that the next flight will be in two hours time. No skiing today and apparently there is powder at Sun Valley. My father has already started a letter to the head of the airline and contemptuously refused a voucher entitling him to a free meal. Mine too. Not best pleased by this, I wander off again through the endless, almost empty corridors. It is an eerie feeling, like being trapped in an Antonioni movie. When I do see a plane out of a window, it scuttles round a corner as if it had no business being there. Maybe something is going on that we do not know about. Perhaps an invasion by a small number of Martians who have taken on human form or, more plausible at Salt Lake City, Jaredites who, instead of becoming extinct in 600 B.C. as suggested by 'The Book of Mormon', may have gone to live on another planet and chosen this afternoon to return and see if the idea of an Olympic Games had caught on.

Clip, clip, clip. A pair of midnight blue high heeled shoes goes past down the corridor. Luckily for my peace of mind there is somebody wearing the uniform of an airline employee inside them. My peace of mind is not great at the moment and this is the kind of natural watershed where a growing boy is obliged to take stock of his situation. Trapped inside what seems like an alien growth from another planet. Guilty of car murder. Confused about the past. Worried about the future. I gaze towards the distant mountains like Christian in 'Pilgrim's Progress'. Only Christian travelled with Faithful while I have my father. Hmn. I suppose Los Angeles could easily double for The City of Destruction, and Christian's destination, The Celestial City, does sound like a studio. Celestial City Pictures. I can see it picked out in spotlights like the Twentieth Century Fox logo. Maybe this is productive symbolism. All I have to cope with is the Slough of Despond, the Valley of Humiliation, Doubting Castle and the Valley of the Shadow of Death. But wait a minute. Haven't I been through them already? It sounds like every day of my life.

I tried to call Zaiferts so that they would know where I was if they wanted me but all I got was an answering machine. Not even his terrifying secretary - I mean assistant. I thought about calling Constance, but after our meeting at the Irvine Ranch it did not seem such a great idea. I could not bear it if she burst into tears again, always difficult to deal with down a telephone.

That leaves my father for immediate dialogue and reassurance. Never a great success in the past. When pressed by my mother to enlighten me about the facts of life - I had told her to 'fuck off!' without having any idea what I was saying - he merely recounted that it was not something dirty but something very beautiful that mummies and daddies did when they loved each other very much. This was fine, but what precisely was 'it'? He never got around to that. I therefore continued to wait with increasing anxiety for my umbilicus to get an erection. I knew that my procreative organ could not be my cock, despite what my dirty little friends said, because you pissed through that and - well, it was obvious. There was also that tacky liquid that emerged when my comrades tipped me off to an agreeable new way of killing the time not devoted to reading 'Coral Island' and re-arranging my birds' egg collection. My mother, ever the pragmatist, solved the problem by leaving a packet of Kleenex by the bed plus an illustrated book that revolutionised my thinking and put an end to me trying to prise my belly button out of its socket with a nail file.

Unhelpful really, my American mother deciding to live and work in London, while my father divides most of his time between France and the States. It does not make it any easier to decide where you belong. And, of course, there is Philippe, the other corner of the international triangle, a Frenchman living in London. He now sells Pernod to trendy young Brits though he would happily live on a houseboat in Nepal if my mother was beside him - in fact, I think he would probably prefer it.

Philippe gives the lie to those who say that people always gravitate to a replica of their ex-spouse. He is much nicer than my father. Sensitive, thoughtful, tolerant, faithful, groomed. My father says that he looks as if he just fell out of an autumnal knitting pattern brochure. It is difficult to adjust to someone like that after twenty years. I am talking as a son, of course. My mother clearly feels differently. For me, it is a little like moving from the middle of Manhattan to Vermont. You wait for the noise and bustle, feel slightly resentful of the peace that you know was not programmed for your benefit. Some kind of changes you never really adjust to.

Career-wise, my mother has thrived. Or rather, she now has a career. She met my father when she was visiting friends in L.A. and he was travelling round the world prior to putting his youth behind him and getting a job. They fell in love and that, as they say, was that. Just back to Nebraska to tell the folks the good news: ''62 Homecoming Queen to wed Brit Voyager. London bound'.

When the marriage broke up she got a job as a secretary in a publishing house. Then moved to a literary agent where she had more responsibility, and eventually set up shop with a partner. They represent Devi Prahn who she discovered via a story he published in The Atlantic Monthly. I always wondered who read The Atlantic Monthly. Aspiring literary agents obviously. Devi has been joined by a bunch of hot young writers - or writers who, in my mother's opinion, ought to be hot - and who, I suspect, are secretly in love with her. I suppose she is very bright but to me she is still the person with the familiar, reassuring smell who used to hug me and grumble at having to sew name tags on my school uniform. Her advice to me? 'Never go into a relationship imagining that you are going to change someone'.

Maybe I *should* make an effort to talk to my father.

"Did you ever see such a stomach-turning load of tasteless rubbish?" He is standing in the doorway of one of the gift shops. "Makes that shop on Santa Monica Pier look like Tiffany's."

"Can I be of assistance to you gen'l'men?" The female assistant with the Man in the Moon earrings has glided to our side.

"I was wondering if you handled wedding lists," says my father.

Luckily, she seems to have no idea what he is talking about so I lead him away and start unburdening my problems. "Do you think I should go into the movie business?"

"I don't know." Helpful start. "It's always difficult to give people career advice, especially when you're close to them. I think if I had my time again-" here we go "-I'd have joined the Footlights when I was at Cambridge. When I think of some of the conspicuously untalented people who've gone on to make fortunes-" right, thanks, dad. "Or the B.B.C. They used to have a damn good training scheme. Of course, the money's zilch but there're the contacts you make and their production values-" when will I ever learn? "I'd be directing my own stuff by now, instead of being at the mercy of some pimply reject from the U.S.C. Film School who's never bumped into an idea north of Magic Mountain."

I nod and, with relief, see that he is closing in on the nearest bar. If you asked him to describe the crucifixion it would boil down to how he had to queue for three quarters of an hour in the rain to see 'Quo Vadis'.

By the time we leave the bar we are in danger of missing the flight. "That's what the bastards want," he says knowingly as if his sinking four margaritas was part of some undefined but carefully mounted conspiracy. Certainly, the woman who eventually - we manage to go to the wrong gate - takes our boarding passes looks upon us with affection. She rips my father's in two like one of Zola's downtrodden *sans culottes* lighting upon the private parts of a particularly detested rent collector.

The plane is cosy and half-full, giving the lie to my father's theory that all the seats would have to be sold before we moved. I begin to perk up again - until I see a mechanic and a middle-aged man in a Windbreaker striding the runway and looking up at the underside of one of the wings. A small puddle of dark liquid is visible on the concrete. My father's eyes meet mine and he sighs through clenched teeth and the soggy remnants of potato chip wedged between them. "Typical," is all he can manage. I begin to feel uneasy. Maybe the strange atmosphere pervading this place is trying to tell me something. All that introspection. Perhaps fate encourages you to enjoy a quick retrospective of your life slightly before the terminal experience (or in my case, the terminal terminal experience);

thus giving your faculties the chance to approach the actual moment of immolation without distraction.

The engines choke to life - and stop. The flight attendant who has risen to her feet and picked up a card - presumably not an eye test to see if we can spot the exit doors - replaces it and turns towards the cockpit door. As if on cue, the middle-aged man in the Windbreaker appears. "Hi, folks." The tone is breezy. "Looks like we got a little problem." We know what he is talking about. "Okay. I'm going to start her up again. You people keep your eyes on the wings and tell me if you see anything." He retreats to the cockpit before anybody dares ask him what exactly we should be looking for.

"That was the pilot?" exclaims my father. "No uniform?"

I know what he means. A few epaulets and a peaked cap with some scrambled egg works wonders for the morale. In fact I prefer not to see the pilot at all. He can never be as impressive as I want to imagine him. I just want that weathered teak, all-American voice that could be God playing Gary Cooper as it tells me how nice it is to have me with him, and how high we will be flying and at what speed and - yes, there may be a little turbulence but, don't worry, folks, with me at the helm you won't come to any harm. He then introduces Senior Steward Raymond Petrawinski who I would like to see sometime but never do.

The engines start up again and every neck in the plane is twisted like the pipes under a wash basin. The wings tremble and one drop of oil falls to the runway. Seems okay. We can spare that. After a couple of minutes, the pilot reappears and stoops to take a quick look out of a window. "Okay, folks. We're going to go for it." He murmurs something I cannot catch to the flight attendant and retires to the cockpit pursued by a faint ripple of applause in which my father does not participate.

I look to the flight attendant. She is arranging small tins of juice on a tray. It seems like a vote for life. 'Bang, bang!' Someone is hammering on the door of the aircraft. The flight attendant hurries forward and there is a collective hiss of exasperation from the passengers. What now? The door swing open and a woman and girl sweep into the plane shepherded by a solicitous airline official two Brownie points below fawn. My heart jumps. The eyes, the hair, that haughty twitch of the shoulders as the girl sheds her poncho and thrusts it imperiously at the attendant. Rashmi. I should want to punch her on the nose but my prime reaction is excitement mixed with relief. This is fate - and I hope she realises it too.

I watch entranced as she and her mother shed articles of clothing like models at the end of a catwalk. It has to be her mother. The features, the way they share space without manoeuvring, knowing exactly where the other one is going to be. Mother looks eastern, talking continents not seaboards. She could have Indian blood and does have soft brown eyes and a bone structure to make Rodin kill for a piece of marble. The bones she has clearly bequeathed to her daughter. She looks calm and sad and remote, several locked doors from the outside world. While the flight attendant hovers attentively, she shakes out her hair from beneath a felt turban and unzips a long baggy outer garment of such striking ordinariness that it must have cost a fortune.

"Last time I saw a coat like that, it had my golf clubs in it," observes my father.

Rashmi turns to give him a look that would mothball a battleship and sees me.

For a tiny second, a very tiny second, her composure slips. Then: "Small plane."

I start to say something but she overrides me. "Look, I'm sorry-" she doesn't sound sorry "-it's not what you think. I broke down on the freeway. I didn't have the number of the restaurant and by the time I could get through you'd gone." By the end of the sentence I feel as if I have stood her up.

"Sure." I try to make it sound like I might believe her or I might not believe her but in either case I remain strong, composed and stoical.

My father is lapping all this up so I introduce him. "Hi." Her eyes barely brush over him as she starts to follow her mother up the aisle. "I didn't have the number where you were staying."

"Right little madam," says my father. "You want to watch yourself there. Family probably own the airline. That's why we're late. They held the flight. Typical."

I ignore him and stare out of the window at the Salt Lake. Something I have the opportunity of doing for the next seventy miles. It is big. Capable of swallowing several Dead Seas before breakfast. There are occasional islands and whorls and flourishes like the surface of a meringue, and a zillion grains of salt sparkle up at us as if hoping that we are a giant potato chip with engine failure.

I am not looking at the scenery a lot. I am wondering how to handle Rashmi. With reserve, I think, in the circumstances. Unless, of course, she ignores me. In which case I will have to think of something else. My vein of morbid romanticism is also weighing up every hum and judder of the aircraft; wondering what the chances are of being reunited with the woman of my unfocused dreams only to be turned into a couple of Lot's wife look-alikes twenty five minutes later.

I rise to go to the lavatory and she waggles her fingers cheerfully. She is wearing faded jeans and truncated cowboy boots decorated with rhinestones. Spectacles are tilted on the end of her nose and one foot stretches down the aisle. Her mother has been given a drink that is not juice. They do look as if they own the airline.

I return to my seat and stare out of the window. The wing seems just fine and the Great Salt Lake has disappeared. Now we are skimming across flat arable land with hills in the distance and I assume that we have crossed the state line and are flying over Idaho, home of the famous potato. Below us must be the Snake River Plain, lightly dusted with snow. Hailey cannot be all that far away. A nasty thought occurs. Supposing Rashmi and ma are flying on to Seattle or some under-populated corner of the boondocks in between?

'Blip!' The seat belt sign flicks on and I am relieved to see the flight attendant drawing back a curtain and laying preparatory hands on the poncho and the zippered coat. The plane is descending under its own power with the engine sounding robust. With a modicum of luck, Rashmi and I will be on the ground together.

The Friedman Memorial Airport at Hailey is a shiny, wooden structure carpeted with lolling bird dogs that prick up their ears hopefully every time the doors from the runway open. It squats anonymously at the end of an industrial estate off State 75 which runs north from Shoshone through Ketchum and Sunbeam to rejoin U.S. 93 and head on north through Carmen, Charlos Heights, Lolo, Missoula, Polson, Big Arm, Kalispell and Eureka all the way to the North Pole. From there you have to find your own way to Father Christmas. I love the names of American towns, the charms on the necklace of the great American road. I wonder where they come from and how you are supposed to pronounce them. Nauvoo, for instance, the Illinois River town that expelled the Mormons. Is it an Indian name or a hand-me-down of 'nouveau': 'new' bestowed by French trappers as they pushed round a bend of the Mississippi before the Louisiana purchase? I must remind myself to look it up.

I keep an eye on daughter and mother at the baggage claim and glance around warily, hoping that neither Larry nor any members of the Godorosky will turn out to meet us. I need not worry.

"They don't seem to have sent a limo," says my father petulantly and unnecessarily loudly.

I don't know where they would find one if they wanted to. The parking lot is full of huge, weathered pick-ups with fenders like Victorian bedsteads and lugubrious hound dogs behind the wheel like undertakers' chauffeurs waiting for a consignment of coffin to be loaded. Apparently, Bruce Willis owns a lot of real estate up here. He must have chosen the place for its calm.

The baggage is arriving and it is not difficult to associate the matching sets of Vuitton with their owners. Our own luggage is less imposing. Intentionally, my father would claim; his reasoning being that expensive luggage serves as a beacon to airport thieves and that the savvy traveller always packs his duds in cheap bags to throw them off the scent. I wish more people knew this. They would be spared the impression that we are destitute and have just dug our bags out a cliff-fall.

I leave my bulging hold-all, perilously secured with a lace borrowed from one of my sneakers, and cast around for Rashmi and her mother. A Marlboro Country clone with droopy moustache, plaid woollen jacket and cowboy hat with a rime of dried sweat round the band is loading himself up with luggage like it was firewood. He bears it outside to a huge station wagon with more wooden panels than Hampton Court Palace. Rashmi's mother follows as if on castors but there is no sign of Rashmi. I turn and nearly fall over her.

"I was looking for you," she says.

I gaze at her and my resolve to be cool and distant breaks up like a dynamited log jam. "I find you incredibly beautiful," I hear myself saying.

"Then let's have that dinner." She waits. "Unless you're still mad at me."

"I'm not mad at you. I'm-"

I'm not quite certain what I am. Smitten, probably. In love, possibly. Confused, definitely. But one thing I do know: Western Rentals, my career, Lucy, these are incidentals, mere midges on the windshield of life compared to what I feel when I look at Rashmi.

"Where are you staying?" She sounds impatient.

Where am I staying? My father did mention it but, of course, I took no notice. I see a poster on the wall and, with relief, 'Warm Springs' jumps out at me.

"Warm Springs."

"I'll meet you at the Creek Inn. Seven thirty."

"Tonight?"

For a second, doubt flickers across her face. Her lips tremble in the semblance of a pout. "I am incredibly beautiful." A petulant flick of the poncho and she moves towards the door.

"I'll see you there." Did my voice soar a couple of octaves in its desire to be heard?

Shit! Why did I have to say 'tonight?' in that quavering, dork-like voice, like I might not be allowed out; like I would not kill to be at her side at the-the-what did she say? Panic grips me. Something to do with water. Rivers, lakes, ponds, streams - creek! The Creek Inn. I must write it down. My brain is turning into Donald Rumsfeld's shredder.

A golden rule in life, one of the few not proclaimed by my grandmother, is 'if in doubt, say nothing', but I refuse to obey it. I always have to fill a silence with blurt. As if conversation was some kind of infernal relay race and the baton had to be snatched up and borne remorselessly towards the finishing line. So foolish when it is always words that leave the scars. Not eloquent, interpretable silences that leave clues but no fingerprints.

"I've got a taxi," sighs my looming father, clearly indicating that it was something I should have done. "They probably met the earlier plane."

But when we get to Little Elk Lodge it is to find that neither Larry, nor Bronski nor Igor have arrived. "We gotta call saying they were held up," says the friendly receptionist with the badge that says 'This spud's on me!' "But they must be coming because they double-checked the address."

I am not paying total attention because I am looking around for slot machines and sinister, square-jawed, potato-faced (hmn) men in baggy suits tossing fifty kopeck pieces and having difficulty catching them. Not a sign. The Little Elk Lodge looks as wholesome as you can get without singing 'God Bless America' through a mouthful of apple pie. It is difficult to imagine anyone round here saying 'panty hose' on a Sunday, let alone playing ballski with the Godorosky. Still, that just might be what makes it all so incredibly clever and sinister. My father's experiences in Hollywood have taught me that nothing is ever what it seems, unless it seems very unpleasant.

Little Elk Lodge is a three storey wooden structure with one of those balconies that bad guys plunge from, through, or out of in westerns. In fact, the whole street looks like something you might find on the back lot at Burbank where you would push back the swing doors of the saloon and immediately hit your head on some scaffolding. But this is not the case at spacious but cosy L.E.L. where a log fire blazes cheerfully in a huge stone fireplace and exhausted but happy guests "eeh!" and "a-a-rgh!" and "o-o-o-h!" as they hobble past on the way to the sauna, massage rooms and Jacuzzi or stretch out cuddling steaming mugs of grog and swapping stories of new runs, ancient aches, incurable deficiencies of style and near death experiences.

I want to rush out and see if I can still do it but the chairlift has just closed and the shadows are lengthening down the mountain faster than the last weaving skiers. I can see the grey wrinkles of mogul fields high upon the slopes, but lower down it is brochure cover time with wide trails carving through tightly massed regiments of conifers.

My father seems depressed. He says nothing when we are shown to our comfortable, stripped pine suite with its own fireplace and kitchenette and photographs of snowscapes on the walls, and unpacks only what he needs to retire to the bathroom. I imagine that the journey has got him down and wait for him to return and suggest that we descend to get fitted out in the ski shop on the premises, thus beating the morning rush. But he tells me to go ahead because he needs to call Larry and the others. There are some packets and bottles sticking out of his wash bag in the bathroom but I barely register them. Creams and lip salves to protect the ageing but still dearly loved flesh from the hostile attentions of sun, wind and cold, I imagine.

When I am through in the bathroom he is lying on one of the beds with a telephone on his chest. "We're on Mountain Time, aren't we?" he muses. "Makes you feel more manly, doesn't it?"

I tell him that I know what he means and head for the door. "Hey." He stretches out a hand for me to approach the bed and grips my arm. "Go and buy yourself a snazzy ski outfit. You can charge it to the room. Then maybe you'll stand a chance with that girl on the plane." I start to blurt out thanks but he releases my arm and waves me away. "It can be your next birthday present. Remind me."

The ski shop is attended by three 'Hi, there! How'y'doin!?' young blond-streaked merchants of groom in cute little leather aprons who are waxing soles, sharpening edges and adjusting bindings like it is tipped to become an Olympic event. They could have been press-ganged from the editorial board of GQ Magazine.

I rent skis, boots and poles while casing the joint and the customers for what the 'in' skier is wearing this season. Ideally, I would like two pairs of skis. An extra long pair to carry around and give the impression that I must be dramatically good, and a smaller, safer pair for the actual skiing. I settle for Elan 205s which will test the upper level of my ability and boots that jut forward so radically that once in them you have to bend your knees and adapt a crapping position just to stay upright. Either that or lean forward at 45 degrees as if into a polar blizzard. I flirt with curved poles but this seems a little excessive when I am no more than a solid intermediate skier. I don't want to promise more than I can deliver. Well, not much more. Rashmi looks like a Sun Valley native and when/if we ski together I need to get it right. Which brings me to the outfit. Hmn. Difficult. I don't want anything too flash. On the other hand, I don't want something that makes me look like I am content to shrink into the background, that I have no faith in my ability. That one piece looks interesting but maybe it is a little too Wall Street, too reserved. On the other hand, the red, yellow and green reworking of the Guinean national flag is, perhaps, a little too vivid. How can I achieve the desired effect of highly visible understatement?

In the end, I settle for what I am told is a *combinaison*, a one-piece in a kind of muted blue with enough zippers to fit out a chapter of Hell's Angels. I hope it conveys tenderness and sensitivity within a carapace of steel.

My father hardly glances at the suit. He has been unable to raise anybody. "Not even Constance. It's ridiculous. She's usually wedded to her desk."

Experience has shown me that people with Hollywood associations often fall prey to unease the moment they leave town. It is not only that they suspect that someone will be emptying the contents of their desk into a brown paper bag and unscrewing their nameplate from the door the moment their car has pulled off the lot, but that the whole place might disappear; that the San Andreas Fault might spitefully choose the moment of their departure to strut its stuff and bury all their deals, all over town, at the bottom of the Pacific Ocean. When I was a child, there was a producer who came to visit my father at Pulignac and he used the phone at the local hotel so much for international calls that he pushed the meter through the roof and into an area never before achieved.

The locals who had started coming to watch stood on chairs and applauded when the big moment arrived. This man didn't have a deal on the boil. He just wanted to check that California was still there and that he wouldn't have to spend the rest of his life in the depths of the French countryside eating goose livers.

"An hour of my life has been stolen," complains my father.

"You'll get it back in L.A."

"I want it now. I might be dead by then. I'm not feeling six o'clock. I'm feeling five o'clock. My gastric juices aren't pinking. We'll have to eat later."

I feel a tinge of guilt. He has just bought me a ski suit. And the Vuarnet shades. And the Bolle goggles. And the gloves and Zinca and the rest of the indispensable stuff. "Sorry. I've got a date."

He does a convincing impression of a sulky five-year-old. "With that girl? You didn't waste any time. Where are you meeting her?" He reads my expression. "I wasn't going to suggest I joined you. I just wanted to know so I didn't turn up there myself. We'll have a drink before you go."

The telephone rings and he snatches it up. "Hello?" He listens and nods and his face turns a deeper shade of grey. He covers the mouthpiece. "It's our lawyer." He continues to listen, clucks softly from time to time and stares at the ceiling. Eventually: "Yes, well, let's just hope it turns up." He holds the telephone over the rest and drops it like a bomb. He turns and looks at me. I feel a familiar sense of guilt. But it was his idea.

Later, it occurs to me that the Creek Inn must be just down the road and that a little reconnaissance might not be a bad idea. Outside, the sun is a pink glow behind Bald Mountain and it is cold. Real cold. Cold you can hear. It creaks like a vice tightening as the earth hardens into ice and a million shards of frost sparkle on the dark trees and wide, deserted slopes. When I breathe out, I wait for my breath to solidify into skeins of crystals and shatter against the frozen ground. The air hurts the insides of my lungs, numbs my cheeks like the aftermath of a hard slap. Just trudging down the icy road seems like more exercise than I have had in weeks.

The Creek Inn is a log cabin as visualised by Donald Trump and stands apart from other buildings amongst the pines. There are stooks of skis stacked outside and it looks like a popular place. I can hear the overflow of energy from the slopes before I force the outer door open. Flickering firelight ripples across the frosting glass and the bar is a scrum of mainly young bodies, hailing, hollering, jostling, canoodling and generally acting as if they were auditioning for a beer commercial. It would be great to be recognised and hauled into their midst but this does not happen and I can skirt the bar, drawing hardly a glance, and advance to check out the restaurant beyond.

It reminds me of a small theatre. Candle-lit, check gingham-topped tables descending in tiers to a huge safety curtain of glass with the stage - an illuminated, snowbound creek - beyond. Some people, older, quieter, are eating already and looking at the clientele it occurs to me that although America is, of course, a classless society, if it was not , these people would surely qualify as belonging to its upper stratum. They project the invisible sheen of wealth and privilege that I recall from Rockingham, and more memorably, my university. They exude confidence without appearing confident. It is below the surface, in the blood. The way that man weighs his knife and thoughtfully dissects his steak, stares through his wife as she stares through him, both of them focusing on distant - inevitably internal - vistas. Ivy on the wall. Grandfather clocks telling the same time with a slightly different tick-tock. Coffee? She shakes her head. He raises a finger. The check arrives immediately - but not too immediately. Onward. *Ad astra sine multa ardua.*

"Do you wish to be seated?" The sepulchral tone as much as the construction makes me feel that I am being invited to participate in a religious experience.

"I'm just looking for someone, thanks." I hesitate and make a reservation, feeling slightly ashamed that my cheapskate eye immediately starts checking out the cheapest items on the menu whilst my name goes in the book. It is even more expensive than L.A. and, thanks to my jaunts with Hadiscomb, I have already overspent my Mastercard limit. But what does this matter? I am dating Rashmi, for God's sakes.

I return to the hotel where my father is explaining to the receptionist, with warmth and assiduousness, that his accent is English, not South African. She seems interested. Maybe he will not be eating alone tonight. It is much quieter now. Everybody must be taking a bath or snoozing. Night has fallen. The snow is grey-blue; the sky violet, dusted with stars. The pines are children's cut out silhouettes.

I draw the shades and take a bath, wondering what to wear. I want to look like myself only slightly better. Something I can live up to and that won't disappoint in the long term, if there is one. Nothing too smart - like I have forgotten to take the hanger out of the jacket. In fact, forget the jacket. Nobody wears a jacket at a ski resort.

In the end I settle for clothes I feel at home in. Brown sweater, beige corduroys - make that greyish-yellow corduroys - and well-worn Timberlands. In fact, everything I have is well-worn. I may not look sensational but I look like someone I have got to know and love over a long period of time.

When I get back to the Creek Inn at seven-twenty-five and thirty-two seconds, there are no skis outside and the jocks have disappeared. I am relieved as Rashmi would surely have known most of them and there would have been introductions and the danger of being sucked into their orbit. I shed my parka and order a glass of white wine. A martini has already been swallowed in the company of my father and Ellen, the receptionist, who comes from Spokane and is mourning a dead gerbil, and has cousins in Cheshire, England whom she has never seen but with whom she exchanges Christmas cards.

I am becoming increasingly aware that I should not have used my father's cologne. It has the subtlety of Agent Orange and seems to gain in intensity the longer it rests on the skin. I smell like my grandmother's antique commode impregnated with lavender-scented furniture polish. To the outside world, the message is obvious: only a guy with a very serious personal hygiene problem would wear this stuff. So go to the restroom and wash it off - but, but supposing Rashmi arrives as I emerge. Is this a positive sighting on what amounts to a first date? What does it suggest? Anxious bowel syndrome? Tiny bladder? A drug problem? Maybe if I dip my handkerchief in my wine glass and-

"Hi."

Rashmi has materialised behind me. Apart from her beautiful face, I am aware of a spiky, bouffant jacket that makes her look as if she is wearing a giant, black sea urchin. I start to put my wine glass in my pocket and then get a grip on myself. "Hi. Great jacket."

"Thanks. You look lovely too." She smiles and I know how an iceberg must feel when it drifts into the Gulf Stream.

"I thought we'd eat here. Okay?"

"Great."

The table we are shown to I would have bribed for - if I had thought of it before. Looking over the deck with glass on both sides and the floodlit creek below. Away from the other diners, but not so far that you feel the management fears that your proximity might kill their appetites. Dimly lit. *Intime*. Very.

"Will you be having an aperitif? "

Rashmi shrugs off her jacket and I jerk my eyes from her breasts. Heaven's sake, Lock. You have seen a woman's breasts before. "I don't know. A glass of wine, maybe."

"Why don't I order a bottle?"

The maitre d' inclines his head graciously. "I'll ask our *sommelière* to visit with you."

So far, so Cary Grant. I am beginning to have the wonderful feeling that this is going to be my night. Our night. "You know something amazing? Those earrings you're wearing. They're exactly the same-"

"-as the woman in the gift shop at the airport was wearing. That's where I got them."

"From the gift shop?"

"From the woman. She sure struck a hard bargain. That's why we nearly missed the flight. Pritty was going crazy. I get a lot of things like that. I need to see something on somebody before I know if I like it. If I do, I ask them where they got it. If it's too complicated, I offer to buy it."

"Right there?"

"On the spot. Makes a change from the Sears Catalogue."

"Hi. I believe you would care for some wine with your meal?" The wine waitress beams down at us beatifically. I pluck the leather tome from her hands and run by eyes knowledgeably over the pages like a man who will be choosing the Oregon Riesling for its understated smoky resonance rather than because it is the cheapest wine on the list.

"Unusual name, Rashmi," I say as the wine waitress willows away.

"You mean, what are my roots?" She gives me a hard look. "My mother's half Indian. Like-" she holds her hands before her eyes with the tips of her spread fingers almost touching and sways her head from side to side "- my father's very ethnic. He believes that the world would be a better place if everybody went to bed with everyone else."

"My father believes the same thing."

"Yes, but with my father it's a creed. You know, like compulsory miscegenation."

"He and your mother aren't together?"

"It's not a great formula for a stable relationship."

"What does he do?"

"My father? Lots of things."

"Business?"

"He gets involved."

"A captain of industry."

"I guess you could call him that." She starts to study the menu and I pull my eyes away from her face. "I wonder what they've got that's freshly deep frozen." She glances up. "You're staring again."

"I'm digesting you little by little."

"I'll stick in your craw."

"You already have."

"The Idaho lamb should be fresh. Or the Idaho trout. They could scoop them out of the creek with a net."

"There's an Idaho Springs in Colorado."

"So knowledgeable. I should have figured you were half British. I went to school in England once. In fact I've been to school everywhere. The Lycée Français in L.A., the American School in Paris. The Montessori

School in Montenegro and the Montenegro School in Montessori. At least, it began to feel like that. I guess I had an education that was second to none. In other words, it was worse than nothing." She laughs. "Pretty funny, huh? I just thought of it." She looks into my eyes. "I'm showing off, aren't I? I must like you."

"I hope so."

"You look so solemn."

"It's my thinking face. I'm trying to come up with a way of expressing how I feel that isn't corny."

"I like corny. It's very underestimated these days. Give me a little corny."

"Well, I feel very relaxed and happy with you. Like I've know you for a long time. Is that corny enough for you?"

"Go on."

"And I'm knocked out by your beauty. It's like you give off a glow I can warm my hands on."

"That's not corny. That's romantic." She takes my hand.

"It's what I feel."

She presses her lips together so that they nearly disappear and squeezes my hand - hard. I think if I had to choose one image of her to keep for the rest of my life, that would be it.

"You folks ready to order?"

"Yes. I was just about to eat her."

She squeezes my hand harder. "I'll have the Colorado trout."

"The trout comes from just up the road, ma'am."

"I'll still have it."

We complete our order and the waiter sweeps up the menus and strides away.

"I think you upset him," I tell her.

"I was paying whatever you pay to your geographical expertise. How did you know that? I mean, about Idaho-whatever?"

"I like looking at atlases."

"Me too." She seems surprised, pleased. "When I was a kid, we had this globe and I used to spin it and close my eyes. When it was nearly done I'd stop it with my forefinger. That was where I was."

"In the middle of the Indian Ocean."

"Right. On a raft surrounded by sharks. But just before I died of thirst I'd reach the Chagos Archipelago."

"And enrol at the Montessori school."

"It was the Froebel Method on the Chagos Islands. I'm surprised you could be so ignorant. Boy, I sometimes wonder how I would have survived if my parents hadn't split. I was the guinea pig for every educational system in the world. Have you heard of the Pestalozzi Method."

"Anything to do with birth control?"

"I'll ignore that. You synthesise experience. Trust me, it's tough when you're eight. You don't have a lot of experience and you can't pronounce synthesis, let alone understand what it means."

"I still can't pronounce it." I try. I can't. She tries. She can't. We try again. We can't. We laugh. We even chortle - and when was the last time you heard someone doing that? We drink a little more. We are having such a good time.

"Then my father tries to 'bond me', I think that was what he called it, to a tribe of American Indians. He said that they were the real owners of the country. That to be worthy of the right to live here one had to have an understanding of their ways and culture."

"And?"

"They didn't want me. Boy, was I relieved. Their reserve was one big parking lot knee deep in mud. And they were living in immobile mobile homes with huge dogs and the TV on all day. It was so sad. Then I was saved. The marriage broke up and I ended up with my mother."

"But you still see your father?"

"Sure."

"What does your mother do?"

"Not a lot. She travels, visits friends they used to have, tells me how like my father I am. I don't think she's ever got over him. I think, inside, she still feels she's married to him. It's the Indian thing. It's for life, so now he's gone, there's nothing left. She might as well be dead. It's funny. I sometimes feel I have nothing, not a thing, in common with her. It's as if I missed out on all the Indian part of her chromosomes."

"Maybe we should get her together with my father." This is a terrible idea. Why did I say that?

"He's weird, isn't he?"

"He never tried to dump me on a tribe of Red Indians."

"Is he all right?"

"What do you mean?"

"He doesn't look well."

"He's fine. He always looks like that. Maybe it was the flight."

"My mother prefers struggling artists."

"I have your man."

"Painters, sculptors, musicians. Their talent has to be unrecognised."

"Most unrecognised talent you've never seen."

"Being gay helps."

"Damn! Still, two out of three isn't bad."

"And he's in the movie business."

"Too commercial?"

"Something like that." She takes my hand and presses it against her cheek. "If there's no more wine, Willum. Give me some more corny."

I don't remember us leaving the restaurant. I think we must have floated out like Chagall lovers. I don't remember the cold. I just remember kissing her the first moment I could after we had passed through the doors and us crunching off down the road wrapped around each other like we were an animal with four legs. The squeak of our footsteps and the time-confusing brilliance of the moonlight. The snow weighing down the branches of the trees. The stillness. The happiness. Standing behind her facing the forest with my arms around her waist. Pulling her to me. "What is this? The Heimlich manoeuvre?"

"'The woods are lovely, dark and deep'."

She twists her head and the words hang before my lips in a frozen cloud. "'But I have promises to keep, and miles to go before I sleep'."

"I fell in love with Robert Frost," I tell her.

She smiles and turns completely to place her mittened hands behind my neck. "Just as long as you understand what the poem's all about."

And then she kisses me.

10.

"The hearty man ate a condemned breakfast," observes my father.

We are in the breakfast room of the Little Elk Lodge - it is the only meal they serve - and bars of dazzling sunshine are crashing through the windows and reverberating off the varnished pine walls. The object of my father's attention is a hefty, middle-aged man in a scarlet lumberjack's shirt who is carefully pouring half a jug of maple syrup over a stack of buttermilk pancakes. "He's already had a bowl of that nut muck and two yoghourts."

"I expect they were low-cholesterol, "I say, studying the menu. "I think I'll have the 'Mountain-Tamer'. 'Broiled six-ounce sirloin steak and eggs served with home-fried potatoes and-'"

"Please! I'm feeling a little fragile this morning."

"Or maybe 'The Salsa Special': '*Huevas Rancheros* served on corn tortilla with-'"

"Don't! '*Huevas Rancheros*' sounds like someone starting to throw up." He takes a defensive nibble at his toast. "I don't know how they do it. There are nine combination breakfasts on that menu. I put on five hundred calories just reading them. Who needs that amount of food? It's obscene."

I have a certain sympathy with him, and when I see the half-eaten pancakes pushed aside to make way for the pan-fried corn beef hash and poached eggs I feel bad. But then, my father and I have been brainwashed at the same source. Whenever I left anything on my plate, English grandmother would always tell me to finish it because 'thousands of little starving children all over the world would love to gobble that up'. I could never understand how me eating it was going to improve their situation, and as a gesture of solidarity it would seem better if I did not eat it. It was going to end up as waste whether I ate it or not and there was no way I could get it to the starving children before it became inedible. And if I got stomach ache from eating food I did not need it seemed unlikely that some strange inverse spiritual osmosis was going to make them feel any better.

Nevertheless, I ate it because, thanks to Gran, I could sense the starving children watching me. When my foot touched something underneath the table, it was them. Huge-eyed and emaciated, huddled in the darkness, poised for the crumbs. If I did not consume every scrap, a skeletal hand might claw above the table and tap towards my plate like Blind Pugh's stick. I did not want that. I would force the food down my throat and hate the starving children. Gran used to wonder why I would suddenly kick out beneath the table as I placed my knife and fork together.

"And everything has to have a nationality: 'Belgian waffle, English muffin, Canadian bacon'."

"And 'Freedom fries'."

"Stupid bastards!" snarls my father. "Don't they realise that they'd still be a British colony if it wasn't for the Frogs?"

"Funny there's nothing Russian," I say. "I suppose Godoroski is a bit of a mouthful."

"Sssh!" My father's eyes dart round the room. "Don't say that word. I should never have mentioned it."

"I can't believe-"

"We'll discuss it another time. This is not the place."

I gaze round at the happy munchers and the bustling kitchen staff and the beaming lady with the 'Spuddy buddy' T-shirt and the coffee pot that is always trying to find some more room in your cup.

"Do they know?"

"Who?"

"The staff."

"Know what?"

"Who owns the place?"

"No. Anyway, they might not own it. It was just an intimation I had, something Bronski said. Forget it." His eyes drift towards the middle-aged man who is now thoughtfully spreading boysenberry jelly on a bran muffin. "How did your date go?"

"Fine."

"Fine good, or fine bad?"

"Fine." I could tell him that inside me a choir of rapturous Disney bluebirds is singing 'Oh, what a beautiful morning' fit to fall off their perches, and that I think I have found the mother of several little Locks but it seems like tempting providence or at least a lecture on the danger of confusing physical passion with love. "How was your evening?"

"Ellen invited me back to her place."

"Really?"

"Yes. That was nice of her, wasn't it? Attractive little house in a patch of snow just outside town. Apparently the elks come down to the back fence, only there weren't any there last night."

"Perhaps you'll see them another time."

"Possibly. It could be the high spot of the evening. She shares."

"How many people?"

"Just one. A man. She's married to him. I didn't realise that at first. I kept thinking: 'Why does the bugger persist in hanging around? Why doesn't he go home?' I imagine he was thinking the same thing about me."

"So why did she invite you back?"

"We got around to that eventually. Vernon, that's her husband, has written a book God knows how. His vocabulary barely stretched to five words."

"And she wants you to read the book?"

"'A Mountain Man Remembers'. That's a title that leaps out and bites you in the nuts, isn't it? I brought it back. Didn't you see it beside the bed?"

"I thought it was a telephone directory."

"It's not as well written as a telephone directory. Got more characters though." He barks a bitter laugh. "God, I ought to have some inkling of the female psyche by this time."

"Never mind. There's always what's-her-name? Karen?"

My father shakes his head. "Now there's a strange woman."

"Over?"

"Suddenly turns round and calls me a drunken, racist fascist."

"Well...." I struggle for the appropriate response. "It's a point of view."

"Yes. But those were the things she liked about me."

"She told you that?"

"Not in so many words. But you know what American women are like. Despite their enthusiasm for the task they're normally hopeless at reading their own feelings." He sighs. "There were moments when her true sentiments revealed themselves. The problem is this raving Puritanism that pervades them all. If you enjoy something, it must be sinful or obscene. I tried to explain this to her but she only became more abusive. In the end, I had to tell her to pull over."

"Where was this?"

"The San Diego Freeway."

"Jesus Christ!"

"Well, I was drunk. It's an indulgence I feel I can permit myself from time to time. Especially when somebody else is driving."

"She left you on the San Diego Freeway?"

"Isn't that a song? No. Well, I was kicking the car; you know how I hate them. I think it helped her to make up her mind. God, it's a terrible place to be dropped, I can tell you. The stink and the trash and that never-ending flood of lights roaring past. And you never see any faces. You can imagine all the devils in hell inside the cars. It's like standing on the platform as an express train goes through. You're drawn towards the edge. I suddenly wanted to see if I could get to the central divider. But with all those lines of cars you can never tell how fast each one is going. You'd dodge one and - WACK!" He snaps his toast in half to make the point. "Nobody would slow down. You'd be hamburger before you could say shovel."

"Jesus," I say.

"So I climbed over the barrier and started down the embankment. The stuff that was lying around. It was like a battlefield. And things were moving - everywhere. Rats, I suppose. Stray dogs, cats, people. There's a sub-culture down there waiting for a Marxist film-maker to turn up. It was really frightening."

"And stupid."

"At last I found a hole in the fencing and crawled through. Into the middle of nowhere. I mean, there were dwellings somewhere behind fences but it was - nowhere. All that traffic thundering past above and nothing at ground level. Just another place you'd never want to live. And how would you get there? It was as if the freeway had siphoned off all the cars. Crazy."

"You should stop drinking."

"I didn't know where to go. And then two people scrambled through the fence behind me. I started walking with ice in my stomach after that. They didn't say a word. Just kept following me. I have stopped drinking, incidentally. Virtually. You just haven't noticed. I saw this Texaco sign way ahead and I started running. It was like miles away. Nobody, nothing on the streets. When I got near, I could see it was closed. Chains all around it. My heart was spilling out of my mouth. I could hardly breathe. And these two shapes were closing the distance between us. Taking their time. Because they knew the station was closed and I wasn't going anywhere. And then it came, just like I would never have dared write it in a script. A huge Yellow Cab like a block of gold. One moment I saw it, the next I was lying on the bonnet. The driver nearly had a coronary. He was going home but he took me because of my accent. He thought I was Irish. Irish! Can you imagine? But by golly, by the time we got to the hotel I was Irish. I told him he was 'a broth of a boy - the crock of gold at the end of my rainbow'. I gave him every last cent I had on me."

"One day he isn't going to turn up."

"But it's in the blood. You know the story about the scorpion?"

"Yes, I know the story about the scorpion. It was in his nature. I'm serious, dad. You need to stop pushing your luck. Rashmi said she didn't think you were looking so good."

"Did she now? How considerate. Well, if it's any consolation to her, I was thinking of taking some exercise today. If Larry and Co. lack the common courtesy to inform me of their movements they can get stuffed. Have you got some free time today?"

"Sure. I'm meeting Rashmi after lunch."

"Good. Then this morning you're booked to ski with your dear old father. I expect the others will roll up around lunch time."

But when I leave him after a plate of pasta at Barsotti's Mountain Café, calls to the Lodge have revealed no sign of them. No messages either. He is clearly unsettled and this adds to the apprehension that surrounds seeing Rashmi again. These are his problems, not mine. It has also not been good for my skiing to be constantly waiting for him to pick himself out of a snowdrift or get his breath back after bobbling over a couple of moguls. Following a few runs, I feel myself descending to his level which, I suspect, is not going to impress Rashmi. I know that I'm being unkind and this makes me feel worse and blame him the more because he is the reason for it. And because I know that I am being irrational I try to think of genuine reasons for blaming him, like the car which was his fault, but which I could/should have stopped and which could/might prejudice my career, about which I have heard nothing, which makes me feel even more uneasy and starts the whole vicious circle all over again, when all I want is to be left alone so that I can fall in love in peace.

He does seem to have stopped drinking though. With lunch he limits himself to one beer when, normally, a bottle of Chianti would slip down without a burp, followed by a double grappa 'to get the knees bending'. After lunch is normally the only moment of the day that my father truly flows down the slopes.

The sun has climbed over the mountain and the ascent in the chairlift is almost cosy compared to the morning journey with my father. Then, the icy slopes were in shadow and glistening like wet knife blades. His beard had a coating of hoarfrost and the cold chiselled under my nails, turning my fingers into throbbing lumps. Now the lift hums benignly where it had clinked and clonked irritably and the sound of skis below is a soft, reassuring swish rather than an ominous icy rattle. Shouts and laughter ring through the trees and occasional splashes of vivid colour show where trails through the woods cross from one piste to the other.

I feel good about Sun Valley. For skiers it has intimations of paradise. The guys who man the lifts dust snow from the seats and smile at you. They ask if you are having a good time as if they really care about your response. There are Kleenex dispensers. The sun shines. The snow is good. As a habitué of European slopes, where the lift people seem to have been recruited predominantly from the ranks of redundant Stasi interrogators praying that Santa will bring them a high voltage cattle goad for Christmas, this is a major breakthrough. And skiers waiting in line actually wave you ahead of them. I was suspicious at first, thinking that a crevasse must have opened up. After skiing in Austria, I had assumed that the first two World Wars must have broken out in ski lift lines and that the Archduke Franz Ferdinand had been assassinated by a Bierkeller of bratwurst salesmen because he stepped on the sales manager's Dynastars. But this is different. It could become habit-forming. It will be different to go back to the ways of the Old World.

My father is scornful of what he describes as the 'Have a nice day!' syndrome but I have no problems with someone who can replicate friendliness and good cheer rather than deliver straight from the heart, totally unfeigned, bloody-minded indifference.

As I approach the summit, I start worrying. Will it be the same? Will she even turn up? Did I dream it all? I nearly fall over leaving the lift and catch an outside edge twenty yards later. I have difficulty skiing on gentle slopes. On the other hand, I am not infallible on the difficult ones. Relax. 'Bend ze ankles', as my old Austrian ski instructor used to say. At least nobody else is wearing my ski suit. Or anything like it. Or anything even faintly resembling it. Maybe it is a little too, too radical. But I can't worry about that now. Though I will. Meet the rest of the gang, little worry. I am early, of course. I could do a run to warm up but there might be a line at the bottom and I then I would be late back and miss her. Best to stay here and ponder whether to wear my shades or tilt them to the top of my head. Maybe I could flip them back nonchalantly as she approaches. I try it and they drop into the snow behind me. I have just picked them up when Clint Eastwood comes out of the restaurant. In the flesh. Weathered, but definitely all his. He is with someone who must be famous because they are wearing a mink parka and huge dark glasses so that you cannot see who they are. Playground of the stars. Wow.

I am still staring whilst pretending to look somewhere else when Rashmi glides over from one of the lifts. Jeans. Floppy Fair Isle sweater. Very uncomplicated. But you can tell. The way she ingests the bumps like the suspension on a '52 Cadillac. She's got it.

"Well, well." She shimmies to a hockey stop in front of me, spraying snow up to my knees. "Little Boy Blue. Is this what they're wearing in Europe this year?"

"Every last son of a bitch," I tell her. "It's like the sky fell on the slopes."

We look at each other and it is still there. Dug in for the winter. Ten foot high neon letters across the front of Macy's. Being towed across the sky above us by stuttering biplanes. We are young, we are beautiful, we are indefatigable. 'Bliss was it in that dawn to be alive'.

"Do your lips only come out at night?" she asks. "What does a girl have to do to get kissed around here?"

"You just did it."

Other people falling in love can be pretty tedious. Like their new car or the condo they are straining to buy with grandpa's legacy. You hope everything works out but you are not all that concerned. What is the big deal? But with your own love affair. Ah, there you enter a state akin to a fusion of 'Spring' in Bambi with the last three minutes and fifteen seconds of 'Tristan und Isolde'. You realise that Shakespeare and all the great writers, artists and composers were creating specifically with you in mind. You are sublime, you are unique - and you are very stupid.

Rashmi skies better than I do but it is of no importance because I start falling just so she can pull me up and I can pull her down and we can neck. We neck on the slopes, we neck in the woods, we neck on the lifts. We blow each other's noses with Sun Valley Kleenex while we wait in line: 'Little Boy Blue, come blow my nose'. We think we are s-o-o-o funny. We are having the best time. And when we nearly miss the last connecting lift and skim down to Warm Springs four inches above the snow and drink hot chocolate and I kiss her goodbye for the fifteenth time and cover the distance to the hotel like my ski boots are five league dancing pumps, I hardly notice that my father is sitting on his bed with his head in his hands.

"It was great out there this afternoon," I tell him.

He picks a letter off the bedside table and hands it to me. Immediately I feel uneasy. Very uneasy. Like my report card has arrived. "What is it?"

"Read it."

"Did it come here?"

"Read it."

Something to do with the car, articulates the pain in my stomach. I read. It is short and couched in arcane legal jargon. "I don't understand. What's 'Miss Butterfly'?"

"It's 'Madame Butterfly' for fifteen year olds. It's a movie I dreamed up and wrote for Larry to produce."

"Larry Sabel?"

"The same."

"So what's this about?"

"It's from Larry. He's firing me from my own project. From our project."

"The letter-"

"-says that I'm in breach of my contract because I delivered the second rewrite two days late and that I'm only going to receive the money I've already had for the first draft, and that they're going to proceed without me. It's technically correct that I delivered two days late but that was because I was finishing a story outline for a project Larry had set up."

"Can they do this? It seems incredible. Your own agent-producer, manager-whatever. Surely you can sue?"

He laughs with a noise like a waste disposal unit digesting glass. "Did you notice who signed that letter? The rat fink lawyer who's representing us in the car business. Larry's lawyer. While you're filling their glasses with champagne, they're pissing on your boots."

"Get another lawyer. Sue them. They can't do this to you."

"They've done it. Suing isn't going to do any good. It's just throwing away money I haven't got."

"But people should know about this. You're supposed to be Sabel's client for God's sake."

"Everybody knows that Larry is a two-timing little shit. He's highly respected for it. Why should I give him any free publicity?"

"But don't you care?" He remains silent. "You thought he was your friend."

He winces as if the word hurts. "Yes, that was stupid, wasn't it? After all I've said. It's amazing. This place never loses the ability to surprise you. You try to imagine the worst so you're prepared for it but somebody always comes up with something a little more ingenious."

"So what about 'War and Peace in Space'?" The question is not posed without a degree of self interest. "Is that finished?"

My father struggles. Pain? Principles? Uncertainty? "Looks like it. As far as I'm concerned. Yes, I suppose so. It doesn't seem as if our Russian chumskis are about to lock shoulders through the door, does it?"

"You couldn't work with Larry again, anyway. Or them." I wait. "What a shit. He probably sent you up here to get you out of the way. The Godorosky. "I attempt a scornful laugh.

My father slowly rises to his feet and rubs his hands over his face as if attempting to rearrange the position of his flesh against his bones. Rashmi is right. He doesn't look so great.

"You have to believe, William. You have to make it your shibboleth. If you don't, you're doomed. You have to plunge your hand into the slim and feel for the thread. Things will crawl against your flesh but you must keep delving. Eventually, with luck, your fingers will close about something and you can start to pull. Normally, the thread will snap immediately and you'll have to find another one. But when you've pulled the twentieth thread, it might just grow into a piece of string, and if that doesn't snap it'll become a cord that will thicken into a rope. And if you keep pulling long enough and nobody axes the rope, one day, one bright and shiny day, a crock of gold will plop out of the slime. The name of the thread is belief. Not hope. Hope isn't strong enough. Belief. God. The Godorosky. Anything that's going to make it happen for you."

I listen to this and think how fate never gives you a break. All I wanted in the world was to be left alone with Rashmi. And now?

"So, I suppose this is it." I wait. "We go back to L.A."

He reads my face and cranks out a smile. "No. Fuck 'em'! We'll finish our holiday."

Boy, what a father. How do I love thee? Fetch me an adding machine.

"Of course, we have no money, but what the hell? You know Alexander Korda's maxim: 'Always stay at the best hotels and eat at the best restaurants and, sooner or later, someone will come up and offer you money'. By the way, there was some good news. They've found the car. The bloody little lawyer rang just before the letter arrived. Didn't mention that, of course. Not a dicky bird. Somebody turned up to rent the house and saw it." He studies my face attentively. "No mention of the police."

"They can't have followed up my call."

"No." He continues to stare at me. "You can't rely on anyone, can you?"

"Seems like it," I say uncomfortably. "So what's-"

The telephone rings. He hesitates, then picks it up. "Yes, surely. Put her on." He covers the mouthpiece. "Constance."

I start to withdraw discretely. "Tell her I haven't heard from Zaiferts."

"Of course." He holds up a restraining hand. "William."

"Yes?"

"I'm glad you're here."

I go into the sitting room and turn on the television which has a special channel with nubile adumbrations of Rashmi flitting around on skis and telling you how wonderful Sun Valley is. I know that. It is the rest of the world I am worried about; Hollywood now shouldering its way centre stage. After what is happening to my father - what always seems to be happening to my father - do I really need a career in the movie business? His response to adversity is admirable and in the guts-it-out tradition of 'Rudolph the Faithful Mosquito', 'Doris the Dedicated Dishcloth' and 'Ursula the Undesirable Ugly Fruit' - Ursula's big problem was her beauty. She was so attractive that none of the other ugly fruit wanted to be seen with her. She was on the shelf because she wasn't on the shelf. Then, one happy day, a pumpkin fell on her face.

I am pretty certain, let's say convinced, that I do not possess the same resilience as my father. I would much rather take Rashmi by the hand and steal back to Pulignac where we would lie in the big brass bed in the warm pink stone house and smell the freshly cut hay and listen to the red squirrels scampering across the tiles and the nightingales singing in the moonlight. You don't need a load of money to live there and it's a wonderful place to bring up bilingual children - unless you're French, of course. I could fatten geese and grow walnuts. Each tree brings in forty euros a year, so if I planted a hundred trees that would be four thousand euros a year which is…approximately…forty-eight hundred dollars. Uhm. Shit. Even the old man who lives in the collapsing caravan on *Le Depot des Ordures* probably brings in more than that.

My father emerges from the bathroom. "The plot sickens. That distribution deal Bronski talked to Constance's lot about. It wasn't for 'War and Peace in Space'. It was for 'That Girl from Minsk'."

"You're losing me a bit."

"That's what they're calling 'Miss Butterfly'. Bloody awful title. They've changed it so that the American rock star flies in to give a glasnost anniversary concert. Glasnost. Who remembers fucking glasnost?"

"You'd changed Pinkerton to a rock star?"

"And his name too. What was Puccini on? Pinkerton? Sounds like a pantywaist with a fir cone up his arse. Anyway, who gives a shit? The bastards must have been cooking this up behind my back while they tried to get 'War and Bollocks' off the ground. Igor is going to direct and do the rewrite. Can you imagine the dialogue?"

"I won't see it," I say loyally. I had taken Bronski and Igor and my father's evaluation and share his sense of betrayal. They are not rough-hewn, good old boyars, misty-eyed before the American dream but like everyone else in town.

"You won't get the chance. It'll never see the light of one fine dayski. But it's a blow, I don't mind telling you. I was budgeting on the money for the revisions seeing us through 'til the end of the year. Now I've got to find something else fast. And I don't have an agent. And there's the bloody car. And the hotel bill. And the lawyer's fees. Not to mention the money a demented, sick society demands that I pay your mother and her snivelling little pimp."

Maybe we should all go back to Pulignac. Instead of Candide, Cunegonde and the Old Woman, there will be William, Rashmi and Lock Senior. He can settle down to that book he is always talking about. We could all settle down to something. '*Cultivons notre jardin*'. Why not?

"Thank heavens there are a few people like Constance about. She's very sweet really. Thoroughly unappreciated. I was thinking of asking her up for the weekend. You wouldn't mind, would you?"

"Not a bit." Great. While he is teaching Constance to snowplough, I can be skimming across the Elysian Fields with Rashmi and a clear conscience. "What did she say about my script analysis?"

"Shit! I forgot to ask her. With all the other stuff it went clean out of my mind. I'll see if I can bring some pressure to bear at the weekend. Okay?"

"Sure." I feel almost relieved. Like discovering that the exam results will be late. I sense that he feels the same way too. All problems present and accounted for, formed into three ranks and ordered to stand easy for a while. He rubs his hands together briskly.

"Right. I'm beginning to feel hungry. Let's brave the hellish cold and hit Ketchum. I'm told that's where the cognoscenti take their beef injections." He sees my mouth beginning to open. "Bring the girlfriend if she'd like to come."

"Er-well, yes, thanks, I'll ask her." I can't keep them apart for ever and, unsavoury thought, even if we are destitute, he is in better shape to pick up the tab than I am. It would also be a lousy night to leave him by himself.

Rashmi expresses herself as being receptive to the idea and says that she will make a reservation and meet us there 'panting like a bitch on heat'. Father and I 'wrap up warm' as Nebraska gran would advise and catch the shuttle bus that winds through the snowy lanes picking up and dropping off people who all seem to know each other until it deposits us in the ordered heart of Ketchum - named after somebody who passed through looking for something better. Dignified dogs still appear to be driving pick-ups down Main Street and what look like the only traffic lights in town are providing the illuminations. The grid of streets is empty of pedestrians which is no surprise as you would have to be hooked on hypothermia to risk walking more than two blocks. The cold presses in like a mould of ice stealing space in my lungs. I can feel my skin tightening as it freezes. We waddle flat-footed along slippery sidewalks like nervous penguins testing the ice and approach the restaurant that has the facade of a western saloon. The exterior portals could guard a mausoleum but beyond, the warmth wraps you in an embrace and there are louvered swings doors leading to a noisy bar with a brass foot rail, spittoons, sawdust floor, and what looks like every brand of Bourbon ever distilled. The patron weighs us up like men with heavy stubble who have just ridden into town on stolen horses and Rashmi emerges from a garland of admirers to buss me on the lips and shake my father's hand. It is a moment to reassess one's worth. Envy and grudging respect are emotions I would like to think I can detect on some of the male faces as we pass through to the dining area where a log fire blazes at the end of the room and there are round tables with oil lamps, wagon wheel candelabra and more balconies for bad guys to plunge over. A glance at what the diners are consuming tells me that the words nouvelle cuisine would be considered an obscenity, given that anyone knew what you were talking about. Steaks droop over the side of plates the size of gongs and the salads could be confused with flower arrangements knocked up by Constance Spry when fighting drunk. Thank God that love on skis has the appetite of a behemoth.

Father is good as gold. Adversity has drawn some of his teeth. He drinks sparingly of a wine tasted with the minimum of glass-swirling and lip-smacking and even winds back his arm and passes the conversational ball rather than snatching it to his chest and driving remorselessly towards an invisible, and seldom discovered, goal line. He does not start every reminiscence with 'As I've probably told you before' - a device employed when he suspects that he probably has told you before but cannot remember when because he is too pissed. He even listens with apparent interest, or at least tolerance, to what other people are saying, an eerie experience for those used to dining with him, and finally, just when I am feeling that the frustration of merely squeezing Rashmi's hand beneath the table and grinding my foot against hers will cause me to explode, he says that he has some calls to make, signs an open check, tips handsomely and walks out into the night.

"I think he's sweet," says Rashmi.

"He is."

"Sweet and kind of sad. He seems unfulfilled."

"He's had a bad day. His agent's just dumped on him. But don't worry. You've been in the presence of the comeback king."

"We should have asked him to stay."

"He'd have refused. He could sense that we wanted to be alone."

"He's your father, William. You should be nice to him in a while."

"I bend over backwards to be nice to him. You have no idea."

Silence. Are we arguing? It would be a good moment for a server to arrive and ask if we want any more coffee but they don't.

"We don't really know a lot about each other, do we?" She is holding my hand, but lightly, like it just drifted into her grasp.

"How much do we have to know right off? I mean, we've only just met-sort of really met. Time…time will tell, won't it? I know it's a cliché. At the moment you're like a beautiful but unopened box-"

"Pandora's box."

"Not if you want to cheer me up. No, you're wrapped in hundreds of pieces of shiny paper. I'm peeling them off one by one."

"That sounds sexy." Her hand comes to life.

"Good." I draw closer and rest my nose against her cheek.

"You're like your father." She runs a finger across my chest. "You both express yourselves in images. You have to borrow the words."

"I want to be alone with you. Somewhere where it isn't thirty below."

"We have to, don't we? Sooner or later."

"Not if you don't want to." I am not certain that I mean this. I wait. "What's going through your mind?"

She smiles. "I've asked so many people that and never got a coherent response. What's going through your mind?"

"I want to make love to you. I want us to make love to each other. Simple biological stuff."

"Simple? Yes, yes. I guess it is simple. Okay. Right. Let's do it." She leans closer and kisses me. "I'm sorry. I could have sounded more enthusiastic, couldn't I?"

"A little bit. I wasn't suggesting we marched outside and did it in the car."

"It would have been a lousy idea. The heater's on the blink. It would have put you under unfair pressure and the worst might have happened."

"Frozen to death in the back seat in the sedentary position."

"A monument to American youth."

"But still smiling."

"Lips permanently parted in a rictus of ecstasy. I think that's what it is. The curse of biological necessity. I hate being told what to do. I feel like a little dog that's being sent off to make itself ridiculous by the side of the road."

"How many bodily functions does this feeling cover?"

"Only that one. But you're right. It probably all goes back to toilet training. Pestalozzi strikes again. Perhaps you're what I need, Willum. Someone who hasn't been screwed up."

I spring to my defence. "I've been screwed up. You must know about English public schools. It's just a different form of screwing up. They all get you in the end." I lose myself in the beautiful violet eyes. "I'd only be screwed up if I didn't think I loved you."

She closes her eyes. Maybe it's a blink. "I need to get used to that word. It frightens me."

"I mean it."

"That's what frightens me." She squeezes my arm. "I'm sorry. Come on. We'll go back to my place."

"If you don't-"

"I do. All right? We don't have to pay anything, do we?"

"It's all taken care of."

The same faces, a tad more blurred by our mutual drinking, wallpaper the bar as we go out. Some of them say goodnight - always to Rashmi. I am taking away their girl - or someone who ought to be their girl. Outside, there seem to be even fewer lights and the wind stalks the icy sidewalks like a maniac with a switchblade. Down these dark streets Hemingway did walk. And in that invisible house up there on the hillside - he blew his brains out. How terrible those words are. The shock never goes away.

We crunch across to the car and scrape ice off the windshield. Rashmi has a de-icing spray but it is frozen. Now I am convinced. The heater definitely does not work. I watch my breath turn into a scrollwork of ferns against the glass and wonder what conversation with Rashmi's mother will be like. How fast things change. One moment you can feel as if another person's blood is making your heart pump, the next, be sitting beside them in frozen silence racking your brains for something to say. I start to pull off my gloves. "Open the window. I'll keep the windshield clear while you drive."

"Keep your gloves on; you'll stick to the glass."

"That's what I want." I press my hand against the windshield and feel the greedy cold snap my finger tips like a thousand tiny sucking mouths. "I want something physical to happen."

She seizes my hand and tears it away. "Oh, William. Don't be stupid. I want it too. I do." She kisses me clumsily. "Put your glove on. It'll warm up. I'll warm up."

I hold her to me. "God, your nose is cold."

"It's because I'm very healthy. Let me go. We'll never get there."

She pulls away and the car snaps from its icy mooring.

"Does your mother have something hot to drink?"

"I'll make you something, little William. You're not going to see my mother."

She drives slowly and I try to keep the windshield clear, peering doggedly ahead out of the open window, going half-blind as my right eye waters and freezes over. It feels as if someone is hammering an iron stake into my brain. Luckily, the streets are empty except for a few bird dogs driving their masters' pick-ups home and we leave the town grid and pass 'Our Lady of the Snows' Catholic Church. The road begins to climb and the snow beside it gets deeper. Home lights glow snug and yellow behind clumps of snow-covered Douglas firs and slimmer spruces and larches. The interval between homes gets longer, and we are in darkness when we leave the road and bump along a frozen driveway with laden branches scraping the side of the car like brushes in a car wash. The snow dumps on my lap and I struggle to get the window closed.

"Don't die on me. We're nearly there."

The house is a forest, trimmed and reassembled as three sides of a rectangle. Big, solid, opulent. The porch light glistens on the banked snow and I recognise the back of the station wagon sticking out of the treble garage. There is a battered pick-up outside one wing of the house and Pink Floyd coming from behind a half-drawn curtain. As I get out and try and rub my face alive, Marlboro Man peers out at us for a second through the icicles before flicking the curtain closed almost contemptuously.

"That's Joe," explains Rashmi. "One hell of an uncomplicated guy. He looks after the place when we're not here." She crunches past the front door to the opposite wing that looks as if it might be a stable block. "This is me. The door always freezes." She puts her shoulder against it and there is a sharp crack as it snaps open and she stumbles forward to the foot of a flight of stairs. I follow in a flurry of snow, grateful for the warmth. She switches on a light, stamps her feet and bolts the door behind us. I like that. "It gets better." I follow her up the stairs and it becomes even warmer. Another door opens into a long panelled room with a combined kitchen/bar at one end and two doors leading off at the other. There are stirring Ansel Adams photographs of the American wilderness on the wall and a scattering of books. My eye alights on 'In the clearing'.

Rashmi picks up a phone and taps out a number. "Hi, I'm back… fine…and you…goodnight." She puts down the phone." That's mother taken care of. Now she can watch Jay Leno." She waves a hand round the room. "How do you like it? It's not bad, is it? A little preppy. I ought to have a Montessori pennant on the wall. I wonder if they do one?"

"It's slightly smaller than Buckingham Palace, but I'm still impressed."

"And with much higher moral values. That's what we pride ourselves on here. Come, I'll reveal the geography of the place. Isn't that what you say in England when you show someone the john?"

She throws open the door to a large, untidy bedroom with layers of clothes piled on chairs and the satin feet of a child-sized patchwork doll protruding from beneath the bed. "That's Hagatha, a relic of my unsullied childhood. She only gets to use the bed when I'm not here. Merely queen-size, I'm afraid. It's mother's compromise between space for a growing girl and a licence to throw orgies." She pushes past me into the bathroom. "Let's see if there's anything I don't want you to see in here."

I go back into the living room. It seems more mature than standing by the bed panting. I am also a little scared. In fact, more than a little scared. I pick up a book of Robert Frost's poems. "How many places do you have?"

Her voice flows in from the bedroom. I hear drawers opening. "There's an apartment in New York, a shed in the Hamptons, a house in L.A. and this place."

I put down the book. "Some might say you're rich."

She comes in and slides her arms round my neck. "Beyond the dreams of avarice. You know, I always thought that avarice was a person."

"Like Avarice Harriman."

"Precisely. I think it's rather a pretty name. Little Avarice. I can see her with her podgy little fingers wedged in the cookie jar."

I gaze into Rashmi's eyes and see two little Avarice Locks. Or maybe, an Avarice Lock and a Cupidity Lock. She backs away.

Before we go any further, there's something you ought to know." She raises her voice. "I'm a virgin." She smiles and waits. "I said that in case my mother has the place bugged. She's fainted now, so we can carry on." She reads my expression. "I'm sorry. Shall we light the fire and have some coffee? They're both artificial, I'm afraid."

She starts towards the kitchen but I hang on to her. "And I used to think Catherine the Great's lovers had it tough."

"We never did rude history. Not at any of my schools."

"She used to have them examined by her Scottish doctor. Then put through their paces by her senior lady-in-waiting."

"Shit. It's the staff's night off. You mean, I'm going to have to do all this by myself?" She start's to ruffle the hair at the back of my neck.

"Then, one day, with one of the putative - or perhaps, in the circumstances, Putinative - lovers, Korsakov, I think it was-"

"Rimsky's little boy?"

"Very possibly. The inevitable happened."

She raises her eyes. "He fell in love with the Scottish doctor."

I love a girl with a sense of humour. It's a great relaxant. But a great relaxant and grand passion are not ideal bed mates and I had set my heart on grand passion. Still, in life you have to settle for what you can get and the grand passion can come later. That's what I tell myself as we help each other out of our clothes and start to make love. I have the feeling that I am overseeing a military exercise in which the equipment is being tested before a battle that could change the course of history. I remain slightly outside my body, watching it anxiously for any signs of mechanical failure, very aware that too much apprehension could precipitate the feared disaster. It does not let me down and Rashmi is beautiful. A slimmer version of any woman I have ever yearned for in a classical painting where you meet a very nice class of naiad. I can imagine her tiptoeing into a pool with the elders peering through the bulrushes or taming wild beasts with an urn on her head. There are no hidden flaws. She does not have a pierced belly button or a tattoo of Alice Cooper on her inner thigh. She is tender and considerate. I am energetic, probably over so. Bounding round her body trying to find switches that will turn her on, desperate to pour feeling into her. I want to mark my territory with my body, make her mine. What she is feeling is a mystery. When I try and talk, she presses a hand against my mouth. Her eyes are often closed. Tight. I hope that time will tell me what she likes.

When it seems to be over and we are lying eye to eye I still cannot read her mind. "That was great," she says. "You were like Tigger in 'Winnie-the-Pooh'."

"Thank you - I think. Is that all?"

She turns and wriggles her back into me so that we are in the spoons position. "I love Tigger."

"Then I guess I'll have to settle for that."

She reaches back and tugs my arm around her. "Hold me for a bit and I'll make us something to drink." I wait for her to say more but she makes a little sighing noise and falls asleep.

The next morning, I call my father and suggest that we all go skiing together. I still have an adolescent feeling of guilt for having stayed out all night. So stupid. Constance is coming up at the weekend and he has got hold of Larry. He is vague about what passed between them but it sounds as if Larry was apologetic and trying to play the whole thing down. Surprise, surprise. What really pisses me off is that father has still not asked Constance about my script analysis.

The other news is that Western Rentals are saying that we have to buy them a new car but that our lawyer thinks he can make a deal. I am just relieved that they haven't dusted the back of the car for fingerprints though with Rashmi on board I feel better equipped to deal with fate's little jabs.

There is no sign of Rashmi's mother when we leave but Joe raises his head from beneath the hood of his pick-up. He looks me up and down like he could eat two of me for breakfast. It is almost as if he is jealous.

Father is waiting in reception at Little Elk Lodge with an attentive Ellen resplendent in a fluffy sweater of caterpillar pink. He looks the better for a night's sleep. "We're invited to a party on Saturday night," He explains with forced cheerfulness. "Ellen's throwing a little hootenannay. Is that the word?"

"Not really," says Ellen modestly. "Just a few folks dropping by for cheese and wine. You make sure to come along and bring your ma, Rashmi."

"Should be a laugh riot," says my father as we head for the elevator. "At least it'll give me the chance to lie to Vernon about his ghastly book."

I let him and Rashmi share the chair in front and watch them chatting as we ascend the first stage of the lift system. It is another perfect day in Idaho. Cold, but the sun will be shining on the far side of the mountain and more snow is forecast for tonight. Father would make a good grandfather. Full of wise saws and a great dandler. Already, I can see Avarice and Cupidity wedged between him and Rashmi on the chair. But maybe Avarice will have a brother? I ponder. Greed Lock. Hmn. I like the sound of it, but...I will have to ponder some more.

We get to the top and I feel myself inflating, eager for challenge. I want Clint Eastwood to be taken hostage by terrorists so I can storm Bartelli's Mountain Café single handed, waste the bad guys and bear him to safety under a tornado of exploding San Pellegrino bottles. I am responsible for all around me. My ageing father, Rashmi, our unborn children. They need me. They have me.

My father wheezes as he snaps his bindings tight. "Let's hope these work better than the last lot."

In fact, this is the reverse of what he hopes. Experience has shown that he always needs at least one item of equipment that can be deemed faulty and thus held responsible for the inevitable deficiencies of style and performance. If he ever put on the perfect skis, boots and bindings there would be nothing left to blame as he continued to face-plant and hold yard sales all down the slopes.

"Now, where are we going to go?" He straightens up awkwardly and adjusts his glasses. I am about to suggest that we ski the bowls but he is already launching himself down a simple blue run like the carcass of an ocean liner rumbling down a slipway. I watch Rashmi go after him, holding herself in check. She does ski beautifully. I feel another surge of male pride and possession. I have made love to that stunning creature. I have ventured where no man - well, not too many, I hope - has ventured before. Certainly none of the deprived hundreds currently whizzing past us like sparks from a grindstone.

Father is skiing within himself, testing the snow to see if it is user-friendly. A series of awkward turns with a clumsy transference of weight from one ski to the other and a jerky up and down movement that comes more from the shoulders than from the knees. Not a pretty sight. He skis like that because the turns slow him down and when he falls it will not hurt so much. Those ageing bones are getting brittle. The marrow is turning into dust. I dig my poles in and jump start like a downhill racer going through the gate. It is frustrating to see the old buzzard plodding down this bowling green like it is the north face of the Eiger. I want to kick snow in his face, reveal how feeble he is. I want to show off to Rashmi.

I skate a few yards and drop into a tuck. Father is a hundred yards down the slope and a further twenty yards below him is a small mogul by the side of the piste. I will schuss past him and take off from that mogul like an eagle. It will give him a mild scare and look impressive. I begin to pick up speed. Faster, faster. The cold stings my cheeks. Father is making a wide turn with Rashmi behind him. He is coming in from my left. Faster, faster. I will just miss him and go into my jump. He hears or senses me, turns his head, sees me out of the corner of his eye, panics, catches an edge, falls-SHIT!! He is sliding across the slope. We are on a collision course. One of his skis comes off. I try to change direction but I can't. WACK! I hit his ski and fight to stay upright. My vision fragments. I am at the edge of the trail. ICE!! Shit! Oh, SHIT! Oh-! I've lost it! HELP! Into the void. I hang in space and, for long seconds, everything seems to be happening in slow motion. The light has turned grey. I can see the valley far below. And the deep, frozen snow like whorls of shaving cream. And the black tips of rocks poking through it. Then-click! I'm back in living time. The second hand spurts forward and I hit the rocks. PAIN! Immediate. Agonising. Terrible seconds. I am static. Have I broken my back? Can I move my legs? Is there anything sticking into me? Out of me?

I am lying on my back and I look up to see my father staring down at me from the rim of the ridge. He is biting his sleeve and talking through the material. "Oh, my God; Oh, my God; Oh, my God!" he mumbles. His eyes are full of tears and terror.

"I'm okay," I shout. I wave one of my sticks which seems very light. I realise it has snapped in two. I am trying to encourage myself. Power of mind over matter. The back of my head throbs and feels wet and sticky. And when I move my legs - aaargh!! That hurts. I have done something to one of my ankles. My father and Rashmi scramble down towards me. I am feeling woozy. I want to throw up. "Poor darling." Rashmi hesitates and touches my cheek gingerly. I try to sit upright. "SHIT!!" My coccyx reacts in fury.

"Careful!" My father pulls Rashmi away and winces as he sees her hand. There is dark red blood on it from the back of my head. He starts to forage nervously. Argh! "All right, all right. I think you've cut your scalp.

It doesn't seem too bad. You'll need some stitches." Now real concern enters his voice. "Can you move your legs?"

I point towards my ankle and his face screws up, anticipating the worst. He is muttering to himself through clenched teeth, half prayers, half curses. His mouth is orange and I think he must have bitten his tongue. Then I realise that it is the dye from his ski suit. He has chewed through one of the sleeves. He unzips the leg of my suit at the ankle and gently eases up the material. "Christ! It's pretty swollen. Maybe it's broken. Thank God." I imagine he means 'Thank God it isn't any worse'. He looks around and I know what he is thinking. Beneath the banked snow, the rocks are huge jagged teeth and I have managed to get myself wedged between two of them. It is a miracle I am not dead. I stare at the white pigment in the rock and begin to feel cold and faint.

My father pulls himself to his feet. Suddenly he seems strong. "I'll stay with him. You get some help."

Rashmi hesitates and drops to her knees beside me. "You be a good boy and don't move. I'll be right back. I love you."

She runs her hand across my chest and kisses me. As she stands up, she kisses my father. He watches her scrambling up the ridge before returning to me. "What the hell were you doing back there?" I start to open my mouth but he drops down beside me and takes my hand. "It doesn't matter. Just don't do it again when I'm sober." He kisses me and I can smell the daiquiri. "I love you too. It must be your lucky day."

I get lifted off by a helicopter, which makes me think of Vietnam and I half expect a hail of bullets to follow us into the air. The guys who do the retrieving could have been there. They look tough and other worldly and chew gum, and you soon figure that this is not the first time they have done this. You are an inevitability, a statistic. Without them there would be unsightly piles of faded polyester and bleached bones all over the slopes.

At the surgery, the first thing they examine is my father's credit card. When that proves healthy, they give me an x-ray and a doctor who has made a bad choice of cologne informs me that I have mild concussion and a cracked something or other in my ankle. Apparently it is bone heaven down there and you can't move for the little rascals. He sews up my scalp - ten stitches - and puts my lower leg in plaster. He, too, appears to have done this many times before and, to my father's relief, restricts himself to treating injuries he can see. He does not run tests for rickets, beriberi or schistosomiasis, thus turning me into a profitable growth industry and forging a bond that could exist for the rest of our lives - at least via our lawyers. In Beverly Hills you can go to the doctor with bunions and come out with a nose bob and a three year programme of preventive surgery.

My father says nothing, but behind his eyes I can see numbers ringing up as on a cash register. All this is going to cost a fortune and he has always spurned medical insurance, claiming that it only encourages you to be sick. Once the body knows that a free hospital bed is available it immediately searches for an excuse to climb into it. That is his theory. On the other hand, knowing that you are going to have to pay an iniquitously large sum for treatment is one of the most effective pain killers conceived by man.

My father believes that most illnesses are psychosomatic - except his, of course - and that Americans would be better off gobbling handfuls of germs rather than vitamins. He argues that their obsession with bodily cleanliness and hygiene is in fact profoundly unhealthy and that by denying themselves the chance to build up useful immunities they run the risk of perishing in droves at the grubby hands of the first itsy-bitsy little germ that the average Englishman would snap up for tea with jam on it.

There was no room for Rashmi in the chopper and she is waiting at the hotel when we get back, having alerted the staff to the near tragedy. Ellen's large bosom wobbles with concern and almost too many hands attempt to support me back to our suite. I feel like the Stars and Stripes being raised at Iwo Jima. All I want is to be left alone with Rashmi, to salvage something from the day, but by the time I am helped out of my tattered suit and into bed, I am feeling like a real invalid. "I'll see you tomorrow," she says, leaning over me and darting her mouth down against mine. "No break dancing, okay?"

I wait for her to tell me once more that she loves me, but she goes off with my father.

11.

The next morning I feel better. Stiff and aching but better. My head has cleared and, in its plaster adobe, my ankle throbs softly like an electric fence. I ease my way out of bed and start to practice walking with crutches. Apparently, after a few days, I should be able to hobble around without them, but the plaster is going to be with me for weeks. That this should happen at this particular point in my life is one gigantic pisser and the only thing that stops me screaming out loud is the thought of how it might have been even worse.

Rashmi shows up after breakfast when my father has 'sallied forth in search of simoleons', as he chooses to call going to the bank, and I am miffed to find her dressed for the slopes. I had visualised her in a cute little nurse's uniform carrying a copy of 'A Farewell to Arms'.

"You look a whole lot better," she says, perching on the arm of my chair. "I think I could go for you with that bandage round your head. You look like John McEnroe when he used to scream. Or maybe Tutankhamun."

"Thank," I tell her. "But I'm choked. You're going skiing? I thought you'd stick around so we could play gin and read Emily Dickinson to each other."

"People don't do that any more." She kisses me. "Be proud of me. I'm going to devote the morning to good works. I'm going to teach your father how to ski."

The idea is grotesque. She must be joking. "Better men than you have tried and failed. Some of them were paid extravagant sums of money. Let him go by himself. Then you can creep into bed with me. Haven't you ever dreamed of having a man in a plaster cast completely at your mercy?"

"Not since I read 'Catch 22'. Listen, William. If your father could ski a little better he might not incite you to kill yourself. Hundreds of lives could be saved."

"The accident was his fault."

"No, it wasn't. You hit him from behind. You know the rules." I chew on this. Technically, she is correct. And if I was a better skier I would have avoided him. "And I'm going to introduce him to mother." She drops to her knees beside me and produces a ballpoint. "I think they might get on. He was so torn apart when he thought you might have killed yourself. It was really touching." She starts to write on the cast.

"Christ. You're a proper little Henry Kissinger, aren't you?"

"Just want to leave the world a better place." She rises and kisses me on the mouth. "Be good and don't play with yourself while I'm gone."

I hang on to her as she starts to pull away. "Do you remember what you said yesterday? On the rocks?"

"Yes," she says. "I remember."

When she has gone, I think a bit and then twist my head to read what she has written on the plaster: an arrow pointing to 'PISSOIR POUR CHIENS'.

Left to my own devices, I struggle into some clothing and go for a little hobble around Warm Springs. Everybody is heading for the slopes and it makes me sick. I feel like a novice eunuch in a harem. And everybody is sympathetic and asks me how I did it, a question they must have asked a hundred times. The only high spot is seeing an expensively dressed and over-made-up woman whose face reminds of how it used to look in the movies they showed on afternoon TV when I was a child. I think it was Janet Leigh or Lauren Bacall (though I am not sure if they are still alive) - or it might have been the ex or future wife of somebody they were previously or subsequently married to. It can get confusing. I know the woman is famous by the way her cold gaze reduces me to a sheet of glass through which she might just notice someone who *was* worth acknowledging.

I have a milkshake and limp back to the lodge to read old magazines. I even start a poem. It must be love. Rashmi and my father show up at one. Just when I am beginning to feel really deserted and peeved. "You won't recognise me!!" he enthuses. "You've got to lean downhill all the time. Rashmo's taught me more in a couple of hours than all the other instructors since the birth of time."

"Four hours," I correct him, vaguely irritated that he dares to mess around with her name.

But he is not listening. "If all the ski instructors in the world were laid end to end," he muses. "Dorothy Parker's estate would sue me for plagiarism."

"I'm hungry," says Rashmi.

After lunch, he takes a nap and she goes home to change. I want to go with her but she explains that this is the afternoon the cleaning woman comes in and she wants Joe to fix the heater in the car.

It is four o'clock in the afternoon when she comes back and my father has gone off for yet more skiing.

"I'm taking you to the movies," she informs me. "'Sun Valley Serenade'. It's years since I saw it. Probably as old as your father."

She is not far off. 'Sun Valley Serenade' is a 1941 movie ostensibly shot in Sun Valley, though it soon becomes clear that the principle players never got within eight hundred miles of the place and that the second unit barely stayed long enough to get snow on their boots. John Payne leans indomitably into a wind machine and we cut to someone doing telemark turns. The Glen Miller orchestra play a few tunes, people dance a lot, and the love interest is provided by Sonja Henie who skates up a storm and has the face of a Cabbage Patch Kid but, unfortunately, not the sex appeal. She is a war refugee in the movie and you can understand why the boys might have preferred to fight on without her.

Maybe I am underestimating Sonja. Her own brother described her as 'Sexually voracious', which added a little frisson to the moments when she does the splits on ice - and close to Hitler (that close?). She also made a couple of movies with Tyrone Power - another veteran of 'Brigham Young, Frontiersman' - and their high jinks in her dressing room could apparently be heard two sound stages away.

The movie is what might be described as a rarity but I would be happy staring at the fire screen if Rashmi was beside me. There is also the considerable period charm of the Sun Valley Opera House where the work is shown daily, a kind of local equivalent of the raising and lowering of Old Glory. We share the auditorium with five other people and neck a lot. It remains one of my favourite cinema-going experiences.

When we come out, it is dark and I vaguely wonder what the world was doing while we were away; though it can't have been very interesting because Rashmi was with me. The rest of the audience separate into the snow and Rashmi helps me back to the car.

I explain to her about the second unit and the wind machine so that she knows I am going to be very big in the movie picture industry but she doesn't seem all that interested.

"It's a cute movie," she says. "I love it when the train pulls into the station with that big cow-catcher thing and they're all driven away in sleighs. Can you imagine coming here by train? Wouldn't that be great?" She stares at me. "What's the matter? Is your ankle all right?"

"Listen."

"I can't hear anything."

I strain my eyes into the violet darkness. The colour of her eyes. Something is coming. Can I really hear it? Maybe I just feel it. There is a 'tinkle, tinkle' like a twitch in the wainscoting and a 'huh, huh, huh' of rhythmic breathing. Then the unmistakeable sound of sleigh bells and a shape, magically billowing into being. Two horses emerge from the darkness pulling a sled, their harness jingling, their breath clouding the air before them. The driver is hunched over them, wrapped like a package, his head and shoulders silhouetted against the sky. And then - snap! - they are gone, like a picture whipped away from before your eyes. The night rolls over them, blankets out the sounds. I strain my ears but I can hear nothing. It is as if they were never there.

"You heard them coming?" She sounds incredulous.

"I felt them. It was weird. Didn't you feel anything?"

She is struggling. "Not quite the way you did."

We go back to her place where Joe is into 'Twisted Sister' and mother is out for the evening. This means that we can scavenge for food after making love - carefully but still painfully - and I call father and tell him that I will not be back until late.

"See you tomorrow then," he says. "Tell Rashmo I'm looking forward to my lesson."

"You're taking the old fart out again? You must be a masochist." We are retiring to her wing with half the contents of the icebox nestling between four slices of rye.

"Why not. He's making progress. Get some into your mouth, please. This rug is on a diet."

I delve for a slice of pickle. "What exactly does your old man do?"

"He doesn't exactly do anything. Not any more."

"You're not exactly forthcoming. I'm beginning to wonder if there's some dark secret."

"Wonder away. I don't feel the need to drag him into every conversation. Not like some people."

"What do you mean?"

"You're always quoting your father. Coming out with little anecdotes about what he did. It's...it's kinda strange to me. He must be a big influence on you."

"I don't know about an influence. He's been around a lot, that's all. While I was growing up. He's a writer. They tend to work from home. Anyway, he'll be back in France soon and, with any luck, I'll be working here." She eats. I wait, "Are you going to carry on being a permanent travelling companion to your mother?"

She shrugs. "Maybe."

"Have you ever had a job?"

"I worked on a magazine in New York. It folded. I'd like to write. Travelling's good for that."

"You could come and stay in France."

"I could." She licks her fingers. "Oh, Willum. You're such a planner, aren't you? Goal-orientated. Everything has to be cut and dried."

"I need to be goal-orientated. I want to make enough money to take you out to dinner."

"Then maybe we're not right."

I feel cold. "Because I don't have any money."

"Because you care about not having any money. It doesn't matter to me. I don't give a shit."

"Because you've got it."

"It's not that. It's because regardless of whether you've got it, just talking about it puts you in a straightjacket, hangs a tag around your neck. It's a form of control and I don't like that."

"So you'd go for me if I was an impoverished free spirit?

She removes a crumb from the corner of her mouth. "Maybe."

Later, much later, I lie beside her as she percolates across the lake of her slumbers making the 'poc-poc-poc' of a distant boat traversing deep waters and I ask myself why she has to be so complicated. Presumably so that I can love her. If she was less difficult, I might not care so much. Poor Lucy dotes on me with totally available passion and I spread her on my bread like peanut butter.

Impervious to every flaw I gaze upon Princess Smug. How peaceful she seems in her ambiguity - or perhaps the ambiguity is mine. The graceful neck a flying buttress to the tilted chin, mouth slightly open, lips poised as if to blow out a candle, her lashes asleep on her cheeks. I want to wake her up and tell her how beautiful she looks.

I can still smell the joint she smoked. She said it would help her to sleep and I said nothing, feeling that I had already offered her a fairly lifelike etching of myself as a control freak. But I was not pleased. Annoyed that, having made love to me, she should crave another opiate, annoyed that she should use a drug, annoyed with myself for saying nothing, annoyed with myself for being a hypocrite. It was only pot for Christ's sake. More than a third of the population of the United States uses it - and me. She was not scoring her fifteenth line of coke or main lining heroine. Her nostrils are impeccable. If she took a sleeping pill, would I be pissed off? Probably. I want to be her drug, her therapy, her panacea.

Not that all is discord. We did decide that we preferred Ollie to Stan - though we like both of them, of course - that Tchaikovsky's First Piano Concerto and Prokofiev's New World Symphony are heart-stirring and toe-tingling, and that we love the end of 'Love and War' when Woody Allen dances with Death along an avenue of trees and it goes on and on - though he should never be allowed to wear shorts or seriously kiss anybody on screen ever again.

That's not bad for three days and it does not even touch upon the fatal happenstance of us both being the progeny of mixed marriages with unusual parents and an international upbringing. Whoah! This is practically incest. And there was that premeditated magic sled tonight. That must have signified something positive. If little Avarice and Cupidity had been with us they would have believed in Father Christmas for the rest of their lives.

When I wake up, it is still dark and Rashmi is leaning over me. "You were having a dream."

"I never dream," I tell her. "Not any more."

"Well you were doing something. Sort of singing in your sleep. Something about cherubim and something else."

"Cherubim?" I think about it. "I know. 'Cherubim and Seraphim, falling down before Thee'. It's a hymn. We used to sing it at Rockingham. My dear old public school. How weird."

"Yes," she says. "But it wasn't 'seraphim'. It sounds crazy, but it was more like 'terrapin'."

I lied to Rashmi. I should have said that I try not to dream. In fact, my dreams are getting worse - and more frequent. Usually, they feature a cat that deposits dead kittens on the counterpane of my bed. I try to brush them off but the pathetic little creatures only proliferate and stick like burrs. Water drips from the cat's bedraggled fur. I think it must be the vicar's cat.

The next day I catch a cold. Through my foot, says Rashmi. Maybe she is right. Nature comes down like a ton of bricks on smart asses who hobble around freezing ski resorts with only a few pairs of socks over their toes. I am put to bed and my father hits the slopes with Rashmi big time. He says that he is making great progress and she does not disagree with him. I am still feeling lousy so he takes her out to dinner with her mother while I doze and drink bottled water until I might as well move my bed into the bathroom.

It is late when he comes in and my ankle is throbbing. Neither of us is able to sleep and I have to listen to him tossing and turning all night. When I eventually do drop off and awake late, it is to find him gone. I am soaking wet but cured. Drinking lots of water always does it for me. My headache has disappeared and I have a rediscovered appetite that hires a dragster to rush me to the breakfast table.

I am half way through my Birchermuesli when Rashmi shows up in jeans and jacket. She looks especially good. No makeup. Very natural. You would demand that she became the mother of your children.

"You look much better." She kisses me on the cheek and drops into the seat opposite.

"So do you. Every time I see you. Why no skiing? Dad's going to be broken-hearted."

"I thought I'd give it a miss today. Spend some time with you."

"Does dad know?"

"Yeah. He's gone off by himself to tame the mountain."

"Let's hope he doesn't lick it into shape with his face. You want some breakfast?"

"Just coffee." She holds up a cup and Ellen sprints over with the brimming pot.

"How did it go last night? Love at first sight?" She stares at me. "Your mother and dad."

"That's just fine, thanks." She steers the pot away with her finger. "I think mother was charmed. She doesn't usually like Englishmen. Her Indian grandparents were killed by British soldiers in a demonstration at Amritsar."

"Christ." I think of father's friend in the car rental business. "Having an empire sure helps when it comes to making friends and influencing people. I don't suppose your father has any Irish blood by any chance?"

"It's possible."

"You don't know?"

"He belongs to a rare blood group - AB Rhesus negative. So he carries eight refrigerated pints of it wherever he goes. Just to be on the safe side. I guess some of it could be Irish."

"Fascinating man, your father. I look forward to meeting him one day. I don't know what blood group my father is."

"It's about the only thing you don't know about him." She starts stirring her coffee vigorously, even though she hasn't put anything in it. Time to change the subject, maybe.

"There was a Frenchman who used to travel everywhere with a cocked pistol in case he got fatally wounded by accident and needed to finish himself off. He was nearly always killing people." I wait. "Imagine having to explain that to the LAPD when you'd accidentally blown somebody's head off. It's like something in a movie, isn't it? I can imagine my father-"

"How much more do you need to eat?" What seems like a restraining hand is on my wrist.

"I'm having the 'Healthy Living Breakfast'," I tell her. "So there's just the low-cholesterol scrambled eggs garnished with fresh fruit and an English muffin. Why?"

"Because I want to go back to the apartment."

We are hardly through the door before she is in my arms. "I'm sorry," she says. "I'm crazy. Let's make love. Please." I am struggling to get a fix on this. I came back to the room not knowing what to expect. She clings to me. "I'm the Lizzie Borden of love. Show me true romance and I give it forty whacks. I'm so lucky to have found you, Willum. You do love me, don't you? Come on." She is pulling me towards the bedroom. "You don't have to make love to me. Just hold me. Tell me about the French guy with the revolver or your first date, or Cambridge. I bet that was nice. I've seen the backs. All those daffodils." She is lying on the bed and I am pulling her jeans over her heels. A sock comes too. The hard skin of her heel rasps my wrist. I have forgotten about my ankle. "And King's Chapel. It's so beautiful it makes you weep, doesn't it? I'd like to go back when the sun was shining. Will you take me, Will?"

"I love you."

"I love you too. Yes. Yes." She wraps her legs about me. "That's good. Don't move. I just want to feel you inside me. Feel buried under you, protected, safe." She tightens her grip. "I don't deserve you but never quote me. I'll swear I never said it. How's your poor ankle? Thank God you didn't fracture your cock. Coarse. Sorry. Those jeans must be killing you. Is that better? You knew at once, didn't you? Because you're smart or you have access to information, or something. I should learn to take advice from the right people - you're moving. All right. Not too much.... please. You're very handsome, Will. It's a pity you can't see yourself from this angle. Delicate little nostrils. You could set fairy tales in them. 'Babes in the Wood', maybe. We're covered in tiny creatures - you probably knew that. They write articles about them every three months when there isn't a serious war somewhere. And your eyes. They're lovely. Sort of green and brown and bloodshot - not too much…not yet. And I don't know if anyone has ever told you, but your upper lip is tattooed with the Dead Sea Scrolls. You're a national treasure, Willum. You should be in a museum, not me. And one day you must tell me how you got that cauliflower ear. Pursuing some manly sport, no doubt. Am I holding you too tight? Get that job in the studio and we'll live together. I'll cook career-enhancing dinner parties. I'll wake up and start baking sugar cakes. You know, like in that old song. You'll take them to the office 'for all the boys to see'. Isn't that crazy?" I think she is laughing but she is crying. "It's all right, it's all right. Maybe we can move into the house. The L.A. house. Mother could come and stay, couldn't she? Parents…" She closes her eyes. "Please… please, William. I want you to come. I love it when you come." She clings to me and I can taste her warm tears, smell the heat of her breath as if it is a potion.

"I love you."

She feels for my mouth. "Come!"

"I love you!" I pull her hand away and we buck and ruck and gulp and gasp until I can tell myself that I have pumped out all her tears and that by the act of pouring myself into her I have made everything all right.

The liquid ceases to bubble. The surface calms. The particles sink to the bottom. If you wait long enough, everything becomes clear.

I hope Rashmi will stay but there is something she has to do. We part with long hugs and I am left to tidy my father's bed and feel the sulking ache in my ankle reassert itself as a centre of attention. I wonder if they are still serving breakfast. I really feel like some scrambled eggs now, maybe with corn beef hash. Or lox and bagels with cream cheese. Why do they bother to have other meals in America? After breakfast, everything is downhill.

I think about what Rashmi was saying. About us living together in the L.A, house. What a fantastic break that would be. I wonder where it is. Brentwood? Belair? Not Beverly Hills, I hope. That would be a little too up-front. I would prefer something more off Broadway. Westwood would do okay. Or Santa Monica. Yes, that would be perfect. I can just see little Avarice and Cupidity trotting down the pier, trying to peer between the planks at the swirling water; slightly overwhelmed by all the hustle and bustle, looking round for the reassuring presence of - me. Dad. He who strolls but a few steps behind with a casual arm around the shoulders of beautiful, smiling mother pushing the baby carriage that contains tiny Parsimony.

At eleven o'clock the phone rings and I immediately think of Constance. She is due in today and I imagine some last minute hitch at the studio. I will take the opportunity to ask her about Zaiferts and my script analysis. Good thinking, Lock.

It is Rashmi. "Hi. Re-hi. Listen, I've just heard that my father's in L.A. I need to see him so I'm flying down."

"Right away!?"

"Yeah. There's a good connecting flight. I can just make it." She sounds very up together.

"When are you coming back?"

A pause. "It depends on my father. He's not always easy to get hold of. A couple of days maybe."

"A couple of days!?"

"Yeah, but you'll be coming back to L.A., won't you? I've got your number."

"Where can I get you?"

"Try my mobile. There's no point in me giving you a sheaf of numbers. I don't know exactly where I'm going to be."

"I can't believe this. One moment we're making love and it's wonderful. The next you're walking out of the door."

Her voice loses a little of its control. "William, darling Willum, believe me, I…I need…I have to see my father. I'll keep in touch. I promise. Now I've got to go or I'll miss my flight. Enjoy the party. Say goodbye to your father for me."

The phone goes down on my voice. I call back immediately but there is no reply. Shit. What should I do? Try and get to the airport? But what am I going to do then? Buy her some candy for the trip? Wave a tear-stained handkerchief as the plane takes off? If she has to see her father, she has to see her father.

My father creaks in an hour later. He looks as if the slopes have given him a hard time. "How are you?" he asks.

I turn off the television. "Pissed off."

"I can understand that." He heads for the bathroom.

"Rashmi's flown to L.A."

He stops on a dime. "Did you have a row about something?"

"On the contrary."

He digests this. "So why did she go?"

"She needed to see her father."

He goes into the bathroom and I hear him rummaging amongst his pills. Water hits the bottom of a glass. "Is she coming back?"

"Maybe not before we leave."

"So you may not see her again?"

"Not up here. L.A. probably. She said she'd be in touch."

"Funny girl - FUCK!" The shower curtain comes adrift and he punches it savagely, slopping the contents of his glass. He adjusts the plug in the bath and turns on the faucet.

"I thought you liked her," I say.

Water is thundering into the bath and I am not certain that he has heard me. He starts to unzip his ski suit. "Any messages?" he asks.

12.

I have never seen Constance so radiant. No comparison with the woman at the Irvine Ranch. She wears a long Lincoln green trench coat trimmed with fur at hem, cuff and collar, a fur hat and fur boots. She looks like part of the environment. If she walked into the woods, someone would shoot her. An ecologist probably.

"Oh dear," she says. "Poor William. What have you done to yourself? If that's what happens to you, I'm not going within a mile of the slopes."

"A chance in a thousand," I say, gamely. "By the way, I was wondering about my script analysis. I imagine Jim Zaiferts is back by now?"

"Yes, he is. And there's a staff meeting next week. I'll make sure it's brought up." She smiles at my father. "I'm very hopeful. You'll just have to be patient a little longer, William. Remember: no news is good news."

In fact, my father has always led me to believe that, in Hollywood, no news is very bad news, but I say nothing.

Despite her reservations, Constance troops off to the slopes with my father who looks as if his minimal reserves of patience have been exhausted by hiring her skis. There is something oddly touching about them as they approach the lift line clutching their equipment like bundles of faggots. I can almost accept the idea of Constance as a stepmother. She is endlessly tolerant of my father and I think that she really does love him.

I do not expect Rashmi to call, or rather, I do not allow myself to expect her to call. In this way I will not be surprised or disappointed when she does not call. She does not call. I call her mobile number and get an answering service. I do not leave a message. Despite my advice to myself, I am disappointed. Still, I draw comfort from the fact that the disappointment would have been greater if I had not prepared myself for it. 'Blessed is the man who expects nothing, for he shall never be disappointed'. Thank you, Alexander Pope. One advantage of a smattering of education is that it affords access to a club where you can share sad moments with a superior class of intellect. Rashmi has problems with her father. No big deal. I have problems with my father. When we are next together I will tactfully try to get a little closer to the heart of the matter.

Right now, for both our sakes I need to concentrate on my own future. Constance's arrival can be construed as a good omen. She seems happy and outgoing. Hopefully, Ellen's party will provide an opportunity for me to further my cause.

Ellen's house is bigger than I had expected and full of wood carvings and mounted animal heads. Moose, elk and caribou look as if they have charged the house from all sides to crash their heads through the walls and be finished off by Vernon with one of the flintlocks mounted over the rough-hewn stone fireplace. Despite his check shirt and frontier affinities, Vernon is a realtor as, it soon appears, are the majority of the guests. Most of them seem to be in semi-retirement having made fortunes in places where the air quality is markedly inferior to that available in Idaho and, once again, I begin to rewrite the history of the West. Now I can see covered wagons full of realtors eagerly scanning the horizon through their spyglasses for prime sites; hardly waiting to leap down and massacre a few Indians before hammering posts into the prairie and sending William Cody galloping back east with a bundle of handbills: 'The rattle of carriages driving you crazy? Tired of waiting for basketball to be invented? Don't delay, invest in the lot of your dreams. Endless vistas, frequent water, DIY buffalo rugs! Hurry! Hurry! Hurry!'

Ellen has prepared masses of brightly-coloured food and the booze available extends far beyond the modest wine originally proposed. There is a table groaning with spirits and my father, hailed as a British literary lion, has champagne pressed upon him. Vernon and Ellen have clearly never seen 'The Dirty Diaries of a Window Cleaner'.

My father's attitude soon begins to cause me concern. I want him to be nice, and I want him to be especially nice to Constance. Her mood is a barometer of their relationship. Rashmi's mother, Pritti, is also present, looking sad and beautiful and out of place in a garment that starts off as a puce sari and ends up as baggy, violet knickerbockers. I want him to be nice to her as well.

Unfortunately, he seems to have forgotten that he is not drinking and has abandoned the New York Champagne - 'tastes like an aspirin dissolved in a glass of gnat's piss' - for stronger stuff. I quickly sense that his comments on 'A Mountain Man Remembers' have impressed Vernon more by their candour than by their charity and he listens with barely concealed tedium as Ellen describes the little literary group that meets each month to discuss a book they have all read and 'battledore ideas'.

"My God," he groans as she darts away to greet new realtors. "I doubt if they could form an opinion on Elton John, let alone *Weltanschauung*."

Constance chuckles loyally but she has the air of someone who has seen the movie already and not enjoyed it over much. Her long fingers run along the rim of her black velvet purse and pick uneasily at its clasp. Better to waste no time in approaching her for a little chat that might well embrace matters filmic, with particular emphasis on the vital role of the script analyst. But first perhaps, a drink to get the verbal juices flowing.

I help myself to a large vodka - made a little larger after reflection - and head towards Constance. En route, I am waylaid by Ellen who thoughtfully introduces me to some of the younger guests. The one with the streaky hair I know from the ski shop at the hotel and other faces I recognise from around town. I am associated with Rashmi and this seems to instil a certain distance. I get the feeling that she is not on great terms with the local young. An out-of-towner, a little stuck-up are the impressions I am left with without anybody being directly hostile. I am her boyfriend, so I must be more of the same they seem to intimate. Fine. I drift away and have another drink - the vodka is nearly history - and look for Constance. The place is filling up now. Wall to wall people squeezing under the moose heads so that from across the room they look as if they are wearing them like hats.

"Yes, he did go to school in Los Angeles for a while...." I realise that my father is talking about me to Vernon and a couple of his bored - but disguising it brilliantly - friends. "We had to take him away because the teachers weren't learning anything."

"That's interesting," observes one of the men.

"It's not interesting," says my father. "It's a joke,"

I move on hurriedly. Why tonight? He has been almost mellow lately. I suppose it was too good to last but it is tough on Constance - and possibly me. Just as well that Rashmi is not around.

Constance has retreated to a corner and is staring at a misshapen piece of wood flecked with grey pellets that Ellen and Vernon might have mounted in the mistaken belief that it possessed some intrinsic artistic merit. Either that or they once owned a parrot.

"A lot of people here," I say.

"What?"

I say it again louder and she nods. "It's hot."

She has a preoccupied look and the lines round her neck seem to run with predestined predictability into the scalloped top of her grey crêpe de Chine dress.

"I was wondering if you'd - you know, you yourself - had had a chance to read my script analysis?"

I am on the verge of shouting. Waves of overlapping conversation and braying laughter reverberate off the walls. Constance is gazing across the room to where my father is waving his arms in animated conversation - or rather, monologue - and slopping scotch. An imposing redhead is cuddling her drink before him in such a manner that the glass seems to be wedged between her generous breasts.

"No." Constance makes an angry clucking noise and ploughs towards them. Great. It looks as if I have already left it too late.

Viewed as an incendiary device, the party that started off as a small pile of damp, smoking leaves struggling to sustain a wick of flame is now a raging forest fire threatening to run out of control. People are laying hands on each other and bellowing opinions regardless of whether any one is listening. Ellen's Technicolor offerings are being spooned, spilt, speared and smeared and sometimes - in diminished quantities - eventually finding their way into mouths. Empty bottles lie felled amongst the splits, the ice is melting and the few intrepid smokers present are cheerfully grinding out their butts amongst a rubble of peanut particles.

All the vodka has been drunk so I switch to Southern Comfort on the basis that one needs to try anything once. My advice to posterity would be that it does not make a natural chaser to vodka and probably deserves to be on a list containing Poire Williams, something else that I try.

Another drink and my body begins to report increasingly frequent acts of sabotage: objects dart aside just as I am reaching for them, people's faces slip slightly out of register like illustrations in a poorly-printed comic book. I have difficulty performing reasonably simple physical functions - like using my crutches to hobble in a straight line. When I move from one place to another it is as if I am trying to clear a path through a cane field.

The younger crowd are pulling on coats and anoraks and preparing to go and eat somewhere - more food? It occurs to me that it might be a good idea if they asked me along. Just for the fresh air. But they don't. Probably just as well. I need to stay here in case there is a chance to get to grips with Constance. And - drink induced maudlin thought - they do not like Rashmi, the most beautiful, life-enhancing girl in the world so they are beyond human redemption and should be spurned like rabid curs. I hope their pizzas are baked hard as roof tiles and teeming with toxicants.

Thinking of Rashmi makes me sad so I have another little drink. Triple Sec, something else that I have never tried. It is all there seems to be left. I can see how the stuff can get a hold of you. Especially when you are in a room full of happy people and deprived of the one you love. Maybe this would be a good moment to approach Constance again. The room is thinning out a bit and I can hear music. My mind is a little woolly but she must have had a few drinks too. I certainly feel relaxed.

Constance is nowhere to be seen but my father is in a corner talking to Pritti. I see people whispering to each other and glancing towards them. It may not just be because they make such an attractive couple. This is the time of evening when father is quite capable of making a pass at Rashmi's mother or insulting her - choose the order. I need to get over there.

I move to put down my glass and watch a table hop sideways so that the glass drops to the floor. I glance down in surprise and pick it up with what I would like to think is easy nonchalance. Like somebody else dropped it and I am merely retrieving it. Ouch. When I stoop, the inside of my head feels like a snow scene paperweight. It takes a moment before the Father Christmas on Ellen's beautifully iced cake comes into focus. I stagger slightly and kind people hurry forward to help me. It's okay, folks. It's just the plaster around my ankle. Makes me a little clumsy. I blunder on, trying to gauge the distance to my father and the obstacles between us. What an inconvenient moment for someone to have replaced my legs with miniaturised water beds. I cover the last few yards like escaping effluent and arrive beside my father.

"Hi," I say brightly. "A lot of people here." It occurs to me that I have heard the words before, but what the hell? I expect Pritti to acknowledge my rescuing presence with relief but it does not show on her face - like lots of other emotions.

"But not as many as there were," says my father coldly.

"It's a shame Rashmi can't be here." I am addressing Pritti with the respectful tone of a future son-in-law.

Pritti's eyes do a little boogy between me and my father. I have no idea what is going through her mind. "You will have to excuse me," she says. "I have some animals to feed. I hope you both have a safe journey home." A bejewelled hand hitches her sari thing over her shoulder and she glides away.

I sense that they were probably talking about me. Pritti does not approve of my relationship with Rashmi and has been passing that information on to my father. Well, tough.

"What was she saying?"

"Nothing very important."

"Was she talking about me and Rashmi?"

"No!" He almost shouts the word and stomps off to where the bar used to be. What has got into him? Perhaps in some strange way, he is jealous. It must be frustrating to feel your sap drying up whilst your son flaunts himself in front of you with a beautiful young woman. I watch him flicking through the empty bottles as if searching for vital information in a poorly conceived card index. At least Pritti has left before something terrible took place. Could it possibly be that she sent Rashmi away to put some distance between us? No, that sounds too old-fashioned, even by Henry James standards. Rashmi is a child of the new millennium, when enlightened mothers do what their daughters tell them, wistfully wishing that it had been like that with their own mothers.

People are beginning to leave and I am relieved to see Constance approaching Ellen with her 'saying goodbye' face in place. Even in my fragile condition I can recognise the solar system smile: a grid of white teeth that has stored away all the manifold joys of the evening and is about to recycle them in one beatific beam that will imbue the hostess with a warm glow of gratitude and self-satisfaction. She starts her pre-bye chat and I brace myself. America is a thrusting place. If you lie back and wait for food to be dropped into your mouth, then the only thing that is sure to happen is that someone will drive over your legs. I take a few deep breaths and prepare my route. If I hobble round the walls I should be all right. I just have to be careful when passing the fireplace.

Constance glances towards my father and I follow her widening eyes. Oh dear. He is talking to another woman, someone I have not noticed before. She must just have arrived. She is no raving beauty but that has never been an impediment to embarrassing incidents in the past. She is standing unhealthily close to him and picking at his shirt like an anorexic plucking a sparrow for Thanksgiving dinner. I detect dangerous signs of instant infatuation. If her fingers are on the narrow side, the rest of her is not. Her large bottom twitches from side to side like that of a boxer bitch on heat and every few seconds she turns and lobs it at him. She is practically turning round and round in trembling circles asking to be petted.

Constance ought to hurry forward with a bucket of cold water but she is being led away by Ellen and Vernon. A door opens and I glimpse a wall of books. No doubt, Vernon is going to show her his first edition of 'White Fang'. My father has proved a disappointment as a source of literary excitement and they have now hitched their star-struck eyes to a prestigious studio executive. Said father is cantilevered forward and softly massaging his new friend's plump upper arm. The one that is still plucking at his chest. His head is tilted slightly to one side and his mouth half-parted as if his lips are about to embark upon an urgent relief mission of ecstasy-bestowal. His eyelids are half-descended awnings on a sun-baked street where hot things happen. This is part-programmed to me by memory. Other evenings, other ladies. I should be watching them from a hide through a pair of binoculars. If your own father wasn't involved, it might be an interesting anthropological experience. Now, his finger brushes across her lower lip and she bites it tenderly. He is inclined over her like a condemned cliff, his shoulders performing an encircling movement whilst someone doubles off to fetch the dynamite. His hand steals round her waist. I must do something. Fortunately, nobody seems to be taking much notice, but they soon could be. My father's hand descends to the ample buttocks. 'Jut butt', yes. Coyly, she rises to kiss him on the mouth. Christ, this is disgusting. He should barely be able to remember this, let alone want to do it, let alone do it. And Constance will return at any minute.

I take a step forward and the room goes into orbit. My head spins and a surge of nausea swirls up from the pit of my stomach. It is not just my father; I should never have finished off the Triple Sec. I didn't care for the label, anyway: 'Distilliat ou infusion plantes ou fruits'. The double 'or'. Weren't they sure? Do they just chuck anything into the stuff? There can be a lot of difference between a plant and a fruit. Deadly Nightshade is a plant, for God's sake. I stretch out a hand and am relieved to find that the wall is still there. Or something. A painting, as I discover when I pick it up at the cost of more gut-wrenching vertigo. I doubt if the glass was cracked before it fell, but still. You give a party, you have to expect a few breakages. I stare with simulated interest at something that Landseer might have painted with a blunt stick whilst undergoing treatment for substance abuse and then - when people have stopped looking at me - prop it against the wall. If there was a hook, I can't see it.

It is becoming increasingly obvious to me that I need to rest. My father must take second place. I feel as if I am about to pass out. Some fresh air would be a good idea but if I went outside and collapsed then I might freeze to death. Having a guest hacked out of the driveway would almost inevitably cast a shadow over the evening as far as Ellen and Vernon were concerned, and I have too much to live for at the moment.

It is weird how it suddenly hits you. The downside. The feeling that your body will shortly be breaking up like a successful pop group. I need to get to the bathroom as soon as possible. Just in case. It seems like the appropriate environment for me at the moment. Virtually aseptic, private. Private would be good. I set my legs in motion and try and keep up with them. I had always assumed that we got on reasonably well but they seem to be trying to get away from me. It must be the plaster and the crutches. Everything is throwing me out of synch. And then there is the inside of my head; like a zoetrope of the charge of the Light Brigade - another disaster when I come to think of it. God, this is awful. Hot flushes, tingling flesh, sweat breaking out along my forehead, trickling down from my armpits. I should have eaten something but it is too late now. One glance at the detritus that was the food table and - urgh! My eye lights on the chewed cigar stubbed out in the remains of the trifle. Another wave of nausea is beaten back at the last second.

Cooler air. I am in the comparative emptiness of a long hallway and can steady myself against a wall. Strange. I had no recollection of having touched anything with red currants in it. Still, I expect it will sponge off without too much difficulty, and my hosts are hardly likely to fingerprint everyone at the party. Now, which way? There are stairs leading up and down. Easy one. I grab the hand rail like an old friend and we go downstairs together. At the bottom, I catch up with the crutch I have dropped and resist a self-destructive impulse to kick it down the corridor. Ahead of me are two doors. The one that isn't the linen closet leads to a bathroom. A bathroom with an elephant trunk faucet that turns in a direction you do not expect, soaks the front of your pants with a spiteful jet of water and is directly responsible for me batting a glass tumbler full of tooth brushes against a wall. Calm, Lock. Fate is conspiring against you as you perspire against yourself but you must try and stay in control. A glance in the mirror makes this marginally more difficult; what I see is like a study for 'The Scream' that Munch rejected because it was too frightening.

I need to lie down. Very much. Very soon. I crunch over the shattered glass and stumble out into the corridor. Facing me is a door bearing a sticker in childish handwriting: 'The Guys'. Nobody is about so I open the door - that red stuff that gets everywhere must be my blood - and take a quick look inside. A den-like room with a poster of Stallone tackling the Third World's over-population problem, high school pennants, and two bunk beds, one on top of the other. I don't recall meeting any younger versions of Vernon, so presumably 'The Guys' are away in college or selling real estate somewhere. This room has been kept as a shrine to their youth. Fine. It is just what I need. I close the door behind me, dump the crutches, and struggle across the room in darkness. A sharp pain in my ankle tells me that I have bumped into the ladder that leads to the upper bank. It is weird, but I immediately start to climb - like the villain in the final reel of the movie who always heads for the highest spot he can find so that he has further to plunge to his death. Maybe I do it because I want to separate myself from all the bad things that exist at ground level.

I reach the top bunk, a little dizzy and queasy, ankle throbbing, and feed myself under the duvet in a kind of peristalsis. I don't feel great but, at least, I feel protected.

The ceiling is less than the length of my outstretched arm above me. It makes me dizzy when I reach up and feel it and it is even worse when I close my eyes. A coffin. Yes, I am thinking of coffins - and 'The Vanishing', the spookiest film ever made. Not a good idea. Think of something nice. Or, better still, nothing at all. Space. Infinity. A black wall of calm. Sooner or later you will go to sleep.

I think I do go to sleep. Certainly, I have the feeling that a period of time has elapsed. But something is happening. Something near me. The black wall is trembling. It is not a mental sensation, not a dream nor a nightmare. It is physical.

The wall is becoming the surface of a liquid and there are ripples running through it, quivering isoseismal lines ruckling the heaving black. I am being shaken, shaken awake. I stretch out a hand and find a flex. Instinctively, I follow it to an egg-shaped knob. An egg-shaped knob with a switch. I press. Click! A bilious gothic twilight floods my face. The coloured light bulbs of cool young people. My body jerks in the air with the motion of what is happening beneath me. I force my head sideways. Look down.

The swollen, balding head of a huge slurping terrapin is devouring a hairy mollusc in the lower bunk. Half-clothed by a latter-day Hieronymous Bosch, their compressed bodies batter and thrust against the shuddering woodwork until it threatens to disintegrate. Bulbs burst inside my head and rasp of sickly nausea stings the back of my throat. My stomach churns and starts to boil over. My mouth jerks open and I croak an involuntary warning message. Father, wet-mouthed, raises his head from the glistening fur. Our eyes meet. The bunk stops shaking. I try and check myself. Too late. I vomit all over them.

13.

The journey back to L.A. is quiet. Very quiet. The loudest noise comes from inside my head where the brass and percussion sections of an orchestra of tone deaf schizoids are attacking the more strident passages from 'The Rites of Spring'.

On the plane, my father and I could be total strangers who found themselves side by side owing to a whim of the ground staff. Constance flew back via Seattle to avoid being on the same flight. I don't know what words passed between her and my father before her departure. Very few, I would imagine.

Ellen was not on duty when we checked out which perhaps was just as well. I have very little recollection of leaving her house, save that I think I did some more damage to my ankle when I fell out of the bunk. I will write a sincere letter of apology from L.A. - or, at least, a postcard in an envelope - and perhaps I shouldn't be feeling too bad about myself anyway. The way civil litigation is going in the States, I could probably sue Ellen and Vernon for attempted murder.

My main concern, selfishly I concede, is that I should get to Rashmi before news of the evening. Reports can become exaggerated. At least her mother missed the grand finale. I had hoped that Rashmi might have left a message. Maybe she did and the Little Elk Lodge staff failed to pass it on. One could definitely sense an atmosphere. Provincial America can be very close-knit. I tried Rashmi's mobile number from Hailey Airport but even her voice mail box was full.

All this is a shame as I really liked Sun Valley a lot and with Rashmi having a home there it could have been a perfect place to hang out. Maybe, by next year, everything will be forgotten, or at least forgiven and we can go back - especially if I swear an affidavit that my father is never going to set foot in the place again.

Another source of distress is my father's treatment of Constance. This is not going to help my cause at the studio. I will have to sidestep her and launch myself directly at Zaiferts. The time for pussy-footing is over. I must put the past behind me and etc., etc., etc. It becomes tedious when you have to be your own private cheerleader all the time. I would like to have Rashmi on the touchline.

The big news at the hotel is that Peter has been discovered. Just as in my casual surmise. A producer did check into the hotel - then checked out the build, the abs, the smile, the notion of limitless inner strength. Now Peter has a walk-on in a sitcom pilot. He hasn't got any dialogue but the whole of his body - in a T-shirt and tracksuit pants apparently - is going to be up there on the screen for several seconds. And he gets to walk. Both ways. It is a beginning. The only downside is that Peter's uncle who acted as his agent has now had to be replaced by a professional. Uncle is pissed but, hey, this is show business not nursery school. And even nursery school is tough around Hollywood where mothers can take out contracts on any moppet who might beat their own little treasure to a Sugarpops commercial. Peter is beyond thrilled and Maria has taken to humming romantic ditties. I even caught her dancing with her mop. I mentioned the good news to José while he was planting pansies the colour of dried blood but he just went on making holes. I definitely think there is something wrong with his hearing.

There is a new girl behind the desk and she practically bubbles over when my father asks for messages. "Mr Lock? 'The Man' called you twice. You just missed him."

"What man?"

"'The Man'!!" She makes it sound like capital letters with lots of exclamation marks.

"You mean 'The Man'?"

I am skimming through the messages. Rashmi has not called. Or maybe they put it in the wrong pigeon hole. That happens. Wait a minute. 'The Man'? Did I hear right?

"Did he leave a number?"

"No. I asked him but he said he'd call back."

"Did it sound like him?"

The receptionist shrugs. "Gee, I don't know. Yeah, I guess so." Her uncertainty is understandable. 'THE MAN'. A screen legend. The greatest actor of his generation - maybe lots of others. He can be anyone. Or rather, he could. When did he last make a movie? Must be ten years ago. What a waste. Why is he calling my father?

"Maybe it's a hoax," I say encouragingly, when we are in the elevator.

"Thanks. Maybe you're right. But I've heard rumours that he's thinking about doing another movie. Christ, I can remember seeing his first film.

When he played the deaf mute. That scene at the end when they put his eyes out."

"'Indifference'."

My father nods. "Something like that. Everybody was going crazy for his next film. Wondering whether he really was a deaf mute."

"Because he stayed in character at all the press shows. People had to write down questions." It is a blunt question but I ask it. "Why would he be calling you?"

"Because he's read something I wrote and he likes it." I wait. It is difficult to imagine 'The Man' becoming enthused by 'The Dirty Diaries of a Window Cleaner'. "Maybe that thing I did on 'The Double Helix'. Though he's a bit old for Watson or Crick. Jesus, can you imagine what it would mean to write his come-back movie?"

I can. Right from the beginning 'The Man' was an actor apart. His very refusal to reveal his own name: 'Who I play is who I am'. The courage to demand that his name was billed like that before he had any box office clout. When people thought that he was crazy or that it was just a publicity stunt.

"Where is he now?"

"I don't know. Didn't he have a boat? I thought he was moored off one of those Polynesian islands. Or was it Greece?"

One has to go back a few years to remember reading about him. The media forget pretty quickly. It is only when one of his old movies turn up on TV that it all comes back: the brawls, the Civil Rights marches, the demonstrations, the studio fights, the holdouts, the walkouts, the women, the scandals, the custody battles and, above all, what an incredibly great actor he was.

My father calls reception the minute we are in the suite. "It's okay. You can put calls through to the suite now. My son and I have found the core to our inner being." There are confused noises at the other end of the line. "It doesn't matter. Just put the calls through." He bangs the phone down. "Bloody people never remember anything you tell them. Did it sound as if I wanted room service?" He takes a couple of deep breaths. "Can you imagine me writing that movie? I could buy out Western Rentals from the TV residuals - incidentally, they're going to take you to court-" he holds up a hand "-all right, all right, us to court. No need to get your knickers in the proverbial. If this comes off, we're free and laughing." He thumbs through the messages gleefully. Well, well. Bernie Bowman's in town. He's throwing a little party."

I had seen the name and it had rung a bell. Of course. Bernie Bowman. The intrepid, and now very rich, soul who produced the 'Dirty Diary' movies.

"I thought you said you never wanted to speak to him again?"

"Did I say that?"

"No, what you actually said was that you'd rather nick your dick and plunge it into a pool of starving piranha."

"Really?" My father chuckles. "The image must have appealed to me. No, I'm really quite fond of old Bernie. If you held a grudge against everybody in this business who's ripped you off, there wouldn't be anybody left to leave messages for. You've got to concentrate on the end product. The movie is always bigger than the pain of its parts. A few knife scars in the back are a bonding ritual."

Once again he is rubbing his hands together like a boy scout with a couple of sticks. The state of happiness has returned.

Sometimes I wonder if Hollywood corrupted him or if he merely tumbled into the right profession by chance.

In my father's elation is something that disturbs me. With typical French cynicism, or praiseworthy honesty, depending on one's point of view, De La Rochefoucauld observed that 'In the misfortunes of our closest friends we find something that is not entirely displeasing'. Unfortunately, perhaps, I can identify with this. As I can with the converse: in the good fortune of our closest friends we can find something that is more than mildly irritating. I am dogged by the unpalatable thought that my father might be about to usurp what should be the upsurge in my fortunes. Of course, I hope that the calls from 'The Man' are not a hoax but-

The phone rings and we both stare at it like twin sisters who have been waiting six months for a date. My father gestures to me to take the call, no doubt hoping that I will sound like one of his P.A.s.

I try to think of Rashmi so hard that it has to be her. "Hello?"

"Oh, Mr Lock. I'm sorry to bother you. Could I speak to-?"

"Lucy, it's me." Disappointment, irritation and guilt join hands around me in a familiar circle. "Hold on a minute." I turn to my father who looks as if he is about to say something and then raises his arms in a gesture of despair and goes out onto the balcony. He is presumably irritated that the line is now clogged up with the trivial minutia of my private life.

"I've just got your postcard. You'll never guess how long it took to get here." She sounds so bubbly and happy I cannot bear it.

"Lucy. I feel an awful shit but I've got to tell you something." That's it. The birch bark canoe pounds into the rapids. No turning back. "I'm afraid I've met someone else." I wait. Nothing. "Hello? Are you there?"

"Yes." A sob.

"I'm sorry. It happened after I wrote." A lie, but what's another one? "Not that it makes any difference, of course, but…I…I…I don't know what to say." This is true.

"You love her?"

"Yes, I think so. Yes." I blunder on because I cannot bear listening to the pain in her voice. "I'm very fond of you, Lucy. You've always been great to me. You deserve better, I know you'll find someone." I have to raise my voice against the sound of her sobbing. "Please don't cry. I'm really sorry. I'd like us to stay friends." Why doesn't she put the phone down? "I'm sorry it has to sound so brutal but I can't go on - I can't lie about it."

"Oh, William. I love you so much." Her voice gouges into me. I feel such a shit. I am a shit. Why does life have to be so cruel?

"I'm sorry, Lucy. I don't know what else I can say."

"I want to be with you always. I want to have your babies."

Christ. "Lucy, please. It wouldn't be any good. Honestly, I'll write. I'll try and explain. It's nothing to do with you." Why can't she put the phone down on this agony? Why does she still cling on? "Lucy, I can't go on repeating myself. It's over."

A terrible wail. "I can't live without you!"

"Yes, you can. You'll have to. Lucy, I…I…" I put the phone down. God, I feel awful. I am sweating.

Out on the balcony, my father has his arms on the rail and is staring down into the pool. He turns and faces me through the window. Difficult to read his expression. Compassion? Irritation? A kind of shared guilt? He tries to come in but the door is locked. I open it.

"That was Lucy."

"I know. She's a nice girl."

"I know that! But I can't have everybody. I'm not like you."

I expect him to explode but he just folds his lips together and stares at a wall. "Oh Christ," is all he says.

The telephone rings and my heart takes another trip to the death house. Lucy is standing on a high stool with a string of tights round her neck.

My father approaches the phone. "If it's her, I'll say you've gone out." He does not sound enthusiastic. I start to head for the door. "Hello?"

I hesitate. There is just the faintest chance that it might be Rashmi. Of course, it won't be, but - my father's face is a blank; then, slowly, it undergoes a change. Like a child who has been connected with Father Christmas. He raises a second hand to the phone as if he is frightened that someone might try and take it away from him. "I can't believe I'm actually talking to you." His eyes bump into mine and he mouths 'it's him!', jabbing his finger against the phone as if a miniature 'Man' was curled up in a foetal position within the receiver. "Yes, yes." So deferential, so awed. "Yes.........no." His expression suddenly changes. From glorious summer to a very discontented winter. "No, that's my son. I'm Adrian Lock." He listens some more, half listens. "Yes, yes. I'll put you on to him." He holds out the phone. "It's 'The Man'. He wants to talk to you."

Is this an elaborate, and rather cruel, practical joke? I take the phone. "Hello?" My voice sounds as it did when it was breaking.

"William Lock? I'm delighted to make your acquaintance, sir. Very delighted indeed." The voice sounds just like Sidney Greenstreet in 'The Maltese Falcon'.

"Hadiscomb?" I say. "That was brilliant. You have a great future in the movies."

"Thank you. But this is not Hadiscomb, whoever he has the good fortune to be. This is 'The Man', as in Homo erectus. Your comments on my talent are flattering, and would be even more so if they were original." Now he sounds like Orson Welles in anything. "You appear to have made rather an impression on my little girl, which is why I'm calling." What is he talking about? "I'm an old fashioned father, William. When the fruit of my loins expresses a more than unusual interest in a young man, I have a proprietorial desire to set eyes on him. What are your movements tomorrow?"

"I'm sorry, the fruit of your loins?"

"Rashmi." It comes out like a sneeze.

"You're Rashmi's father?"

"Somebody has to be. Now, what about tomorrow?"

"Yes, of course. Fine. What time?"

"Someone will call you. I'm glad we've made contact, William."

"Yes, so am-" He has disappeared before the end of my sentence. I put down the phone, half-missing the rest the first time. "Did you hear that? Rashmi is his daughter."

"Yes." My father's face is a catalogue of emotions, most of them associated with disappointment.

"I'm sorry," I say, lying a little. "I mean, that he didn't - that it wasn't - maybe something will come out of it. You know? Who knows?"

"Who indeed?" He smiles a bitter smile.

"It could still be a hoax." I feel an obligation to be pessimistic. A good egg gesture of commiseration and, more honestly, an insurance against outrageous fortune.

"What we need is Rashmi," he says.

The telephone rings. That must be her. On cue. She was probably standing beside her father when he made the call. Clinging to his arm affectionately. Craning her neck to listen. Smiling as my father waffled on. But, wait a minute. It could be Lucy again. Standing on a high window ledge with the telephone flex so stretched that the coils have disappeared. I look to my father but he doesn't move. I pick up the phone.

It is Hadiscomb. At first I am suspicious. Then I relax. He could never have accumulated all the information to mount such a complicated hoax. Hadiscomb is eager to tell me about his weekend at Palm Springs. The number of swimming pools per house - he seems fascinated by pools - the local tennis champ he nearly beat, the incredible girl he nearly seduced, the fantastic weather. It seems a very English weekend. I manage to interject that I have shattered my ankle and he sympathises in a typically British at-least-it-wasn't-any-worse way and asks about the car. The news that my father and I might go to prison is probably the highlight of his day.

"Why don't we do a movie?" he says. "It might be the last chance."

I think he means before I get locked up but he is referring to his imminent return to England. He suggests tonight but I am pretty certain that Rashmi will call so we make it tomorrow. I can always cancel. He rings off and I feel depressed. Hadiscomb has that effect on me. He takes me back to Rockingham and the freezing cold and driving rain. The sodden playing fields. The boredom, the bullying. Voyce. It is strange but Hadiscomb is beginning to appear in my dreams. With the vicar's cat.

Rashmi does not call. I even go down to reception to make inquiries. Just in case. On the way, Peter and Maria are coming out of one of the rooms in the corridor that leads to the new wing. I want to say something encouraging to Peter but they seem pretty engrossed in each other so I don't bother. I don't think about it at the time, but Maria isn't pushing her trolley.

At reception, the English girl is on duty. Probably having heard about 'The Man' she beams at me encouragingly and asks me where I come from in England but I can barely respond. She reminds me of Lucy.

All evening, I sit in front of the television aimlessly switching channels. I could be Gabriel trying to find some glad tidings to bring someone. My father has gone out. He did not suggest that I should join him and I do not feel broken-hearted. In fact, I would have refused anyway. I know it is not very nice to vomit over your father, but sometimes a gesture really can be worth a thousand words.

I switch channels again. I never knew there had been so many 'Planet of the Apes' movies. Rashmi's silence is beginning to annoy me. She could make a little more effort, especially considering that I have just sacrificed my long-term girlfriend. Not that she knows that. Not that it ought to make a lot of difference. It boils down to a question of simple good manners, of respect for other people's feelings. How can you be humping the nuts off somebody one minute and then just disappear? She can't have had an accident otherwise daddy would have said something. If it really was daddy. Shit.

I pace round the room and am confronted by the tray of miniature spirit bottles that is always placed strategically to tempt you. I nearly throw up. Never again. I need to be more assertive with Rashmi - and with the world in general. I will call Zaiferts tomorrow without fail - and before Constance can get to him. Not that I see her as the vindictive type. It is just that someone might ask her if she had a nice weekend and...and-

I change channels again. Burt Reynolds. What is he in? I pick up The Television Times: 'A stock-car racer tries to extricate himself from the iron-clad contract he signed that requires him to wear the chicken suit symbol of his fast-food sponsor'. Pass. I am not looking for 'Crime and Punishment', but still.

What does KPBS have for us? 'Artie's schizophrenic wife, a deaf movie star, a band of marauding nuns and a bomb upset his plans for the Pope's visit to New York'. Timely, maybe, but I don't think so.

So how about KOCE? '"Life in the Balance." Scientists explore man's impact on the ecosystem and possible evolutionary consequences'. Uh, uh. This is not going to be 'Happy Days' I can smell mutants down the line.

So what is left? What rib-tickling fare is good old KCET proposing? '"Testament." A typical American family try to survive a nuclear holocaust winter'. Not even late autumn, poor bastards. Where is 'Laughing Gravy?' when you need it?

I switch off and take another turn round the room. I wonder who produces the synopses of all these thousands of programmes and movies.

There must be an incredible staff turnover as their minds atrophy and drop out when they pick their noses. I glance in the bookcase, purely there to bulk up a blank wall. Its total contents are two 'Mickey Spillane's' and an ancient National Inquirer. 'Is Hitler's grandson alive and living in San Diego?'

I check to make sure that there is still a dialling tone and go into the bedroom. Somewhere, on one of the channels, there must surely be an old 'The Man' movie. I glance through the listing but, no, not tonight.

It's weird how long ago it all seems. His career. At the beginning he was always holding out for better roles. Then he made some funny choices. Then he made money. Then he took the money. Then he disappeared. Apart from at the beginning he did not make all that many good films. What was the one with his second wife who couldn't act? 'Life Class'? Jeeze. Could that have been Pritti? No, of course not. That wife killed herself.

All in all, it's depressing how many lousy movies are made. As if to remind me of that fact, Bernie Bowman's name stares at me from the mirror where my father has tucked his message like an invitation card. I suppose that neither of us would be here if it had not been for him reading 'The Sexy Diary of a Window Cleaner' on the 7.42 from Basildon and realising that it was screaming to be turned into a great movie. 'Great' in the best sense of the word. The lucrative sense.

Andy Groper. How I hate that stupid obvious name. It certainly changed my life; right from the moment my father was interviewed on TV and 'The Dirty Diaries' were dragged inevitably into the conversation.

Voyce and his cronies at Rockingham did not watch book programmes but one of the masters did. The next morning I was addressed as 'The Shakespeare Kid' and asked if I had the same literary bent as my father.

Somebody once observed that nobody would teach at a boys' boarding school unless he was at least a latent homosexual. I am not so sure. Drunkards, psychotics, sadists and total incompetents, yes. Men dedicated to the protection of dandruff as an endangered species, possibly. But surely someone who lusted after boys would be nicer to them? Perhaps it is counter-phobia, a tendency to loathe what you despise yourself for yearning after, or merely an attempt to disguise the preference.

Either way, Voyce was presented with the ideal excuse to make my life even more miserable. Not only did I speak with a funny accent and have the presumption to live in poncy France but my father was a rich pornographer. It was useless, and I was too frightened, to point out that having a father who made road signs was hardly the first step to being poet laureate. One-eyed bastards comb the streets for blind men to kick, especially if they are already lying in the gutter.

I find myself brushing my teeth so hard that I make my gums bleed. My hand knocks against a glass and I am back in that bathroom at Sun Valley. Opposite 'The Guys'. And the terrapin.

Voyce had a terrapin. Terrified small boys used to be despatched to collect tiny frogs and toads and drop them one by one into the creature's tank. Pink new-born mice from the pet shed were another speciality. It was a bloody business as the terrapin was as clumsy as it was voracious and the more sensitive kids frequently burst into tears. They were the ones Voyce sent out to collect more prey.

Why do I have to think about this now? When I haven't even gone to sleep. Stuff like this should be locked away in the oubliettes, wasting away until it disappears completely. Now it is escaping from my dreams. Voyce. The terrapin. The cat is out of the vicar's bag and it is all Hadiscomb's fault. Hadiscomb who Voyce hated almost as much as me. I am not quite certain why; I think it was because he would not let Voyce into his bed.

Voyce. I can see him lowering over me in that loose scrum. His ugly pig face with its tiny eyes and lank, blond hair. I was wedged under a mass of bodies, the ball against my leg. I couldn't move. The referee was on the far side of the scrum. I saw the metal studs gleam through the mud as Voyce drew back his boot; just for a second before he stamped down with all his weight. Youch! I can feel the pain now. The same ankle I have plaster on. They carried me off on a stretcher and Voyce kissed the tips of his fingers to me. That was the moment when I knew what I was going to do.

All this makes me frightened to go to sleep and I almost wish that my father would return so that I could get up and engage in banal conversation to break up my mood of deepening gloom but when, half-dozing, I glance at the bedside clock it is one o'clock and there is still no sign of him.

It is strange, but when I do fall asleep I do not dream. Maybe thinking about things when I am awake is the answer. My father must have been unusually sensitive when he returned because it is only when I wake up around nine that I hear him turning the bathroom into a no-go area. He emerges, drowning a handful of pills in a glass of water, and informs me that he is going to see 'our' lawyer. He looks awful. God knows what he has been doing during the night. He does not ask if Rashmi called, which is typical, and says that he has no idea when he is going to be back. I imagine that the idea of me getting together with 'The Man' is more than he can stand. Good.

I wait until I hear the door slam and get up and do fifty push-ups off one foot. Not easy, but it makes me feel that I am earning Brownie points with God. He likes you to cherish your body. I have now dispensed with the crutches and can move around in a kind of Quasimodo lurch; my damaged foot on its little metal platform swinging out as if I am trying to carry a canon ball on my instep.

Rashmi and 'The Man' to call me. Me to call Zaiferts. It would be great if I had some good news to tell Rashmi. Five to ten. Even now, Zaiferts will be sliding his white Porsche into his reserved parking space and gazing with satisfaction at his newly stencilled name. Or maybe he has already been there for several hours. If he worked for Disney he would only go home on his birthday.

I wait until precisely ten o'clock and call the studio. The number I usually dial does not get me through and I end up at the switchboard. Making the words trip off my tongue like he is my oldest buddy, I ask to talk to Jim Zaiferts.

"Jim Zaiferts is no longer with the company."

WHAT!? There must be some mistake. They can't do this to me. "I-er-Christ, let me talk to his secretary - I mean, assistant."

"I'll see if there's someone who can help you. What is it concerning?"

Of course, the assistant would have gone too. They are inseparable. They roam the studios like knight and squire.

I make a clumsy job of explaining that I have submitted a script analysis with a view to being taken on as a reader.

"Hold on." The woman can hardly keep awake.

"Yeah? Maddox."

I start explaining how I-

"You need Constance Tilly."

"She's taken over his job?"

"No." A snort suggests that this idea is too risible for discussion. "She's been handling reader recruitment for nearly a year."

I greet this news with the silence of the pole-axed and the line goes dead. *Et tu*, Constance. And I always thought you were so nice. Wrong again. Zaiferts was a front and you were holding me hostage to your relationship with my father. I could still have been trying to get into the studio when the Dodgers won something. Now I'm a long shot for a job neutering the commissary cat. This is so unfair. I should be considered for a job on my merits. This is America, for God's sake. Constance owes me an explication.

I get through to the studio again and ask to speak to her. It is strange, but I have the feeling that they are expecting my call. This time, the woman on the switchboard sounds almost solicitous. "Oh, yes. I'll put you straight through."

But not to Constance. I am listening to a woman who sounds uneasy. "Are you a relation?" she asks. Funny question. And it is not delivered in a chatty voice. I suppose my mid-Atlantic accent tallies with that of Constance who sounds more British than American. Still, studio people rarely express interest in those kind of details. I say who I am and the woman's tone changes immediately. "We'll have to get back to you."

I gabble my number but the line goes dead almost before I have finished. What is going on here? Do they think I am my father? Has Constance vetoed all calls from anybody called Lock? 'We'll have to get back to you'. In Hollywood this usually means: 'Drop dead, and if anybody trips over the corpse we'll sue your dependents'.

I go down to reception and pick up a Hollywood Reporter. Zaiferts is banner headlines. He has 'ankled' to Paramount and appears to be virtually running the studio.

Well, well. My old buddy, Jim, pressing the sucker of his basket ball hoop to a bigger wall. Maybe he will have two of them and be able to intercept himself and shoot baskets at both ends of his office. Bounce. Would he remember me if I rang him up? Er...silly question, William. Oh well, perhaps I can work our relationship into a conversation from time to time

I drag my weary heart back to the suite and wait. The telephone rings. I hesitate to let my heart beat drop below the two hundreds and snatch it up. Larry Sabel's office are sending over a script that needs a re-write. My father should call if he is interested. I have to admire Sabel's chutzpah. I can imagine him mugging you and saying 'Have a nice day' as he shook the blood from your wallet.

Midday comes and there is still no word from 'The Man'. Looks as if lunch is out of the question. Of course, I had not expected lunch, but...you never know. It would have been nice to walk into Valentino at the shoulder of a legend. My father-in-law. Boy.

At twelve-fifteen the phone rings. I pick it up. "Hello?" How studied my voice sounds. Like an actor who has waited too long for the audition.

"Darling?"

"Rashmi." Relief.

"Will, is that you?"

"Where the hell have you been? I thought something had happened to you."

A pause. "It's been frantic. I'm sorry. How are you? How's the poor ankle?"

"It's fine. Just hearing your voice makes it feel better." I know. I was going to be tough, assertive but- "But listen, you never told me about your father."

"I told you lots of things about my father. I just didn't tell you who he was."

"Why not?"

"Think about it. Who needs that kind of competition? I'd like to be liked for me. *Tout simple*. Isn't that what you say in France?"

"I'm not exactly flattered - for either of us. You think I wouldn't be interested in you unless you were the daughter of somebody famous?"

"It's happened. Trust me."

I wait. And wait. "He called me. You know that?"

"Sure. I told him about you."

"He's supposed to be calling me today. He wants us to meet. You must know that, too. Are you going to be there?"

"No." There is a pause and, for a moment, I think that there must be a fault on the line. "I don't think he's going to be able to make it today."

I feel an ache of disappointment. "But he sounded so…so sure about it."

"His mind can go off on a tack. He can drive you crazy, believe me. When we talked he was thinking about going home."

"Where's that?"

"Saint Francis. It's in the Virgin Islands. Near Puerto Rico."

I try to digest all this. "So I'm not going to see him."

"Not on this trip. Not unless I can wangle you an invitation. Would you like that?"

Is she kidding? Hand in hand along sloping white sand, between bending palm and cobalt blue ocean, love walks. "That would be wonderful. We're talking Caribbean, right?"

"Yo, mon."

I try and contain myself. "How soon can I see you? I've been going crazy?"

Another long pause. "What are you doing this evening?"

"I was going to a movie with Hadiscomb, but I can cancel it."

"Your English friend? No, you mustn't do that. I can meet you afterwards. I have to have a drink with somebody anyway. I'll come round to the hotel about nine. Is that too early?"

"It's too late. I can't wait that long."

"You'll have to."

"I love you. You know that?"

"Yes, I know that. Enjoy your movie, my sweet William. Hey-" she laughs "-you're a flower. I only just thought of that. I'm going to look you up and find out what you look like. Goodbye, darling."

It is towards the end of the afternoon when my father returns, strangely sober, and I pour out the happenings of the day; the good stuff first: Rashmi has rung and is tripping round this evening.

"Wonderful." He sounds like the captain of the Titanic learning that he has won the mileage sweep as he steps into a leaking lifeboat. "Things are less than good with those bubonic rats at Western. They cancelled the meeting I was supposed to be having with them. They're trying to pull something."

I jerk my mind back to the dreary quotidian. "They're trying to scare you."

"Us. I'd like to hear the 'U' word, William. Don't forget, it's your laxity that's at the root of this situation. You should have had the youthful sapience to restrain me. Astute children are supposed to rebel against their parents' imbecilic ideas. And they've got our passports, remember. I could be applying for citizenship if this drags on much longer. Jesus Christ." He lunges for the gin bottle. "When are you meeting 'The Man'?"

"Doesn't look as if I am at the moment. He's gone back to his island in the Caribbean." I consider mentioning that I may be joining him but decide to hold this information back.

"No surprise there. 'The Man's' totally unreliable. He had to be chained to the set on his last movie." Some more gin joins the first inch. "Any more glad tidings?"

"Zaiferts has gone to Paramount and Constance was in charge of reader recruitment all the time. She's been sitting on my analysis." I glare at him challengingly.

For once, his face reveals genuine concern. "Shit! I had a great idea I wanted to pitch to Zaiferts. Now, I'll have to try and set up another meeting."

"Constance!" I shout at him. "What about me and Constance? My career."

"Yes." A dew of tonic is allowed to descend upon the gin. "That's not good either. I'd better give her a ring. Poor old Constance. It was a shame what happened up there." He takes a lip-smacking gulp of gin. "I feel quite bad about it, I really do. Normally, I like to think of myself as some kind of roving, unpaid ambassador for the old country."

"Are you serious? Jack the Ripper with Ebola Virus would make a better ambassador."

My father laughs. "That's the spirit, Will. Don't let the bastards get you down."

"You're the bastard who's getting me down!" I yell at him.

"Steady on. No need to get things out of proportion." He takes a ruminative swig of his drink. "If we lose our sense of humour, we're lost. It's the only thing that separates us from the animals. Have I ever told you that?"

"About a hundred times."

"Not that there's anything wrong with following your animal instincts, of course. I mean, we're all animals, aren't we? It's natural that we should react viscerally sometimes. We have to start with what we can understand."

"Sounds like the Marquis de Sade."

"He was very misunderstood." My father sluices gin through his clenched teeth. "Very few of his critics have read 'Justine'."

"Have you?"

"No. That's why I refrain from censure."

Apparently, in his youth, Descartes stopped reading books and emptied his mind of all that it had been taught so that it would be ready to receive the truth in whatever form it presented itself. It occurs to me that, inadvertently, my father has placed himself in the same position. He has read little, forgotten most of it, and knows practically nothing. Perhaps, despite his detestation of philosophers, he is about to embark on a great journey of the mind.

"'Blood of the Lust Crazy'." He has picked up Sabel's script. "What's this?"

"Larry Sabel had the cheek to send it round. Wants to know if you interested in doing a re-write."

My father is weighing the script in his hand like a cut of meat. "Was there any mention of money?"

"Are you kidding? After what the little fink has done to you? You swore you were going to find another agent."

"I could knock this off while I was looking." He checks the number of pages and starts reading at random.

"Don't you have any principles?"

"They're out of my price range at the moment."

"Larry Sabel is totally despicable."

"So's a dung beetle in a sense. But it's doing a job that nature especially equipped it for. Would you like to be a dung beetle?"

"There must be nicer dung beetles than Larry."

"'Nice' and 'dung beetle' don't usually go together."

"He made a pass at me, for Chrissakes."

"Try and look at it as a compliment." My father checks back a couple of pages. "Larry's sexual proclivities have nothing to do with his talents as an agent. He could be a drug addict-"

"He is a drug addict! He offered me drugs at…at that party at Santa Barbara. I told you that!"

"For God's sake, Will. I don't employ him as your baby sitter."

Something inside me snaps. "You've no guts!" I shout at him. "Everybody screws you and all you do is take it and get drunk and whine about everything!"

The script smashes down on the edge of the table. "And all you do is spend the money I make. So until you're head of Dreamworks or you can get off your arse and find some means of supporting yourself, I might as well go on re-writing this crap!" He heads for the door and spins round. "The world is a fucking sight more complicated than you think, William. I hope you never find that out." His mouth stays open as if he is about to say more but he merely shakes his head and storms out, nearly colliding with Maria's cleaning trolley. Half a dozen 'Freshly sanitized for your comfort and safety' paper sashes flutter across the balcony. My father starts to pick them up but Peter is hovering nearby with a broom. "I got it, Mr Lock. Have a good one." My father nods and mumbles something before flailing on towards the elevator.

Peter stoops gracefully, sweeps up the sashes and bears them through the open door of the next suite which Maria has started cleaning. I am left feeling angry and slightly guilty which makes me even more angry. Family rows always leave a bad taste in the mouth. I have to get away from my father, with or without Rashmi. I keep saying it but that's not enough. I must do it.

One of the sashes has blown along the balcony and lodged against the balustrade and I go out to retrieve it. José is staring up from one of the flowerbeds around the pool. In need of human contact, I wave to him but there is no response. Maybe the sun is in his eyes. He turns and walks into shadow leaving another tray of brightly coloured flowers to await extinction.

The door to the suite that Maria is cleaning is now closed. It seems stupid to bang on the door. I take the sash back to our suite and flush it down the lavatory.

Hadiscomb is looking disgustingly healthy and suntanned. No comparison with the pallid freak I bumped into on Santa Monica Boulevard. He even seems to have grown a couple of inches. You can tell that he is a tourist. Apart from the surf loonies, they are the only ones who work at a suntan. It is going to last all of ten days when he gets back to England. Unable to restrain myself, I casually slip in the information about Rashmi's father.

"I thought he was dead," says Hadiscomb.

This is not the response I would have preferred. "I've talked to him," I say, firmly.

"In person?"

"On the phone."

Hadiscomb shrugs. "It could have been anyone, couldn't it? I mean, I can do a pretty good imitation. What would you like? The poor sap who stands up against the mob?" He half opens his mouth and adapts a look of congenital imbecility. "Duh-er-duh-"

"Okay, okay. Don't call us, we'll call you." Hadiscomb is such a pisser. And he is wearing the shirt he must have bought at 'Esprit' on that first day.

"I could have sworn I read something in the paper. Leukaemia."

"That was somebody else."

"You remember all that stuff about Howard Hughes? When he disappeared and people started getting these calls, and nobody knew whether it was him?"

"Why would anybody go to the trouble of pretending that their father was 'The Man'?"

"To impress people, to wangle credit. It happens all the time. I don't want to be unkind but maybe she's a bit unstable. She stood you up, didn't she?"

"She didn't stand me up. Her car broke down.

"Of course." Hadiscomb smiles and I want to punch him. And yet - and yet - maybe it's not the right moment to mention the Caribbean trip.

"Perhaps if you heard it from her own lips," I hear myself say. "We're meeting after the movie, back at the hotel. You want to come along for a drink?"

"Why not? Yes, that would be good. Let's hope she turns up this time."

The movie we see in squealing, crowded, y-o-u-t-h-f-u-l Westwood does not make me feel any better. It is so frustrating to be watching crap when one's own creative genius is being denied expression. And the audience love it. They are yocking up a storm. The guy behind me is kicking a hole in my seat and spraying popcorn three rows in front of me. And Hadiscomb likes it. 'Refreshing' is a word he uses.

I am still fulminating when we get back to the hotel - and not just against the movie. Why did I have to finagle myself into inviting Hadiscomb to meet Rashmi? Dumb move. Supposing she doesn't turn up? And if she does, how long before I can get rid of him? We drive into the garage past the TV scanner which is never working and take the elevator up to the fourth floor.

The first thing we see as the doors open is a row of backs along the balustrade. People are gazing down into the pool area. There must be a reception, or perhaps they are shooting a TV commercial. Maybe this is Peter's big moment. I glance down and see what looks like a grip with a sound boom.

My father stands with Rashmi outside our apartment. She must have got here early. Her face is red and blotchy as if she has been sobbing. I have never seen her looking like this. My father looks strained. What is going on?

I move to Rashmi. "Are you all right?"

Hadiscomb turns from the balustrade. "Are they shooting a commercial?"

"No," says my father. "One of the staff."

I look again. The grip with the boom is a paramedic with a plasma feed. The shape of a body on a gurney becomes visible through a cluster of people.

"Who is it?"

My father agitates his hand as if trying to pluck the name out of the air. Rashmi looks as if she is coming round after an anaesthetic. "The blond guy with the slow delivery."

"Peter?"

"Yes."

"Oh, no."

"Seems like your classic *crime passionel.* He was having a relationship with one of the maids and her husband didn't like it."

"It's terrible, isn't it?" Rashmi takes my hand. I begin to understand.

"Maria," I say. "How did the husband find out?"

"Used his eyes, I imagine. He was the gardener."

"José?" My brain turns a somersault. "Her husband? I thought he might have been her father. He was such a happy little guy."

"'Was'. They just took him away."

"Is Peter?-" As I speak, I see that a sheet completely covers the gurney. "I put my arm round Rashmi. We are both shaking. "Did you see this?"

"No. We-we-I-"

"I thought it was a car backfiring at first." Father takes Rashmi by the hand and leads her into the suite. "Come on, you need to sit down." He continues to talk to me over his shoulder. "You know, that's your first reaction. But when you hear five bangs."

Peter and Maria. I think of all the times I saw them around each other. And I never thought. Poor Peter. What a lousy break.

"Gosh," says Hadiscomb. He continues to look down at the crowded Astroturf and I can imagine him recording every last detail for the folks back home.

Peter's body is being wheeled away, carrying people with it like iron filings on a magnet. Those watching from the balconies turn to each other to compare impressions and exchange observations. There is a buzz of excitement and, yes, camaraderie in the air. We have stood shoulder to shoulder in the presence of death and we are still alive.

I introduce Hadiscomb and sit next to Rashmi. She is pale and still trembling. The air conditioning is hammering away. I get up and turn it down.

"Who wants a drink?"

Rashmi shakes his head. Hadiscomb prevaricates in his typically British way. He will have something if somebody else is going to have something.

"I'll open some wine," I say.

"That would be splendid," says Hadiscomb. He is gazing admiringly at Rashmi. I think he believes me now.

"It's already open," says my father. "In the fridge."

"I still can't believe that José would do that. He seemed such a sweet guy."

"He's Mexican. He probably is a sweet guy until you start messing with his old lady. Then he whips out his snickersnee."

"I will have some wine." Rashmi has found a glass.

"I think that's what depresses me most about the whole sorry business. The pistol instead of the knife. It's a rejection of your heritage, isn't it?"

Rashmi looks at him and shakes her head. I can imagine what she is thinking.

"Sad to think that when you cross the Rio Grande, you turn your back on your culture."

"Yes," says Hadiscomb politely. He raises his glass. "Cheers."

"And apparently they weren't even *in flagrante delicto*, him and the lady. Doesn't show much respect for salty drama, does it?"

"You can be a real pain in the ass, can't you?" says Rashmi calmly.

Hadiscomb stares at her, embarrassed by such disrespect. I am a little surprised but more angry and upset. Why does he have to behave like this, now? And Peter, poor Peter.

"How astute of you to have noticed." He is emptying the dregs of a gin bottle into his smeared, sticky glass. A bottle that was full this morning. He is pissed. Pissed. Pissed. Pissed.

"If you're going to kill someone, you might as well do it with a bit of style, mightn't you?"

Hadiscomb realises that he is being addressed. "Er-yes. I suppose so. Definitely." He sips uncomfortably. I try to catch Rashmi's eye but she is staring at my father with what I interpret as a superior smile.

"And the location. The gardener, with a pistol, in the laundry room. Hardly very glamorous."

"Doesn't your father say naughty things?" says Rashmi. "Isn't he so wickedly outspoken?"

"The only good thing was that he died just as his tremulous fingers were reaching out for stardom. That could be his apotheosis - in the hands of a decent writer. Me, for instance."

I stand up. "I'll take you home."

"Where you're spoilt for choice, aren't you?" says my father.

"I've always been a great admirer of your father." Hadiscomb has plucked up courage to address Rashmi. As usual, it has taken him a little time to get the measure of his surroundings.

"Do you have a preference?" She is locking eyes with my father.

"'The Difference'," says Hadiscomb.

"'Indifference'!" My father's and my voice overlap.

"Anyway, he got blinded at the end. I couldn't look."

"Neither could he," says my father.

"Yes," says Hadiscomb. "And he was brilliant playing the mad scientist. You know, in-"

"Okay?" I am willing Rashmi to her feet.

Up until now she has barely glanced at Hadiscomb, but now she turns and her eyes pounce on him. "Perhaps you'd like to meet him? I've got to fly down tomorrow. Hey, wouldn't that be fun?" Her gaze expands to embrace all of us. The life has flowed back into her lovely face. "You could all come. Can you imagine? There might be more drama. We could talk about it incessantly."

My father stares at his glass, as if noticing for the first time how filthy it looks.

"You're joking," breathes Hadiscomb.

"I was voted the most serious girl in my class."

"It sounds tremendous but I couldn't come anyway. I'd never be able to afford the flight." His eyes dart towards mine but I am staring at Rashmi. What is she saying?

"No problemo. We'd be taking the plane that flies down his provisions. He's nearly out of Bath Olivers and St Yorre. There'd be plenty of room."

"I can't believe this." But I think Hadiscomb does. And I think I do, too. She couldn't make this up. Not unless she was stark, raving mad. Could she? Is she?

"Santa Monica Airport. 0600 hours tomorrow. Lift off. And that means you too, Mr Grumpy." She takes the flesh of my father's cheek between finger and thumb and kisses him on the nose. "I know you'd like to meet my daddy." She pauses a second. "A successful failure."

I wait for him to sock her, but he just shakes his head.

"Will I need my passport?" says Hadiscomb.

"What are you doing!?" I screech when I eventually get her outside. Behind us, Hadiscomb is politely answering my father's questions concerning the incidence of drug-taking and homosexuality at Rockingham. "Why did you have to ask them?"

"Why did I suggest we have dinner? A whim, a hunch, a caprice? That worked out pretty okay, didn't it? They'll be an alkali - I mean, what's that thing that helps a reaction?"

"A catalyst. I don't see Hadiscomb as a catalyst. An alkali, maybe."

"Perhaps I'm just terribly attracted to him. He is handsome."

"Are you serious?"

"Of course not. He's too stupid to be attractive. I'd just fuck him a few times."

"He's not stupid. He's just - just British. And he's a little overawed by you. Who isn't? Oh, God. I hope my father doesn't come. He's driving me crazy at the moment."

"Poor guy." I am about to give her an argument when I look down at the pool. There is still a section of the Astroturf with sand sprinkled on it.

"Yeah, it was our maid, you know. Who he was - you know. With whom-"

"Yeah."

Something glitters in one of the flower beds. A trowel. Nearby, the pool lights pick out the dark rectangle of a tray of flowers waiting to be planted. "Where are we going?" I move in and slide my arm around her.

"Tomorrow we're going to Saint Francis."

"What about tonight?"

She kisses me quickly on the lips. "Tonight I've got to pick up my mother. She's flying in late. You know what it's like when you have parents to look after."

My heart sinks. "Surely she can get from the airport by herself?"

"I promised." She disengages and heads for the elevator, trailing me behind her by one hand. "Don't be mad, you've only got to wait twenty-four hours."

"I want you now." I press the button.

"Urgh! Look at that. Ice-cream on the carpet. People are pigs." The door slides open.

"I want to make love to you." This is a euphemism, but I do love her. I take her in my arms and she wriggles to press 'P' for parking.

"Oh, Willum. What am I going to do with you?"

"If we get all the way down without stopping, you're going to have to make love to me."

We watch the floors tick by. It is the slowest elevator in the world. Without the floor numbers flashing, you would never know you were moving. I have lots of time to think about Peter. But I don't.

"I have to go. I can't spend the night with you."

I push my hands up inside her sweater so that I can touch flesh. I need to do that. The door shudders and slides open slowly. Beyond is the dimly lit garage and rows of cars. The traffic hums by on Wilshire, screeching and revving as the lights change. There is an acrid smell of exhaust fumes waiting to put on weight and become smog. Her mouth is hot and the scent of her body strong.

"Oh, William." She sounds like a mother talking to a difficult child. "Come with me."

Halfway down the garage is a fantasy car, a dream machine, a collaboration between Heath Robinson and Arthur Rackham with silver tubing sprouting out of its engine housing and huge headlights and everything shining. It looks like the Pompidou Centre on wheels. Rashmi leads me towards it and opens the back door. She gets in. I follow. It smells of leather and pot and decadence and there are crystal decanters in a rosewood holder and glasses with a filigree of vine clusters. We could have brought a pool table with us and still had space to work out. The seats creak as we settle into them and the carpeting tickles our ankles. I wonder what period of 'The Man's' life this belonged to.

Rashmi is suddenly very close. "I lied to your little friend," she says. "I wasn't voted the most serious girl in my class. I was voted the girl most likely to succeed - or maybe it was 'suck seed'. I was never certain." She kisses me and tugs gently at my lower lip with her teeth. Her hand runs down to my knee and then up inside my thighs. "I looked you up, Sweet William. You're really 'Dianthus Barbatus' and you come from Eurasia, did you know that? You're usually cultivated but you can grow wild. 'Barbatus' sounds a little wild, doesn't it?" Her fingers tug down my zipper and I can feel myself growing into her hand.

"Get on to me," I tell her. "I want to look at you."

But her head is slipping down my body. "Lots of varieties. And there's one called 'Scarlet Beauty'. How appropriate can you get?"

I stroke the back of her head and feel the incredible silkiness of her hair. I love what she is doing but I want to see her face. Saying 'I love you' now seems like tossing the words into space. I say them anyway, and a few seconds later I start to come, crying out at the same instant, flinching and flexing as the shock waves spread out through my body. She releases me gently, like a cat putting down a newly born kitten, and swallows my seed. I fold her to me and hold her tight, feeling tears against my cheek and half-wondering whether they are hers or mine. We stay like that for minutes, and then she draws away. "Tomorrow."

I feel sad. A little empty, a little foolish. With Rashmi, I always want to be strong. To give rather than be given. And to do it here. In the basement. In this replica of a Las Vegas bordello where I have just lived out the fantasy of every fourteen-year-old in America. The trouble with me is that I always want more.

We get out of the car and I pat the hood. "Quite a car."

"Yes," she says. "I wonder who it belongs to." She heads for a battered jeep parked opposite.

I take another look at the heap of chrome and, for some strange reason, feel better. Now it seems like a discarded condom. The jeep's engine surges and she leans out towards me.

"Six o'clock tomorrow. Clover Field."

"I'll be there. Hadiscomb will probably sleep on the runway. I don't know about my father."

"Whatever." She kisses me hard on the mouth and jolts away. I follow her around the corner and watch the jeep revving impatiently as the grill slowly starts to swing open. I wave and she screeches forward into the night. A Californian girl.

14.

The nose twitches, the jaws tremble rhythmically, the piece of lettuce disappears slowly as if being fed between a set of rollers. The soft brown eyes watch warily. I push a finger through the bars and it is sniffed cautiously and found to have no nutritional value. I feel a strange, electric, not unpleasant, tickling sensation as the damp nose touches my skin.

There are twenty of them. Chinchilla rabbits. Ten bucks and ten does, though they have to start humping each other before I can tell the difference. Their makeshift cages are piled amongst stacks of Badoit, Perrier, St-Yorre, Evian and Vittel. Rashmi was not kidding about the mineral water. Piled along the fuselage are bulk packs of bran, brown rice, whole wheat flower, vitamin supplements, yeast pills and homeopathic products I have never heard of: 'Wheat Grass' and 'Dragon Eggs'. 'The Man' must be a grade one health freak.

My father should be depurated by his very proximity to all this stuff. He sits by one of the windows, with a pencil, chuckling over a copy of 'Blood of the Lust Crazy', not at the script but at what he is doing to it. Hadiscomb has talked himself out and is dozing a few rows back.

We have been flying for nearly seven hours, refuelling at places I never knew had airports. Now we have left San Juan - 'I know a boat you can get o-o-o-o-o-o-n!' - and we are on the final leg. It is a little less glamorous than I had anticipated, what with half the plane taken up by natural laxatives but, hey, I am not complaining. I had only been barely aware that this kind of flying existed. That airports had back doors you could pass through to pick up a charter or fly off in your own plane; just like sailing your boat out of a marina. Rashmi merely says that the plane has been 'made available' to her father. I feel that it would be vulgar to ask if he actually owns it.

Hadiscomb's presence irritates me but does not surprise me. It is my father I am pissed off about. Not only is it like taking your mother-in-law on your honeymoon but he would be much better employed staying at the hotel and taking steps to dodge the shit storm that is about to break out in L.A. Western Rentals are refusing to get back to our lawyer and that can only bode ill. They still have our passports and, despite Rashmi's reassurances, I am not convinced that we will be able to get into Saint Francis without them.

"I hope they last longer than the llamas." Rashmi has appeared beside me and is gazing at the silky-haired rabbits.

"Llamas?"

"Father's always trying to set the local population up with something they can turn into an industry. He thought the men could raise the llamas and the women weave their wool into garments."

"What happened?"

"They ate them. At least, I think they did. They disappeared anyway. Everything does. Though we see the minks sometimes. They come down and kill the chickens."

The rabbit has stopped nibbling. "Maybe we should-"

Rashmi has been following my eyes. "Yes, it would be more considerate, wouldn't it?" She moves towards my father. "Do you want a drink, Adrian?" It seems strange to hear her call him by his Christian name.

"Yes, if there's anything other than lukewarm orange juice. We'll be landing soon, won't we?"

"About twenty minutes."

"I'll wait, thanks."

He touches her hand and she drifts forward to talk to the pilots. This casual freedom of movement seems strange to me. I have difficulty remembering I am on a plane. My father gazes after Rashmi and then down at the sea. A tug is towing a barge weighed down to the gunwales by a towering mausoleum of containers.

"I remember reading this book review by Anthony Burgess," he says, talking to space. "He managed to drag in the doctrine of New Immortality. Apparently, the ego survives death because, according to the theory of psycho-neural parallelism, it has no cerebral counterpart and can't be snuffed out with the body. It's comforting to know that there are minds capable of grappling with that kind of thing, isn't it? I sometimes wonder what good it does them unless they write a lot of book reviews, but I suppose that's not the point. When you've absorbed all the simple stuff...." His voice tails away and he pulls his eyes away from Rashmi and turns to me. "Give me three synonyms for treachery?"

We haven't done this for some time. I reflect. "Betrayal...treason..."

Rashmi leaves the cockpit and closes the door behind her. She leans against it, gives a cute little wriggle of her upper body and mimes the fastening of a seat belt.

"I was thinking of betrayal," says my father. "Betrayal, love and fucking bad luck."

I wait for an explanation but he does not provide one. Sometimes he ventures where the other guides do not take you. How old and tired he looks. "You need a drink," I tell him.

He smiles at me not unkindly. "Maybe."

The few clouds are very high or banked along a horizon that is virtually obscured by haze. The sea is a brilliant juggled palette of blues and greens. The colours overlap in layers like the plumage of a tropical bird. We start to descend and a scattering of cays appear; then small islands, the foliage so thick and all-pervading that the small circles of land seem like huge drowning trees. White razor nicks fleck the surface, hinting at currents, shoals and a lively wind, and suddenly there are beaches and people, clusters of houses and cultivated fields amidst foliage, dense and green and succulent. Corrugated iron roofs dazzle from hilltops and I feel a familiar but too easily forgotten excitement. Another world moored in its own time. Different smells, different accents, different history. Rashmi buckles herself in beside me and I take her hand. The rabbits are sitting upright with only their noses twitching. They can sense that something important is about to happen.

The plane lands and we file into a building that has the air of a shabby but friendly art supermarket. Everybody seems to know Rashmi and the pilots, and passports are not mentioned. Most of the tour operators' booths are closed or unattended, but there are piles of leaflets everywhere offering trips in midget submarines, visits to the - presumed - sites of buried pirate treasure or a cruise on the yacht where Bing Crosby once crooned to Grace Kelly. When all that palls, you can invest in real estate.

Rashmi bustles around greeting people and Hadiscomb informs me what time it is in England and how the island used to be a Danish colony before it was sold to the United States who were wary of its strategic proximity to the Panama Canal and feared that the Germans might move in and build U-boat pens. I immediately cancel plans to buy a guidebook.

Outside, a middle-aged, dignified black man is waiting beside a truck that has been converted into a bus by the addition of a few rows of benches and a striped awning, and he and a silent companion load our luggage and the rabbits and provisions. I notice the way the silent companion is gazing at the rabbits and wonder how many of them are going to be around to read bedtime stories to their grandchildren.

"'Kay, Mis' Rashm'."

We scramble aboard and chug out into the bright sunshine. Bougainvillea, hibiscus and coral vine are sprouting from the rusty wire fences like weeds. An untidy sprawl of nondescript houses splashed with desquamated stucco squat beside a pot-holed road. There are patches of cultivated land but no obvious demarcation lines between them. We rise in broad zigzags through the colourful vegetation, thick enough to be jungle, and suddenly tip over the edge as on a roller coaster. Below us is a wide bay dotted with ocean liners and yachts at anchor. Houses are tacked to the steep slopes and clutter the waterfront as if some have worked loose and tumbled down to land on top of each other. Far out to sea, there are islands and cays lost in haze. That is where we are going.

The brakes squeak nervously and we start our descent. A few streets back from the waterfront the houses become grander. Crisp white wedding cakes with tiers of wrought iron balconies, painted shutters and string of pearl cornices. They are fronted by small, dignified palm trees and privet hedges. Not the vulgar riots of creeper that obscure lesser dwellings. We pass a neat, pink fort, so ordered in its square design, gothic arches and ordered crenellations that it seems like a giant version of a child's toy.

Now we are nearly at the quay and there are lots of people. Not locals, but tourists from the cruise ships who have come ashore to sack Benetton or buy another Rolex. Loaded down with booty, they are trudging from the narrow alleys and waiting for the launches that will ferry them back to their air-conditioned floating palaces. Most of them look as if the fun is wearing a little thin. They jostle to get on the gangplank and snap at their partners. Perhaps they should have bought that camera three ports back; when the wife told them. Still, in a couple of days they will be in another port and maybe the prices will be better and their stomach bug will have cleared up.

We stop further along the quay from the milling crowds, where there is a grown-up launch with two levels of deck moored broadside to the waterfront.

"This is us?" exclaims Hadiscomb, incredulous, thrilled.

"Every nautical inch," says Rashmi. "Hi, Samuel. You got the rum punch?"

"He's got, Mis' Rashm'" A grizzled black guy skips ashore and a keyboard of white teeth beam up at us. "How y'folks doin' dis fine eve'nin'?"

"Fantastic," says Hadiscomb.

"Dat's good." The response is slightly muted. Samuel has obviously been fazed by Hadiscomb's enthusiasm. Another man comes ashore and lazy high fives are exchanged all round.

We load up and Rashmi hands over some cash to the driver of the bus who seems pleased though he hardly says anything. Daniel's assistant delves in a zinc bath of ice and retrieves a bottle of pinky-brown liquid that he proceeds to decant into glasses already equipped with two cocktail cherries. Rum punch. I accept a glass and mount to the upper deck. The motor splutters to life and we cast off and nose away from the quay.

Not for the first time in my life, I contemplate how nice it must be to be rich - provided that you can appreciate it, of course. With the taste of nutmeg on my lips and the sun sliding down a chute of flamingo pink it is difficult not to feel like a man sailing under the flag of a rare and gilded destiny.

I return to the lower deck where Rashmi is refilling my father's glass and Hadiscomb trying to feed one of the rabbits his cocktail cherry. I stop him before he can kill it and look back towards the receding shore. The tourists are scrambling over each other to get into a launch and it occurs to me that I have forgotten the postcards. This was where Ellen and Lucy were going to receive a statement of my regret - in that sentiment-enhancing envelope, of course. Perhaps it is no bad thing. There is always a danger of reopening healing wounds. Ellen has almost certainly got the bedding back from the cleaners by now, and the very sight of an exotic postcard could remind Lucy of what she was missing and plunge her into an even deeper abyss of depression. No, nothing was the right thing to do and, instinctively, I did it.

A launch flying a Technicolor pennant cuts across us and my father snorts. "'Senior Cruises'. God, can you imagine anything more disgusting? The orchestra launching into a tango and the artificial limbs hopping out of their sockets. The rubber knickers sloshing like maracas. The cumulous clouds of incontinence pads dancing in the wake. Those special fridges groaning with geriatrics who popped off on the poop deck. The crew scurrying to sweep up the bits that fall off - defunct pacemakers, failed prosthetic limbs, lost wigs, ejected false teeth, clapped-out hearing aids, stained surgical supports. All stinking and rattling like skeletons in some ghastly floating charnel house-"

"All right!" cries Rashmi. "We all have to get old!" She calms down a bit. "People's infirmities aren't funny."

"Then surely that robs them of their only point?" He stares at her and waits. "What's the grand design?" He shakes his head and stomps towards the upper deck.

"Super punch," says Hadiscomb.

Rashmi tells him to have some more and follows my father. I am touched by her compassion. She must realise how lonely he feels sometimes and how he can make a scene just to keep himself company. I think she rubs him up the wrong way, too. Because she is young and rich and beautiful - and mine. It must be difficult for him.

He may even want to punish her for leaving me in Sun Valley; he can be strangely protective sometimes - though perhaps it is more realistic to interpret it as part of his patriarchal nature.

Hadiscomb is expounding on the failings of the current West Indies cricket team to an apparently disinterested Samuel and I climb to the upper deck. Rashmi and my father are leaning against the fore rail with their arms spread wide and a few inches between their finger tips. They move aside so that I can join them and we stare ahead into the broad channel that leads to the open sea. Once beyond the headland, the wind buffets our faces and the boat begins to pitch and toss. A strong swell is running and a rib of white water, stirred like cream in a bowl, reveals where a reef or sand bar bisects a shoal. We steer straight for it and the rusty buoys and mooring chains clang and bob and outriders of foam race into the algae coated rocks and send spray soaring. The waves are pinched tight and high and the bow thumps down rhythmically like a cleaver hacking through the channel. Womp! Womp! Womp! I am clinging on with all my force, craning down into the pits of foaming water and ahead to the bar. It is dramatic and exciting; and with the motion of the boat and the wild wind hurling seabirds round the heavens like boomerangs, and the land and seascapes leaping and cavorting, tension and fatigue are snatched away and the air rushes through my lungs, charging me with the joy of being alive, convincing me that this is, incontrovertibly, the best of all possible worlds. I look to my father and his eyes are watering. Perhaps he is feeling what I am feeling.

Rashmi's hair blows across her face and she plucks it aside and jabs a finger ahead. There are several islands on the horizon and it is impossible to see which one she is pointing at. We slash across the lip of white water and sand swirls to the surface in a long brown lick. The sea turns grey-green and heavy and the troughs stretch ahead with the pattern of opaque glass. We shake off the islets and the cays and steer into the setting sun.

I usually feel uneasy in the open sea but here it is less intimidating because in every direction there are islands. Some are British and some are American, but they all look the same.

After about forty minutes, we approach an island with low, thickly-wooded hills and long empty beaches fringed by overhanging palms. The sun has almost disappeared and the pink sky is turning grey. The wind has dropped and the sea is calm. Soon it will be dark. We round a point and there is a jetty and a couple of bungalows glinting from thick vegetation. No other dwellings are visible, though a small cove is peppered with white canvas beach chairs all facing the sea. Some have sunk into the sand almost to the seat, as if they have not been used in a long time.

"This is it," says Rashmi. She sees me looking at the chairs. "It was going to be a luxury beach resort, only the developers ran out of cash. That was when my father bought it."

I look towards the jetty. Somewhere in my mind I had formed a picture of him being there to greet us, like the French Lieutenant's Woman with balls; but there are only two black kids, one of whom runs into the palms as we get closer.

"Feeling better?" Hadiscomb has turned the colour of the rabbits and been on the point of throwing up since we hit the open sea.

"I'll be fine," he says stoically. "I think it was something in the drink."

We draw alongside the jetty and a comfortable black woman with granny spectacles and her hair in a scarf comes towards us, wiping her hands on a tea towel. Rashmi embraces her and makes introductions. "This is Mrs Tunker. She looks after us here. Is my father joining us for dinner?"

"Don' know, Mis' Rashm'. He say he call down."

It is dark by the time we have got everything ashore and the small boys refuse to be helped and stagger off with our luggage towards the bungalows. I notice that Rashmi's bags do not accompany them. Mrs Tunker clucks over my ankle and hissing hurricane lamps appear, borne by what I assume are more family retainers. A procession forms and we are conducted along a path through sweet-smelling lady of the night, already being courted by large moths. Smaller insects flutter around the lamps and there is a sudden flurry of raindrops that makes Mrs Tunker cluck some more.

The bungalows are a hundred yards back from the sea amongst tall palms and divided into suites with slow-turning ceiling fans and heavy mahogany furniture. There is a faint odour of damp and decay as if the buildings are not totally at home in their tropical surroundings and have contracted a wasting disease. Father, Hadiscomb and I are shown to rooms next door to each other and Rashmi says that she will collect us for dinner in an hour. She steps into my room for a few seconds and I want to seize her and mould her to the bed; but the entourage are peering round the door in layers and I have no chance to mention the rest of the night.

I feel strange when the door closes and I am alone. Then I realise why: because I am alone. For the first time in weeks there is no father commandeering the bed nearest the bathroom, emptying his socks into the top drawer, tossing his dirty underwear where I have arranged my things. Not that he is far away. When I have unpacked my bag and run a bath - brown water that slowly begins to clear - a familiar figure has appeared on the adjacent balcony, staring into the night and pouring the contents of a small packet into a glass of what I assume is water. He tosses it back with an audible grimace.

The fronds of the palms slither and slide as the breeze comes up and the ocean hisses against the shore like it wants to remind you that it is there and not to be taken lightly. Out to sea, there is a single stationary light. Maybe a moored boat or a nearby island. Perhaps the light at the end of Nancy's dock. I would like to have some contact with my father but I want him to make the first move. A comment about the rain that finds its way into the wind, or the rhythmic warble that could either be frogs or night birds. But he continues to act as if I was not there, so I go back inside and close the shutters and run more liquid rust into my bath.

At least the bath is hot and presumably the same colour as the one our host is sinking into. One tincture suits all. The island is more island than I had anticipated. As if winking their approval of this thought, the lights flicker. Rashmi could well be happy in Pulignac if she is used to this. There, storms bring down the power lines and the water not only runs brown but disappears altogether when the farmers are watering their young tobacco plants. That is when my father launches himself at the telephone and screams to the water people that they are nourishing a weed that destroys millions of human beings whilst he and his loved ones are condemned to die of thirst. They say that they are *desolés* and the sprinklers go on sloshing water across the thick, juicy leaves. Meanwhile, down at the *Syndicat Intercommunal d'Adduction d'Eau*, they are probably congratulating each other on their contribution to a display of the famous British eccentricity.

Perhaps we could spend most of the year at Pulignac and come here in the winter. It will be different tomorrow, when the sun comes out. That is the main charm of arriving at an unknown destination in the dark: the anticipation of discovering it in the morning, when you will both be at your peak. Now, it is four hours later than it says on my watch and I can hear the drumming of rain through the rise and fall of the bustling wind. Something scampers across the roof above my head. I say 'scamper' to myself rather than 'run' because it suggests the progress of an endearing, pretty little creature rather than, say, a rat. 'The isle is full of noises, sounds and sweet airs, that give delight and hurt not'. Urhmn.

I dress and wait by the door, like a cat before a mouse hole. A soft, sweet smell seems to be pushed under the door by the rain. There are adjustable slats in the walls so that the breeze can enter from one side and leave via the other. Tentacles of vine poke in like searching fingers.

There is a light tap on the door and I whip it open. Hadiscomb is revealed in his 'Esprit' shirt. I could slug him. "Are you all right?"

"I'm fine."

"You looked-"

"Come in."

Hadiscomb does so and gazes around. "I found a huge centipede in my bath. I didn't want to kill it so I eventually chivvied it down the plug hole. It'll probably come up in your bath."

"Thanks a lot."

"Either way, I'd keep the plug in." He rubs his hands together and takes another look round the room. "Place reminds me of Rockingham." I confess that the resemblance had escaped me. "I mean the rain and the sense of being cooped up." He studies me patiently. Every time he mentions Rockingham it is as if he is handing me a key and waiting for me to unlock something. "I never thought of bringing a raincoat." He has given up on me. "In fact, I don't have one. Not here, I mean in Los Angeles, not on the island."

"Yes," is all I can think of to say.

Further attempts at conversation are avoided by the arrival of Rashmi with my father, a hissing lamp and some tired golf umbrellas. I wait for her to sidle up to me and slip a note into my hand but all I get is an umbrella.

"Don't put it up inside, it's bad luck," says Hadiscomb.

My father bestows a withering look from the porch and extends a hand into the night. You won't have to put it up. It's stopped raining."

Slipping and sliding, we make our way through dripping shrubbery. The ground rises and we emerge onto a grassy hillock surmounted by a square stone house with an elegant, pillared portico. It is surrounded by spreading trees from which dangle long beans that rattle in the wind. Dark shapes are moving across the grass and disappearing into holes in the ground.

"Hermit crabs," says Rashmi as I touch her arm.

I am bracing myself for my first sight of 'The Man'. I imagine him glimpsed from behind like Rochester in the movie of 'Jane Eyre', one hand resting on the arm of a huge leather chair that is facing an enormous fireplace, two hounds lolling at his feet.

The dogs are there, an Airedale and something less easy to pin down, but there is no sign of our host when we leave the high-ceilinged entrance hall with its brass candelabrum and enter a dining room with cool green walls and louvered shutters over French windows. Fans turn slowly against the dried blood ceiling and hanging in discreet shadow is a painting of a bowl of fruit that reminds me of Gauguin. I think about it and decide that it probably is a Gauguin. Rashmi suggests how we should sit and she and my father flank the polished Chippendale dining chair at the end of the table where a fifth place is set. Rashmi seems uneasy and I feel vaguely usurped by my father taking preference. Still, he is my father.

A door opens and my stomach tightens. It is Mrs Tunker.

"Any word?"

"No, Mis' Rashm'. You wan' I try an' call him?"

"No, Sarah. It doesn't matter. We'll start without him. Maybe he'll join us later. Oh, and Sarah, we'll have some wine in honour of our guests."

Mrs Tunker nods and goes out and I see Hadiscomb looking at me. I know what is passing through his mind: perhaps Prospero does not exist. There is only Miranda. Maybe we have stumbled into an Anouilh play. Maybe 'The Man' is watching us through a hole in the panelling. Maybe it is all a dream.

"My father's stomach isn't rigged to an alarm clock," says Rashmi. "You have to hope that a pang of hunger coincides with a meal time."

Mrs Tunker appears with a bottle of St Emilion and my father becomes more animated. We learn that we are in what used to be the estate house when the island was a sugar plantation worked by slaves.

The slaves rose several times and on one occasion stormed the house and hacked everyone inside it to death with cane knives.

"Good help is hard to find," sighs my father.

"The ringleaders were tortured with hot pincers, mutilated, impaled, sawn in half and burned to death slowly," says Rashmi.

"By which time they were probably beginning to get the message," says my father.

"I suppose their ghosts roam the island," says Hadiscomb.

"I wasn't going to mention that." Rashmi pelts her soup with pepper.

"Jumbies no got de power to kill you, but deh sur' can make lotsa trouble." Mrs Tunker chuckles as she plumps down the giant bowl of what smells like fish chowder in front of me. "But don' you lissn' her. Dis is one happy place. You see dat tomorrow."

I hope she is right but doubts are beginning to creep in. I stretch out a discreet foot towards Rashmi and Hadiscomb kicks me in the ankle. "Sorry," he says, peering under the table. "Was that you or one of the dogs?"

I begin to understand why Voyce hated him so much. It probably had nothing to do with a refusal to grant sexual favours.

The wall lights flicker and Mrs Hunker hisses in exasperation and snatches up a strategically placed box of matches. She stands poised, daring the lights to go out and I sense a woman who has learned to gobble up adversity like a tasty snack. Another protracted flicker and we are in darkness.

"Jumbies," says Hadiscomb.

As if to prove him right, there is a muffled shout of frustration from somewhere in the recesses of the house. Mrs Tunker chuckles in the darkness and swiftly lights one of the candlesticks. "He never find hi' matches," she says cheerfully and departs, another candle in hand.

"I imagine her ancestors were whacking away with the old cane knives," says my father.

"Mrs Tunker is wonderful," says Rashmi. "She's been like a mother to me. More than a mother."

All the candles are lit but darkness has now taken control and our faces gleam in shadow as if we have come together to hatch a plot. I have the feeling that I am slipping to the edge, losing contact with the centre of things. I stretch out a hand to feel the reassurance of Rashmi and encounter my father's death head stare louring out of a cowl of darkness. I put my hand on the table where everyone can see it. Footsteps approach and I brace myself. I am not ready for 'The Man'.

It is Mrs Tunker with a roast chicken. "He enjoy'n his new waters," she says. "Tinks de rabbits is jus' fine." She laughs as if at a private joke and leaves to return with a bowl of sweet-tasting vegetables and more claret.

My father tastes the chicken and kisses his fingers. "I'm going to marry your Mrs Tunker," he says. "I'm going to hide the cane knives and she's going to make me live happily ever after."

"Over my dead body," says Rashmi. "Anyway, how do you know there isn't a Mr Tunker?"

"She looks too happy."

Rashmi appears about to say something and then pushes her glass towards him for a refill.

"Do you remember that storm at Rockingham?" says Hadiscomb. "We had to eat by candlelight then."

"We should have done it all the time," I say. "It wasn't food you wanted to look at."

Hadiscomb extends his fork towards me out of the shadows. A strange gesture. There is a small piece of chicken impaled on the prongs. "That's when I knew you'd done it. When I remembered you taking the piece of meat."

There is a silence.

"What's he talking about?" asks Rashmi.

They are all staring at me, waiting.

"Nothing important," I say.

When Rashmi walks us back to the guest house the electricity has come on and there are bats picking off the moths around the porch lights. I have the feeling that the evening has been a liquid I have spilled and that will be mopped up in the morning. Then, I will see more clearly and, hopefully, the stain will be less obvious. Now, I am tired and the island is gnawing at my spirits.

Rashmi kisses us all goodnight and says that breakfast will be available when we want it. I search her eyes for a look that belongs only to me and yearn to feel a secret pressure in her touch but I know that we will not be sharing the same bed tonight. It is not serious. She is our hostess, the island's major-domo - how masculine that sounds - and as such has other responsibilities than to nurture my love. She seems a little strange in that role but I will attend to the re-wooing in the morning. I do not have to mount her every ten minutes to indicate my feelings, though it would be a pleasant way of doing so.

I try to close the wall slats but one set are sealed by creepers and I cannot extricate them all from inside my room. I go outside to the balcony. On one side I can hear my father coughing but there is neither sound nor light from Hadiscomb's room. He drunk a great deal - but not as much as my father, of course - and is probably sprawled out across his bed. 'The Death of Hadiscomb'. A pleasing pre-Raphaelite notion. Hadiscomb. Yes, I now see clearly the path that he is treading and where it might end. His smudged footsteps mingle with the stain, a kind of Rorschach test that I have no desire to take tonight. I start tugging at the vine and there is a sound behind me. A breath, a snort. I take a step forward and strain my eyes into the darkness. There is a scary, desperate panting as if a wounded creature was poised to attack. Then a rasping bellow that explodes in my face in a gust of foul breath and something huge crashes away into the undergrowth pursued by frantic barking.

"What is it?" My father appears on his balcony.

"I don't know."

We listen and the barking gets fainter and fainter until it merges with the sounds of the night.

"I'll try and ring Constance in the morning," says my father. "See if I can sort something out."

"Thanks," I say, wondering what has jerked forth this sudden expression of paternal feeling. He grunts and retires to his room and I forget about the slats and go to bed.

I sleep badly and awake to my father singing, "'Fling 'ope the gates of paradise, and let the glory of the dawn shine in!'" He is a bit late for the dawn but spot on for the glory as I find when I venture out onto my balcony. Sparkling azure sea semaphores through a glade of palms fringed by beds of scarlet frangipani and poinsettia. The grass is bright green, the light pure and dazzling. Birds warble cheerfully and there is a clean, scrubbed edge to the air. I shower and dress quickly so that I can get to Rashmi before the others.

She is sitting on the wide terrace of the estate house with Hadiscomb. Her hair is held back by nacre clips and her skimpy beach dress is a converted flower sack that looks as if it was tailored by Dolce & Gabbana.

"We were wondering what to do today," she says brightly as one of Mrs Tunker's acolytes replaces a coffee pot. We could start with a boating accident, I reflect. A drowning starring Hadiscomb. "Of course, it's a little difficult with your poor ankle."

"Apparently there are some wind surfers," says Hadiscomb, carefully picking marmalade off his Lacoste alligator with the tip of his knife - don't slip now. "But I suppose that's out of the question in your condition."

"You go ahead," I tell him. "Some of those cays look very reachable."

I glance around for any sign that our host might have made an appearance. Nothing. Rashmi pours me some coffee and my imagination extrapolates the gesture into a breakfast ritual. "Did you sleep okay?"

I tell her about the monster and she laughs. "Must have been one of the donkeys. There are nearly a hundred of them now. They were originally brought in to work the cane fields. When that folded they went native."

"European sugar beet destabilised the market," says Hadiscomb.

"That's right," says Rashmi. "Your friend is very knowledgeable."

"That's only part of his charm," I say. "That and his penchant for remembering the old days."

Hadiscomb continues to butter his toast. He doesn't even look up.

"I don't think there's one native animal on the island apart from a species of bat. This guy's a real villain, aren't you Gus?" Rashmi indicates a bushy-tailed, weasel-like creature that scuttles out of the hibiscus to bear away the piece of bread tossed to it. "Mongooses were brought in to control the rats that were munching the sugar cane. The only problem was that the rats lived in trees and slept during the day while the mongooses got vertigo six inches off the ground and started stacking Zs the instant the sun went down. It was an ecological disaster. Part of a rich tradition that my father has been fostering ever since. The island is crawling with escaped animals that don't belong here and spend their time trying to eat each other."

"If Mrs Tunker and Co. don't get there first," says Hadiscomb.

"I thought mongeese were Indian," I say.

"Mongooses," corrects Hadiscomb.

"Right again," says Rashmi. "That's the plural."

I wonder how Hadiscomb would look with the butter knife sticking out from between his eyes. "A charm of nightingales is a plural, I like. And a murmuration of starlings." These gems of fifth form learning are delivered solely to Rashmi and I realise that the floppy-haired Rupert Brooke look-alike is trying to seduce her with his intellect.

"How about a ballsache of pompous pedants?" I ask.

Hadiscomb looks at me disdainfully, as if I am lowering the tone and my father arrives. He looks awful. Bags under the bags under the bags under his eyes; furrows where there used to be merely lines. He has cut himself shaving and what looks like a tiny scrap of blood-soaked bog paper adorns one sagging cheek. Despite his appearance, his manner is brisk. He refuses a cup of coffee, drinks a thimble full of grapefruit juice with the expression of a man swallowing hemlock and, on being assured that the United States can frequently be reached by cell phone, states that he is going to make a few calls and then explore the island. This news brings twofold happiness. My father lost in the jungle, Hadiscomb borne away by trade winds, Rashmi to me.

My father stumps off 'to do what a man has to do' and Hadiscomb departs to check out the wind surfers. I am left alone with Rashmi, two increasingly bold mongooses and a black and white crow. I draw closer immediately.

"I can scarcely believe it. Apart from the burgeoning animal life we're alone." I kiss her as the girl arrives to start collecting the breakfast things.

"And the staff," says Rashmi.

The maid is darting glances at us, half cheeky, half bashful. "How many do you have?" I say, willing the girl to hurry up.

"It varies according to romance, whim, family relationships and what jobs are available on the neighbouring islands. Always enough, sometimes too many, never too few."

I gaze at her, lulled by waves of tenderness. "I'd love to show you Pulignac."

A spray of creeper is hanging near her and she starts picking at a blossom. "What about your job?"

"I was going to tell you about that. It doesn't look good at the moment. Problems at the studio. I may have to start all over again."

"Poor William." She rests a hand on my arm. "What are you going to do?"

"Forget about it while I'm here. With you around, I always feel something positive is going to happen."

She moves her hand and pats me on the cheek. "One huge optimist."

"That's what being half-American is all about, isn't it?"

"That's what we're told."

I move to kiss her but she draws away and glances into the house. "You're very sensitive about the staff. They don't look easily shockable."

"They're not. They're not." Her beautiful eyes are looking at me but they don't tell me what they are seeing.

"Or maybe it's your father. Surely he wouldn't be shocked to see us exchanging a chaste kiss?" I wait. "When I am I going to meet the guy? Hadiscomb doesn't think he exists."

"That's very profound of him."

This is not what I want to hear. "What do you mean?"

"The other day we ran one of his old films for Mrs Tunker. She didn't like it. 'It wasn't him'. That's what she said. We were surprised, but it's obvious really. She sees more of him than any of us. All those different roles he's played, all those different people, they're strangers to her. I sometimes wonder if he hasn't become a stranger to himself. Do you see what I'm getting at.?"

"Sort of." She is worried about her father. Like a good daughter. It is reassuring. "But you mustn't let it get you down. You have your own life to lead - our life. My father has a ton of problems but there's not a whole lot I can do about them."

She mulls over this but does not seem any happier. "William-"

"In fact, me worrying too much would just make him feel worse. It's probably like that with your father."

"Oh, William. Why is life such a bucket of shit?" This is the kind of philosophical question that has always thrown me, especially when the person asking it is beginning to cry and gripping my wrist like her fingers are a tourniquet.

My father chooses this moment to reappear. "What's happening?" he says.

"Nothing. Did you get through to Constance?" I goad him. It had never occurred to me that she could get on a list of his first ten calls.

He does not reply immediately but continues to look at Rashmi. She sniffs like a child trying to be brave and runs the back of a hand across her eyes. "No," he says eventually. "She's in hospital. She took an overdose and set fire to her office."

"Christ! That's horrible." I think about it and begin to understand the strange response when I called. It must have just happened. "Is she burned?"

"No. The smoke alarm did its stuff. They got her out in time." He shakes his head. "Poor Constance. Trying to commit suttee on the funeral pyre of a million rejected ideas. There's a dedicated studio widow for you."

"Poor woman," says Rashmi.

"Yes," muses my father. "She might as well chuck away the key to the executive washroom." He gazes at Rashmi. "Suicide is always a lousy career move in Hollywood. Unless you're a washed up actor, of course. Grand larceny, shop-lifting, murder or a smattering of incest can always be excused as executive stress-related, but suicide suggests that your heart's not in the job. And that's death."

Something snaps. "So's the way you talk!" I shout at him. "Constance loved you and you treated her like shit! Fucking that hag at Sun Valley under her nose! Humiliating her!" I have never seen Rashmi's face as it is now. "Now you talk about her like this when she's just tried to kill herself. Doesn't it occur to you that you're responsible?" He is looking at me patiently like he wants to make sure that I have finished before he says anything. The staff are peering round doorways. "Am I getting through to you? 'Responsible'! Remind yourself to look it up in a dictionary!" I turn to Rashmi but she has disappeared.

"Maybe you have a point," says my father. "Maybe I am partly responsible."

"'Partly'!?"

"Nobody in their right mind decides to kill themself. There has to be a little worm in the apple first."

"How did the worm get there?" He doesn't say anything. "What are you going to do?"

"I don't know." He kicks a piece of bread towards a skulking mongoose. "Perhaps go for a walk while I ponder." He starts to walk away.

"You're a bastard!" I shout after him but he merely waves a dismissive hand over his shoulder.

I sink down on a chair and the sparrows move in on the crumbs. I feel drained, or rather, battered. Peter, Constance. Shit! *Delicta maiorum immeritus lues*. Old Horace certainly knew what he was talking about: 'Though guiltless, you must expiate your father's sins'.

I go into the cool, dark house and approach the foot of the wide stone staircase. Chunky knives with broad blades are mounted on the walls. Cane knives.

"Yes, sah?" Mrs Tunker makes me jump.

"I'm looking for Rashmi." I nearly said 'Miss Rashmi' but it would have sounded like something from 'Gone with the Wind'.

"She go out." She gestures towards the sea and jabs a bony finger beyond the wrought iron banisters. "That hi' place." I get the message. Private.

"Thanks," I say because I have to say something and go out under the spreading poincianas. My feet are on a path and I follow it; through mangoes, lime palms and kapok trees, their twisting ridge-backed roots rearing up their trunks like feuding lizards. The clouds are high in the sky and the ever-present breeze rustles through the undergrowth like a stalking animal. I came out on the shore and a narrow strip of white sand plunges steeply to aquamarine sea. The wavelets barely have the strength to nibble at the beach and I hobble down to the water's edge and shade my eyes to scan the length of the beach. There is no one there.

How bitter the taste of unhappiness in paradise. How infuriating to be shackled by the plaster round my leg. I can understand why the Serpent chose the Garden of Eden. Nearby is a low outcrop of rock and beyond it another bay. Perhaps she will be there. I find a narrow, overgrown path and negotiate a sharp descent that brings me out at the corner of the cove I saw from the boat. It forms a natural amphitheatre with its untidy rows of chairs facing towards the ocean as if arranged for some aquatic spectacle that never took place. Many are beginning to rust, some almost completely buried where the wind has banked the sand high. It is sad and a little sinister, especially as the sun has yet to invade the beach. Bizarrely, there is a pile of laundry on one of the chairs. I am about to move on when the pile of laundry flinches. The wind? I feel uneasy. Then it moves.

It is not a pile of laundry but a man in a grubby, white caftan. He turns towards me and I start. The flesh is bloated and the features look as if they have floated to the surface of a bowl of whey, but I recognise them. I am looking at 'The Man'. Inflated to the limit of anatomical possibility as if by a powerful bicycle pump. A balloon with nose, eyes and mouth chalked on it. His hand drops beside the chair and fumbles for something. It comes up with a richly-worked, double-barrelled shotgun, a filigree of silver glinting about its hammers.

"Good morning," I say, noting how the prospect of a few hundred lead pellets jostling each other in the pit of my stomach immediately polishes my manners.

'The Man' digests me and then slowly turns his face towards the open sea. "Sometimes bad things go by an' 'ah shoot 'em." The accent carries a breath of magnolia with it. Southern gen'lem'n. I approach, wondering how to reply to this. I do not want to be confused with a 'bad thing'. "Ya' hurt ya' leg." He says it like he is tipping me off to something.

"Skiing accident. I did it with your daughter, Rashmi. At Sun Valley." It seems a good idea to pack in as much credential-building information as possible."

"You have come to offer me money. A great deal of money." Now his accent has changed completely. He sounds like Omar Sharif playing someone wily.

"Not really," I say.

"The larger the sum, the smaller the man. Is it not so, my friend?" Such observations might well pass the time while we waited for the camels to be watered but I am beginning to feel out of my depth.

"You called me in Los Angeles."

'The Man' closes his eyes and groans. A tremor passes through his body. "Wild tings, when dey die, burn 'n hell an' leave der skins behin'. Der was a crack in th' floor o' heav'n 'n I fell through." Now we are back in the Deep South. "Who said that?"

"Tennessee Williams?" I hazard. "Eugene O'Neill?"

His face reveals surprise tinged with disappointment. I imagine that my ignorance has shocked him. When he eventually speaks it is with an accent that I do not associate with anybody. "I thought I did."

"Well, I suppose you could have done." I clear my throat and search desperately for the appropriate response. "Perhaps it was from something you wrote?"

He says nothing but continues to stare out to sea and I wonder if he is deaf. I remember hearing how, when he was playing Moses, he used to wear earplugs so that the voices of the other actors would not interfere with his concentration. One day, he forgot to take them out and walked off the set under a truck. The whole unit had to wait six weeks in the Kalahari Desert before he could fly back from New York and carry on.

"Sit yourself down, boy." We have left the Deep South and moved again; maybe west to Texas.

I do as he asks and my chair sinks deep into the sand until my arse is almost level with it. Now I am lower than he is. Like a vassal before his master. His watery eyes threaten to slop out of the swollen flesh.

"Tell me all about yourself real quick."

"I'm William Lock, a friend of Rashmi's, your daughter. You called me in Los Angeles-"

"Enough." He raises a silencing hand like a couple of pounds of pork sausages and, discovering it before him like a providential tool, starts to scratch an armpit. Folds of flesh like ruched curtains have to move aside to make this possible. "I can fill in the subtext." He sighs. "She was talking about someone." He sighs even louder. "And I thought you were offering me work."

"I love her," I say firmly.

If he is impressed by this declaration his face does not show it. He continues to gaze out to sea until his head suddenly jerks forward like a vulture spotting lunch. Hadiscomb has appeared round the rocks on a wind surfer. He skims across the sparkling ocean and waves gaily. He is good. I wait with mounting interest to see if he will be designated 'a bad thing' and shot.

"You know something?" I wait respectfully. "Round here they reckon I'm the reincarnation of a pre-Columbian Arawak priest martyred by the Caribs."

I struggle to digest this. "That's fascinating." I wait. "Why do they believe that?"

"Because I told them." He raises the gun, but Hadiscomb has disappeared round a headland. "Word of mouth never fails. Trust me."

"I can see that," I tell him.

"They're simple people but they respect me." Now we are sitting round a camp fire poking flames under a billycan. "I've always identified with the underprivileged. 'Be rich, think poor'. It's one of my credos." He turns and on close inspection his face has more lines than a collapsed Chinese lantern; he looks like a two thousand year old man dug out of a peat bog. "You can have it if you like."

"Thank you." I try to sound grateful, but not desperately so. A man who has his own credos, lots of them, but who would never slam the door in the face of a worthy, homeless notion.

"Rashmi and you." I perk up as his eyes wander over me, doubtless evaluating prospective son-in-law material. Perhaps we are getting to the nitty-gritty. "Crabs."

For a second I am not sure that I have heard him right. Then I feel myself blushing. Is this why she has avoided making love? Why did she tell her father and not me? And why haven't I experienced any of the symptoms? Could it mean - terrible thought - that she-?

"Advertising crabs."

A surge of relief. There must be a cannery around here. Some kind of export business.

"Who for?"

"Who for what?"

"Who would we be advertising the crabs for - or to?"

Reading expressions on 'The Man's' face is like trying to spot a ripple on a bowl of porridge but I think I am looking at someone who has discovered that he is addressing an idiot.

"The crabs would be doing the advertising. I could oversee it but I've got too many other things on my plate."

"Sounds great." I wait hopefully. "But I'm not quite certain I understand."

"What?"

"About the crabs."

Hadiscomb is returning. His brown body arches back athletically and he dips the back of his head in the ocean. He straightens up and waves. 'The Man' glances at his gun.

"Crabs?"

"Yes. You were talking about advertising and crabs." It is difficult enough holding the man's attention without fucking Hadiscomb skimming backwards and forwards. I feel like snatching up the gun and blowing him away myself.

"You mean the hermit crabs?" I don't argue. The ocean is now empty save for a distant yacht disappearing behind a palm-fringed cay. "Once a year they come down to the sea to lay their eggs and change shells. That's the moment." Now, his voice is settling into another rhythm. It comes from somewhere in the middle of America. It is simple and unadorned. A 'get up early, work hard, go to church on Sunday' voice. I wonder if this is the voice Mrs Tunker hears. "There aren't enough of them. Shells."

He stares at me with what I assume is expectancy, as if struggling to come to terms with the fact that his daughter has fallen for a retard. "So that's where the ecologically-minded companies come in. They'd provide artificial shells in return for having their products advertised on them. You'd run the scheme and take a cut. You imagine? Everywhere you went, little moving advertisements."

His lips flutter and tiny bubbles appear at their corners. This is the man whose face never quits the racks of movie postcards in Westwood. Right now he looks like the death mask of a death mask.

"You'd feel real good about buying a product that was subsidising shelter for an endangered species, wouldn't you? Of course now-" he picks up his gun and cranes towards the spot where Hadiscomb disappeared "-you'd have to be careful 'bout what products you selected. No cigarettes, no liquor. And the designs would have to be tasteful. You'd probably need to set up a panel of distinguished artists to approve them. I know some of these people." I can see him when he played the wrestling coach in 'Catch'. Not a spare inch of flesh, profile of a Greek god, eyes of a hawk. "The only problem I've hit is that the crabs might go for one design rather than another, or a colour, maybe."

"You'd have to do some tests," I say. "I don't think it would be a problem. It's a great idea."

"It's helping nature to help itself to help you." He reflects. "That would make a pretty damn good slogan, though you'd probably never get it all on one shell. Not with the manufacturer's name as well."

"Probably not," I say.

'The Man' holds out his hand. He sounds tired. "You need to go now." Shaking the flesh is like picking up a bunch of rotting bananas.

I struggle to my feet and point out to sea. "He's a friend."

"Who is?"

"The guy on the wind surfer."

"Really?" He obviously has no idea what I am talking about. Hadiscomb is on his own.

"See you." I make a gesture of farewell and start to turn away.

"The only way back is forward, Mr Hawkins. Your Frenchie has no taste for cold steel." The accent is impeccably cut-glass British and for a moment I think that someone else must have sprung up out of the sand. But it is still him. He smiles a strange smile and doffs what I assume is an imaginary cocked hat.

"Right," I say and continue to trudge back the way I have come, thinking strange thoughts. I do not look back. Out to sea, Hadiscomb is far away and on a tack that will bring him in near the jetty. Somebody up there must like him.

I don't think I will tell Hadiscomb about my meeting with my future father-in-law. Father-in-law. I digest the title and begin to understand why Rashmi has been behaving as she has lately. It makes it even more important that I should find her and tell her that the meeting has taken place. She will be relieved.

The palms open up ahead and I can see Mrs Tunker hanging out washing that billows like the sails of a galleon in the wind. Something tells me that it is not the reincarnation of a martyred Arawak priest that she sees when the electricity goes off and she lights the candles. It is a bloated, ageing man who sits on an empty beach dreaming up wacky schemes to avoid acknowledging the fact that, somewhere along the line, he blew it.

I look back towards the cove, and in my mind there is a shot and an image of screeching birds exploding into the air. But that is the end of a movie about Van Gogh and real life is more prosaic.

Beyond the bungalow, the local kids are waiting on the jetty for Hadiscomb to come in. They wave and holler and I am jealous. Hadiscomb has it easy. He looks good out there and all he has to do is grip, lean and balance. There is no time/need to think about other things when you are skimming across endless blue at sixty miles an hour. And Hadiscomb grows in strength the more his complacency gnaws away at you. As if he is feeding on your disdainful inertia. I have a feeling that something terrible is happening and that I am powerless as a storm builds in an unseen corner of the sky. Sand has got into my cast and I need to wash it out and think for a while. 'The Man' is still churning around inside my head. It is like the aftermath of driving past a bad road accident.

I am about fifty yards away when Rashmi runs from the direction of the bungalows. I call her name but she is gone and I cannot run after her. The breeze is shaking the poinsettia like pompoms so maybe she did not hear me. My father is standing in the doorway of his room. He looks as if he has been crying.

"What's the matter?" I ask him.

"Come in. I need to talk to you."

My heart starts to do its stricken albatross impression. I was right. Something terrible is happening. Has happened. Is about to happen. I follow him into the room. The place is a mess. Clothes and bedclothes everywhere. And pills.

I look at him and suddenly understand what is happening. He is dying. That is why he was gobbling all the pills, behaving so badly. He was lashing out at the injustice of what was happening to him. And I never realised. I was too wrapped up in myself. So many things I've never said to him. And now, when I say them, it will sound as if I am only saying them because - shit!

"I'm sorry, dad, "I say. "I'm so sorry." He stares at me, his face haggard, his eyes red. "I know - I know, you're not well."

I move to put my arms round him but he takes a step back. "No!" He regains control. "It's not me. It's Rashmi."

I feel as if I've been kicked in the pit of the stomach. Prompt cards from the past pop up like targets on a rifle range. The changes of mood, the refusal to be committed about the future, the departure from Sun Valley. She had to see a specialist.

"She's got cancer," I say.

"Worse than that. We're in love."

He goes on talking but I can't hear anything. It's like the aftermath of an explosion when you are dazed and stunned and bombarded by endorphins; before the pain kicks in and you start counting how many limbs you have left.

"That's obscene," I hear myself say. "Ridiculous!"

"Do you think I don't know that?"

"But she loves me."

"Not enough. I'm sorry, Will. I've done everything I can to break it. Everything that's humanly-inhumanly possible to make her see sense but I can't fight any more. We're doomed for each other. I can't...we can't escape. It's passion, it's destiny...it's tearing us apart!" He buries his face in his hands.

"You're old enough to be her father! It's a... it's a fucking joke!!"

He faces me, tears running down his cheeks. "You don't have to tell me any of that. I've told her. I've shown her. She agrees with me. There's nothing we can do. Believe me, it's the last thing I would have wanted to happen. But we have to have each other. We're invaded by demons. My God, I hope it never happens to you."

"But it has happened to me. I love her!"

"Love is an animal that comes in two halves, Will. You have to have both of them." He looks at me sadly. "I hate to cause you pain, Will. We both do."

"Where is she?"

"She's packing. We have to get away from here. Now it's...now it's... now that you know."

"I can't believe this."

"Neither can I. You're probably right. Maybe it is ridiculous. Three weeks and it will all be over. I don't know." He reaches for a bottle of aguardiente and knocks a litter of pills across the room. "Absurd. That's the word."

"And I thought you were dying and I hadn't noticed. That's funny."

"Ironic, I think, would be the better word."

"For Christ's sake! Don't start!-"

"I'm sorry, I'm sorry." He holds up a hand that restrains and surrenders. "Don't worry about the pills. They were the legacy of one of those little designer sexual maladies you can pick up." He starts to sing out of tune to the melody of 'Perfidia'. "At l-a-a-a-a-s-t, I'd never had Chla-a-a-mydia! It's all right. The treatment finished weeks ago. I'm just finishing up the pills to get my money's worth. You don't have to worry." He reaches out to pat me on the shoulder. "You're not going to catch anything."

It is not the best punch I have ever thrown but it catches him in the mouth and he goes down, dropping the bottle. Blood spurts from his split lip and I kick him in the ribs as hard as I can. I feel a scorching flame of pain and realise that I have done something very stupid. I should have used the other foot. Now I have broken my ankle again.

My father writhes on the floor clutching his ribs and I am crying out with the pain and trying to cling to something to stay upright and something very strange happens. We both start laughing. I want to kill him but I cannot stop myself. Laughter is a strange creature; a breed of jackal that hangs close waiting for part of us to die so that it can feed, reminding us with its gross yaps and yelps and yawls that we are not lords of creation, resolutely in control of our destinies, but often weak and faintly ridiculous victims of events that we might otherwise have held ourselves responsible for.

My father hauls himself onto a bed and snuffles blood into a sheet and I hobble back to my room. I lie on my bed and weep, just as I did when I was a child and I thought about dying - although I had not imagined this kind of death; one that takes place before the breath has left the body.

I cannot believe that it is over. That we are never going to - that I can't - that there won't be - that she - that she doesn't love me. That she loves him. How can she when I love her so much? Can't she feel it? The very intensity of my feelings should make them impossible to reject, a kind of force majeure of nature. What didn't I do or say that would have made her understand that I was - that I am - exactly right for her?

I continue to lie there thinking painful thoughts until I have the sensation that there is someone else in the room. I turn my head, and there she is, her face slippery with tears.

"Will," she says. "I'm so sorry. You can hit me if it makes you feel any better."

"Give me a break." I realise that I have made another joke. The jackals are hunting in packs today.

"I don't know what to say. This is terrible for me too."

"You've come to the wrong person for sympathy."

"Don't be cruel."

"Cruel!? Me!?" She starts to cry and I have to conquer a desire to stretch out a comforting hand. What an idiot. "Why did you leave Sun Valley like that?" When I was a child there was a medical text book at home that contained the photograph of a man in the advanced stages of smallpox. I was terrified of that photo, but I always had to turn to it.

"It was starting to happen. I had to get away from both of you. But back at L.A. things...I...I-"

"That time at the hotel you were calling my father not me, weren't you?"

"I can't remember."

"Of course you can. You thought I was out of the way with your father. But I guess he let you down - as he probably always does."

"Don't!" She covers her face with her hands.

"And while I was at the movies with Hadiscomb and that guy was getting shot, you were…you were…in the apartment! But you could still suck me off afterwards. You're a whore!"

"Will!" She is wailing. "Can't you understand? I couldn't have you inside me. Not after…after-" she scratches at the air with her nails as if trapped inside a glass box "-Oh Will, Will, I can't explain it. It's just that with him I don't have to think."

"That's it! I can't listen to any more of your crap." I thrust out an arm. "Goodbye. Go!"

She starts to say something but it is drowned in sobs. I turn towards the wall and when I look back she has gone. Wonderful. A man who can't think and a woman who doesn't want to. They are made for each other. But even then I am praying for her to appear through the door, to say that she made a terrible mistake, that she is sorry, that she wants us to be together again.

But it is my father who returns, mumbling through a bloody handkerchief. As if to cheer me up, he tells me that he thinks I may have broken one of his ribs. He and Rashmi will send over a doctor from the main island and he will leave some money at the hotel in L.A. He does not know where they will be going (a lie, surely, but what's another one?) and he is very sorry. He will be in touch. I say nothing and he goes away.

Minutes pass and I twist my head and peer out through the slats. Storm clouds are building along the horizon. Maybe a hurricane will spring up and blow them over the edge of the world. I try to think bad things about Rashmi. Her face was puffed up when she left. Like her father's. Maybe it is hereditary. Perhaps one day she will float off like a blimp and my father will have to shoot her down with an air rifle. It does not seem to help.

I drag myself out onto the balcony and, through the palms, the launch is just visible pulling away from the jetty. I can make them out on the lower deck. He seems to have his arms around her protectively. Shit! Why doesn't 'The Man' pop up and blow them away? 'The Man'. Le Man. Leman. That could be it. A morbid father-fixation that has transformed itself into an infatuation with a kindred disaster area. Sigmund would have loved this.

I pour water that could be colder over my foot and hobble back to bed. My ankle is throbbing painfully and has expanded against the plaster cast. I wonder if I should try and take it off. For the last few minutes I have forgotten the existence of physical pain. I close my eyes and wonder how I am going to get through the rest of my life.

"Hi." It is Hadiscomb looking purposeful and personable. Not quite an orchid behind his ear but it is only a question of time. He has clearly groomed himself meticulously after his exertions on the wind surfer. He looks as if he has something on his mind. "Great board that Wave Tool."

"You looked pretty good out there."

"Thanks." He clears his throat like he is done with the small talk. "I've been hoping for some time that you were going to say something."

"Really?" What is he talking about? How much does he know? Surely, he can't be involved in-

"Yes. I'm fed up with waiting for you to do the decent thing. You know what I'm talking about."

"Hadiscomb, this isn't a very good-"

"Shut up! For you it's never a good moment. You're always wriggling." He waits and his voice becomes calmer. "I'm not asking for an apology. I just want you to face up to the truth."

I look at the probing fingers of creeper poking through the slats. There seem to be more of them than there were yesterday. I do know what he is talking about. Of course I do. The sleeping dormitory, the creaking floorboards, the smell of floor polish in the hall, the rush of cold, damp air as the kitchen door cracked open. Gravel crunching underfoot. Wet foliage. The house louring behind, the shed before. Wet grass brushing against the pyjama bottoms. The damp-swollen door jolting open and the nostril-invading stench of small animals. Mice rustling in their cages, the whirr of a rat spinning inside its wheel, the soft glow of the aquarium lights. The sheen of the terrapin half-immersed in water. The gobbet of meat dropping into the tank. The creature's head lunging out-

"All right," I say. "I killed Voyce's terrapin. Is that what you've been waiting for me to say? I drove a compass through its miserable frog-eating head and I wish it had been Voyce's." Relief. The vicar's cat scrambles up the bank, shakes itself, and disappears. "I shoved the compass through its eyes after it was dead – just to make it more gruesome for Voyce."

"Why did you leave it on the doorstep?"

"Because I hated the whole fucking house. The whole fucking school."

"But I got the blame! Everybody thought I did it. I was the one who got persecuted - more persecuted!"

"I'm sorry," I say. "I'm sorry for you. I'm sorry for the terrapin. I know it couldn't help eating frogs and mice. I should have killed Voyce. But I didn't have the guts. I didn't have the guts to own up. I suppose I was ashamed. No, I was scared. It was later I was ashamed. I made myself forget it had ever happened. I ripped the pages out of my mind."

"But it doesn't work, does it?"

"No. Because you had to turn up as a male prostitute on Santa Monica Boulevard."

"What!?-"

"It doesn't matter." Because even if you can extirpate something that did happen, something just as bad that you never dreamed about will spring up like a dragon's tooth. Like Constance. Like Peter. Like: "Rashmi's gone off with my father."

He stares at me. "You mean, like eloped?"

"Yes. But I prefer 'gone off with'. This isn't 'Pride and Prejudice'."

Hadiscomb nods as if he understands. "I'm sorry. I mean, I'm sorry it's happened and I'm sorry I chose this moment to raise the bloody Rockingham business. I don't want to kick a man when he's down."

"That's my speciality," I tell him. "And God doesn't like that either. I've broken my ankle again."

"God, how awful." Hadiscomb looks genuinely concerned. He pulls up a chair and sits by the bed. Visiting time. "You didn't see any of this coming?"

"No. Why? Did you?"

"Well, I thought there was some kind of tension between them. That can be a sign.

It's probably why she invited me, when you think about it. So I'd be some kind of company for you." We digest this. "I did wonder why he was being so nasty to her. I suppose it was to warn her. To make sure she knew what she was taking on. You don't mind me talking like this?"

"I asked you."

"What are you going to do about your ankle?"

"They're sending a doctor from the main island."

"Was that them on the launch? Christ, you mean they've gone already?"

"Yes." I feel a sharp pang of gut-wrenching emptiness. "It's just you and me and…and-" I change my mind "-Mrs Tunker."

It has started to rain and the wind delivers a flurry of drops through an open window. I wonder if 'The Man' is sticking it out or stumping back, visualising the Technicolor hermit crabs scuttling about their business. It suddenly occurs to me that with phosphorescent lettering you would be able to read their messages at night.

"I think my father's having an affair," says Hadiscomb. "He's a consultant at a private nursing home and I caught him with this sister in her office. He had his hand up her uniform."

"Maybe he was giving her a free consultation."

"She'd need to have her brain in her vagina. He doesn't know the names of any parts of the body below the chin." I realise that I am smiling. Hadiscomb is not such a bad guy when you get to know him, despite the 'Esprit' shirt. He turns towards the door. "I think I'll go and see Mrs Tunker, persuade her to cook us something delicious for lunch. Maybe dig out some more wine. One of the girls is falling in love with me. Maybe she has a friend."

"Let's hope she fancies damaged goods"

Hadiscomb pauses in the doorway. "And who knows? Maybe we'll break bread with 'The Man'."

"If he exists." I struggle to change the subject. "I wonder what happened to Voyce."

"Probably pretty high up in the North Korean Police by now. Do you remember his face when everybody sang?"

I think, and suddenly it comes back to me. I start to sing and Hadiscomb joins in and our voices soar to drown out the sound of the wind and the rain drumming on the roof.

> Holy, holy, holy, Lord God Almighty!
> Early in the morning our song shall rise to thee.
> Holy, holy, holy! All the saints adore Thee,
> Casting down their golden crowns around the glassy sea;
> Cherubim and terrapin falling down before Thee,
> Which wert, and art, and evermore shall be!!

15.

I do not see 'The Man' again and, with the passage of time, I begin to wonder if I might have dreamed the encounter on the beach. I am gingerly allowing myself to dream again. They are not always very pleasant dreams, but at least there are no vicars, cats or terrapins in them.

The last meal Mrs Tunker serves us is a delicious stew and it makes me think that I have not seen the rabbits since we left the plane. She never mentions Rashmi, nor my father and says, "You come back'n see us a'gin real soon," when we leave. She says it more to Hadiscomb than to me but that is understandable. She is a class act, is Mrs Tunker.

We have to get up early to catch the plane and the beauty of the dawn as we pull away from the jetty is sufficient to bring tears to the eyes - if any other reason was needed. The sea is smooth and pink-impregnated and the sky rose petal with one huge dragon of damask cloud trailing its long tail above the cays and islands, dark nearest to us, and then receding grey, purple, red and lastly yellow where the alchemist sun rises to pour gold across the heavens. I think of my half-countryman, Sir Francis Drake, sailing through these islands four hundred years ago, on his way to attack the Spaniards at San Juan. Three thousand miles away from a home he was never to see again; a handful of cockleshells to carry him and his men. What infinite wonder must have been their companion as they sailed these scarce-charted seas; when the world was still a mystery and they could reach out like children spoiled for choice, touching and tasting everything.

When I think about it, there was something very American about Drake: take from the rich - and keep it.

Against my wishes - the smallpox syndrome - I glance into the cove as we pull away from the shore, but it is empty. Even the sand seems smooth and unsullied by the imprint of a foot. It makes the quavers and crotchets of the sinking chairs seem even more bizarre.

If, on the way down, we stopped at places I never knew had airports, on the way back, we stop at places that do not have airports, or maybe they are not even places, just landing strips in the jungle that we seem to light upon like a parting in a giant Afro. We pick up bales and packages and consignments of bananas, and Hadiscomb - who has something to live for and is paying attention - says that many of these places do not export bananas and that it would be too expensive to send them by air anyway. I tell him to shut up because I am already expecting the police to be waiting at the airport and if I am busted for drug-running as well as pushing rented cars into canyons, Western Rentals might as well burn my passport because I am never going to need it again. Not that a passport is of great importance to someone who has already reached their destination before they even got on the plane.

The police are not waiting at the airport and I say goodbye to Hadiscomb with restrained regret and go back to the hotel. Generously, he offers to accompany me but I say that I can look after myself and that we will meet for a drink before he goes, or we go. Or whatever.

The hotel is just the same except that we have a new room maid and the flowers look in great shape. Californians are excellent at getting it together after unfortunate incidents. It must be all the earthquakes. Nobody seems to want to talk about Peter, which is perhaps understandable, but it is disconcerting that they seem reluctant to acknowledge that he even existed. Maybe I should be able to understand this. All I do learn, and that from the English receptionist just before she leaves to work as a barmaid at the John Bull Arms in Santa Monica, is that he was born in Hungary and that his real name was Bela Sztojay. Or maybe it is more appropriate to think that his real name was Peter. He was able to choose that.

No surprise is evinced that my father departed without me and I am handed a thick envelope containing a letter, money and - to my surprise - my passport. I inquire casually if he has left a forwarding address, but he has not.

My dear Will,

I cannot go on saying that I am sorry, so let this be the last time: I'm sorry. Sorry too, if in my distress and confusion I gave the impression that I was merely a hopeless, pathetic victim struck down by the deadly disease of passion and unable to help himself. There is obviously more to it than that. Though, in a certain sense, it may be painful for you to hear it, Rashmi and I do love each other and I believe that her presence in my life will help me do some good work. Really good work. That famous book, perhaps. I am certainly going to try.

On a more positive note - as far as both of us are concerned - our problems with Western are over. YES!!!!! They have been swallowed by Last Hope which means that Messrs Shankel and Gallow: Sherlock Shit and Doctor Poo, are now history, along with most of the staff, and were only too happy to saddle their successors with every red ink debt and liability down to the oil stains on the office carpet.

The car, therefore, has been written off and all charges against us dropped. In fact, by a stroke of what in any other town might be termed irony, I have now entered into a working relationship with Messrs Shankel and Gallow - or Lenny and Rick as I will be calling them when we next meet. Based on their experiences in the rental business they have come up with a notion for a movie which I have tickled into a story outline which, if successfully pitched, could be stroked into a screenplay. Larry is drawing up a contract. Yes, I know. You are absolutely right but this is Lalaland and they do things differently here. Did I tell you about Sean Connery and the taxi driver? - probably several times.

Well, my dear boy, I guess that's it for now. Don't hate me too much, or if you must, hate me with such intensity that it burns itself out of your system quickly. I would loathe to lose you. Rashmi sends her love. I hope we will all be able to get together at some time in the future - a future that I know will be good for you because you have talent and a brave, honest heart. Despite the latter, you could still succeed in this town.

My love - always - Daddy XX

P.S. My rib is only cracked.

I feel like having another weep but there is a limit to how much you can indulge yourself. Rashmi's skills do not, apparently extend to writing letters. I should have married my father. There are probably parts of California where you can do that.

I screw the letter into a ball and sky hook it towards a distant waste basket. If it goes in, Rashmi will come crawling back to me on her hands and knees within a week. It misses. Strange about the car. The thing I was most worried about; the thing I really deserved to be punished for. God's preoccupations are difficult to fathom sometimes.

Not that I'm grumbling, deity. I have some money and an airline ticket back to Europe. Things could be worse.

I could plunge straight into the search for a job but I think that I need time to take stock. And I would like to see my mother. It seems a long time and I could probably travel back to London with Hadiscomb and his sister-groping father and, presumably, unsuspecting mother. It is eleven o'clock there now and ma will almost certainly not have gone to bed. I get her sweet, reassuring voice on the answering machine and leave a message saying that I will be coming over soon and would like to stay and will call her at the office when I have a flight. This time, I am sad that I have not been able to talk to her, though there is not a lot I could have said on the phone. I must remember to tell her about my ankle so that she does not get a shock when she sees me. I now have a new plaster with no writing on it.

The apartment seems huge and unnaturally tidy without my father. I would have preferred to change but it seems too much of a hassle when I am only going to be here for a few more days. I go into the bedroom and try and avoid looking at the beds. Bernie Bowman's invitation is still there, tucked into the side of the mirror. A housewarming. This evening. Why not? It would help to kill the time and get me out of this hygienized, sanitised sewer of carnal memories. I might even meet somebody useful. And I have a talking point: a thrice-broken ankle. Hadiscomb can come, too. There should be a fair smattering of his fellow countrymen there. 'Brits'. Sticking together in the Land of the Free - or the freeload, at least.

I call Hadiscomb and tell him about the car and the party and my plans for going to London. He is enthusiastic about the party and tries to be encouraging about the state of my life in general. He uses words like 'catharsis' and 'moral regeneration' which makes me wonder if he has been discussing me with his parents or signed on for a quick course with Santa Barbara Esme. The crux of his argument is that by coming clean about the terrapin I have taken some kind of spiritual laxative that is going to make everything better.

This is a solid theory for him because it puts him centre stage but I am not so sure. Despite the car resolution, I still have a nagging fear that things may need to get worse before they can get better. It may not totally equate with the unquenchable optimism of my American ancestors but when your father runs off with the woman you love and you break your ankle for the second time in two weeks and your main hope of employment tries to commit suicide, a lurch towards European fatalism seems not only pragmatic but almost healthy.

It is not an appealing trait - how many appealing traits do I have? - but it often takes feeling sorry for myself to make me think of other people. I can't get in touch with Peter but I do write a letter to Constance, via the studio and also to Ellen at Sun Valley. Lucy I do not know what to do about. Would she feel better if she knew what had happened to me? Being Lucy, probably not.

I had been expecting early Tudor Byzantine but Bernie Bowman's house is more late Neasden Odeon. It looks like one of the great north London cinemas he must have gone to as a boy, before it was mugged by television and turned into a bingo parlour, and then boarded up, and then torn down to become a shopping mall. This building is whiter than the Californian teeth my father despises and rises in rectangular tiers, some with their corners blunted into quadrants. Windows are wide and low or high and narrow so that their slits and dashes look like something written on the walls in runic script.

It is smog-pink early evening when Hadiscomb and I arrive and huge automobiles and garishly clad guests mill around the already clogged driveways. Parties start and end early in Hollywood. There are scripts to be read, calls to be made, deals to be done and, of course, that exhausting drive home. We are moving slowly towards the huge front doors when a lapis lazuli Jaguar jolts out of the crowd and nearly mows me down. I stoop to abuse the driver and do a double take. I am gazing into the matinée idol features of Ganna, now clad as a car jock. He glares at me and scorches away down the road to park the car. Well, well. Protean Jim must have leaked out of Ganna's follicles and gone in search of greener pastures. A new bucket is being lowered into the bottomless well of Esme's inner being.

Security guards check us out against a list and we find ourselves in a huge pillared room dominated by a chandelier slightly smaller than the spacecraft in 'Strange Encounters of the Third Kind'. The furniture has been given the night off and the room is wall to wall people. As surmised, the British contingent is here in force. On all sides I hear people talking about Green Cards and how you cannot get a decent cup of tea for love nor money and why does the beer have to taste like piss and be so cold it freezes your balls off? Neither Ralph Fiennes or Jeremy Irons seem to be in attendance. Male Britons are recognisable by their ruddy complexions and predilection for yellow or light blue safari suits as made popular by Roger Moore. Their women are less easy to pick out, conforming to the local mix of three parts clothing to two of flesh and one of expensive jewellery. Beautiful girls in mini-togas - they could be peering through slits in sacks for all I care at the moment - struggle through the throng with trays of drinks; though the evening has yet to reveal any other sign of a Roman theme.

"This is great," says Hadiscomb.

"Yes," I say, injecting a note of weariness into my voice; as if I had attended so many of these occasions that it had become a penance. I glance around and recognise Bernie, fatter and sleeker than the last time I saw him, in earnest conversation with two security guards. They are frowning and looking in our direction. Clearly, our faces do not ring a bell. Shit, I do not need any more humiliation at the moment. Bernie plucks at the lapels of his green silk smoking jacket and move towards us purposefully, flanked by his two gorillas.

"Good evening, Mr Bowman," I say politely. "Fabulous party. I'm William Lock. My father couldn't come so-"

Bernie looks puzzled. Then his face splits into a comprehending smile and he snaps his fingers. "Adie!"

"That's right. This is my-"

I am trying to introduce Hadiscomb but Bernie is waving the security guards away.

"'Ow lovely. Oy, Rosie!" He draws a woman away from the people she is talking to.

"This is Adie's kiddy. You remember? Adie Lock? 'E wrote all the 'Dirty Diaries' for us."

I vaguely recall Mrs Bowman who has been at her husband's side for more years than either of them would care to remember. Her nipped and tucked features pay homage to the fading memory of a once beautiful and much-desired starlet and her piercing eyes strip you down to the lowest figure on your bank balance. The dress gracing the becoming-ample body rises in tasselled sections like a pagoda with the wearer's head poking through the roof. "Oh yeh," she says. "Wot 'ave you done to yer leg?"

I don't have time to tell her because Bernie has started to reminisce. "Right load of laughs, yer old man. Too bad 'e can't be 'ere tonight. I always remember, oh dear-" he starts chuckling in anticipation "-it was when we was shooting 'Driving Instructor'. We 'ad this right ponce of 'n actor, reckoned 'e was a bit of a ladies' man. 'Do you knew' 'e says one day-" Bernie is essaying an upper class accent "'you can kill a woman by blowing up her vagina?' 'Depends if you've got a stick of dynamite', says your dad. Laugh? I thought I was going to die."

"The dirty sod!" cries Rosie joyfully, looking at me with rekindled interest as if I might be a chip off the old block."

"It sounds like him," I say.

"Certainly does," says Hadiscomb unnecessarily.

"It's funny bumping into you boys." Bernie lowers his voice conspiratorially. I've just 'ad some Australian interest in another 'Dirty Diaries' movie. I think the money's Indonesian actually but if they put their rupiahs where their mouths are, who gives a monkey's? Your dad should give me a ring."

"I like the Australians," says Rosie, who I notice has quickly expanded her range of vision to include Hadiscomb. "They don't mess abowt. No airs an' graces. They call a spade a spade."

"An' they won't let 'em in the country!" Bernie and Rosie shriek with laughter and he slaps me on the shoulder. "Just talking about it all gets the old 'umouristic juices flowing."

"You remember Tristram and Benedict?" says Rosie. "My boys?"

I think about it and vaguely recall two pimply, thirteen year olds with hair down to the shoulders who were put on probation for holding up a convenience store with a switchblade. "Of course."

"They've done ever so well," says Rosie proudly. "Benedict's got as far as 'e can in the Young Conservatives so 'e's going to be a Euro M.P."

"Of course, 'e knows sweet F.A. about Europe," chortles Bernie.

But what do the Frogs know about us?" says Rosie triumphantly. "It's swings and roundabouts, innit?"

"Anyway, 'e's getting in on the ground floor," says Bernie enigmatically. He is glancing around and I sense that our audience is nearly over. "C'mon, my angel. Duty calls. 'Spose we'd better circulate."

"Nice to talk to you," says Rosie. "Give my love to your dad. An' your mum." She looks deep into Hadiscomb's eyes. "Nice to meet you."

Hadiscomb mumbles something appropriate and Rosie follows her husband who is already bear-hugging a swarthy man in wraparound shades who is even fatter than he is. My mother once accused my father of having had an affair with Mrs Bowman - those were not the actual words she used - and I begin to believe it.

"What was that all about?" asks Hadiscomb.

"My father made him rich and he gave some of it back. He produced all the...the films."

"Villiam!" I turn and it is Bronski in denim jacket, decidedly non-designer jeans and a very old Budweiser T-shirt. He greets me warmly like every other man in Hollywood who has stolen all your money, raped your wife and sold your children into slavery. Igor is with him, looking even more like a hen-pecked ghoul than usual. I would like to watch them both being flayed by cack-handed fish gutters armed with Victorian gardening tools, but what the hell? This is Hollywood. "How's the movie going?" I ask.

Igor shakes his head. "You should not think even of asking that question. It is like asking soldier if he has killed man in battle. He might say 'no'. It would make him sad."

"It is in turnaround," says Bronski. "Maybe we do it with animals."

"Like Rubarov," says Igor. "He do it with animals." They laugh for a little while.

"What about space?"

"It is too expensive and people are bored with it," observes Bronski.

"'War and Peace' with animals is good," says Igor. "People are like animals." At least, that is what I think he has said. In fact, I realise that he really said "People always like animals" which is more debatable.

Bronski taps his nose. "An idea your father should have had. The producer cannot everything do."

This observation clearly alerts him to the fact that he may be in the contaminating presence of hereditary incompetence. Tugging Igor by the sleeve, he makes incomprehensible farewell noises and they dissolve into the scrum, almost certainly in search of liquor and slim young women in togas.

I look around for Hadiscomb and find him in the company of an intense Larry Sabel. For a second, I think I have caught Larry's eye but I must be mistaken. Either that or I have ceased to exist.

"Funny sort of chap," says Hadiscomb when he returns. "Said he tried to talk to me at that Mahlathini concert. Kept squeezing my arm and asking me if I'd like some pot."

"Let's go outside," I say.

The terrace is less crowded and surrounded by cypresses and rose trellises that provide views of ornamental gardens and a croquet lawn that I would wager my father's life - no collateral required - Bernie has never set foot upon. At one end is the obligatory pool and I gaze at it and look again. And again. Then I look to Hadiscomb and we gaze together. Speechless.

Poised gyroscopically at a vertical angle just above the water towards the far end of the pool is a gleaming white Rolls Royce Phantom looking as if it has been dropped nose-first and frozen in time a split second before it pierced the surface.

"What do you reckon to it, my old son?" Bernie has appeared beside me clutching what I recognise as a remote control in his podgy hand. "I think it makes a statement. Don't you?"

"It's no good 'aving something that's just artistic with the Yanks," says Rosie who has popped up next to her husband and chosen the moment to clutch Hadiscomb's arm. "Oops! I need to be careful, don't I? I'd forgotten your mum was American. She never liked the films, did she?"

"She had to type the books," I tell her.

"I wanted something that said: 'I've got as much as you 'ave, I'm goner get a bloody sight more, an' I don't give a tinker's toss 'bowt art or any of that bullshit!' I know what people like! I think the Yanks can relate to that - in fact, I sodding well know they can! Watch this."

He presses the remote and there is a deafening blast of rock music from inside the house. "Sod it!" He presses the control again and the huge chandelier goes out, plunging the reception area into semi-darkness.

"Bernie!!"

"Give over, Rosie! Sodding thing!" He presses again and the lights come on and the Rolls begins to revolve slowly on its axis. Its lights flash and coloured jets of water spray from invisible holes along its body, the effect achieved by the water passing through beams of light emanating from the same openings. Water sprinkles down into the pool as from a spinning fountain. Guests who are present burst into admiring and obligatory applause.

"We got the idea when we was looking for a place to rent for my nan," explains Rosie. "Mind you, they'd made a diabolical job of it. It looked as if they'd dropped the car in the pool from a plane."

"That's the wonderful thing about this country," chips in Bernie. "We just told the contractors what we wanted and they did it. Imagine trying to create something like this in England. You'd 'ave all the bleeding heart pinkos jumping up and down an' saying you should 'ave given the money to the Third World."

"So they could buy more weapons from Russia and shoot each other," says Rosie.

"This is the bit I like," says Bernie. "I don' mind tellin' you, it brings tears to me eyes."

He presses again and the jets of water turn red, white and blue. The sound of massed choirs singing 'Rule Britannia' booms out and the Rolls starts to spin faster and faster. Perhaps too fast. Those standing nearest to the pool are suddenly soaked to the skin and the booming massed choirs shrink to a single, strident banshee wail. Bernie curses his remote whilst Rosie shrieks at him.

I look at Hadiscomb and we take the opportunity to withdraw into the background. The problem is quickly overcome, and as the Rolls slows and starts to spin to a halt, those admiring guests who are still relatively dry press forward to congratulate Bernie and pump his hand. In a way, I am sorry that my father cannot be here to see this. It would have pleased him at many levels and perhaps I am gazing at the sole monument he will leave behind to record his passage through this world - apart from the prototype of the Rolls, of course. Perhaps that applies to both of us, but I hope not. In my case I would prefer to see it as an omen, though quite what it signifies does not immediately occur to me. That things are unlikely to turn out as you expect seems a little generalized for an omen and I already know that.

When the Vikings sailed towards what would one day be America they were in sight of its grey, mysterious shore when they came across a totem pole floating in the sea. They gazed down in awe and foreboding at the menacing carved faces and strange symbols and decided that it must be a message from the Gods. So they turned back. I have already been turned back on this voyage so the omen, whatever it means, will not change that. Maybe it is for somebody else or maybe, like so many things in life, it is merely a diversion.

Later

It is eight months after Bernie Bowman's party and I am now working for a local newspaper group in North Wales. I cover everything from soccer matches to funerals and it is said to be excellent training. Exactly what for I am not certain. Being patient, perhaps.

The countryside is pleasant and sometimes, on a cool autumn evening, the breeze carries the scent of burning English cottages fired by Welsh Nationalists. It helps preserve the feeling of alienation from all races and cultures that I increasingly feel must be my birthright. I owe the job to Lucy's uncle who is chairman of the group that owns the newspapers. She comes up at weekends and we go for long walks in the hills. She is a fine girl and it is difficult to resist her loyalty and generosity of spirit. We will have to see what happens.

My mother was surprised to learn about my father - I, of course, gave her an edited version of events (something that I now do professionally, of course) - but I think that whoever he settles down with, if he ever does, she will feel a pang. Apparently, Philippe would like a child and there is talk of him moving into his own apartment. I thought that relations between them were a little strained the last time I saw them but perhaps that was my imagination. Work-wise, she has a new partner and her discovery, Devi Prahn, has left her, poached by a rival agent with the promise of a three book deal and far more money. It seems very difficult for caring left wing writers deeply concerned about problems of world poverty and the exploitation of the downtrodden proletariat to resist large sums of cash. Presumably they must identify with the aspirations of those they write about. Despite such setbacks, my mother's career thrives though she works too hard and tries too much. She always did.

English grandmother has died. There was a splendid rook-cawing funeral in Somerset that Robert Frost would have approved of and which my father did not attend because nobody knew where he was. I hope that there is a heaven and that she has gone to it. She was very certain that she would, but from what one sees of the way God works it is clear that he does not like to be taken for granted.

Hadiscomb has found a job in television - everyone I know is in the media or advertising - and has written a novel. He never mentioned it but, quite by accident, I read a review in the Western Mail. The story follows the adventures of an accident-prone young Englishman in Los Angeles and the reviewer described it as rocambolesque - though it might have been picaresque. Critics like words like that. I abandoned ship after seventy pages when the hero is rescued by a beautiful, young nymphomaniacal heiress to a newspaper fortune whilst trying to windsurf to Santa Catalina Island.

He, Hadiscomb, has written, suggesting that I accompany him to the celebrations in aid of the four hundredth anniversary of Rockingham's foundation as a foundling hospital for the unfortunate bastards spawned by a rich aldermanic precursor of Rousseau afflicted by conscience, but I am still thinking about it. It seems like recidivism and I am not sure how I would handle Voyce even now. I am also a bit miffed about the book.

News from L.A. is less easy to come by - Americans are not great letter writers - but I hear that Constance has opened a bookshop with another woman. Considering the rate at which bookshops close in Beverly Hills it is difficult to believe that she has totally shaken off her death wish.

There were rumours in the trades that 'The Man' was making a come-back to play Oscar Wilde on Masterpiece Theater but I am inclined to discount that. None of the projects that my father was associated with have come anywhere near the screen, which is not at all unusual, but I did notice recently that 'Dirty Diaries of a Sexy Surf Bum' is going before the cameras in Australia. The screenplay is by one 'Piers Absolom' and it does seem like the kind of nom de plume my father would choose. Maybe he and Bernie Bowman did make contact.

The last word from my father was a postcard from Nebraska. Strange coincidence. I had always thought that my mother was the only connection he had there. Maybe it is something to do with 'The Man'. In the books, it gives his birthplace as New York but the voice I heard when he was talking about hermit crabs came from the solid heartland of America. Maybe Rashmi is taking my father back to her father's roots. The postcard gave no clues and was of the cathedral at Albi in southwest France. My father never sends postcards of places he is in. He saves them up until time and generous memory have imbued the spot with a patina of happiness and well-being. They become talismans. It is a wrench for him to send one; a mark of esteem to receive one. I miss him, but not as much as I will when he is dead. Then all the bad stuff will have sunk to the bottom and there will only be the good memories left. Like in his postcards.

I have not been back to Pulignac because I have a fear that he and Rashmi might suddenly turn up on the doorstep or already be ensconced and I could not handle that. Not yet. Sometimes they play a song on the radio, or I pass a girl in the street who looks a little like her, and I know that if I was helping the Virgin Mary pull Jesus Christ out of a train wreck I would have to break off for a silent weep. This, of course, is corny. But corny is the cliché of love and no more than the timeless reiteration of experiences universally shared. And Rashmi liked corny.

Of course, I do not talk about any of this to Lucy but sometimes, when I fall silent on our walks, she must know what I am thinking about and I start to run or hurl stones or make love to her or do anything physical to jolt myself into another mood. All this will surely pass and perhaps, one day, I will go back to America. It is just a question of taking stock and deciding what I really want to do. A question of time.

OTHER BOOKS AVAILABLE FROM TWENTY FIRST CENTURY PUBLISHERS

SINCERE MALE SEEKS LOVE AND SOMEONE TO WASH HIS UNDERPANTS
by Christopher Wood

Colin Fisher is long-divorced with two grown-up children and an ageing mother in care. He is not getting any younger. Perhaps it is time to get married again. There are hordes of mature, nubile, attractive, solvent (hopefully) women out there, and marriage would provide regular sex and companionship, and someone to take care of the tedious domestic details that can make a man late for his golf and tennis matches. All Colin needs to do is smarten up a bit, get out more and select the lucky woman from amongst the numerous postulants. What could be easier?

International best-sellers by Christopher Wood include: A Dove Against Death; Fire Mountain; Taiwan; Make it Happen to Me; Kago; 'Terrible Hard', Says Alice; James Bond, the Spy Who Loved Me; The Further Adventures of Barry Lyndon; James Bond and Moonraker; Dead Centre; John Adam, Samurai.

Christopher Wood has written the screenplays for over a dozen movies, including The Spy Who Loved Me and Moonraker, two of the most successful James Bond films ever made.

"Laugh-out-loud-funny...deeply touching...I really enjoyed this book. Mark Mills, author of Amagansett."

ISBN 1-904433-18-9

RAMONA

How did a little girl come to be abandoned in the orange scented square of the Andalusian City of Seville? Find out, when the course of her life is resumed at age seventeen.

Ramona catches the mood of Europe in transition, as Ramona, brought up in a quiet village in southern Spain, moves into the cosmopolitan world. Her strange background holds a mystery, revealed as the novel develops, but then events take on a different hue as a new perspective emerges. But that is not all, and reality seems to bend further, but does it?

From a novel within a novel, we move on to ... well, let's not say. Read it, and the author challenges you to predict each step of the unfolding plot, and just when it defies belief, read on – you will believe.

Ramona by Johnny John Heinz

ISBN: 1-904433-01-4

MEANS TO AN END

Enter the world of money laundering, financial manipulation and greed, where a shadowy Middle Eastern organisation takes on a major corporation in the US. As the action shifts through exotic locations, who wins out in the end? Certainly, the author's first hand experience of international finance lends a chilling credibility to the plot.

As well as being a compelling work of fiction this book offers, in a style accessible to the layman, a financial insider's insight into the financial and moral crisis, which broke in the early millennium, in the top echelons of corporate America.

Means to an End by Johnny John Heinz

ISBN: 1-84375-008-2

THE SIGNATURE OF A VOICE

The Signature of a Voice is a cat-and-mouse-game between a violent trio, led by a psychopathic killer, and a police officer on suspension. Move and countermove in this chess game is planned and enacted. The reader, in the position of god, knows who is guilty and who plans what, but just as in chess, the opponents' plans thwart one another. The outcomes twist and turn to the final curtain fall.

There is a sense of suspense but also anger as the system seems to be working against those who are fighting on the side of right, while the perpetrators of vicious crimes seem able to operate freely and choose to do what they wish. They choose the route of ultra-violence to stay ahead of the law in an otherwise tranquil community: they plan and execute, in all senses of the word. Is it possible to triumph over this ruthlessness?

The Signature of a Voice by Johnny John Heinz
ISBN: 1-904433-00-6

TARNISHED COPPER

Tarnished Copper takes us into the arcane world of commodity trading. Against this murky background, no deal is what it seems, no agreement what it appears to be. The characters cheat and deceive each other, all in the name of grabbing their own advantage. Hiro Yamagazi, from his base in Tokyo, is the biggest trader of them all. But does he run his own destiny, or is he just jumping when Phil Harris pulls the strings? Can Jamie Edwards keep his addictions under control? And what will be the outcome of the duel between the hedge fund manager Jason Serck, and brash, devious, high-spending Mack McKee? And then one of them goes too far: life and death enters the traders' world........

Geoff Sambrook is ideally placed to take the reader into this world. He's been at the heart of the world's copper trading for over twenty years, and has seen the games - and the traders - come and go. With his ability to draw characters, and his knack of making the reader understand this strange world, he's created an explosive best-selling financial thriller. Read it and learn how this part of the City really works.

Tarnished Copper by Geoffrey Sambrook
ISBN 1-904433-02-2

OVER A BARREL

From the moment you land at Heathrow on page one the plot grips you. Ed Burke, an American oil tycoon, jets through the world's financial centres and the Middle East to set up deals, but where does this lead him? Are his premonitions on the safety of his daughter Louise in Saudi Arabia well founded? Who are his hidden opponents? Is his corporate lawyer

Nicole with him or against him?

As the plot unfolds his company is put into play in the tangle of events surrounding the 1990 invasion of Kuwait. Even his private life is drawn into the morass.

In this novel Peter depicts the grim machinations of political and commercial life, but the human spirit shines through. This is a thriller that will hold you to the last page.

Over a Barrel by Peter Driver
ISBN 1-904433-03-0

THE BLOWS OF FATE

It is a crisp clear day in Sofia and three young friends are starting out in life, buoyant with their hopes, aspirations, loves. But this is not to be, as post war Eastern Europe comes under the grip of its brutal communist regime. Driven from their homes and deprived of their basic rights, the three friends determine to escape ... but one of them cannot seize that moment. It may seem that life cannot become worse for the families who are ostracised and trapped in their own country, but the path of hopelessness descends to the concentration camps and unimaginable brutality.

For those who escape there is the struggle to survive, tempered by the kindness they encounter along their way. We see how talent and determination can win through. Yet, though they may have escaped those terrible years in Bulgaria, they can never escape their personal loss of family, homeland, friends and love that may have been.

While life is very difficult for the three friends, they do not forget each other. After forty years of separation, they meet. For each one fate has prepared a surprise....

Can beauty, art and love eclipse the manmade horrors of this world? You will think they can, as Antoinette Clair brings out the beautiful things in life, so that the poignancy of her novel reaches into the toughest of us, and moves to tears.

This is a tale of beauty, music and a grand love, but it is also expressive of the sad recurring tale of Europe's recent history.

The Blows of Fate by Antoinette Clair
ISBN 1-904433-04-9

THE GORE EXPERIMENT

William Gore is not a mad scientist: he is a dedicated medical researcher working on G.L.X.-14, an AIDS serum. He is on the brink of a major breakthrough and seeks to force the pace, spurred on by his knowledge of the suffering to be spared, if he is right, and the millions of lives of AIDS victims to be saved. But as things begin to go askew, how far dare he go? What level of risk is warranted? What, and who, is he prepared to sacrifice? The answers become worse than you can imagine as William Gore treads a path to horror.

The Gore Experiment may be fiction, but it addresses real issues in the world of experimental vaccines, disease-busting drugs and genetic engineering. Is science unknowingly exposing us to risk through overconfidence in ever narrowing fields of expertise, ignorant of ramifications? Or is the red tape of bureaucracy signing the death warrants of the terminally sick? Well, William Gore at least is confident. He is convinced of what he must do. Should he do it?

This is not a book for the faint-hearted. H. Jay Scheuermann adds a new high-tech dimension to the traditions of vampires, Jekylls and Hydes as William Gore paves his own road to hell. But there is a twist....

The Gore Experiment by H. Jay Scheuermann
ISBN 1-904433-05-7

CASEY'S REVENGE

Is this the best of all possible worlds? Well, almost, or so Casey Forbes thinks. She is a college professor with a successful career and good friends; boyfriend trouble in the past, perhaps, but who hasn't? And her prospects are excellent.

But no woman can expect to descend into the real life nightmare, that envelopes Casey ... out of nowhere.

Mary Charles's heroine is forced to confront the darkest side of human nature and the most bestial of acts committed by man. Yet it is the strength of will, the trauma inflicted on Casey's personality and the resourcefulness of the female psyche that Mary Charles explores in this novel. What does it take to survive overwhelming adversity and does Casey have it?

Many dream of revenge but wonder if they have within themselves the capacity to carry it out. Can Casey? And is the price going to be too high?

Read this thriller and one thing is certain: don't ever let this happen to you.

Casey's Revenge by Mary Charles
ISBN 1-90443-06-5

SABRA'S SOUL

From the heart of the California rock music scene comes this story of much more than just love and betrayal.

Does Sabra know who she is? She thinks she is a loving mother and a trusting wife, but her husband Logan, a powerful figure in rock music, seems consumed by commitments to his latest band, 23 Mystique. Sabra begins to feel that something is missing, to feel a yearning for something more. Is she too trusting and too slow to spot Logan's lapses in behaviour?

When Sabra meets the pop idol of her sub-teen daughters, things begin to change. She can't believe the attraction growing in her for this youthful figure, her junior by several years.

Lisa Reed paints a picture of virtue and vice in this tale of love, lust, betrayal and drug-induced psychosis, set amidst the glitter of the rock scene. It is not fate that leads these people on but their own actions. Can they help it and where does it lead?

Who better than Lisa Reed, with her access to the centre of rock, to weave this tense plot as it descends from the social whirl into the deadly serious. If you are a successful rock star, this is a book for you, and if not ... well, read on and dream.

Health warning: this book contains salacious sex scenes demanded by its setting.

Sabra's Soul by Lisa Reed

ISBN 1-90443307-3

FACE BLIND

From the pen of Raymond Benson, author of the acclaimed original James Bond continuation novels (Zero Minus Ten, The Facts of Death, High Time to Kill, DoubleShot, Never Dream of Dying, and The Man With the Red Tattoo) and the novel Evil Hours, comes a new and edgy noir thriller.

Imagine a world where you don't recognize the human face. That's Hannah's condition - prosopagnosia, or "face blindness" - when the brain center that recognizes faces is inoperable. The onset of the condition occurred when she was attacked and nearly raped by an unknown assailant in the inner lobby of her New York City apartment building. And now she thinks he's back, and not just in her dreams.

When she also attracts the attention of a psychopathic predator and becomes the unwitting target of a Mafia drug ring, the scene is set for a thrill ride of mistaken identity, cat-and-mouse pursuit, and murder.

Face Blind is a twisting, turning tale of suspense in which every character has a dark side. The novel will keep the reader surprised and intrigued until the final violent catharsis.

Face Blind by Raymond Benson
ISBN 1-904433-10-3

CUPID AND THE SILENT GODDESS

The painting Allegory with Venus and Cupid has long fascinated visitors to London's National Gallery, as well as the millions more who have seen it reproduced in books. It is one of the most beautiful paintings of the nude ever made.

In 1544, Duke Cosimo de' Medici of Florence commissioned the artist Bronzino to create the painting to be sent as a diplomatic gift to King François I of France.

As well as the academic mystery of what the strange figures in the painting represent, there is the human mystery: who were the models in the Florence of 1544 who posed for the gods and strange figures?

Alan Fisk's Cupid and the Silent Goddess imagines how the creation of this painting might have touched the lives of everyone who was involved with it: Bronzino's apprentice Giuseppe, the mute and mysterious Angelina who is forced to model for Venus, the brutal sculptor Baccio Bandinelli and his son, and the good-hearted nun Sister Benedicta and her friend the old English priest Father Fleccia, both secret practitioners of alchemy.

As the painting takes shape, it causes episodes of fear and cruelty, but the ending lies perhaps in the gift of Venus.

'A witty and entertaining romp set in the seedy world of Italian Renaissance artists.' Award-winning historical novelist Elizabeth Chadwick. (*The Falcons of Montabard, The Winter Mantle).*

'Alan Fisk, in his book Cupid and the Silent Goddess, captures the atmosphere of sixteenth-century Florence and the world of the artists excellently. This is a fascinating imaginative reconstruction of the events during the painting of Allegory with Venus and Cupid.' Marina Oliver, author of many historical novels and of Writing Historical Fiction.

Cupid and the Silent Goddess by Alan Fisk

ISBN 1-904433-08-4

TALES FROM THE LONG BAR

Nostalgia may not be what it used be, but do you ever get the feeling that the future's not worth holding your breath for either?

Do you remember the double-edged sword that was 'having a proper job' and struggling within the coils of the multiheaded monster that was 'the organisation'?

Are you fed up with forever having to hit the ground running, working dafter not smarter - and always being in a rush trying to dress down on Fridays?

Do you miss not having a career, a pension plan or even the occasional long lunch with colleagues and friends?

For anyone who knows what's what (but can't do much about it), Tales from the Long Bar should prove entertaining. If it doesn't, it will at least reassure you that you are not alone.

Londoner Saif Rahman spent half his life working in the City before going on to pursue opportunities elsewhere. A linguist by training, Saif is a historian by inclination.

Tale from the Long Bar by Saif Rahman

ISBN 1-904433-10-X

COUSINS OF COLOR

Luzon, Philippines, 1899. Immersed in the chaos and brutality of America's first overseas war of conquest and occupation, Private David Fagen has a decision to make - forsake his country or surrender his soul. The result: A young black man in search of respect and inclusion turns his back on Old Glory - and is hailed a hero of the Filipino fight for independence.

Negro blood is just as good as a white man's when spilled in defense of the American Way, or so Fagen believed. But this time his country seeks not justice but empire. Pandemonium rules Fagen's world, Anarchy the High Sheriff, and he knows every time he pulls the trigger, he helps enslave the people he came to liberate.

Not just an account of an extraordinary black solider caught in the grip of fate and circumstance, Cousin*s of Color* tells the story of Fagen's love for the beautiful and mysterious guerilla fighter, Clarita Socorro, and his sympathy for her people's struggle for freedom. *Cousins* also chronicles Colonel Fredrick Funston's monomaniacal pursuit of victory at any cost and his daredevil mission to capture Emilio Aguinaldo, the leader of the Philippine revolution. Other characters include the dangerously unstable, Captain Baston, particularly cruel in his treatment of prisoners, and Sergeant Warren Rivers, the father Fagen never had.

Himself a Vietnam combat veteran, author William Schroder hurtles us through the harsh realities of this tropical jungle war and provides powerful insight into the dreams and aspirations of human souls corrupted and debased by that violent clash of cultures and national wills. Based on actual events, David Fagen's pursuit of truth and moral purpose in the Philippine Campaign brings focus to America's continuing obsession with conquest and racism and provides insight into many of today's prevailing sentiments.

Cousins of Color by William Schroder
Hardcover - ISBN 1-904433-13-8
Paperback - ISBN 1-904433-11-1

EVIL HOURS

"My mother was murdered when I was six years old." Shannon has become used to giving this explanation when getting to know new arrivals in the small West Texas town of Limite. She has never hidden the truth about her mother, but she is haunted by the unresolved circumstances surrounding her mother's murder and the deaths of a series of other women around the same time. It is when she sets about uncovering the truth, with the help of an investigator, that the true depravity of Limite's underbelly begins to emerge.

The very ordinariness of the small town lends a chill to *Evil Hours*, as revelations from a murky past begin to form a pattern; but much worse they begin to cast their shadow over the present.

As Shannon delves behind the curtain of silence raised by the prominent citizens of Limite, she finds herself caught up in a sequence of events that mirror those of the previous generation...and the past and the present merge into a chilling web of evil.

In *Evil Hours* Raymond Benson revisits his roots and brings to life the intrigue of a small West Texas Town. Benson is the author of the original James Bond continuation novels: *The Man With the Red Tattoo*; *Never Dream of Dying*; *DoubleShot*; *High Time to Kill*; *The Facts of Death*; and *Zero Minus Ten.* He has recently released a thriller set in New York, *Face Blind.*

Evil Hours by Raymond Benson

ISBN 1-904433-12-X

PAINT ME AS I AM

What unique attribute dwells within the creative individual? Is it a flaw in the unconscious psyche that gives rise to talent, influencing artists to fashion the product of their imagination into tangible form, just as the grain of sand gives rise to the precious pearl? Or is it more?

To the world around him, Jerrod Young appears to be a typical, mature art student. He certainly has talent as a painter, but hidden within the darkest corners of his mind are unsavory secrets, and a different man that nobody knows.

H. Jay Scheuermann, author of The Gore Experiment, gives us another great psychological thriller, delivering a chilling look inside the psyche of a man whose deepest thoughts begin to assume control over his actions. The needs of the darkness within him seem to grow with each atrocity, his ever-increasing confidence fueling an inexorable force for evil.

Hell is not a place, but a state of mind, a state of being: it exists within each of us. We like to believe we can control it, but the cruel alternative is that our choices have already been made for us. Jerrod has accepted his truth, and is resolved to serve his inner demon.

Special Agent Jackie Jonas has been given her first assignment, a case that may mark the beginning and the end of her FBI career, as it leads her into a web of violence and deception, with each new clue ensnaring the lives of the ones she loves....

This gripping story brings to life the awful truth that the Jerrod Young's of this world do, in fact, exist. It could be one of your co-workers, the person behind you in the supermarket checkout line, or even the person next door. Can you tell? Are you willing to stake your life on it?

Paint Me As I Am by H. Jay Scheuermann

ISBN 1-904433-14-6

EMBER'S FLAME

"He could focus on her intelligent conversations and the way her aqua blue eyes lit up when they were amused and turned almost gray when they were sad. It was easier to admire the strength she carried in her soul and the light she carried in her walk. Now, seeing her in five inch heels and hot pants..."

Ember Ty is majoring in journalism. Graced with stunning looks, she finances her studies by dancing in a strip club. She has a hot boyfriend in a rock band, a future writing about the music world, and yes, she's working hard to achieve it.

But it all starts to go wrong. There is a predator on the loose, and Ember is sucked into a nightmare that none of us would care to dream, let alone live.

Vulnerable and threatened, Ember is drawn into a love triangle that might never have been, with the man she is to marry and the man she knows she can never have.

Ember's Flame by Lisa Reed
ISBN 1-904433-15-4

THE RELUCTANT CORPSE

"Stewart Douglas could not, under any circumstances, be considered your average human being. He'd always been a fan of agony as long, of course, as it wasn't his own." Well, Stewart is the local mortician, and maybe he has a less than healthy interest in the job. Every community has its secrets, and Savannah, Georgia, is no exception. The questions are: exactly what are those secrets, and who do they belong to?

Mary Charles introduces us to a community of characters, and although we do see the mortician at work, everything is comfortably tranquil, or so it seems. But strange things are afoot. Who can you trust? It may be best to let things rest, but events have their own momentum.

There is a foray into the antique art market, which gives the plot a subtle twist, and as the sinister undertone begins to take on real menace, you will be unable to put down this exciting suspense novel.

"Set within the confines of Savannah and Southeast Georgia, The Reluctant Corpse confronts the reader with frightening images lurking just

behind closed doors and stately homes. Well written and enjoyable." William C. Harris Jr. (Savannah best-selling author of Delirium of the Brave and No Enemy But Time).

The Reluctant Corpse by Mary Charles
ISBN 1-904433-16-2

THE AFFAIRS OF STATE

A philandering president. Rumors about The First Lady. Public lies about private lives. Talk about impeachment. Unstable world events that could lead to war. Sound familiar?

It should. It was all possible in 1940.

Immediately after Franklin Roosevelt won an unprecedented third term and World War 2 was heating up, a brand new radio network aired information about the First Family that was true but had never been made public.

Michael Audray, the network's high-profile host of the most listened-to radio program in the country, asked *the* question that set off a chain of events that changed modern history before and after Pearl Harbor.

The Affairs of State is about power politics, broadcasting, private lives and the public's right to know. It's fiction, but it meshes with the historical record and asks questions that challenge us to face the moral ambiguity that emerges.

The Affairs of State by Tim Steele
ISBN 1-904433-17-0

ARCHIPELAGO

If you haven't yet, you soon will hear about the Archipelago Company. They run the utopia that is the independent economy orbiting London and the whole raft of money-making schemes that goes with it. Let London sink under the weight of congestion charges, an uncontrolled building boom, high prices and limited employment. The Archipelago doesn't need to help it along. It can just help itself to bits of the action that come floating by. Simple!'

So for the man on the M25, and business, this utopia can only be a win-win, or so it would seem. Perhaps we should take a closer look at the conflicting interests of the members of the team running the Archipelago

Company. In this best of all possible worlds of tomorrow that is here today, we see a financial institution that has come down in the world, a university that wants to be a business, an IT company, not too ambitious, that just wants to run the country.

There are rich pickings for the bottom feeders: a language school with delusions of grandeur, a mysterious firm of Swiss lawyers and individuals participating in this grand scheme who are seeking to connect with their inner demons.

Virtue has to be its own reward, since no-one will give it the time of day.

Archipelago by Saif Rahman
ISBN 1-904433-22-7

GUY DE CARNAC: DESCENT

The character from the Dr Who New Adventure, Sanctuary, and the audio drama, The Quality Of Mercy, returns in a full-length novel.

Set in 1303, young Templar Knight Guy de Carnac begins a long and life-changing journey when everything he holds dear is torn apart into mayhem and intrigue between the French crown and the Papacy.

Guy de Carnac: Descent by David McIntee
ISBN 1-904433-19-7

Please visit our website to learn more about our authors and their books. We welcome your feedback by e-mail.

www.twentyfirstcenturypublishers.com

Lightning Source UK Ltd.
Milton Keynes UK
UKOW05f2057021213

222267UK00001B/151/A